# The Death Detail

## Part one of The Securus Trilogy

## By Anthony Maldonado

# DEDICATION

For my wife, Bernice. You are my strength and
inspiration.

# CONTENTS

# ACKNOWLEDGMENTS

Thank you to all those who helped and encouraged me throughout the process of writing this book.

Bernice, without your support I would have never even finished it. To my readers, Sommer White, Tho Le, Karen McDowell, Diane Harris, and Bahar Abbassi, thank you all for your encouragement and input. Howard Chung, I would thank you, but I am not sure if you have finished reading it yet.

Mariann Yattaw, thank you for the awesome cover.

For the first time I can remember, I wake up before the blare of my morning alert. Sleeping is usually an escape from my bland world, bringing dreams filled with vivid colors and exciting landscapes to explore. It is normally difficult to tear myself from those dreams and face my stark reality, but today is not going to be a normal day. For the first time in months, I was able to obtain a permit to go into The Caves with my friends. Leadership has been much more restrictive with access lately, especially with groups, so this evening's excursion will be a rare escape for us.

My eyes are open, but the room is veiled in darkness. With all of Securus being deep underground, there are no windows or light except for the barely perceivable shimmer penetrating the seals of the entry door. By the time I sit on the edge of the bed, the main power is activated and the lights turn on, emitting their familiar warm glow. Years ago they were altered to provide a substitute for the Sun's rays after it was discovered that the lack of natural sunlight was leading to depression and vitamin deficiencies. The bland walls of my quarters are not much more stimulating in the light than they were in the darkness.

The bunk above mine is empty. I can hear my brother, Arluin, already awake and in the bathroom. As usual, he is the first to rise. Despite our ten year age difference, people often say how we are so alike. We do share the same olive skin tone and short cropped hair, but this early in the morning, that is where the similarities end. Even when I was a teenager like him, I was never such a morning person. I sit back on my bed and wait for Arluin and my mother to get dressed before taking my turn. By the time I come out of the bathroom, they are both waiting for me in our usual seats in front of the television monitor in the far wall.

Arluin looks back at me with his deep green eyes. "You got up fast today," he says with a hint of jealousy in his voice. He knows where I am going and that he is still two years away from the mandatory minimum age requirement.

"You'll be able to go soon enough" I say while sitting down, trying not to make him feel too bad. It is hard on all of us to constantly be surrounded by the same bland, steel walls, and going into The Caves is the only time we can temporarily escape them.

"Yeah, yeah," he says, shifting positions in his chair to look me in the eye. "So, Kagen, when are you gonna trick some girl into marrying you so you can finally get assigned you your own quarters and give me some space?" he says with a mocking exasperation.

"You and mom would be lost without me," I reply.

"We would manage just fine, and it wouldn't hurt for you to give some of those nice girls a chance," my mother says from her chair next to Arluin.

Before I can respond, the short high-pitched tone that indicates the announcements are about to begin sounds, mercifully cutting our conversation short. We all divert our attention to the screen in front of us, just in time to see the image of Mr. Vaden appear. For a moment, he remains silent while looking through the screen, as if waiting for our full attention. As always, he is wearing the

2

official uniform of Leadership. It is a clean line uniform with a mineral grey base combined with differing accents on the sleeves and collar to indicate rank and occupation. The accents on his uniform are royal blue indicating his rank as the official leader of Securus.

Like all of those in Leadership, he also bears the distinctive insignia on the left breast of his uniform. It has an eight pointed Sun with a yellow center that melds into orange tips. The sun is surrounded by its glowing light and is nestled in the center of a sharp black biological hazard symbol. It is a reminder of the terrible biological weapon, known as The Agent, which has driven our people underground. The inspiration for the emblem was taken from the unique, metallic biohazard marker stamped into the massive outer doors that once served as the lone entrance to Securus. At first, the stamp was meant to keep others away by making them think the facility was already infected. Now, the Leadership insignia is meant to symbolize the light and strength that has come from the tyranny of The Agent's devastation.

Seeing Mr. Vaden, stare into the camera, waiting to speak, often makes me feel uneasy. He possesses an air of authority that is augmented by the streaks of silver interspersed in his hair, and even on the artificial screen, his calculating eyes seem to stare directly into you.

"Good morning, I am Mr. Vaden," he starts as always, even though he needs no introduction. "I am pleased to announce our food and water levels remain above minimum levels. Energy generation remains sufficient. No defects were identified in the air filtration system diagnostic.

"However, not all news is good today. There has been some minor seismic activity, and I advise increased caution if venturing into The Caves. Not all areas have been reinforced and there is always the danger of a collapse in the more remote chambers. Because of this, we will be closing off the upper tunnels to the public and limiting permits for access until everyone's safety can be assured. Any infractions of our policies while in The Caves will not be tolerated.

"I also regret to inform you that this week's surface air test shows that The Agent is still present and active. That is all for the morning announcements, may you all have a safe and productive day."

The screen turns off, but I remain in my seat. Mr. Vaden's warning during the announcements is completely unexpected. I have been in the upper tunnels before, and they never seemed to be unstable or dangerous. There have not been any incidents out in The Caves, so it makes me wonder why he is so concerned with that area. There has to be something more behind his decision. Since I am headed out there today, this is a troublesome change.

Arluin taps my shoulder, reminding me it is time to go. We all head down the hallway to our designated breakfast hall. There are many of these halls spread throughout Securus, and they all look the same. The three of us enter the hall and once inside, we were are again surrounded by more plain steel walls, but at least in here the uniformity is broken up by a mobile food service area as well as built-in partitions. This designed flexibility allows it to be used for multiple purposes throughout the day. With limited resources, we must always be creative and flexible with what we do have.

Today, our breakfast consists of the usual mix of a synthetic nutrient drink, small piece of bread, and a porridge-like substance. Not our best meal of the day, but it always gets me through the morning. After some idle talk amongst our neighbors, I leave the hall and make my way to work. Securus has numerous levels and with the infirmary being six flights up, I use one of the many stairways to get there. There are some elevator platforms centrally located for our use, but I prefer the exercise of the stairs. When I arrive to the external waiting area, the warm smile of Rana McPheeters, our senior Healer, greets me.

"We have a busy morning ahead of us with a full schedule of appointments. Can you take care of them for me?" she asks with a faint wink from behind large eye glasses that do nothing to conceal the keen perception behind them.

"Of course, to what do I owe the honor of filling in on your favorite duty?" I reply suspiciously. Once assigned to the infirmary from the general aptitude testing, our training circulates us through all the jobs in the infirmary, but we typically settle on the particular function that suits us best. Rana has always greatly preferred the appointments over the walk in visits, so I cannot help but wonder what surprise she has waiting for me.

"Oh, I just wanted a change of pace for the day," she says nonchalantly.

We both entered the main door into the infirmary and turned down the central hallway that connects all of the various exam and treatment rooms. Like most other areas in Securus, the walls are undecorated except for labels to the individual rooms and sections. Just after the sterile surgical room, I turn and enter the appointment exam room. It has been a while since I worked in here, but the setup is still ingrained into my mind. The small gurney for examinations sits adjacent to a row of cabinets filled with medicines and other essential equipment on the far wall. I check the schedule and then turn to check the equipment that will be needed for the day.

Before I can get started, there is a crash in the hallway. I run back out to find a man with a crazed look in his eyes, on the floor, and crawling toward Rana. She looks at the man and then at me with confusion. We have both seen people like this before, except he is somehow covered with dirt. The only way that should be possible is if he was in The Caves recently. That does not make any sense, because he is not wearing a research uniform, and no one else is allowed out there this early.

I go to help him up so we can get him into the treatment room. The reason for the rest of his weak and disheveled appearance is not so elusive. His frazzled, rusty brown hair has matted, dried blood clots in it, and the stains have dripped down his back. Cracked lips and sunken eyes give away his dehydration. My guess is he was injured out there and ended up stuck in The Caves all night. But if he was, then why did none of the Guards help him get here?

I grab his arm and help him to his feet. He stagers and nearly falls before leaning heavily on me. He lifts his head from my shoulder and starts to talk in a whisper. "They didn't see me, but I saw them. They shouldn't be out there. You have to stop them."

His words seem like the product of his weakened physical state, but still, they grab my attention. "Stop who?" I ask him.

"The shadow-men in The Caves. They'll be the end of Securus," he says before his voice trails off.

Inside the exam room, I help him onto the gurney. I want to ask him more, but Rana is giving a look meant to remind me that she is more than capable of handling this herself. Taking the hint along with a deep breath, I force my mind to clear, and then make my way back to the appointment room. In this profession, one must be able to mentally move on from whatever we encounter to make sure we can do our best for the next person that comes in. This time, that is harder than normal because his words mark the second unusual warning that centers on The Caves. It is hard to ignore the coincidence on the very day I am scheduled to go out there.

Despite that, my job now is to focus on the scheduled appointments. Today, they largely consist of yearly blood screens for health maintenance and outbreak protection. It is not my favorite task, but it is essential none-the-less. There are multiple groups of collection tubes to separate, and each one reminds me of a disaster from the past. Our sophisticated biological filters protect us from the poisonous surface atmosphere, but The Caves are directly connected to the lower levels of Securus, bypassing their protection. Along with new resources, The Caves brought new microbes that when mixed with the old, created deadly strains of disease that nearly devastated our entire population.

The first set of tubes is intended to screen for continued immunity from vaccinations to a severe flu that wiped out one fifth of our population in a matter of months. The second set is to screen for any signs of a deadly hemorrhagic fever that was previously spread from tiny mites that invaded Securus. The screening for this one is geared at identifying any cases before anyone develops the full disease, with profuse bleeding from every possible orifice, both internally and externally. Since the mites have been eradicated and there has not been a case in years, I always felt like the testing was overkill. But, because it was such a visually terrifying outbreak, our Research Department insists on it. The third set of tubes is for the general health maintenance, and is probably the only truly useful part of the screening.

All of the testing equipment is in order, and the vaccines are ready. I again fight to push aside my curiosity to Rana's intentions and the weird coincidences with The Caves while gearing up for the day. I am not looking forward to covering in this area and have to remind myself that the benefit of being assigned the appointments is that you have a parade of people to interact with. But, I also know the downside is that other than any side conversation you may have, the visits will all be the same. Extract enough blood for analysis; listen to the sounds of their heart and lungs, then move on to the next person.

Even before starting, I already want to go back to my usual station where there are infinitely more possibilities. Random injuries, which for some reason always seem to be occurring to our younger men, and acutely ill people trickle in throughout the day. Each person and situation is always unique. It can be stimulating work, and there is also another added benefit. In between these visits, I occasionally have the time to access the internet interface. It is a rare privilege, since there are so few access points and most of those are restricted to Leadership personnel. The Healers are granted an exception to look for information that may improve our effectiveness in treating patients, so they do not typically monitor our use. Now with the regimented schedule of the appointments, there will be no time for me to access the internet and search for the images that so often fill my dreams.

Even so, I would never decline Rana's request and need to figure out what she has in store for me today. She has a reason for nearly everything she does, and it is part of my continuing training to decipher her lessons. The morning moves faster than expected, and as the end of the morning appointments nears, I begin to appreciate why Rana enjoys these visits. Instead of focusing on the repetitive actions of the task, she relishes the opportunity to simply enjoy the company of those she sees. I wonder if that was the purpose of the switch all along. To give me more chances to connect with our people. While considering this and waiting for my next appointment, Rana appears in the doorway.

"I am so forgetful today! I neglected to add one more name to the morning list," she says while entering the room. There are many ways to describe Rana, but forgetful is not one of them. She may be older, with a head now full of long grey hair to prove it, but she remembers every word we have spoken to each other since I began as an understudy with her eight years ago. This seemingly incidental comment worries me. I make a mental note to speak with her later and make sure she is not feeling ill. Rana adds the name to the appointment list on the computer and leaves the room. I try not to stare, but there is no mistaking her watching me out of the corner of her eye as she leaves. My curiosity compels me across the room to the list. I scan it and find the name she has added. It is Talia Vaden.

Unfortunately, I have not had the opportunity to speak with Talia for years, ever since we finished our primary education courses. Just seeing her name brings back a flood of memories. I remember the last time she filled in for her father, Mr. Vaden, during the announcements. The screen beamed her long flowing black hair, deep brown eyes, and naturally tanned skin that completed the image of this stunningly beautiful woman. Her elegant confidence while speaking commands attention.

I shake my head, trying to refocus my attention.

Needing something to do while waiting for Talia's appointment, I wander over to the cabinets, and start shuffling the phlebotomy supplies into a more logical order. There is not much to fix since this was already done as part of the morning check, but the mindless activity helps keep my mind on track. My attention is diverted back to the door by the sound of footsteps drawing near. I turn just as Talia enters the room, and my knees almost give. She is radiant as ever.

## 2

"Hi Kagen, I didn't know I was going to see you today! It's been so long," Talia says with a warm smile.

"I-I'm filling in for Rana. She wanted to change things up for the day," I stutter for a moment before regaining my composure. "So, how are things in Leadership, you whipping everyone into shape?"

"It's been great. With my growing responsibilities, I can better influence and organize Leadership. I have so many ideas to try to improve our life in Securus," Talia says without any hint of insincerity that often accompanies those with political ambition. Listening to her speak makes me grin. She has always had a way of sounding so proper and formal, only to surprise you with an offbeat or playful joke when you least expect it.

"You always did love a challenge," I reply while beginning the testing. Carefully, I fumble my way through the rest of the routine. "Are there any special projects you're working on?"

"Well, I've been studying The Caves. I think there's a lot more potential there that we have not yet harnessed," she carefully explains. "But, I don't want to get too excited about it until I'm sure. I need to find some time to get back out there to collect more samples."

"I'm going to head out to The Caves during free time today with some friends. You could come with us if you like. We could help collect whatever samples you need," I blurt out while labeling the samples.

"Sounds like fun, but I'm kind of busy. I have some meetings, but I'll see if they can be rescheduled. I'll let you know," Talia replies causally. She gives me a brief hug, and then heads off.

After my knees regain their stability, I leave my exam room and find Rana in the front room of the infirmary where she is still finishing some paperwork. I give her a suspicious stare, and she responds with an embellished expression of innocence. Even though Talia and I were friends in the past, I have always known there could never be anything more because of the unspoken law that those in the highest positions in Leadership do not mix with someone from the worker class. Being the daughter of Mr. Vaden and having a ranking position in the developmental section of the Research Department has her on track to succeed her father. That still never stops the tingling sensation in my stomach every time she is near. I never spoke of this with Rana, but it is hard to hide anything from those penetrating eyes.

With the morning appointments finished, I motion that it is time for lunch. We do not have the same scheduled lunch breaks because there always has to be someone present in case of emergency, so she waves me off and continues her work. I start to leave, but before reaching the exit, a lingering thought in the back of my mind stops me.

"Oh, just out of curiosity, what happened to that confused guy this morning?" I ask Rana.

"He wasn't that bad. I gave him some fluids and stapled his scalp lacs. There were no internal injuries. When I finished, some Guards came to get him. They said he had been hiding in The Caves, trying to avoid going the Detention Center. I'm sure that's where he is now," she says and then looks back down to her work.

That explanation does make sense, but even so, his warning felt real. What could he have meant? Is this somehow connected to the odd closure of the upper tunnels? There are no creatures out there big enough to be mistaken for a man, so that could not be what he saw. Most likely it was just the Guards chasing him or some research workers checking new tunnels for safety. But how could he mistake them for anything else, or think they were a threat to Securus? Realistically, it had to be either delirious rambling or him faking delirium in an attempt to stay in the infirmary instead of going to the Detention Center. I cannot blame him for that, just hearing Rana say the name of that place makes me uneasy, and most people would make up any story to avoid going there. I force my mind away from the disheveled man, since given his current situation it is unlikely we will ever hear from him again.

I leave the infirmary and replay the rest of the morning in my mind. The work was more pleasant than expected, and it was nice to see Talia again. Thinking of Talia and remembering Rana's clever setup brings my smile back. With extra energy in my step, I depart the infirmary.

As expected, my friends are already there when I reach the lunch hall. A tight schedule must be maintained in the various food halls in order to rotate enough people through so everyone gets their daily ration. Because of that constraint, they cannot wait long for me or they will miss their meal. This particular lunch hall is larger than my breakfast area but otherwise looks quite similar to it, and just like most of the larger areas, it serves various functions. I walk over to the food dispersal station and scan my identification key to gain access to my allotted meal. Such strict rationing is needed to make sure we do not exhaust our food and purified water supply, as we nearly did before the discovery of The Caves saved us with its added resources. I pick up my ration consisting of purified water, a potato-like vegetable and a synthetic sliced meat. The warmth of the meal helps distract from its lack of taste.

"Hey Kagen, any unexplained foreign bodies at work today?" shouts a voice from across the hall. I hold in a laugh and try to hide my face while making my way to the table, knowing there is only one person it can be. When I reach the table, a stalky man with spiked hair is waiting for me, grinning from ear to ear with satisfaction at my embarrassment. Despite our unnatural circumstances, Hadwin is always in a good mood and often finds ways to entertain our group, usually at the expense of one of us.

"No Hadwin, you weren't on my schedule," I chide while sitting down. "But, I did have an interesting visitor today."

Sitting at the table with Hadwin are the other regulars in our group, Merrick and Sayda. "So, who was this interesting visitor?" Merrick asks.

"Talia Vaden," I answer casually.

Without having to look, I can feel Sayda's attention fixate on me. I turn and find her striking crystal blue eyes studying me with curiosity. She brushes back the few strands of golden blonde hair that has escaped her ponytail as she asks, "Really? What warranted a visit from the daughter of Mr. Vaden?"

"Nothing special, just routine stuff. I was filling in for Rana," I respond. "I invited her to go with us to The Caves later, but she probably won't be able to make it. Anyway, anything interesting going on with you guys?"

"I'm just waiting to get back into The Caves. Last time I was in there I found a new rock face we can climb. I haven't tried it out yet, but I bet you'll all be far behind me when I reach the top!" Merrick boasts with a confident smile.

"Can we make it with the new closure?" I ask, intentionally not mentioning the words of the man in the infirmary. There is no point in bringing up his failed attempts to avoid the Detention Center.

"It's not in the upper tunnels, although it is close to them. I'm pretty sure Leadership doesn't even know about it yet. So you can't use that as an excuse to get out of losing to me," he says.

We all have our own way of distracting ourselves from our circumstances. Merrick often consumes his time with activities created by his fierce competitiveness and stubborn determination. If Merrick thinks it is going to be challenging, we will definitely have an interesting time. We continue on with our banter while finishing our meal and afterwards we all head our separate ways, returning to work for the afternoon shift.

*

That night, when my shift in the infirmary is over, I meet my mother and Arluin in the dinner hall. These halls are usually the same as the lunch halls, but the assigned locations for individuals varies between the two depending on work and living locations. The hall is, as usual, lively with conversation. It is always filled to capacity since more people share the same time assignment. We are at a large table, surrounded by the other families that reside near our quarters. Dinner is typically the best meal of the day, and tonight is no exception. There are fish from some of The Caves' vast pools of water as well as a mixture of mushrooms grown in some of the smaller side chambers. It is not often we get an entire meal without an artificial substitute, so we all consume it eagerly.

"Why are you in such a good mood?" Arluin asks me while he finishes the last of his food.

"No particular reason. It was a decent day and it's almost free time," I respond elusively.

"Who's going with you?" asks my mother.

"Hadwin, Merrick and Sayda," I reply while devouring the last bits of my meal. "I invited Talia, but she probably won't be able to make it." Looking up, I see a knowing smile on Arluin's face.

"Why don't you invite some of the girls from our sector like Lana or Abira?" my mother pleads. It takes a lot of effort not to roll my eyes, since she is always trying to fix me up with someone. I pretend not to hear her question, and since my food is already finished, excuse myself from the table.

Our scheduled free time is starting, and I am anxious to get to The Caves. I rush down the stairs, descending further and further. It is not long before I pass the welded lines which mark the point where the original facility ended. Despite Leadership efforts to limit population growth, our numbers have climbed to the thousands, and we have had to expand the facility further into the depths to accommodate it. That is how The Caves were discovered in the first place.

Reaching the bottom of the stairwell, I arrive to the exit point before the others. Anxious to keep moving, I rush past the arranged lounge and lingering research workers to the massive outer doors. After checking in my reservation with the stationed Leadership Guard, I make my way into the main chamber of The Caves. As soon as I am outside the rigid structure of Securus, a weight feels like it has been lifted from my shoulders. No matter how many times I come here, it always evokes a sense of awe. Even in the largest halls that Securus has to offer, there is nothing that can compare to the openness of this space.

High above, there are rocks that seem to be flowing down from the ceiling. Others are reaching out from the floor slowly extending their spires toward the ceiling. The random patterns and rounded shapes that naturally arise throughout The Caves are a profound contrast to the linear and symmetrical structure of Securus. Out here, there are always new formations to discover in the many uncharted tunnels and chambers throughout The Caves. That is why we love coming out here so much. It is our escape. Luckily, despite its enormous size, the system is an isolated one. No traces of The Agent have ever been found in any of the tunnels and chambers down here.

The main path is easily navigated with use of the lights from the outer structure of Securus. Not far from the entrance, I encounter some of the natural, flowing bodies of water. In front of me is one of the larger standing pools. These collections of water interconnect with various others through tunnels deep in the pools as well as cracks in the cave walls that allow them to flow freely. I have always found the sound of the flowing water and constant trickle from above much more soothing than the mechanical groans of our facility.

While moving further into the chamber, I stop to marvel at some water bound creatures who, like the people of Securus, have adapted themselves to this unique environment. From the pictures I have seen on the computer, the fish in The Caves look very different than the ones on the surface. Evolving in the darkness has drained them of all color and has shrunk their eyes to functionless decorative beads. They have developed sensory organs near their numerous short whiskers that help them navigate without the use of sight. As if to remind me that not all of the creatures here have such a bland outer appearance, a few of the shrimp-like creatures we call Glow-runts, swim by. They emit a natural glowing light that is easily visible in the dark waters, creating shooting swirls of dramatic color as they move about.

The Leadership Guard at the secondary station is watching me closely while I walk by the water. We harvest the various pools on a rotating schedule to collect these creatures for our nutritional needs. Like most other things in Securus, fishing is tightly controlled by Leadership to prevent depletion of the pools' resources. The Guard and a few security cameras keep watch to enforce the restriction, but that is not really needed. Our people understand that we cannot afford to jeopardize this fragile ecosystem that is so vital to our own survival.

There are some manufactured sitting areas near the entrance to The Caves, but I prefer to wander farther in. Rounding the path, past the water and some massive stalagmites, I find a raised formation that has been broken in half. The exposed, flat surface serves well as a bench. Waiting for the others to arrive, I spend the time admiring the intricate rings that make up layer after layer inside the formation.

With no one else to distract me, my mind replays the warning from the man in the infirmary, *'The shadow-men in The Caves. They'll be the end of Securus.'* I look all around. Off to the right, far behind the secondary Guard, is the closed entrance to the upper tunnels. Other than that, there is nothing out of the ordinary. There are no diabolical figures lurking in the shadows. Even looking for them makes me feel a little foolish. My eyes go back to the formations around me, and soon my solitude is interrupted by the sound of voices growing near.

"Do you ever do anything other than complain?" Even from a distance, the annoyance in Merrick's voice is obvious.

"I'm not complaining, just pointing out the truth." The man's voice is familiar, but I cannot place it.

"And you guys say I'm cynical," laughs Sayda.

"Ok, guys, take it easy. No need to argue. Let's just relax and have some fun." There is a slight flutter in my heart when I hear her voice. Talia has been able to escape her evening plans after all.

They come into view with Hadwin and Sayda walking next to Talia. They are wearing their work uniforms which look like bland, well-fitted jumpsuits of different colors. Hadwin's is a deep blue, Sayda's black, and Talia's is the standard Leadership grey. On the opposite side of them are Merrick and the person he was arguing with. The unexpected addition is a thinly built man with dark eyes and carefully styled hair. His appearance is a stark contrast next to Merrick with his dark complexion, short, tightly curled hair, and strong build.

I try to hide the scowl that creeps across my face when I finally recognize who this unknown man is. It was his Leadership uniform that gave him away. It is made of the same mineral grey base as the others, but has a burnt orange trim indicating a medium level rank. It is Aamon. I have only had minimal interaction with him in the past, but even so, there is something about him that makes me leery. If there are any shadow-men out here, he would be it. His name is not on my permit, but Leadership members are free of some of the restrictions that apply to the workers.

"At least you're not waiting for us naked again," exclaims Hadwin when he sees me, pretending to be relieved. I can only shake my head, where he comes up with these things I will never know. If nothing else, his antics always lighten the mood. I greet my friends and

Talia with brief hugs and then shake hands with Aamon, using enough force to cause a slight twinge in his expression.

"Don't see you in The Caves much," I say, watching him shake the feeling back into his hand.

"When Talia told me she was coming to The Caves, I thought it would be a good opportunity to do some investigating of my own. Maybe I can help with the logistical aspects of harvesting The Caves' assets," he replies while examining the surrounding area. Aamon's extra attention to his outward appearance and rigid posture make him look completely out of place. It makes me wonder if there is another reason why he decided to come along.

"Alright, let's head in," I say, not wanting to let his presence affect our trip.

We continue around the end of the path to the end of the main chamber where a tunnel leads to the other chambers deeper in The Caves. The light from Securus does not penetrate this deep into The Caves, so we affix our illuminators and turn them on high. They look and feel like a simple headband, except they have a row of lights engrained into the lining. Their combined light floods the tunnel, making it easy to navigate.

As we walk, the lights reveal small signs placed along the walls of the passage that help guide us to the different sections and also warn of potential dangers. Only the initial parts of these connected tunnels are marked like this. Deeper in, beyond the last pools, the passages have not been fully mapped or secured, so we will need to rely on our own markings and memory to return safely.

"There's a specific chamber close by that I wanted to visit, if you guys are okay with it?" Talia asks as we walk.

"Sure, we have more than enough time. Just point us

in the right direction," I tell her.

We form a line and steadily make our way through the unmarked tunnels. Eventually, the group manages to traverse a particularly low, narrow, and unmarked passage that opens to a small cavern. Wriggling myself out of the tunnel, I stand up and survey the surroundings. There is a faint glow in the chamber that is not coming from our lights. As each member of our excursion emerges into the chamber I have them turn down their lights. When all the lights are out, the glow intensifies. The cavern fills with a vibrant, sparkling teal light emanating from the walls. The many crystals jutting from the rocks above, reflects the light in brilliant patterns all around us. It is easy to see why this cavern is of particular interest to Talia.

"Like some of the creatures in The Caves, the microbes in this chamber have evolved to emit a biological fluorescence. The mechanism of their light is different than that of the fish and may have promise as a supplemental light source. This could help diminish our energy needs significantly," Talia says in her usual formal tone.

She turns her light back on and moves to the side of the chamber where she can collect her samples. Aamon, who had been slowed while navigating the passage, is just entering the chamber with an annoyed grimace. As he dusts himself off, Merrick laughs. "Took you long enough."

Aamon looks as though he wants to respond, but thinks better of it. Sayda and I go over to join Talia, while the others scatter to explore the rest of this area.

"This bioluminescence is beautiful, but it'll be difficult to convert for our use," Sayda states bluntly as she moves away to study an area with a more intense glow, leaving Talia and I alone.

"I thought you were too busy, Talia," I say with a gentle nudge.

"Well, sometimes I have to just do what I want," she replies with a sly smile.

After a few minutes, Aamon wanders over and begins inspecting an unimportant appearing rock formation immediately next to Talia, obviously trying to listen to our conversation. I am getting the feeling he is more interested in Talia than anything else in The Caves. From the look on her face, that feeling is not mutual. After a few minutes, Talia finishes her collection, so we leave the chamber and start off to Merrick's new climbing area.

# 3

We walk, crawl, and climb our way through a seemingly endless maze of passages. The entrance to Merrick's cavern is well hidden, so it is no surprise that it has gone undiscovered until now. Upon entering the cavern, we all turn our lights to the highest dispersal setting to illuminate the area. It is instantly clear that Merrick has not let us down. Before us is an expansive cavern with an amazing natural beauty. Everyone stands in awe-struck silence while absorbing the view.

My eyes are immediately drawn to the daunting vertical wall on the far side that is divided by a magnificent waterfall. I have only seen waterfalls during my internet musings and some of my more pleasant dreams, certainly never before in person. The water forms a stream that continues on through a fissure in the lateral wall leading out of the chamber. The enclosed surroundings intensify the soothing rumble of the falls. Merrick watches the stunned contortions of our faces with a smug smile.

"Ok Merrick, you win. This is our best find yet," I admit while giving him a firm push on his shoulder.

I can hardly believe the fortune of finding this area. The excitement makes me want to run around like a schoolboy, but I am able to restrain my enthusiasm before embarrassing myself. Hadwin does that well enough, and there is no reason to make myself an easier target for him. As we walk through the cavern, I admire the unique formations we encounter. There are mineral deposits that look as if they were bubbling out of the ground, now frozen in mid drip. Other spires have box-like pieces stacked upon each other reaching impressive heights. On the other side of the cavern there are stone flowers and draping mineral leaves protruding from the rocky walls.

"Let's rest up a little before we tackle that beast," I suggest to the others. We find a suitably flat area to spread out and relax. I nearly fall asleep while enjoying the continuous murmur of the falls. Moments like these are both a joy and torture to me. While it is beautiful and stimulating to have these intricate caverns to explore, it is only a temporary escape. It reminds me of what could have been if the wars never broke out and mankind was able to resist its compulsion for self-destruction that led to the release of The Agent nearly one hundred years ago. In the end, we always have to return to the claustrophobic and drab surroundings that consume our existence in Securus. Still, I enjoy the moment for what it is, knowing it cannot last.

While I relax, Talia remains alert, constantly finding new features in the chamber to grab her curiosity. Sayda and Merrick both spend their time keeping an eye on Hadwin, who seems to be waiting for one of us to fall asleep so he can play a prank on them. Aamon does not speak much and looks even more uncomfortable in this cavern than he did in the others. It is easy to lose track of time while in The Caves. Luckily, Leadership is typically not rigid with the curfew as long as we do not disturb others and maintain our daily production. Even so, there are limits to their leniency and we are starting to push it, especially given Mr. Vaden's warning during the announcements.

"It's getting really late guys. Should we climb or save it for next time?" I ask the group.

"I can cover for us," Talia says. "I'll tell Leadership you were helping me collect samples. I'm not a good climber so I'll just hang around here and fill my sample containers until you guys get back." If I did not know better, by the nervous look in her eyes, I would think she was afraid of the climb.

"I'll keep you company," Aamon quickly interjects. I am not surprised by that since he has been closely shadowing Talia the entire trip. The disappointed look on her face makes it obvious she was hoping he would join us on the climb. Whatever his reason, it is probably best he does not come along. He does not look to be the most agile climber and would probably be a liability for us trying to keep him from falling.

"Afraid to get beat by a girl, Aamon?" Sayda quips before turning to the rest of us, not waiting for an answer.

"Okay, let's make it fast," I say while looking at Merrick. "Are you up for the challenge?"

"Merrick's coming in last this time," Hadwin proclaims.

"We'll see," Merrick says with a confident smile. He turns to face to wall. "Look over to the left of the falls, there's a plateau there that we can climb to."

The plateau he points at is twice as high as we have ever climbed before. I feel both excitement and apprehension at once. It is an intimidating climb, but the challenge is too enticing to decline. We head over to the rock face to study its surface and plan our route to the ledge high above us. Mercifully, the section we plan to climb is not completely vertical. There is a slope and numerous ledges that we could use to rest on if needed. Emboldened by a more favorable course, we begin our ascent. Merrick is the first to start, intent on beating the rest of us to the top. I hesitate long enough to be sure of my path, and then join the race. Hadwin is strong, but climbing is not one of his more accomplished skills. I quickly overtake him and begin closing in on Sayda.

"Don't look back, I'm coming for you!" I shout to the others.

"Never gonna happen," mocks Merrick.

I make good progress and despite my speed, fatigue has not yet set in. With only Merrick left to catch, I push harder, concentrating on my hand and footholds while making sure to regulate my breathing. As I get close to Merrick, my concentration is shattered by a sound that instantly halts my movement. To my right is the distinctive crash of falling rocks. I turn to look for Sayda to make sure she has not been hit by the debris. My glance brings the realization that she was not in the path of the falling rocks, but was the cause of them. She had veered over to a completely vertical section in her efforts to catch back up with us. I can see the newly broken rocks on the tip of a ledge that gave way under her hands, but she has fallen below my line of sight.

"Sayda!" I call out. My heart sinks when there is no reply. I cannot believe we were so reckless to let this happen. I hastily descend toward the ledge, hoping to find her.

"I can see her!" shouts Hadwin. He is on the opposite side of the ledge and luckily was not beneath Sayda when she slipped. "Hold on, Sayda; we're coming!"

"Is she hurt?" I ask Hadwin.

"She hit the wall hard. I think it knocked her breath out, but she's hanging on like a little spider monkey!" Hadwin chuckles.

My tension instantly releases. Hadwin may have an

odd sense of humor, but he would never joke if he thought Sayda was in any real danger. I exhale, now realizing why she had not screamed. She only fell a short distance and had her wind knocked out in the process, robbing her of her voice. I maneuver myself down onto the ledge she is beneath and look past it to find her. She was stuck in an awkward position, unable to climb up or down. She has fallen too far below the ledge for me to pull her up on my own, so I guide Hadwin up and around the other side of the ledge to help me. While Hadwin makes his way up, Merrick finds his way down to the ledge. We position ourselves and together lift Sayda up onto the ledge.

"Are you okay? Any injuries?" I ask while looking her over. She has some minor abrasions and bruising that stands out against her fair skin, but there are no obvious broken bones. There is still a slight tremor in her hands from the shock of the near fall. This is the first time I have ever seen Sayda seem fragile.

"I'm alright. Just give me a minute to catch my breath," she replies gruffly, starting to become annoyed we are all so concerned for her.

"Now that's the Sayda we know." Merrick smiles, relieved by her return to form. "You always were a tough one!"

With this unexpected change in events, we lose our enthusiasm for racing up the wall. We are ready to head back down, but Sayda insists we continue on. She already feels embarrassed by her misstep, and we know turning back would make her feel even worse, so we decide to finish the climb. I call out to Talia and Aamon to let them know we are all okay, but there is no response. Being this close to the falls, the roar of the water drowns out our voices. They are unaware anything has happened at all.

With Sayda safely recovering on the ledge, Merrick and I prepare to finish the climb. This time we decide to be more cautious and forget racing. Hadwin insists on waiting with Sayda on the ledge while she continues to recover. Merrick is to go up first and I will follow. We tell Sayda and Hadwin that after we reach the top we would let them know if it is worth the effort for them to join us. The words are more for her sake, because I have no intention to have them follow us, even if it is an impressive view. There is no point in Sayda risking a climb with any physical or emotional impairment.

I let Merrick get far enough away so there will not be any danger of falling rocks before following him up the wall. The remaining section feels stable, making the climb easier. Merrick reaches the top of the wall while I am still far from it, and disappears from my view as he walks onto the ledge. When I do reach the summit, it is empty. There is a tunnel at the back of the landing that Merrick must have gone in. Before following him I glance back toward the others. Hadwin and Sayda look comfortable resting on their ledge while Talia and Aamon's lights are moving far off in the distance continuing Talia's 'research.'

I enter the tunnel and follow the tortuous path looking for Merrick. Deeper in, the sounds of the waterfall become muffled and eventually go silent. I tilt my head and strain to hear anything besides my own breath. Suddenly, the silence is disturbed by another low rumbling. It seems to be coming from all around me. The intensity of the rumble increases and the ground begins to tremble. It is an earthquake! These tremors are dangerous even when in the relative safety of Securus, but here in decrepit tunnels, they can rapidly turn lethal.

Above me, large rocks and pointed stalactites threaten

to shake loose. I shout for Merrick but do not hear a response. I start to turn back, stumbling from the shaking in the ground. My foot trips on a loose rock, sending me crashing to the floor. As I turn to get up, a spear-like deposit the size of my leg brakes free from the ceiling and falls straight at me. I roll to the side just in time to prevent it from goring me as it strikes the ground. Back on my feet, I start to run for the exit. As I do, the earthquake stops, just as abruptly as it had begun. Catching my breath, I check my surroundings. The tunnel has shed many rocks but the main structure of it seems to be intact. I was lucky, but still need to find Merrick.

"Merrick, are you okay?" I call out, moving deeper into the passage. This time, there is a muffled reply. After turning the corner in the passage, I realize why his voice sounds that way. There is a complete collapse in the path blocking the way. The rubble is so thick that there are very few breaks in it for the light from his illuminator to penetrate. Luckily, there are a few cracks large enough that I can see through by positioning myself close enough to get a proper vantage point.

"Did any rocks hit you?" I ask, pressing my head to a small portal.

"No, I'm okay, just trapped," he replies. "I'm gonna look around and see if there's another way out."

I survey the structure of the collapse hoping to find a way to break through, but it is too solid and the rocks are too large. There is no way I could move the debris, even if Hadwin was here to help. Hoping he has found another passage, I again look through the small portal to check his progress.

What I see freezes me in place. Merrick is standing with his hands raised in a surrendering pose and with his eyes focused on something beyond my field of vision.

Beads of sweat gather on his dark skin, dripping down from his forehead. Something is making him nervous, but he remains still. His agitation spreads to me. *Why is he standing like that?* I think to myself before realizing there is an external light shining on him. He is not alone!

I turn my light off so it will not give me away, and then shift to another crack in the rubble to see who is there. I almost jump from the shock of seeing two dark figures standing before Merrick with their frightening assault rifles trained on him. *It's the shadow-men. They're real!* The realization stuns me. At the same time, questions race through my mind, *Where did they come from? Who are they?*

The two men are wearing pitch black uniforms with a rigid form that looks to be armored plating. Their faces are concealed behind helmets connected to tinted visors and a filtered breathing apparatus. With the light pointed on Merrick it is hard to see more detail on the soldiers, but there is a brief reflection from something on one of their breast plates that looks like an insignia made of an eight pointed sun. It is not the same as our Leadership symbol, but the similarity is disturbing.

They look like soldiers, and are nothing like the people from Securus, but there is no one else left. Everyone else died many years ago when The Agent was released and spread across the surface of the planet. Ours was the only underground facility that was operational in time to escape the deadly biological weapon.

Behind these figures, where there had only been the darkness of the tunnel before, a glow of light reveals a distinctly man-made tunnel. The view of the tunnel is limited and most of the details are obscured except for the metallic shine of railway tracks on the floor.

"Who else is here?" demands the menacing figure to

the left in a low growling voice.

"Just me and a friend, but he already left to get help. The earthquake caused a collapse, and I thought I was trapped," Merrick says in a low and steady voice as he slowly backs away from the men. Despite his fear and confusion, he is trying to keep the rest of us safe.

The figures position themselves so he cannot pass, giving him nowhere to go but back against the rocks behind him. My mind races, as I desperately try to figure out a way to help Merrick. Without warning, an intense flash of light erupts from the barrel of the gun on the right. There is almost no sound from the weapon. I watch in horror as Merrick collapses to the ground. I nearly yell out as it happens but cannot find my voice. Even from my position behind the rubble, I can see the blast in his chest and instantly know that it is a fatal injury. There is nothing in Securus that could repair the damage.

I desperately want to break through the wall and get to Merrick in the vain hope of comforting him in his last moments, but deep down I know he is already gone. Frantically, I struggle to regain rational thought and suppress the overwhelming rage and sorrow that is threatening to consume me. I am a moment away from losing reason and giving in to panic, but then the faces of the others flash through my mind. I need to stay calm and get them out of here. If these soldiers killed Merrick so callously, there is no reason they would not do the same to the rest of us. I need to try to save the rest of the group.

I tear myself away from the sight of my fallen friend and silently maneuver out of the tunnel. With my mind stunned by the event, my body moves on its own without me even realizing I am descending the rock wall. Halfway down, the presence of Sayda and Hadwin coaxes me back to reality.

"Where's Merrick? Is he okay?" Sayda asks warily as she rises to her feet.

"He went into a passage behind the top ledge. There was a cave-in during the earthquake," I reply. I cannot tell them the truth, at least not now. If I did, they would heedlessly rush to Merrick, only to share his fate. Withholding the truth is the only way to get them to safety.

"He's walled in. I tried to get to him, but it's impossible. I couldn't even hear him through the rocks. We need to go get help now." The words feel like poison in my mouth. I hate the deception but cannot think of a better option. I have to fight myself from telling them the truth, at least until we are all safe.

"One of us should wait in the passage with him," Hadwin insists, not wanting to abandon our friend.

"That tunnel is *not* safe," I tell them, trying to keep my voice from trembling.

This at least is true. I think they can sense my desperation and decide to trust my judgment despite their hesitation to leave Merrick in there alone. We descend the rest of the wall and rush over to where Talia and Aamon are waiting for us. I repeat my tale of the collapse and reiterate the need to get others to help rescue Merrick. The group remains silent as we return through the tunnels as quickly as we can. Even though Talia does not know Merrick well, she is obviously just as concerned as the others are for him and his situation. Aamon, on the other hand, has stopped shadowing Talia and seems more interested in watching my reactions as he repeatedly asks me about what happened. I ignore his questions and the suspicious stare he gives me, trying to focus on getting everyone back to safety.

We encounter one more collapsed passage that blocks our return, but the rubble of this second collapse is much smaller than the first. We are able to clear a path wide enough to pass and continue back to Securus.

When we reach the initial chamber of The Caves, we rush over to the Leadership Guard. I mentally compare his uniform to that of the soldiers', but there is no similarity between them. This Guard had the same basic uniform that those in Leadership wear. The crimson trim that lines his uniform indicates his occupation as an armed member of the Leadership Guard. There is no armor and his helmet does nothing to hide his face like the soldiers' helmets do. The small pistol protruding from the holster on his right hip seems laughable when compared to the terrifying weaponry the soldiers carried. Even the bright insignia on the Guard's chest looks different. I must have been mistaken about the symbol on the soldiers' uniforms. *They couldn't have been part of Leadership, could they?* I ask myself, searching in vain for another explanation.

When the Guard sees us coming, he jumps back and pulls out his gun. There is a nervous twitch in the corner of his eye as he raises it and aims directly at me. Hoping to keep him from accidentally firing, I calmly explain the situation to the Guard, leaving out any mention of what was really in the passage. With a gun in my face and a shaky man behind it, I do not want to say anything to make him more suspicious. After absorbing my explanation, he starts to calm down and holsters his weapon, realizing we pose no threat.

Now that he is calm, I momentarily consider telling the truth of what happened, but then decide against it. I cannot get past the uneasy feeling from watching one of the typically stoic Guards be so edgy for no apparent reason. That combined with the nagging thought of the symbol on the soldiers' armor keeps me quiet. If they really were part of Leadership in any way, all our lives could be in peril for having discovered them.

The more I think about it, the more I realize they have to be part of Leadership since none of the workers could have attained that kind of equipment. Aside from that, there are no other surviving colonies except for Securus. Even if there was another facility we did not know about, it would be too far away for them to make it to these tunnels through the poisonous atmosphere. The nearest underground facility to Securus was being built nearly seven hundred miles away. Regardless of their origin, my focus is to keep the others safe and retrieve Merrick's body. In case I am wrong and the soldiers are not involved with Leadership, I need to convince them to bring a big enough rescue team so we will not all be in danger when we go back out there.

## 4

Knowing the danger that waits in the tunnels, it feels wrong not warning the others. But with a large search party there will be significantly less danger if we encounter the soldiers again. My plan is to keep vigilant when we return for Merrick and warn the others of danger if need be.

I look back to Securus and the massive steel door that serves as the only entrance from The Caves. It can be closed at a moment's notice, and that is reassuring. If I am wrong and the soldiers are not part of Leadership, they would not be able to penetrate that barrier, even with their impressive assault rifles. Securus is well designed to keep all else out. The facility was originally meant to protect for a nuclear threat, but when The Agent was released, it was modified to protect against it. The builders knew that panicked hoards would try to get in and overwhelm the capabilities of the facility, so they made it into a sturdy fortress. When we expanded into the depths, we made only this single, secure entrance from The Caves with the same security in mind. We are most vulnerable when we venture away from Securus' safety.

After hearing our explanation and plea for help, the Guard speaks into his communicator, requesting clearance from his superiors for the rescue mission. There is a long pause as he waits for a reply. After the voice in his ear responds, he informs us of the decision.

"We're going to get a team here soon and attempt a

rescue. You all need to return to your quarters immediately. If I were you I'd expect some punishment for breaking curfew," he says, sounding as if he were reading from a script.

"It's not their fault," Talia says firmly while stepping in front of the Guard and presenting her sample containers. "They wanted to return, but I insisted they stay and help me collect these samples."

There is a spark of recognition from the Guard, who becomes much more courteous with the realization he had been scolding Talia Vaden. "I apologize, Ms. Vaden. I'll inform my superiors of this, I'm sure it will be accepted as mitigating circumstances. However, I still must insist that everyone return to their quarters immediately."

"You need us in there," I demand. "You'll never find Merrick if we don't lead you to him. He's deep in an unmarked tunnel system." My frustration is mirrored in both Sayda and Hadwin who are standing beside me looking as if they are ready to attack.

"It's okay, Kagen," Aamon says calmly. "I remember the way and I'll stay to lead the search team." He points to the Guard, "Contact your superior and let them know that Aamon Tiran is here, and I will lead them to where they need to go."

After another prolonged consultation with his communicator, the Guard informs us that his superior in Leadership finds this acceptable. For the first time, I am almost thankful to have Aamon around. At least he can lead them to Merrick. Sensing our frustration, Aamon assures us he will get them there quickly and will make sure they give every effort to save Merrick. Realizing the rest of us will not be allowed to return with the search party, I begin to regret not telling them about the soldiers, but at this point it is already too late. Who would believe that tale now? It would just sound like I was making it up so they would let me join the search party. Plus, a voice in the back of my mind keeps warning me to keep quiet. Something about the Guard is not right. We stand there, still not believing they are keeping us from helping. As we do, a small aftershock shakes the ground. It would normally have sent us scurrying for safety, but with our attention still focused on the Guard, we barely notice.

"Make sure to bring a large group," I caution. "There are a lot of large boulders that need to be moved and it may get worse with these aftershocks." This is true, but I want to make sure that there will be enough members of the Leadership Guard present in case the soldiers are still there.

Growing impatient with us, the Guard again insists that we leave, promising we will regret it if we do not comply. This time we finally do. As we turn to leave, Talia gently squeezes my shoulder and gives me an empathic look to convey her well wishes for Merrick. Hadwin and Sayda do not make eye contact with anyone as they stomp off, their disgust with the situation blatantly obvious. Some of their anger is directed at me for not allowing them to stay with Merrick, but there is nothing I can do about that now. Their exasperation is understandable, with us being forced to stand helplessly by while others set out for Merrick. In their situation, I would also be incensed by being forced to abandon our friend. Only I know that it is already too late for Merrick. Only I know why we had to rush away.

Now that the others are safe, the thought of that tragic loss cannot be avoided. Sullenly, I turn and start off to my quarters. It feels like a terrible nightmare that I am unable to wake from. One of my best friends has been executed.

*Why? Who are those soldiers?* The questions return to my mind repeatedly. To make matters worse, I may have also alienated myself from my friends in a desperate attempt to protect them. When I arrive at my quarters, my mother and Arluin are already asleep. Though I try to be silent, my entrance disturbs their rest.

"Where have you been?" my mother asks while looking me over. Arluin remains silent on his bunk watching for my reply.

I brush her away. "I'm fine, but Merrick isn't," I say with a heavy heart. I force myself to repeat my altered tale of the events one more time. Until I am sure that there is no more danger it is best to conceal the truth, even from them. "There's nothing more I can do tonight. We have to wait for the morning and hope they got him out." I collapse on my bunk and pretend to go to sleep, though I cannot. They do the same.

\*

The scattered minutes I am able to sleep are restless. It feels impossible to come to grips with what happened. An overwhelming fear and anger constantly stirs me, leaving me unable to calm the fury of thoughts swirling through my mind. It all happened so fast. Merrick, one of my best friends since childhood is dead, and with him, my grip on reality feels like it is fading away. None of it makes any sense. The only thing I do know is because of last night, everything has changed. I want to find the man who warned of the shadow-men that turned out to be soldiers. Did he see them in the upper tunnels? Is that what caused Leadership to close them? Those are questions I will never be able to ask. He is locked away in a place that few return from, leaving me with no way to find out what he really knows.

It is getting close to morning, and I cannot force my

eyes closed any longer. The lone blanket covering me on my hard bunk feels stifling. I get up, careful not to hit the bed above me. I do not want to disturb Arluin. Judging from the restful pattern of his breath, he must still be sleeping. My legs are ready to run, but there is nowhere to go. I am stuck in my box-like quarters. Leadership would not tolerate me running the halls of Securus at this hour, especially after what happened last night.

The main power has not yet been activated, so I stand in darkness. Unable to adjust to the minimal light, I put on my illuminator and turn it to the lowest setting. Its faint glow now permeates the darkness. I look to the other side of the small room and see my mother, Cordella, asleep on the remaining bunk. The look on her face causes me to pause for a moment. There is a sadness that often emerges in her expressions while asleep that she would never allow us to see otherwise. It mirrors my own emotions and the shoulder length, charcoal hair framing her face seems to intensify it. She is a warm, strong willed woman, but so much time in this peculiar environment has taken an emotional toll on her. Until now, I never understood why it always felt like she was trying to protect us from the effects this place.

Quietly, I maneuver into the only other area I can go, the small attached bathroom. The space in here is significantly smaller that the main quarters, making me more anxious. One would think living in an underground facility for my entire twenty-six years of life would make me immune to the cramped spaces, but right now everything feels like it is collapsing onto me. I fixate on the small mirror that overlooks the sink and lock onto the face staring back at me. I see his familiar short black hair, olive skin, slightly unkempt facial hair, and eyes with a golden brown center encased by a green outer ring. The face is mine, but even with this simple fact, I feel a whisper of doubt. Apparently, things are not always what they seem.

My eyes remain anchored to the mirror, but my eyes no longer see my reflection. Instead, I see the image of Merrick standing alone in that tunnel and then collapsed on the floor. They killed him and I was powerless to stop it.

A spark in my vision snaps me back to the uncertain reflection in the mirror. Taking a deep breath, I try to calm my mind. Of course it is me. I am Kagen Meldon and I have not yet gone crazy. It is not my self-image that needs to be doubted and this was not a bad dream. I need to figure out who those men are and make sure they pay for what they did. After his sacrifice, I owe nothing less to Merrick. There must be clue out there I had not noticed.

A sudden creak from the pipes within the walls jolts me from my concentration. Deep in thought, I had not heard the footsteps behind me until now. I turn and face Arluin with his scrutinizing stare. He has always seemed to possess an uncanny ability to read others' emotions, and he knows I did not tell him the entire truth last night. I desperately wanted to tell someone what really happened, but if my suspicions are right, that could put him in danger.

"What really happened last night?" he asks in a low controlled whisper. "It wasn't just some accident, was it?"

"I'm not sure what really happened. All I know is something isn't right, and I need some time to sort it out. You have to be patient and keep this between us. No one can know anything's wrong. I'll let you know when I figure this out, but for now it's safer for you to let me deal with it," I say firmly. Arluin narrows his eyes and prepares his rebuttal, but before he has a chance to speak, I place my hand on his shoulder and lean in to whisper, "Trust me on this, I need you to stay strong, especially for mom. I don't want her to worry."

His resistance melts away, and he returns to bed. I cannot let Arluin become involved in this. It is far too dangerous. Even so, I can only keep him in the dark for so long before his patience will run out and he ends up doing something impetuous. That makes it even more urgent that I find a way to understand what really happened and figure out what to do next.

There were a couple things about the trip to The Caves that was unusual from the start. Talia's presence with us was unexpected, and she is a major figure in Leadership. But it is hard to imagine her having anything to do with this because, in my heart, I feel there is no malice in her. Aamon, on the other hand, was acting odd the entire time. My trust in his motives is not so strong, even if he did help out in the end.

From the other room, I hear the morning alert. With it, the main power has been activated, so I take off my illuminator and turn on the bathroom lights. I am no longer standing in the shadows, but my thoughts feel as if they still are. I long for the warm glow of the lights to bring me clarity, but they do not. I am no closer to the truth of why Merrick was murdered or understanding why those soldiers and rail tracks were even there. With the fatigue from the lack of rest, my concentration is faltering. I begin to dress and await the morning announcements, hoping that Leadership will have found the answers that are eluded me. My mother and Arluin are both already dressed and ready for the announcements by the time I emerge from the bathroom. In silence, I take my usual place beside them and wait. We hear the familiar tone and watch as the screen comes to life.

"Good morning, I am Mr. Vaden. Unfortunately, I bring sad news this morning. As you are all certainly aware, there was seismic activity last night. There was no structural damage to Securus or to our energy generation equipment from this. However, some of our people were in a structurally unsound passageway deep within The Caves at the time the seismic activity occurred. There was a cave-in and Merrick Dunn was caught among the falling debris. When the rescue team was able to reach him it was already too late. He had been trapped under the falling rocks and the resulting injuries were fatal. We are unsure if his injuries came from the initial collapse or if they were a result of further falling debris caused by the aftershocks. There will be a funeral service planned for this evening. Specific details for the service will be disseminated later in the day.

"As a result of this tragic accident, it is necessary to restrict all access to any unsecured sections of The Caves. Leadership and our research workers will continue to further explore The Caves and open new areas for general purposes only after the safety of these passages have been confirmed..."

The words echo in my mind, '*He had been trapped under the falling rocks and the resulting injuries were fatal.*' I did not know what I expected Mr. Vaden to say, but that was not it. Standard procedure would dictate that Merrick's body be examined by the Healer who was on shift at the time. Even if the soldiers tried to stage the death as an accident by piling boulders on top of Merrick, they would not have had enough time to fully disguise the gun blast. There is no way the injury could have been missed by a proper exam. Either the exam was never done or Mr. Vaden is purposefully lying to us. If he is lying, that confirms Leadership is definitely involved. This realization is disconcerting. Even though I had suspected it, I had not wanted to truly believe it. If Leadership is up to something in The Caves, I need to find out what. I owe it to Merrick to discover the truth and make sure everyone knows the real events that led to his death.

Seeing my internal struggle, my mother and Arluin come over to console me. Even though I had already known Merrick's fate, the inexplicable circumstances surrounding it has kept me from fully facing the loss. My thoughts were preoccupied with concern for the others as well as my struggle to understand the presence of the unknown soldiers and hidden tracks. There is something about this moment that strips away all of my defensive mental barriers and forces me to confront the reality that Merrick is gone. My initial emotional shock has run out and the strength of my emotions becomes amplified. For a while I just sit there, my head tilted down and my eyes closed. Our mother and Arluin simply embrace me and each other. No words are spoken. My family knows I prefer it that way.

Our mother is the first to get up. "I'll meet you two for breakfast," she says while preparing to leave. She remains stoic as usual, but I can sense the grief she is suppressing. Merrick was like family to all of us. As she exits the quarters, Arluin turns and looks expectantly at me.

"I know, Arluin, you want answers, and so do I," I say carefully. "Whether intentional or not, information was withheld in the announcement. I want you to stay out of The Caves."

"You can't say something that cryptic and expect me to just accept it," Arluin interrupts.

"Look, something bad is going on, and I'm worried Leadership is involved. That's why it's better for you to stay out of it until I figure it out," I sternly reply. "I promise, as soon as I do, I'll let you know. For now, you can help me by just keeping an eye out. I don't know what you should look for, just anything that seems off."

"Okay, I can do that," Arluin replies. "But promise you'll be careful. I don't want you to do anything that'll get you in trouble."

He is obviously not happy with my request and even less so with me withholding information, but I think he will go along with it for now. With this temporarily agreed on, we leave to start our daily routine. Even with tragedy, Leadership demands we maintain productivity.

## 5

The atmosphere at breakfast is somber and the hall is completely absent of its usual chatter. I finish my meal quickly and then head over to the infirmary to start my shift. Rana is already in the appointments room, so I head to my usual exam room. This area has the same general layout as the appointments room, except the equipment is strikingly different. I take stock to make sure everything is in order. There is a range of diagnostic machines that scan the body for different abnormalities as well as a host of devices designed to heal. Many of these devices are so bizarre in appearance that they could easily be mistaken for tools of torture to those unfamiliar with their use.

Other than the equipment, the room is empty. Rana must have already relieved Trent Riley, the nightshift Healer that was on duty last night. I was hoping he would still be in so I could ask him about Merrick's condition when he examined him. No one has come in for an evaluation yet, so I decide to look up Trent's charting. Sitting at the computer, I open the records database and type in 'Merrick Dunn'. Scanning the documents I find the last entry:

*Patient has extensive external signs of trauma. There are diffuse abrasions, contusions and hematomas. Left parietal scalp region is depressed with an underlying skull fracture. This is most likely the fatal injury. There are multiple fractured ribs and evidence of intra-abdominal crush injuries. There is also a deformity of the right elbow, likely representing a fracture/dislocation. Other extremity injuries appear superficial.*

It is not a particularly thorough report and does not help me much. Conspicuously absent is any mention of the chest wall wound from the gun blast. While scrolling through the records I am interrupted by the chime that indicates someone is checking in for an evaluation. I abandon my search and walk toward the check-in area to meet my newest patient. Before reaching the waiting area, there is an unexpected man walking toward me in the hallway. When I recognize him my muscles instantly tense and an electric pulsation races through my shoulders to my neck. It is Mr. Vaden.

"Hello, Kagen," he says casually as he paces toward me. Though his tone sounds benign, the intensity of his stare is not. "I would like to speak with you in private, if you have a minute." Contrary to his words, the look in his eyes suggests that this is not a request.

"Of course, Mr. Vaden, we can speak in my exam room. It is empty at the moment," I reply while carefully turning and retracing my steps, trying to conceal my surprise at his appearance. We enter the room and he closes the door behind us. Under normal circumstances this is one of the places where I feel most comfortable, but now the walls suddenly feel constricting.

"As I am sure you have already surmised, I am here to speak with you regarding the events in The Caves last night," he says while walking toward the medical equipment.

He lifts an automated suturing device and holds it up for examination. The metallic shine and spider-like extensions holds his attention for a brief moment. A slight shift in his expression signals his recognition of its function.

"My consolations for the loss of your friend, Merrick,"

he says while continuing to rummage through the equipment, now looking at the portable ultrasound. The screen appears identical to our portable computers, except it has an attached ultrasound probe.

"It is a difficult loss for us all," I reply.

"There are some details I would like to clarify," Mr. Vaden says. He now turns to focus his gaze directly on me. "It concerns me that we had such a large group of our people that deep in the caves after curfew, even if Talia was conducting research. Is this a common occurrence?"

"No, we were so excited with the new area we discovered that we lost track of time," I reply. I take a seat near the computer interface. This is my usual spot when I am interviewing patients and for some reason sitting here helps me feel more at ease. It appears Talia has maintained her cover story even with her father. Still, I do not want her to endure the blame for choices that were my own. "For that I take full responsibility. It was my obligation to oversee the schedule of the trip since it was my permitted access time," I tell him.

There is a hint of surprise that fleetingly penetrates Mr. Vaden's otherwise stoic expression. Either he actually believed that Talia was solely responsible for the lateness of our expedition, or he simply thought I would let her take the blame for it. Watching his reaction and the renewed intensity of his glare, I believe it was the latter. Talia may be persuasive, but Mr. Vaden is very perceptive.

"Have you been to that portion of The Caves before?" he asks.

"No, Merrick had discovered it recently and held it as a surprise for us," I answer.

"Of course," he says doubtfully. "Both Aamon and

47

Talia said they were not nearby during the cave-in, but Aamon noticed only you and Merrick made it into the passage that collapsed during the earthquake. What exactly happened?" he asks as he slowly walks toward me. His stare never falters as he stops in front of me, awaiting my response.

"Sayda nearly fell while we were climbing, so she stopped to rest. Hadwin stayed with her while Merrick and I completed the ascent. Merrick went into a tunnel system on the top ridge just before the earthquake." I pause, trying to suppress my anger. "He became trapped by the collapse. I tried to get to him, but the rubble was too large for me to move. My only option was to return and assemble a rescue team. From there, you will have to speak with members of the search party."

"I see," Mr. Vaden mumbles. His attention returns to the equipment in the room. He holds up part of a device meant to hold extremities up while setting fractures or dislocations. The five coils in his hand are used to suspend an arm by holding onto the fingers. "Did you notice anything unusual in the passage before or after the collapse?"

"No, it seemed just like any other tunnel I've been in. Why? Did the search team find something?" I shift my position to try to read his expression, but his reflection in the glass cabinets reveals nothing. His question makes me wonder if he is fully aware of the soldiers and the tracks that were concealed in the passage. That must be why he closed the upper tunnels.

"Nothing of concern," he says sharply. "As far as your responsibility for the events that led to this tragedy, I am restricting your access to The Caves until further notice. I would advise you to let Sayda and Hadwin know they need to be more prudent in their actions or they will also gain my attention."

It takes every bit of reasoning and restraint that I possess to hold my tongue. My impulse is to demand he reveal his experiment in The Caves and why he is hiding it from us. Those soldiers are the ones responsible for *"this tragedy."* How dare he place the burden of responsibility for Merrick's death on me when I was powerless to stop it? Even as the thought races through my mind, another whispers in the background. There had to have been something I could have done to prevent it. I *am* responsible. The fight that was surging within me subsides and is replaced with sorrow mixed into self-doubt.

I look up and am surprised to find a satisfied smirk in Mr. Vaden's reflection. I stand and begin to march toward him, not sure of what I intend to do. He sees me coming and turns around. There is no alarm or concern in his eyes at my aggressive posture, only an intense curiosity. When I near him the patient chime again sounds, signaling that someone is checking in for an evaluation. The sound triggers an internal recognition that helps me regain a calm focus. This has been important in my performance as a Healer, but now serves me in this unexpected conversation.

"Duty calls," Mr. Vaden says, as he turns and walks toward the door. He stops before he leaves and adds, "Oh, by the way, it would be wise of you to leave Talia to her research and Leadership duties. My daughter is much too important to Securus to be distracted from her pursuits, understood?"

"I understand, Mr. Vaden," I say evenly.

Restricting me from The Caves and threatening me to stay away from Talia will do nothing to weaken my resolve for discovering the truth. *Yes, Mr. Vaden, duty does call. More than you know*, I think to myself. He leaves and I walk toward the waiting area to meet my new patient.

\*

I continue on through the morning caring for the steady flow of patients. One man lacerated his forearm down to the bone while working in the Deep Vents. Another has developed a significant skin infection that is threatening to overwhelm his cardiovascular system. I navigate the injuries and infections through to my lunch break without any spare time. The rush of people deprived me of the opportunity to further investigate Trent's charts. But at least I was able to accomplish something worthwhile in helping my patients. Rana has also finished her morning appointments, and my meeting with Mr. Vaden did not go unnoticed. She appears in the doorway.

"How are you holding up, Kagen?" she asks.

"I'll be ok," I respond tersely, not wanting to relive the details of Merrick's death again.

"What did Mr. Vaden want?" Rana is not usually this direct, but these are not usual circumstances.

"He was just trying to get more details on what happened last night. I assume Trent told you that I was in The Caves along with Merrick last night," I tell her, intentionally leaving out any mention of Talia. She nods at my assumption and waits for me to continue. "Did he mention anything about Merrick's condition?" I ask, not expecting her to have any new information. I just need to change the focus off of Mr. Vaden's visit.

"No, he didn't tell me anything more than what we learned from the morning announcement," she says, appearing distracted. She hesitates for a moment, carefully choosing her words. "Though he said nothing more, I had the distinct impression that he was withholding something. Did this have anything to do with Talia being out there with you?" she asks without any attempt to mask her concern.

"No, it had nothing to do with Talia. Actually, things may have ended up much worse for Hadwin and Sayda if she wasn't there," I reassure her. "None of this is your fault, Rana." She does not seem satisfied with my response, but does not probe any further.

"If you need some time off, I can cancel some appointments and extend the hours of the other Healers to cover your shift," she offers.

"Thanks, but I would rather keep working. It keeps my mind occupied," I answer. Besides, I'm already in trouble with Leadership, so I don't need the extra attention that would be brought by hampering the workflow. On top of this added problem, I still need to face Hadwin and Sayda. That is not going to be easy either.

I head off to the lunch hall hoping to find the two of them. I walk inside and scan the room. It is nearly filled to capacity with the lunch rush, but there is no sign of my friends. Dejected, I make my way to the food dispersal center. The bland aroma of today's lunch fails to elevate my mood. Nestled amongst the stainless steel counters and below the artificial glass shields is my waiting meal. There is an artificial meat wrapped in a cabbage-like substance, along with a small serving of a nutrient rich, but tasteless slurry. At least there is clean water to wash it down.

I take my food and maneuver through the hall, again looking for Hadwin or Sayda. This time I spot them in the far corner facing the back wall. They are sitting alone at a table made to accommodate eight people. This is a welcome sight because with less people around there may be enough privacy to explain what really happened. I reach the table and set my food down across from the dejected looking pair. Neither of them bothers to look up to see who joined the table.

"Hey," I say, intending to continue, but the words elude me.

"Kagen," Hadwin mutters. He is always the one that lightens the mood for us when things are bad. Now, his lightheartedness is gone, and there is only anguish in his expression. He looks up from his food long enough to nudge Sayda. She finally looks up but says nothing. The rage radiating from her eyes pierces me as she locks onto me with her stare.

"I know I have a lot of explaining to do," I manage to say before Sayda interrupts.

"Explaining? You're damn right you do. *Explain* how we left Merrick for dead in that tunnel. *Explain* how you didn't even let us try to get him out. *Explain* how we let Aamon be the one to lead the search team when he can barely find his own shadow. Explain!" she demands.

"I'm mad too, Sayda, but try to calm down," Hadwin interjects. "We all lost a friend last night, and we're all upset by what happened. There's nothing we can do to bring him back. Right now we should try to focus on the memory of Merrick's life and not the circumstances of his death."

With his words, her fury breaks, giving way to sorrow as she lowers her head. Hadwin leans toward her and puts a comforting arm around her shoulders. She rests her head against him, and I can see a tear slowly trickle down her cheek. The sight of Sayda crying nearly overwhelms me. She has always so been fiery and strong, ever since the first day that Hadwin and I meet her when we were young children. Back then, there was an older boy that had a particular dislike for Hadwin. The boy would go out of his way to confront him. Most often there was name calling and pushing, but on that day, the bullying went further. The boy had pushed me down and then pounced on Hadwin. The bully was sitting on top of him when we heard a high pitched shriek, and out of nowhere the fleeting blur of a little girl came running full speed. She leveled the bully with her attack, and stunned by the blow, he started crying as he ran off.

"You leave them alone," she yelled at him as he disappeared around a corner. "Or I'll come back for you!"

Hadwin and I just looked on in disbelief. This little thing just saved us. From then on Sayda joined our group of friends. Neither of us ever asked her why she decided to intervene, we were just thankful that she did. The little girl who saved us from the bully was now a grown woman who still has maintained her tenacity, but now my actions have led her to this sorrow. Seeing her tears hurts more than her anger ever could.

"Now is not the time, Kagen," Hadwin says as he and Sayda get up to exit the hall. Though he is calm, with his firm tone, it is clear how upset Hadwin is with this whole situation. The lump that has been expanding in my throat steals my voice. With no words left to respond, I merely nod in understanding. For the rest of my lunch, I sit in silence. No one joins me, and no one consoles me. They have all heard Sayda's words and now everyone knows that I am to blame for leaving Merrick in The Caves. I wanted to tell Hadwin and Sayda what really happened last night, but as Hadwin said, now is not the time. They are not ready to hear what I have to say. It leaves me feeling utterly alone and confused. We have always shared each other's secrets and fears. Without them, I am left alone to deal with the true depth of my burden and the uncertainty that it brings.

I make my way back to the infirmary. At least it will give me something else to do besides fixating on my anguish. Despite Rana covering during my lunch break, the waiting area is now full. I go back to my exam room, and discover why. There is a critically ill person who came in just after I left for lunch. Sweat streams from his pale, exposed skin, drenching his clothes and the gurney under him. He appears confused and is rambling incoherently. Despite his current disheveled appearance, there is something familiar about the man. I study his disoriented expression and try to place him. The image slowly contorts in my mind and I see him. It is the Guard from last night.

# 6

"What's wrong with this man, Rana?" I ask while reviewing his vital signs and initial diagnostic data that Rana has been collecting. The man's heart is racing, his temperature is elevated, and his blood pressure is dangerously low.

"His name is Leland Gibbon. I think he has some type of meningitis or encephalitis, but it's unlike anything I've ever seen. The progression of his condition is exceedingly rapid. He only started showing symptoms this morning," she says pensively while motioning me to put on my mask and gloves for protection against transmission of the infection. "I need to do a lumbar puncture and analyze his cerebrospinal fluid so we can confirm it."

"He's the Guard that helped us arrange the search party in The Caves last night," I tell Rana while starting to examine him. "He appeared fine then, from what I recall."

"Leland, do you remember me from last night?" I ask, but he does not respond. His eyes are looking toward me, but there is a ghostly hollowness in his gaze.

"I can do the lumbar puncture if you like, Rana," I offer. I know she prefers to finish what she starts, but this case is intriguing, and the mental distraction would be helpful to me. Not to mention it will take a long time to stabilize his condition, and she could use the break.

Rana considers my offer for a moment. "Okay, but keep me updated on the results. I'm very interested in the outcome of this case, especially to see if he responds to our treatments."

I am surprised that she agreed to my request. By even if she is willing to let me take over her patient, she will still be watching closely.

"Absolutely, Rana, I'll finish stabilizing him and then work my way through the others. You can take a break and finish up your appointments when you get back. I'll check in with you when I get the rest of the results," I tell her. She seems satisfied with this and leaves me to continue working on Leland.

After Rana has left, I return my attention to Leland. The lumbar puncture is my next step. I wrap his fidgeting body with the multiple strips of our soft-strap system attached to the gurney to keep him still in a fetal position for the procedure. We have had to find ways to be self-sufficient since we do not have the luxury of having a team of people to work on a case together except in the most extreme circumstances when an emergency is called. This straps system was devised to cradle patients in whatever position we place them in, removing the need for extra helpers during procedures like the lumbar puncture or spinal tap, as most of the workers call it.

I review the scan of his brain to make sure it is safe to proceed. He is already sick enough and the procedure could not be attempted if there were any signs of increased pressure in his brain. If that were the case, draining the spinal fluid could trigger a deadly condition involving a brain herniation. With the guilt I am already carrying, it would be overwhelming to put that on my conscious as well. There are no abnormalities on the imaging, so I take a deep breath and mentally prepare. Even knowing this is necessary to help him, whenever I need to perform an invasive procedure like this, the irony of having to inflict pain in order to better heal the patient always strikes me.

After applying a sterilizing and numbing solution I begin the procedure by inserting a long, thin needle into Leland's lower back. My hand is steady as this procedure has become routine for me, but that was not always the case. Putting a needle inside a person's spine can be anxiety provoking, especially when first learning it. He does not move, flinch, or even notice the movement of my needle. The pressure changes as I penetrate the layers of tissue encasing the spine vibrate through the needle to my hand. There is a familiar pop as I reach the spinal canal and the fluid begins to drain into my waiting sample vials.

It is instantly apparent that the sample is not normal. Instead of the typical clear water-like fluid, my vials hold a cloudy, almost sludge-like liquid. After finishing the collection I plug then needle and begin to remove it from his spine. Before I can finish, Leland suddenly moves. His entire body begins contorting with rhythmic contractions that can only be from a seizure. I rush to pull the needle out, but the force of his movement is only partially contained by the straps and his harsh movements unsteady my hand. With one more pull, the now bent needle is released from his spine and the tip jumps from my control, piercing my glove.

With Leland's increasingly violent thrashing, there is no time to check for a puncture. I try to suppress the fear that I might have just directly injected his infection into me and administer another medication into his intravenous line to calm the seizure. Soon after the injection, his contractions subside, and I reposition Leland to allow a more natural position of comfort.

Now that he is relatively stable, I can tend to myself. I

remove my glove and repeatedly sanitize my hand. My hands begin to tremble and my heart speeds up as I face the thought of becoming infected like this. The cleaning feels like it takes an eternity, but I need to follow the protocol to try and decrease my risk. After finishing the sterilizing process, a thorough inspection relieves my growing fear because there is no puncture wound. The needle narrowly missed penetrating my skin. I feel a little irritated with myself for letting it get that close. I need to be more careful next time. Turning my attention back to my patient, I review the medications that Rana had already begun. She initiated treatment with broad spectrum antibiotics and antiviral infusions. I add some additional medications aimed at supporting his failing circulatory system. After inserting the sample into our specimen analyzer, it is time to shift my focus to the remaining people in the waiting room.

The rest of the patients are not as ill as Leland and do not share his same infection. After minor treatments they are all able to return to their various duties. By the time I finish treating them, the analysis of Leland's cerebrospinal fluid is complete. The results are worse than I had feared. He has an overwhelming infection that is aggressively attacking his central nervous system, which explains the seizure. It appears to be of viral origin, though we will need a more detailed analysis in the Research Department to confirm it. This virus is acting more destructively than any other that I had ever seen or even read about. It must be a novel mutation of an old virus. I can only hope that it is not easily transmitted, for if there were an epidemic of a strain this virulent, it would be more than Securus could bear.

I return to check on Leland and find that his vital signs are only marginally improved. He is alert enough to try to speak, but his words come out mangled. Despite my suspicions of Leadership, I cannot help but to feel for Leland. I do not know much about him personally, but it is doubtful he has a significant role in whatever is going on in The Caves.

"Leland, you have a really bad infection. We're doing everything we can to try and treat it," I tell him, not expecting a reply. I always talk to my patients even if they cannot respond because it feels more respectful that way.

For a moment his eyes meet mine and this time I do not see the vacant gaze that was there before. He again tries to speak, but the words are barely audible.

"It-it…not" he strains to finish, but is already slipping back into his delirium. "Not… right. I'm sorry."

His focus has eroded and his words trail off into incoherent mumbling. What did he mean? What was he sorry about? Even though he seemed to have a lucid moment it is impossible to tell if his words were truly meant for me or if he was still in the grips of confusion. Still, the words echo through my mind, feeling just as purposeful as the warning the other man gave me about the shadow-men.

With his initial diagnostic evaluation and treatment completed, I decide to transfer him to the small intensive care unit we have in the far end of the infirmary. Because we are limited in space, most people are returned to their designated quarters for continued treatment. We have another Healer that makes daily rounds through Securus to continue care for those that require it. In cases as severe as this in which more constant attention is required, they remain in the intensive care unit with another group of Healers that are assigned day and night. I check the schedule before going. Today the Healer is Adara, which is good because she is a competent and caring Healer from the Leadership caste. As I am wheeling Leland and his gurney to the back of the infirmary where the intensive care unit is located, Rana appears in the hall.

"Hey Rana, the results of the CSF analysis were really bad. The infection looks viral, but it's more severe than any I've ever heard of. He even seized when I was doing the LP," I say while continuing the transfer.

Rana continues to walk with me, helping guide the gurney. "I thought it was going to be a bacterial infection. Interesting," she says, sounding more like she is thinking out loud rather than talking to me directly. After a reflective pause, she says, "I'll take him from here and fill in Adara on his condition. You need to get ready for Merrick's service."

I thank her and head to the decontamination chamber before leaving the infirmary. It is an uncomfortable process, and we only use it when it is absolutely necessary. The chamber is the size of a hallway pass through and is accessed by clear doors on either side. I enter the chamber, close the door behind me, and activate the system. There is something about the thick fog of sterilizing chemicals that now fill the chamber that I have always found uniquely unnerving. My vision becomes blurred, and the warm, sweet smelling mist fills my lungs, setting them ablaze. An intense paresthesia shoots down my arms and legs. Just when I start to feel as if there is no oxygen left in my lungs, the vents activate and mercifully, the mist recedes. My vision returns and the paresthesias subside. I am now safe to exit the infirmary without exposing others to the new pathogen.

I had not wanted to think about the service, but now there is nothing left to distract me. The images of Merrick stuck in that passage replay incessantly in my mind. The feeling of helplessness I had when the soldiers murdered him returns and permeates through my being. I find my way back to my quarters despite the mindlessness of my walk. My mother and Arluin have yet to return, so I lie on my bunk to wait for them.

My mother is the first to arrive. I hear her enter, but still remain motionless on my bunk. She walks over and sits beside me.

"Kagen, I know you don't want to talk about what happened, so please just listen for a moment. When your father died I felt lost, but I had you and Arluin to keep me from surrendering to my grief. We were able to endure as a family." Her words tremble as she speaks and tears start to form. She usually hides her sadness from us, but this time she makes no effort to conceal it.

"Life in Securus is challenging. We were not meant for this kind of environment, but we do the best we can. It will help to think of the joyful moments that you shared with Merrick. Don't let his memory fade, he will continue on through you as well as the rest of his friends and family." The meekness in her voice fades, and her words grow stronger. "And remember, there are still many others who care for you and will help shoulder the load of anger, grief and burden, no matter what."

*

When Arluin arrives, we all leave our quarters, heading to the main hall for the service. There is a large number of people already gathered, waiting for it to start. The faces in the crowd reflect the wide mix of ethnic origins that makes up Securus. It is an accidental diversity created by The Agent itself. These were not the people meant for this place, but in the chaos created by The Agent, most of the intended inhabitants were unable to reach Securus except for those who became the founding members of

Leadership. After that, whoever made it here first was allowed to stay, until it was filled to capacity. Though the faces are all varied, the people are unified with a singular purpose and expression, remembrance and grief.

This hall is the largest Securus has to offer. It has a much higher ceiling than the others, allowing for a less constricting feel that reminds me of the large open areas in The Caves. Its primary purpose is community meetings or other occasions, such as this one, in which a large gathering is required. Up front there is a stage with large screens strategically positioned for visual displays.

Merrick's parents are on one side of the stage along with his older sister, Rowyn. They are holding each other, attempting to soften the blow of their loss. Mr. Vaden and Talia are seated on the opposite side of the stage, solemnly overseeing the proceedings. Between them is a sturdy, plain wooden table with a crimson velvet cloth carefully placed on top. Wood pieces are a rarity in Securus and are only used for specific ceremonies such as this one. In the center of the cloth, sits a multicolored urn that has been skillfully carved out of stone taken from The Caves. Cremation has become our method of burial more out of necessity than tradition. It is far too dangerous to venture needlessly onto the surface for an in-ground burial. The urn itself is a beautiful piece of craftsmanship. I cannot see the writing from here, but I know carved into the face will be Merrick's name. I have always thought our urns were a fitting resting place for the people of Securus because it mirrored our lives. Forever encased within a solid structure born of the earth but crafted by man.

I look around to spot Hadwin and Sayda. They are on separate ends of the hall and are both surrounded by their families. When the flow of mourners entering the hall ceases, the doors are closed and Mr. Vaden walks to the podium to start the service. The screens above the stage now display the identification image of Merrick. His vibrant smile and warm spirit fills the hall.

"Thank you all for coming tonight," Mr. Vaden begins. "We are here to mourn the tragic loss of a valuable member of our community, Merrick Dunn. He is survived by his loving parents and sister. At this time I would like to invite anyone who would like to come to the stage and share your thoughts or memories of Merrick."

Before he can finish the sentence I feel myself rising from my seat. Everyone can see that his family is in no condition to speak right now and someone needs to start. I feel the room watching me as I reach the edge of the stage, where Mr. Vaden waits to escort me to the podium.

"The stage is yours, Kagen," he whispers while placing a firm hand on my shoulder. I know that gesture is meant to appear reassuring, but somehow it feels unnatural and bereft of true empathy. He leaves me at the podium, but not before taking the audio controller with him. It may seem insignificant, but I know better. He is making it clear that while I may have the floor to speak, he is still in control. While waiting for him to reach his seat, my hands become clammy and my hearts pounds against my chest wall. I have no prepared speech and have always feared speaking in front of groups of people. Trying to buy some time, I fidget with the microphone, pretending to adjust it. I look back again to see Mr. Vaden watching me from his seat and then notice Talia next to him. The warmth and reassurance in her eyes are urging me to speak. Telling me she knows I can do it. I take a deep breath and picture Merrick in my mind.

"Merrick Dunn has been one of my best friends for as

long as I can remember," I say, still searching for the words to describe his essence. "He was an intelligent and caring man. He was a friend that you could always count on to do what was right, even if it wasn't the easiest thing to do. He was driven by a powerful spirit that even Securus could not contain. His competitive nature compelled him to excel and improve in every endeavor. This drive was contagious, and pushed us all to better ourselves along with him. His friendship and actions enriched our lives. I will always remember his strength and courage. Merrick was a good man who has been taken from us far too soon. I will carry his memory with me. Through all of us, his spirit will endure." I desperately want to continue, to demand justice and answers for his death. But now is not the time, and even if it were, Mr. Vaden would not allow it.

While leaving the stage, I silently renew my promise to Merrick to find those responsible for his death and hold them accountable. When I reach my seat, another voice begins to speak, it is Hadwin.

"Thank you for your words, Kagen. Merrick was like a brother to me as well. We grew up together, always competing with each other. He was very patient and forgiving as well. Like the time I hid all of his clothes the same day his father's clothes were being cleaned so he had to go to school wearing Rowyn's extra uniform," Hadwin says with a reminiscing smile.

The memory of Merrick stuffed in the way too small and entirely too revealing outfit sparks laughter throughout the hall. Even his family fondly remembers that day. Hadwin chuckles and continues to share more stories of his endless pranks on Merrick. Hadwin has always had a way of making us laugh, and we need that tonight more than usual. After Hadwin finishes, there is a parade of others who share memories of special moments with Merrick. When there are no more people waiting to talk, Mr. Vaden again takes the podium.

"Once again, thank you all for coming to celebrate the life of Merrick Dunn. This concludes tonight's service. Dinner hours have been extended to accommodate those in attendance. Thank you and good night."

The gathering disperses. Most of the people go to the dinner hall. I am physically and emotionally exhausted from everything that has happened in these last two days as well as from the lack of sleep last night, so I decide to skip dinner and return to my quarters. Planning my next actions will have to wait until my mind is rested and clear.

## 7

Again, I awaken before the morning alert. This time I did manage to rest for most of the night. Since it is only a few minutes before the morning power up, I start preparing for the day early hoping to make it to the infirmary before Trent finishes his shift. The water system is always active even when the power is not, so I shower in the darkness. The warm water soothes my mind and eases the tension in my shoulders. I stand still for a while, letting the relaxation continue while considering my options. Soon, the time limit activates and the water automatically turns off. That is another of the controls Leadership uses to preserve resources.

My next objective has to be to find a way to get back into The Caves. I need to investigate the tracks those soldiers were guarding if I am to discover what they are trying to hide. It sounds so straightforward, but finding a way to subvert my restriction will not be so easy. It is going to be difficult to avoid the Leadership personnel long enough to make it past the initial cavern and even harder to find a way past the collapse.

Just as I finish dressing, the power and lights turn on. My mother and Arluin rise to begin their morning routines. When our mother is occupied in the bathroom, Arluin seizes his chance to speak with me alone.

"Kagen, why did Mr. Vaden make a point of keeping the audio controller with him when you spoke at the service last night?" he asks in a whisper.

I let out a small laugh. "You really are observant, aren't you? I didn't think anyone else noticed that. He came to talk with me in the infirmary. He was upset that Talia was out there with us, so he revoked my access to The Caves." I want to leave it at that, but Arluin holds his ground, demanding more of an explanation. "I think he was making sure I didn't make a scene because I was upset over my restriction." That would have to be enough of an explanation for now.

The chime for the morning announcements sounds, so Arluin takes his usual position in front of the screen. Our mother quietly emerges from the bathroom and joins him. I have heard more than enough from Mr. Vaden as of late and have no intention of staying for the announcements.

"I'll see you both later, I want to get a quick breakfast and catch up with Trent before he leaves the infirmary. We have a really sick patient I want to talk to him about," I tell them while heading toward the door.

"Kagen, you know the announcements are mandatory," my mother warns.

"Yeah, I'll be quiet. No one will notice me since they'll be watching the announcements themselves. If anyone does ask, I'll just tell them that I'm needed in the infirmary," I say and immediately exit our quarters, not leaving any time for a prolonged argument.

The muffled tones of the announcements come from the many doors lining the hallway on my way to the breakfast hall. By the time I arrive they are nearly done. I pause and wait for the tone that always signals the end since the food will not be uncovered until after Mr. Vaden finishes. I am the first to arrive, but the cooks pay no attention to me. The food is the same bland combination of artificial porridge and nutrient drink we had been served all week. I am hungry from missing dinner, so the lack of variety does not bother me today. The regular flow of morning visitors begins just as I am leaving the hall. My mother spots me from a distance, so I give her a wave on my way out to let her know that no one noticed my early departure.

The first thing that strikes me outside the infirmary is the indicator for high level pathogen protection has been deactivated. At least I do not have to go through the decontaminator today. Hopefully that means they discovered the cause of Leland's illness is not easily transmitted from person to person. Rana has not arrived yet, so I walk through the rest of the infirmary in search of Trent. The braying of his snoring makes him rather easy to find. He is leaning back in a chair in my exam room with his feet propped up on the gurney. His head is tilted back displaying his unkempt and thinning ash blonde hair. I ring the patient alarm to awaken him, and the tone nearly causes him to fall from his chair. He catches himself, steadies his chair, and looks around the room with confusion. My laughter seems to jar him to attention. He stands and adjusts his clothes and hair to a satisfactory position. With such a limited and regulated diet, it has always puzzled me how he manages to support such a portly stature.

"Kagen, I didn't hear you come in," he says aloofly.

"Yeah, I noticed," I say with a smile still stretched across my face. "Did you happen to check on Leland's condition?"

"I didn't have to," he replies. "He didn't last very long. He died around one o'clock last night." Trent's words sound so indifferent he could easily be speaking of the death of some insignificant insect.

Leland's death is not a surprise given the severity of

his condition, but it affects me none-the-less. It is our charge to heal, and in that, we have failed him.

"I knew it would be difficult to save him, but I didn't think he would go so fast. Did we get any more results from his sample analysis?" I ask. Maybe we can find some way to learn from this and be better prepared if we encounter this illness again.

"No, most of the samples were destroyed with the terminal cleaning after he died. The few remaining tissue and blood samples that weren't incinerated were sent to the research lab," he replies while gathering his equipment, preparing to end his shift.

"We spent half the night with that terminal clean," he says, shifting from indifference to annoyance.

"Trent," I say then pause, waiting for his attention. When he notices the prolonged silence, he turns and faces me.

"Kagen?" he urges. At least he has enough tact to sense I have something substantial weighing upon me.

"That night in The Caves with Merrick," I trail off. Even though I had planned this conversation carefully, the words are still difficult to get out. Trent waits for me to finish.

"I keep replaying the events in my mind, trying to figure out what I could have done to save him. There had to be a way to get to him in time. Maybe I could have stabilized his injuries long enough to get him back here." The remorse in my voice keeps Trent silent. Even though my guilt over Merrick's death is real, I know there was no chance to save him from his real injury. But, I need to know if he is involved in the cover up.

"What was his condition like when you examined him? Be honest, I need to know the extent of his injuries and what you think the fatal one was," I compel his answer.

"Kagen, he was crushed nearly beyond recognition," Trent says sympathetically. "I examined him from head to toe and any number of his injuries could have been fatal. He had a significantly depressed skull fracture along with a large epidural hematoma, both lungs were collapsed, and he had a splenic rupture."

I hold my clenched fist behind my back, trying to hide the fact that his response enrages me. Not only does he have the audacity to lie directly to my face with all these contrived injuries, but he also is feigning sympathy for my feelings. Whatever is going on, this convinces me that he is part of the cover up. I bite my inner lip and fight to calm my emotions. It would be disastrous for me to lose control and reveal what I suspect. With a deep breath, I suppress my anger and compose myself.

"There's nothing you could have done; you can't beat yourself up like this," Trent says with the same manufactured empathy. At least he is not perceptive enough to understand my response was more than simple guilt over a lost friend.

"Okay, thanks," I tell him, wanting to allow him to leave before I lose control. "Any patients left from overnight to follow up on?"

"No, no one's left. I'm going to get some sleep," he says and leaves the infirmary.

I am alone in my exam room, left to absorb the added layer of deception. Now knowing that he is involved, I need to be more vigilant with Trent and watch for any other discrepancies. After my usual routine of checking the equipment and replenishing the supplies, I hear footsteps in the hall. I look out to find Rana headed toward the intensive care unit.

"Rana, Leland didn't make it," I say. "I already spoke with Trent. They did a terminal clean and released all remaining samples to the research lab. There's nothing more we can do."

"I figured that was the case since the infection control protocols were inactivated," She replies, looking off to the side, as if still in thought.

"There's something else I would like to talk to you about, in private," I say in a low voice. Her attention had been distracted with the news of Leland's passing, but my tone refocuses her.

"Of course, Kagen," she says matching my low tone.

I lead her to her appointment room instead of my exam room. If leadership is involved in a cover up, they may be monitoring my work area since I seem to have their attention. Being that I so rarely work in the appointment area, it should be safer. I am probably just being paranoid, but it does not hurt to be cautious. I briefly scan the room, making sure everything is in its usual place before speaking.

"What's going on Kagen?" she asks, watching me intently.

"Something's not right, Rana," I say and move close enough to speak in a whisper. "I asked Trent about Merrick's injuries this morning and something seemed off. I think he was lying, and there's something going on that Leadership wants kept quiet."

"Well, he was acting funny the morning after it happened, but I didn't know why. What I do know is that you need to be careful. You already have Mr. Vaden's attention, and you don't want to do anything to make it worse," she warns.

"I'll be careful, but I need to ask a favor of you. It may be asking too much and I would understand if you choose to say no," I say. Rana's eyes narrow, and she looks increasingly concerned as I continue. "I have to get back into The Caves, but my access is restricted. It will only take me a couple of hours to get to the site of the collapse, look around, and come back."

"Kagen, if you're caught, your punishment will be a lot worse than activity restrictions. You'll be invited to the Detention Center," Rana says. She must be really concerned because she is bringing up that place again. Everyone knows of the seldom used facility, but it is rarely spoken of by the workers. An invitation is essentially a sentence, but like with many other things, Leadership likes to choose words that seem less dark. I have seen firsthand the effects that the Detention Center can have on a person, and Rana is well aware of that.

"I owe it to Merrick to find out anything I can about his death. I would never forgive myself if I didn't try, and that would be just as bad as a stay in the Detention Center," I counter, trying to suppress the painful memories stirred up by the repeated mention of its name. "The only time I can go is during working hours. There are very few workers and will be way less Leadership personnel out in The Caves then. If I leave at the beginning of lunch, I can make it back well before the end of my normal shift," I step back and face Rana. "I just need someone to cover my patients while I'm gone. If anyone asks, you can just tell them that I felt ill and told you I was going back to my quarters. That way you won't be liable if I get caught."

Rana sighs in resignation. "I see there will be no stopping you with this, so I'll help. I already rescheduled most of my appointments today because I wanted to work with Adara on Leland's case, so it shouldn't be too hard to take care of everything on my own." She leans forward again. "You realize you could have just fabricated an illness and went anyway. You didn't have to say anything. What made you decide to tell me what you're planning?"

"I trust you, Rana. Plus, you deserve to know the truth if I'm going to use you for a cover story," I tell her. A smile creeps onto my face as I continue. "That, and I'm not a good enough actor to fake being sick with you."

She stifles a small laugh. "Well, thank you for being honest, Kagen. Now get to work. You're not getting the whole day off."

The truth is I feel a debt to Rana as well as a very strong bond. She has always been a thoughtful and kind mentor, but our bond has developed further than that. In her younger years she was a driven woman. So much so that she did not marry until she was well into her thirties, which is not a particularly unusual occurrence in Securus. Leadership strongly encourages the workers to master their crafts and focus on the good of the colony over individual desires. Combined with the regulations placed on reproduction because of the lack of space and resources, it is easy to wait so long that fertility is compromised. This is exactly what happened to Rana.

By the time we met, she had already accepted that she would never have her own child. Through her mentorship with me I think she filled part of the void she felt from her misfortune. Rana has treated me like a son and for many years we have spent more time together in the infirmary than we have with our own families. I have come to strongly value her caring friendship, fierce intelligence, and compassion as a mentor. Because of that relationship, I had to tell her the truth, at least as much of it as I could without endangering her.

*

The rest of the morning passes quickly. There are only routine cases and no unexpected visitors. As my lunch time approaches I search through my cabinets for a change of clothing. Normally, I wear the same uniform throughout the day, consisting of a smoke white shirt and matching pants, both lined with a cobalt blue trim to indicate my primary occupation as a Healer. But with my current intentions, I cannot allow myself to be so easily identified. I find an old set of garments and squeeze into them. They are snug, but the dark coloration will be much less conspicuous in The Caves.

I rush to the lunch hall to get some food before my search. If my timing it right, I can finish lunch and get to the entrance of The Caves just after the Leadership Guards change shifts. The flow of people is just beginning to trickle into the hall, so there is no wait to get to the food. I pick up my ration of artificial nutrients and make my way to the far end of the hall, hoping to remain unnoticed.

At the edges of my vision, I notice a slender figure headed for me. I try to remain inconspicuous, but the figure continues toward me. She catches up to me and positions herself next to me as I walk. I look over and meet the gaze of her amber eyes. She whisks away strands of dusty brown hair and gives me a gentle nudge with her shoulder.

"Hi, Kagen," she says cheerfully.

"Hey, Abira," I reply.

"Interesting uniform you have there," she says while examining my attire. Her amusement makes me feel exposed and more than a little embarrassed.

"Yeah, I spilled some chemicals on my regular uniform. My spare is still in my quarters so I had to rummage these from the cabinets," I tell her.

I have known Abira since we were both very young. We never had schooling together but her family's quarters are close to mine, and we often cross paths. She works as a Teacher for our younger children. I have always enjoyed her company, but now is not a fortuitous time to be drawn into a conversation. I need to keep this short and focus on the task ahead of me.

Balancing my tray with one hand, I rest the other on her shoulder. "It's good to see you, Abira. We need to catch up, but I need to get out of these uncomfortable clothes and get on my regular uniform before I lose circulation in my legs."

We both laugh. Then, she pauses while considering her next words. "Okay, Kagen," she says meekly. "But before you go, can I ask you about Merrick?"

This is unexpected. She had not spoken with Merrick much, even when she and I were closer friends. But with such a contained living arrangement, tragedy is often shared among most of Securus.

"Okay," I tell her, finding an empty table to sit for a minute.

"I know you see a lot of crazy things at work, but it has to be hard seeing a close friend get trapped like that. Did you actually see it happen?" she asks with her head lowered.

I hesitate and she looks up for my response. She has a pained expression and is nervously rubbing her fingers. It looks like the subject makes her even more uncomfortable than me. At first her question seemed suspicious, but it does not take long for me to feel foolish for being so paranoid. She has been a friend for many years, and is just concerned for me.

"No, he was too far in the tunnel. When I made it to where he was I couldn't see him through the rubble of the cave-in. I couldn't see anything." My voice lowers to a faint whisper. "And I couldn't get to him."

She does not probe any further. "Well, if you need someone to talk to, I am always here," Abira says as she embraces me with one arm and rests her head on my shoulder.

"Thanks," I say.

"Well, I'll let you hurry up and get out of that extra layer of skin you're wearing," she says, trying to change the subject and lighten the mood.

Abira leaves to go get her own food. By the time she picks it up, I am already finished with mine. I take the opportunity to leave the lunch hall. My direction is toward my quarters to keep in line with my cover story. When I am far from anyone's sight, instead of following the winding staircase to my floor, I exit one level down and briskly walk toward the stairway that leads to The Caves.

## 8

I am careful to avoid eye contact with others while walking. The stairway in front of me is relatively empty, so my rapid pace does not draw any attention. I reach the access level and slowly open the door. On the other side, there is a short hallway that shields me from the main area just around the corner. I slide along the edge of the wall and peer into the room. As I was hoping, most of the normal Guards stationed here have already left for their lunch break, and the room is about as empty as it ever gets.

The research offices that line the far wall are all empty, with most of the people now in the lunch halls. There are only two research workers currently sitting in the expansive lounge in the center of the room that lies in shadow of the enormous, retractable steel door. Getting past the impenetrable barrier is my target, but there is still one Guard there. He is stationed just outside the control room that is adjacent to the outer door. *At least they still have the lounge set up,* I think to myself. Sometimes the entire area is cleared and used as a loading station for importing resources in from The Caves, which would have left me no cover at all.

The research workers' conversation is becoming increasingly animated. From my hallway the sounds of their words mingle, and I am unable to decipher the content of their discussion. Whatever it is, they are completely absorbed in it and should pay little attention to me if I walk on the other side of the lounge. The Guard, on the other hand, is alone and his attention unoccupied. Passing him will be more challenging.

My resolve had been unbreakable when forming this idea. As I descended the stairs, adrenaline filled my system and carried me undaunted to this point. Now, faced with my first obstacle, my confidence is not nearly as unshakable. My breathing rate starts to increase, and my feet begin to feel heavy. Before doubt can paralyze me, I force myself forward and attempt to appear confident while strolling through the lounge. As suspected, the research workers seem oblivious to my movements. I quickly walk past them and watch the Guard out of my peripheral vision. He is still looking out into The Caves and has not yet noticed me. I sit at a corner table facing outward, careful to keep the Guard in view. From here, I can watch his movements and wait for an opening while my face is hidden from anyone else that enters the area.

I sit and wait, hoping for the Guard to relax enough for me to sneak out, but he remains watchful. As time passes, my window of opportunity feels like it is starting to close. I need to do something soon, or else the other Guards will return or this one may recognize me. I am sure Mr. Vaden has informed them of my restriction. The Guard finally stops watching The Caves, but now he is surveying the lounge. His eyes stop when he notices me. I pry out the camera that was secured in my pocket. I hold the two cylindrical pieces and slowly pull them apart, unrolling the flexible screen that was contained within them. I look down and pretend to study an image, trying to make myself look like just another research worker on my break. Out of the periphery of my vision I see him start walking toward me. A sense of dread fills me. Unless he believes my impromptu cover, I will be discovered and sent to the Detention Center. Then no one will ever know the truth, and I fear my confinement would be more than my mother can bear.

Though I try so vehemently to forget, the thought of the Detention Center causes the circumstances of my father's death to revisit me. I was too young to fully understand at the time, but still old enough to remember. He was a supervising worker in the Deep Vents, one of the main power sources for Securus, along with the Solar Panels. One day, there was an explosion that destroyed a large generator and killed one of the members of his work team. Even though the cause of the explosion was never discovered, my father was held responsible by Leadership and was invited to a six month stay in the Detention Center. His punishment was made more severe because the loss of the generator was a significant blow to our energy production, which affected the entire colony.

The time he was gone was exceptionally difficult for my mother and when he did return to us, he was not the same. Every night, I would hear him tossing and turning from the nightmares that haunted his sleep. Though he remained distant and distracted, as the months passed, eventually he began to break free from his invisible torment. The occasional sparks of his prior strength became more frequent and his nightmares less severe.

Just when there was some hope of getting back to normal, tragedy returned. My father became consumed with investigating the cause of the explosion. He said he wanted to find out what really happened and prevent a recurrence in the future. During his search, another accident occurred. He was scaling some of the large energy generating equipment in the vents when his foothold gave way causing him to plummet to his death.

Since then, my mother hides her sorrow from us and tries to stay strong. But in her sleep, the loss and sadness becomes visible in her expression. My mother blames the Detention Center for what happened and for changing my father. The only time she mentions him now is to tell me how much like him I can be.

Until now, I never understood what compelled him to risk his own life in search of the truth. After what happened to Merrick, I finally understand that his overwhelming need for answers was not only for himself, but for us all. It was not just the madness from his time in the Detention Center that led to his compulsion. It is the same compulsion that has led me here to The Caves despite my restriction. It turns out my mother was more right than she knew.

I shake the thoughts from my mind. There is no time for it now. My focus needs to be on the task at hand. The Guard continues toward me. There is nowhere for me to hide or escape. I can feel the depths of the Detention Center calling for me. I plant my feet and prepare to run. Just before he reaches me, a voice calls out for his attention.

"Grant, help us settle an argument," says one of the workers as he approaches the Guard from the opposite side. He is a lanky man with glasses that appear to be clinging to the tip of his nose. The other worker stands with his arms folded in front of him and is regarding the lanky man with an impatient stare that is partially hidden by his thick, woolly beard. The Guard turns his attention to the men.

"What are you two arguing about today?" the Guard asks, obviously exasperated by the men.

"This man thinks it is acceptable that his son-" the bearded man grumbles but is interrupted by the other worker before he could finish.

"I didn't say that it was acceptable, I just said-" the lanky man protests, but he is also cut off by his partner.

As they continue to interrupt each other they become increasingly aggravated, and their voices escalate in order to continually prevent the other from finishing his sentence. Eventually they tire of yelling at each other, and both of the men attempt to tell their side of the story to the Guard at once. Their words become mangled together along with those of the Guard's, who is futilely attempting to calm the men down.

I instantly recognize my opportunity. While they are occupied, I rise from my chair, place my camera back into my pocket, and head for The Caves. Sliding along the edge of the wall and out the main door, I am careful to avoid the watchful lens of the security cameras. Just as I pass the door, the Guard's voice barks out. I quicken my pace and steal a glance back. They are all still huddled together, distracted by their discussion. Not wanting to stay in sight for long, I veer off to the poorly lit trails on the periphery, avoiding the revealing lights that focus on the main path and initial pools. Soon, I am safely shielded from their view. It is getting hard to see in the shadows of the towering stalagmites, so I affix my illuminator, but do not dare turn it on yet. I break into a controlled trot, increasing my distance from the arguing men.

Carefully, I circle through the winding paths that have been forged by the many visitors since the discovery of this chamber. It would be useful to check the upper tunnels, but they are on the other side of the chamber and it would be impossible to make it to them without being caught. My pace slows as I near the main exit passage to the tunnel system. Though the opening to the passage is far from the sight of the primary security post, it is still visible from the secondary post. I peek around a grouping of thick, tawny stalagmites that rise to nearly double my height and look back toward Securus. The secondary post is empty, so I dart into the passage. I start off fast, but have to slow as the light continues to fade. Still, I do not turn on my illuminator. If anyone saw the glow of my light in the tunnel, it could trigger an investigation, and that would make an already difficult return impossible.

I have been through this passage many times but never without the aid of light. Needing another way of navigating, I find the wall and run my hand along it as a guide. It turns out I am less adept to moving in the darkness than anticipated. Though Securus is underground and away from the Sun's light, there are many lights constantly shining throughout the facility. The hallways always have a faint glow that traces the various paths from level to level. The only time we are close to complete darkness is when we sleep. Even then, we are in the familiar surroundings of our quarters and still have the use of our illuminators to augment the faint light creeping in from the exterior doors. Now, this deep in the tunnel, I am deprived of all light. Moving through the damp tunnels entombed in utter darkness, waves of panic rise within me. The darkness is starting to feel palpable, like a black sludge, slowing my movements.

Closing my eyes, I concentrate on the ground beneath my feet and the feel of the tunnel wall against my hand. This focus helps to calm me while continuing through the passage. After going in far enough that my light should go unnoticed, I finally turn on my illuminator. Looking around, there is a sign on the wall that tells me I am not as far in as if felt. It is too late to turn the light off now, so I rush further into The Caves hoping it has gone unnoticed. Being able to see the path before me allows my movements to be much faster, and it is not long before I reach the end of the standard marked tunnel system. Out here it is very unlikely to run into anyone other than scattered researchers, and most of them should still be in Securus on their breaks, so some of my tension releases as I continue. The path ahead has a loose, rocky floor and a continuous incline that makes my steps cumbersome. I lean over and use my hands to steady my body while crawling up the path.

By the time the path levels out, I am panting heavily and in need of a rest. Because my thoughts were occupied, my pace had become more rapid than intended. I lean against the side of the tunnel and rest to catch my breath and let the burning in my muscles subside. Sitting here, I realize this trip is not as planned out as it should have been. I need to investigate Merrick's chamber, but do not have a way past the collapse. They must have made a hole in the barrier when they retrieved Merrick, unless they lied about bringing him back as well.

When my breathing slows to a normal rate, I get up to continue. The next passage is flat but very narrow. I turn and squeeze myself through it by sidestepping. Emerging from the narrow crevasse, I enter into a cylindrical chamber that, by all appearances, is a dead end. This means my destination is close. Just above me is the veiled passage that leads into Merrick's chamber.

Walking into the chamber, I remember the pleasure Merrick took as he watched us absorb the awe inspiring view. Despite the beauty of the chamber, the joy I had the first time we came here is lost. Instead, only sadness emerges as this place is forever tainted by the needless tragedy that has brought me back here to investigate.

I retrieve the camera from my pocket. When telling

the others what really happened, visual evidence will be more persuasive than the absurd allegations of a grieving friend. I carefully document the chamber while making my way to the far wall beside the thundering waterfall. This time my climb is slow and meticulous, knowing that if I were to fall, there would be no help. I try to concentrate on the climb, but my thoughts keep going back to Merrick. My distraction is amplified when I reach the top platform and am faced with the passage where it happened. My legs become anchored to the ground, unwilling to carry me in. The image of Merrick, falling before the soldier's gun, burns before my eyes. The thought of those men getting away with their crime causes a seething rage to build within me, powering my legs to break free of their invisible chains. *I will find the truth, Merrick. No matter what it takes*, I think to myself while entering the passage.

Making my way through the tortuous tunnel, I near the site of the collapse. The rubble still blocks the way, but the arrangement has changed. There is more of a structure to the wall of debris and now there are multiple new boulders lining the floor on this side of the tunnel. I crawl over the fallen rocks and peer through the cracks in the wall. The area does not look the same as it did before. I contort my head and neck, searching for the man-made tunnel, but there is no sign of it. That end of the passage now ends abruptly to form a sealed chamber. Even with the unpredictable arrangement of natural tunnel collapses, this seems odd. It is as if it were intentionally sealed off.

I continue to take images of the area while looking for any mechanisms to uncover the passage to the tracks. Everywhere in the chamber, there is nothing but solid rock. Frustrated, I examine the manipulated collapse before me and notice an area on the side where the boulders are much smaller than the ones that originally fell. That must be where the search party went through. The fact that they took the time to reinforce the wall is revealing. I grip one of the rocks and pull with all of my weight. There is only a slight movement before my hand slips, nearly causing me to fall down. I cannot move them by myself. With some extra help, we may be able to get past this wall. That may be useful if I return, but right now it does nothing except add to my mounting frustration. I am stuck on the outside, just as before.

At least the pictures are something to show Hadwin and Sayda, though I was hoping to be able to get proof of the tracks themselves. Failing at passing the collapse, I resign to a defeated return to Securus. Before I can turn, a mechanical hum begins to emanate from the walls. I turn my illuminator off and listen. The walls continue to vibrate and a section retracts into itself. Inside, I see the same mad-made tunnel and shimmer of the tracks that was there before. My excitement instantly turns to dread when I realize the lights that are allowing me to see inside the tunnel are moving. A shiver runs through me when I hear a voice.

"Make sure it's clear," the voice says. The mechanical manipulation of his words by his mask is unsettling.

"Nobody's going to be out here after what happened last time. Besides, who could get past that cave-in?" another voice growls. "What they need to do is seal all these cross tunnels off and save us the trouble of these patrols."

I crouch behind the rubble, hiding in the darkness. The sound of the second man's voice resonates in my memory. He is the one that killed Merrick. I position myself near the base of the wall, and find a small crack to see the soldiers. They are wearing the same armored uniforms as before, but their position and the low light keeps me from confirming the insignia on their chest. I take out my camera to get a picture, but the glare of their lights keeps washing out the image.

"Like they would waste the resources it would take to patch up tunnels no one will ever find. It's cheaper to just keep the extra patrols. That's all they care about, the bottom line. Everything's quiet here. Check the supply room and let's go," the mechanical voice says.

Slowly, I push myself from the floor to move to a higher position to get a better view and hopefully a picture. One of the soldiers pushes upward on a rock, positioned high on the side wall, and another chamber appears. As I strain to see what is inside, my movement jars loose a fist-sized piece of a rock. In the quiet tunnel, the echoing thud of its fall fills the air.

Both soldiers snap to attention and raise their weapons. Their lights pierce the cracks in the barrier, searching for me. One of the soldiers inches toward the rocks for a closer vantage point. It is useless to run. I would be spotted and executed instantly. My only chance is to try to hide. My stomach tingles and my body screams for me to run, but I force myself to move slowly. Crouching further, I lower myself onto the base of the collapse, hoping the sharp angle will shield me from the soldiers' view. Now on the floor and facing up, a beam of concentrated light radiates from the small portal that I was just looking through. The light continues its search for me while I lay motionless, just below its revealing glow.

The barrel of the soldier's weapon now penetrates the wall. An intense light flashes from it, and explodes on the far wall. With the kick of the barrel another loose rock plummets down and catches me on the lower end of my sternum. The hallow thud it makes is masked by the sounds of the crumbling rocks in the passage. With the blow, my breath leaves me, and I am unable to regain it. I struggle for air as the weapon withdraws through the crack and the light changes its focus. I know the mechanism of this injury but am still powerless to stop it. My only option is to wait through the intense suffocation for my stunned diaphragm to awaken. Only then will my breath return. My analytical thoughts help keep me from panic, but the lack of breath is making me lightheaded.

"Just some falling rocks settling," the growling man reassures the other.

They close the secondary chamber and return where they came. As the wall closes, my diaphragm awakens, and I gasp for air. My lungs fill with oxygen as the constriction in my chest eases. After a few deep breaths the dizziness subsides, but with the clarity I start to feel an intense throbbing in my chest that morphs into a piercing pain every time I take a breath. My ribs or my sternum must have broken under the weight of the falling rock.

I rest my head against a large boulder and lay still for a moment to compose myself and absorb my new discovery. There are two doors hidden in the passage and I know how to get into one of them. That is more than I had before. Finally, there is something of substance for me to work with. Despite the protests of my chest wall, I get up and make my way out of the tunnel.

After getting far enough from danger I turn on my illuminator and examine my injuries. My shirt is tattered and there is blood oozing from the center of my chest. Lifting the cloth reveals a deep contusion spreading across the center of my chest. More importantly, the unified movement tells me there is not a free floating segment of ribs detached by the blow. That gives me some hope that the injury is less severe than it feels, but that is something that can be investigated more on my return to the infirmary. For now, I have to endure the pain and find a way back there.

## 9

Retracing my steps, I make my way back toward Securus while considering my options. The only plan that seems feasible is to try and blend in as a research worker. To do so, I will need something to pass off as a sample or research material. Along the path back, there is nothing available that would be convincing. My plan is getting ready to fall apart before it even gets started when I remember the small chamber that Talia had shown us to that night. Collecting some of the bio-luminous bacteria she discovered may be enough to convince the Guards of my cover story. Getting the sample will use up precious time but should be worth it.

The constant pain in my chest wall continues to slow my progress, but the return trip is physically easier with more downhill paths. Upon reaching the low, narrow tunnel that serves as an entrance to Talia's chamber, I kneel down and painfully snake my way through it. Every time I reach out with my arms and pull myself forward, a searing pain drains all my strength, making the effort particularly grueling. Halfway through, the thought of having to continue and then do this again to get out almost makes me turn back. The only thing that keeps me going is the threat of the Detention Center. If I am not convincing enough, this injury will be the least of my worries. I push forward and do my best to endure the pain.

Just before I make it into the chamber, a faint noise

stops me. I turn off my illuminator and carefully inch my way in. Fighting my injury, it is a struggle to try to be as quiet as possible. If I just stumbled onto another soldier, my only chance is if he does not hear me coming. There is a shadow that stands out on the opposite side of the room, conspicuously blocking the glow of the microbes. The figure has not seen me yet and has an illuminator on a low setting. A hand reaches up to turn it off and the glow of the microbes intensifies, lighting up her face. The curious look in Talia's eyes while she studies the microbes makes me smile despite the sadness of my trip and the agony from lying on my injured chest. I have seen that look before, and it reminds me of when we were in school together.

Whenever alone, Talia was always engrossed in some project or study material. She would intensely consume knowledge while always staying eager and curious enough to search for more. I often stumbled onto her when she had same look she has now. Whenever she saw me coming she would stop and greet me with a smile that never failed to brighten my day. Talia was always busy, but somehow she managed to make enough time to talk with me.

As time passed we did find each other more regularly. I knew nothing could come of it, but still enjoyed our time together. One day, she asked me to accompany her to a celebration at the end of one of our school cycles. I was stunned by the invitation, but agreed instantly. That night, while the ceremony was commencing, there was a low light that shone on her, just as the light does now. She looked into my eyes and reached her hand to my cheek. She leaned in toward me just as our instructor came to speak with her. He interrupted and insisted that she was needed by her father. I did not see her again that night or for weeks afterward. The next day is when I heard of her transfer into Leadership as well as my new assignment in the infirmary. That was the last time we were able to speak alone, until she showed up in the infirmary two days ago.

I return my focus to the present. Considering my current situation, there is no time to dwell on the past. Though it hurts to move, I force myself up and all the way into the chamber. The rustling of my movement breaks her concentration, and she turns in time to see me standing at the chamber entrance.

"Who's there? Announce yourself or I will call the Guard," Talia says sternly.

"It's me, Kagen," I reply softly, wincing in pain.

"Kagen! What are you doing in here?" she asks, confused by my unexpected presence.

"I'm trying to figure out what you're doing over there, all by yourself, lurking in the darkness. Why were you standing there with no lights?" I ask, avoiding her question.

"The microbes we collected died while in the lab. I think it has something to do with our lighting system. These organisms have never been exposed to actual sunlight or even our artificial substitute. I was watching how their glow changes with and without a direct light on them," she answers. "And you still haven't answered my question. What are you doing out here? You could get into a lot of trouble," Talia adds, with her voice shifting from surprise to concern.

"Yeah, I know," I start to say, walking toward her to begin my explanation. "I feel responsible for leaving Merrick in that tunnel. I had to go back and see it again, to know what happened and to see if there was any way I could've done something differently," I tell her, trying to be as honest as safely possible. I sit down next to where she is standing.

"It wasn't your fault, Kagen, you did the right thing," Talia says as she sits beside me.

"Thanks, I appreciate that. And I know that if your father finds out that I broke his restriction order, I'll pay severely. But this was something I just had to do," I add hoping that would be enough for her to understand and keep my secret.

The compassionate look that was in her eyes vanishes and is replaced by a vexed annoyance. "Restriction order? When did that happen?" she asks.

"Your father came to see my in the infirmary the morning after we were in The Caves," I tell her. "I appreciated you covering for us, but I told him it was my responsibility to get everyone back on time. After that he gave me the restriction."

"I'm sorry, Kagen. I know how much you enjoy time in The Caves. I'll see if I can get him to remove your restriction," she promises.

"That may make it worse. I think he was more upset because we endangered you," I say while trying to suppress the spasm in my chest wall.

Talia notices my discomfort and turns her illuminator up to look at me. She gasps when she sees my ragged, blood stained shirt.

"Kagen, what happened?" she says while hastily looking over me for any more injuries.

"I'm okay," I assure her. "You know me. I've always had a special talent for hurting myself," I say trying to alleviate her worry. "A loose rock fell on me. It may have cracked a rib, but I'll be fine. Just gonna be sore for a while."

My reassurance eases her concern, and she even starts

laughing. "I remember that," she says, still giggling. "You used to suffer from vicious sneak attacks by random doors and tables. You would always say that they had it in for you."

The radiance of her smile makes me forget my pain, and I cannot help but to laugh with her. Though I would rather stay and continue talking with Talia, I need to get back to the infirmary before my absence is noticed. Cautiously, I rise to my feet.

"I have to get back soon before anyone starts to wonder where I am. I hate to ask you this, but can we keep my little excursion between us?" I ask sheepishly.

"You shouldn't ask something like that, of course I have to report you," she says with an incredulous stare.

My heart sinks, and I can already feel the walls of the Detention Center closing around me. Then, when she can no longer hold it, Talia smiles again. How could I have forgotten how mischievous she could be?

"You had me for a second there," I say with a playful nudge on her shoulder.

"It's time I should go back as well. Take this," she says, handing me a small box. It looks like a large sample container, but the clear walls have been covered with a firm black lining. Talia notices me inspecting the curious box.

"The lining is to keep the light out so I can see if that is really the cause of the problem," she explains. "Hold the box up in front of you when we get back and make sure to walk behind me. That way, no one will see your shirt."

"Thanks Talia, I owe you twice now," I say as we begin our trek to Securus. Her help makes me much more confident in my return now than when I first entered The Caves.

We emerge from the tunnel system into the main chamber. The secondary Guard has resumed watch and turns toward us when our motion catches his attention. Talia is calm as ever, and I try to maintain a confident stride behind her. The Guard shows no interest in me but does wave at Talia as we pass. She waves back and continues toward the main entrance.

The primary Guard has changed from when I entered The Caves, and this one is even more alert than the previous man. His eyes follow us closely as we near the outer door. Inside, the lounge is now filled with people. There are research workers and additional patrolling Guards scurrying about, all preoccupied with their own tasks.

"Hello, Talia," the primary Guard says with a smile as he meets us at the entrance. "Who is this with you?" He points in my direction but does not bother to look at me.

"Just another assistant," she says. Looking back at me, she commands, "Go put the sample in my lab. If you take too long and ruin another sample I'm going to have you reassigned."

My scolding amuses the Guard, and he returns to his post after flashing me a satisfied sneer. Talia gives me a subtle look that makes me think she is also enjoying the ruse at my expense. No one else stops us as we pass through the lounge and enter the stairway. When we are alone, I give Talia back her sample box.

"Here you go, boss," I cannot help but to grin at her clever improvisation.

"You go take care of yourself, Kagen," she replies pointing to my blood stained shirt.

With that, we part ways. I am anxious to get back to the infirmary, but it would be better to stop by my quarters first to change back into my work uniform. Since most of the people that pass by are busy with their daily duties, no one disturbs me on the way to my quarters. Even now while changing in the safety of my own bathroom, I am not sure if I ever really expected to be able to make it to The Caves and back without being caught. Deep down, I think that part of my purpose was as a form of penance for failing to save Merrick. But now, being this close to a safe return gives me new hope. If I can pull this off, maybe there is a legitimate chance for me to actually bring the truth to light. My intentions are starting to feel more like purpose than punishment.

Tempering my relief, I leave my quarters and return to the infirmary. The entrance appears just as it did this morning. There are no warning signs and no one in the waiting room. I continue in and find Rana in her usual exam room where she is in the middle of what looks to be one of her appointments. My movement catches her attention, and she briefly acknowledges me before returning her attention to her patient. I go to my normal exam room and wait while she finishes.

Now that there is time, I can further evaluate my injury. With little else to distract my thoughts from it, the pain is intensifying. I remove my shirt and examine my chest wall. The bleeding has nearly stopped and there is only a single small laceration that had been the source of it. A quick suturing and that will be done with for good. All around the laceration is a deep red welt, mixed with some dark purple bruising that traces the outline of the rock that hit me. My next step is to get an X-ray and an electrocardiogram to make sure there are no internal complications from the injury. Even if the initial signs look good, there is still some concern because these types of blows can collapse a lung, either fully or partially, as well as cause bruising to the heart itself. With the degree of pain in my chest, anything is still possible.

I set up our portable X-ray machine. It has a fully maneuverable chair for me to sit on, along with a mechanical X-ray arm that can finely adjust its position for any angle needed. When the position is correct, I activate the machine and an automated lead barrier rises, sealing me inside until the X-ray is taken. This function typically protects the Healers from the radiation when we are caring for others, but now it just annoys me because it is moving too slow. When the X-ray image comes up on my computer, the result pleases me. There is only a small crack in the rib and no other visible damage. Adding to my good fortune was a normal electrocardiogram.

Satisfied that no significant damage has been done, I tend to my laceration. After applying a numbing salve, I clean the wound thoroughly. Lying on the ground rubbed dirt into it and it needs to be removed to prevent an infection. The position of it is awkward for me to manually repair it so I use the automated suture device. The spider legs of the device grip the skin of my chest and squeeze the wound together. From the body of the machine another arm emerges with delicate articulations for suturing. The movements almost look like it is spinning a web as it quickly repairs my wound. I secure a bandage over it and redress in my uniform.

"Rougher trip than you planned?" Rana's voice startles me.

"Yeah, a falling rock fractured a rib and gave me a small lac," I replied. "How did you hold up without me? I hope the place didn't fall apart." I give her a reassuring smile.

"Oh, it was horrible, but somehow I managed," she says sarcastically.

"Did anyone notice my absence?" I ask.

"No, it was a rather slow day. Just a few urgent cases and no unexpected visitors, although I did see some Leadership personnel lingering outside the waiting room," she says. Rana walks toward me and sits down. Looking directly into my eyes, she asks, "Did you find the answers that you were looking for?"

"I found answers, but not to all of my questions," I reply honestly. "Don't worry though, I'll be very careful from here on out. Sorry I involved you in this, I promise not to do that again."

"It's not me that I'm worried about," she counters.

She gets up and heads for the door. There will likely be another scheduled patient already waiting for her. When she reaches the doorway, I call out to tell her, "Oh, by the way, I was saved again by a friend that I recently reconnected with." Rana's smile let me know she knew exactly who I meant.

After she leaves, my worry returns. No one came in, but why was a Leadership member hanging out in the waiting room?

## 10

Alone in my exam room, I lean back in my chair and struggle to keep my eyes open, a task made even more difficult since it has been an unusually quiet day in the infirmary. The physically and mentally exhausted from the excursion hits me. The weight of my eyes is too much. I abandon my resistance and quickly drift off to sleep.

*I am back in The Caves, following Merrick through a long twisted passage. He is running too fast for me to keep up. I yell out for him to stop, but he does not hear me. The light from my illuminator begins to fade, obscuring the path ahead. Determined, I push ahead, sprinting toward the disappearing shadow of my friend. The ground shakes, but my legs keep moving, unable to stop until I catch him. The intensity of the earthquake increases, but I ignore it and sprint even faster. Suddenly, the ground comes alive with the rocks reaching out to stop me. My foot gets caught, knocking me over. I struggle to get up but the ground is too unstable. My feet sink into the fluid rocks below, becoming anchored within them. My light rapidly fades until it is extinguished, leaving me in utter darkness. Panic grips me.*

*There is a break in the darkness as a single light moves toward me. I hear Merrick's voice calling out to me from behind the light, urging me forward. A sparkling glow begins to peak through cracks of the moving floor. Just as Merrick is in sight, a cage of solid rock erupts from the floor and surrounds me. I look back for Merrick, but he is gone. In his place is a massive soldier with his weapon trained on me, taunting me to try and escape. The sound of his voice morphs from a low growl to a distinctively familiar tone. He removes his visor and reveals his face.*

*It is Mr. Vaden.*

"Kagen!" an unseen voice shouts to me, "Kagen!" The cage disappears and bright light washes out the dream as I awaken in my exam room. I shake myself from the fog of my dream and focus on the figure in front of me. Judging by the look on his face, he is amused.

"Nice to see you're keeping yourself busy, Kagen," Aamon laughs.

"It's been a really slow day," I tell him while straightening myself in my chair. It is interesting that Aamon had not triggered the chime to warn me he was coming as Mr. Vaden had. "I see you're doing well with Leadership," I comment, pointing at his new uniform trim. It is now dark gold, signifying that he has been promoted. I wonder if that is related to what happened in The Caves.

"It's a well-earned promotion," he says, dusting a small piece of lint from his uniform.

"I'm glad you stopped by, Aamon. I wanted to thank you for volunteering to lead the search party back to Merrick," I say, trying to be kind, hoping to get further by appealing to his ego than by challenging it.

"I just wish we could have gotten there in time," he replies.

"What did happen when you found him?" I ask.

"Nothing eventful. By the time we reached the collapse, the aftershocks had already stopped. At that point, it was just a matter of getting enough manpower to move the boulders that had fallen on him and bringing him back. We made it out there and back rather quickly, considering the task. I assure you we tried everything we could, but it was too late," Aamon says. He grabs a chair and takes a seat next to me.

"Well, thanks for trying, that means a lot to me," I tell him. Aamon is being unusually kind, and that is unsettling. He is up to something, and his lies combined with his timely new promotion tell me that he is definitely involved in the cover up. "I'm sure a busy man like you did not come all the way to the infirmary without a purpose. What can I do for you, Aamon?"

"Ah, straight to the point then," he says. As he leans back in his chair, the overly kind appearance he had starts to shift into a foreboding confidence. "As you know, the events of that night in The Caves have caught the attention of Mr. Vaden as well as others in Leadership. There has been much discussion about the leniency that Leadership has showed in enforcing certain policies. The rash of tardiness in The Caves was noted as a particular focal point. We feel that for the safety of our people that leniency must end, especially since Mr. Vaden specifically warned everyone that very morning during the announcements. It has been decided that the best way to show the sincerity of our intentions is to make an example of someone. Unfortunately, you are that someone."

"I'm sure you're devastated by having to bring me that news. I guess we can't have the terrible rebel who dared to try to have some fun with his friends go unpunished. That would make Leadership look bad. Don't you agree, Aamon," I sarcastically sympathize with him. There is no longer any point in trying to play nice.

"I understand you have been through a lot, so I will let that one slide, Kagen. But the fact remains, your punishment will not be limited to the restriction from The Caves. I have been sent to inform you that you will also be added to the Solar Panel maintenance detail for the next two maintenance cycles. Failure to comply with either the restriction from The Caves or your Solar Panel duties will result in an indefinite invitation to the Detention Center," he says. I get the feeling from the smug look on his face that he is enjoying this.

"I accept that. But tell me, why does Leadership feel so strongly about this? Seems like a simple general warning would have been sufficient," I say trying to conceal my surprise at the unusually harsh punishment. I do not want Aamon to get any more pleasure out of my responses.

"It's just an accumulation of many things combined with patterns of behavior," he replies. Aamon gets up to leave, but before he does he asks, "Oh, by the way, am I mistaken or did I see you headed to the lower levels in a much different uniform than the one you are now wearing?"

"I had to go to my quarters to change because of a chemical spill on my uniform. Would you like to examine my dirty clothes as well, Aamon?" I offer him.

"That will not be necessary. I am sure you will be very mindful of the rules as well as Mr. Vaden's concern for Talia, and take special care not to cause any further hardship to Leadership. It would be a shame if we had to extend your punishment to your friends as well," he says while walking out the door, leaving me no chance to respond.

It is obvious that Leadership is suspicious of what I know or have seen, but they do not yet know about my most recent activity. The Solar Panel maintenance detail assignment is a worrisome change. It is an exceedingly dangerous task, so much so that as kids we used to refer to it as the death detail. It is rare to be hand-picked for it, and I have never heard of anyone being assigned to two cycles. But I would still prefer to take my chances in the poisonous atmosphere than spend a single minute in the Detention Center. Aside from that, I find it humorous that he is concerned for Talia, and can only imagine her annoyance with his attention. The thing that bothers me the most about all of this is the mention of my friends. I do not want anyone else to suffer because of my actions. I need to be mindful of that while planning what to do next.

*

When my shift is over, I rush out the door and down the stairs. I have wanted to tell Hadwin and Sayda the truth since it happened, but they were not ready to hear me out. Now that they are being threatened by Aamon, it cannot wait any longer. Hadwin, Sayda, and I all have different assigned halls for dinner, so there is only enough time to find one of them before my absence will be noticed in my own hall. Considering the two options, I decide to speak with Hadwin. There is a much better chance at getting through to him than Sayda. She is way too angry now to really hear what I have to say. There are no security checks to enter the hall, only to get to the food, so I maneuver through the maze of people in search of Hadwin. The hall is filled with unfamiliar faces. Despite being such a small population, our segmented facility can lead to groups of people being relatively isolated from one another. I find him walking back from the food dispersal area toward a table to meet his family for dinner.

"Hadwin, I need to speak with you," I call out to him. The sound of my voice startles him. He turns toward me, obviously surprised.

"I didn't expect to see you here, Kagen," he says. There is no hint of the cheerful friend that usually greets me.

"I just need a couple minutes of your time, but we need to be alone. It's really important," I plead.

His eyebrows rise with a trace of curiosity breaking up his hesitation. "Okay, just let me set my food down first," he answers.

I watch as Hadwin makes his way to his family's table, where his parents are patiently waiting for him. He sets his tray down and tells them something while pointing in my direction. His father waves him off, and he comes back to meet me. As he walks, his expression shifts back to the serious look he had when he first noticed me.

"Okay, Kagen, let's go," he says, walking to the hallway without stopping to check if I am following.

There is a tense silence held between us as we walk. We exit the hall and turn the corner. There are less people out here, but it is still too crowded to talk privately. Hadwin sees my hesitation and continues further down the hallway to a small maintenance room. He keys in his entry code, the locks release, and we enter. I sweep the room to make sure there are no cameras or other potentially intrusive devices of Leadership. It appears to be safe, so I turn to Hadwin, who is watching me expectantly. I am not sure where to start. How can I really put into words everything that has happened?

"I wanted to talk with Sayda too, but I know she's not in any mood to hear me out now. I was hoping after this you could convince her to give me a chance," I start out.

"Depends on what you have to say, Kagen. If it's not good enough, I'm not going to waste my time trying to calm her down. You know that as well as I, so just go ahead with what you have to say," he replies.

"Okay, I don't have enough time to tell you everything right now. Leadership is watching me, and if I don't show up for dinner soon, they'll get suspicious," I say. He seems confused by this, but does not interrupt. "I lied to all of you and for that, I am deeply sorry. I was only trying to do what was best for everyone at the time," I say. The guilt wells up and threatens to steal my words.

"Wait, what did you lie about? If you tell me that we could have gotten to Merrick, we're gonna have a problem," he says. Even in the low light, I can see his stance tense up with his agitation. He looks just like he did on the night Merrick died; ready to attack me at any moment.

"No, Hadwin, there was nothing we could do about Merrick. He was already dead before I made it out of that tunnel." My words cut off. I look up at him trying to find the courage to explain what happened.

"If he was already dead, then why did we have a giant charade of rushing back for the search party? And why couldn't we go back to get him?" he demands with mounting frustration.

"We were all in danger," I say. "We weren't alone in that cavern and it wasn't the collapse that killed Merrick." My words feel as if they linger in the air before hitting him with the full implication of the message.

He steps closer to me and lowers his voice in an eerie whisper. "There was someone in that passage that murdered Merrick, and you let him get away?" He buries his index finger into my chest as he demands an explanation. The pressure of his finger on my fractured rib floors me. My collapse stuns Hadwin slightly, but his intensity does not falter.

"That's why I didn't tell you guys," I say, clutching my chest and struggling to get back to my feet. "I knew there would be no stopping you and Sayda from going after Merrick. But the men in there were different. They were heavily armed soldiers, and they would've killed us all."

Hadwin is at a loss for words. I can see his mind racing, just as mine has been ever since this revelation. Being able to finally tell someone makes me feel as if my burden is somehow lessened. I am no longer alone in my knowledge of these sordid events, and that is somewhat of a relief. But it still will not help unless he believes me.

"We have to be careful, Hadwin. I am certain that part of Leadership is involved with this," I warn him.

There are voices now in the hall. We both turn and listen. The words sound like random conversations of passersby, but it no longer feel safe in this room.

"There is more, Hadwin. I need you to get Sayda to meet us during lunch tomorrow and I'll explain the rest. Okay?" I ask.

"We'll both be there," he assures me.

Before leaving, we check to make sure no Leadership personnel are in the hall. Once we are satisfied that the way is clear we both exit the room. I do my best to try to remain casual in order to deflect any attention from our meeting.

"By the way, thanks for poking me in my broken rib," I add just before he walks into his dinner hall.

"You better hope that's all Sayda does when she sees you," he shouts while walking out of view. He seemed to listen, so that is a good sign. He has always been an understanding friend, and I am counting on that now. Hopefully he can forgive me and convince Sayda to do the same.

While still in the hallway, I get the uneasy feeling someone is watching me. I turn in time to see someone duck around the corner. *Were they watching me, or am I being paranoid?* I ask myself. Trying to ignore it, I go to the stairs and head down. My usual dinner hall is filled with people and alive with conversation. After getting my food, I look for my mother and Arluin. They are in the middle of the hall, and they are not alone. Abira is with them and looks to be entertaining everyone, since they are all laughing. On the other side of the table are two of Arluin's friends, Reed and Varian. They are brothers and are both near the same age as Arluin, with Varian being slightly older.

As I near the group, Varian shouts out, "Speak of the devil!" The entire table turns and when they see me coming, everyone starts laughing again. This cannot be good. I put my mix of synthetic nutrients on the table and await the inevitable explanation of why they are laughing at my expense.

"Okay, I give up. What's everyone laughing at?" I ask

"Nothing," Arluin says with an ear to ear smile. "So, how's your circulation, Kagen?" he asks. The table again bursts into laughter.

"Better, thanks," I say adjusting my clothes and playing along. My eyes meet eyes with Abira's, who is blushing.

"Well, I gotta get back to my table. See you later, Kagen," Abira says.

"I'll walk with you. I haven't spoken with your mother in a while anyway," my mother offers.

They both get up to leave, and I cannot help but think that is going to be trouble for me later. Abira has always been a favorite of my mother's ever since she and I became friends as children. My mother would always find ways to get the families together. Both of our mothers see us as a natural match, but now is not a good time to be consumed by such matters. While Abira is an attractive woman and has a fun sense of humor, there are more urgent events for me to attend to.

"Yeah, we gotta go too," Varian adds. The brothers make their way back to their family tripping, pushing, and smacking each other the entire way.

For the time being, Arluin and I are left alone at our table. He is still smiling, but I can see his humor starting to shift. I can only keep his curiosity at bay for so long, but it is too much of a risk to include him in these potentially dangerous events at this point. I start eating my food hoping he will let things be for now.

"So, any updates for me, Kagen?" Arluin asks.

*So much for leaving things alone*, I think to myself. Well, I have to tell him something to satisfy him before he gets too aggressive. "Yeah, there's some bad news. I'm officially on Leadership's watch list," I tell him.

"Really, how did you find that out?" he asks.

"My first hint was the visit from Mr. Vaden. Then today Aamon Tiran also came in to speak with me. My restriction from The Caves wasn't enough, so they assigned me to the next two cycles of the Solar Panel maintenance duty," I say, watching Arluin's expression. As he realizes the severity of the situation, his enthusiasm for pressuring me begins to wane.

"Well, at least you didn't get invited to the Detention Center," he says, looking for a silver lining.

"I got the distinct feeling that they are waiting for a reason to do just that," I say. "Now do you understand why I'm being secretive about this, Arluin?"

"Yeah, but I still want to know what's going on," he says resolutely.

"I'm working on it. I want to make sure everyone knows when the time is right. For now, stay the course," I say. "What would happen to our mother if both of her sons ended up in the Detention Center?"

"Yeah, yeah, I get it. There was something else that I wanted to talk to you about. I don't know if it means anything, but you said to keep an eye out," he says.

"Earlier, during one of the breaks at school, I overheard a group of the Leadership boys talking. There were three of them, Warren, Mayner, and Balum. They were talking about volunteering for the death detail. I know that some of the Leadership members volunteer to serve, but these guys are not like that at all. They only care about themselves."

"They're probable just spouting off to each other, trying to act brave," I say. "Or maybe their fathers told them it was a good way to gain favor in Leadership."

"I didn't think of that. Well, I did consider the spouting off part, but it didn't seem to fit since they were in such a small group with no one around to show off for except each other. It seems like they would do that with a bigger crowd," he says, looking to the side, as if he were still replaying the events in his mind.

"Thanks for keeping an eye out, but be careful to make sure you're not obvious about it. Since I'm going to be on the Solar Panel detail anyway, I'll look into it and let you know if anything becomes of it. Okay, Arluin?" I ask.

He reluctantly agrees. I can tell Arluin feels better since he contributed something, though the conversation was likely just the rambling bravado of young boys. While many higher officials of Leadership volunteer for the Solar Panel detail to show solidarity with the workers, it is uncommon for the younger ones to do so because of the high risk of a fatal accident on the surface. I do not like thinking about the Solar Panel detail, but at least there is no way for them to pick me for service in a future lottery since this assignment will remove my name from the draw list. I push the thoughts out of my mind and concentrate on my food.

Not long after we stop talking, our mother returns,

and we finish our meal before returning to our quarters for the night. I will wait until tomorrow to tell her about my added punishment. She is in a good mood tonight, and there is no reason to spoil it for her. Before we go to bed, I tell them both a fabricated story of how I tripped and fell earlier today. That was the cause of the chemical spill and of my broken rib. I feel a little indignant that they both so readily believe the story. Neither of them thought to question it at all. *I am not that accident prone!* I think to myself. Well, at least I can settle in for some much needed rest, before being forced into another uncomfortable conversation.

# 11

I awaken the next morning and mindlessly complete my morning routine, still half asleep. While sitting in front of the television screen, waiting for the announcements, the fog of my sleep finally begins to dissipate. The soreness in my chest returns as soon as I make a sudden movement. This is going to be annoying to deal with. The tone for the morning announcements goes off, and Mr. Vaden again appears on the screen.

"Good morning, I am Mr. Vaden. Today I am pleased to announce our food and water levels continue to remain above minimum levels. Energy generation has decreased slightly, but still remains sufficient. The air filtration system diagnostic was satisfactory.

"However, not all of the news this morning is good. Upon reviewing the events that led to the untimely death of one of our workers in The Caves, it has come to my attention that the group was in an unsecure area well beyond the allotted time on their permit. Infractions like this may have been overlooked in the past, but with such disastrous results, that cannot continue.

"I mentioned before that Leadership intends to enforce these policies, so as a result of this tragedy, and with our commitment to prevent further occurrences, the offending permit holder has been disciplined. Kagen Meldon has been restricted from all access to The Caves and will be assigned to two consecutive positions on the Solar Panel maintenance detail team. Let this serve as a reminder to all of us the dangers of disregarding policies that were put in place specifically to keep everyone safe. That is all for the morning announcements. May you all have a safe and productive day."

I was planning on breaking the news to my mother during breakfast, so the announcement of my punishment catches me completely off guard. When I turn to plead my case, she is still staring at the blank screen.

"And when did you plan on telling me about this, Kagen?" she asks, still not looking at me.

"I wanted to tell you last night, but the timing didn't feel right. I was planning on telling you today at breakfast," I answer contritely.

"Don't worry, Mom," Arluin interrupts. "Kagen may be clumsy when he doesn't pay attention, but not when he focuses. There's no way he would let anything bad happen on the surface. Everything will be okay, you'll see." His words feel more like hopeful wishes than a confident statement of fact.

"The detail is not my biggest fear," she says.

I know what she is thinking. The haunted face of my father when he returned to us from the Detention Center flashes in my mind. By the look of my mother and Arluin, the same memory visits their thoughts as well.

"You don't have to say anything, Mom," I reassure her. "I'll do everything possible to make sure we all stay safe."

"That's what I'm worried about. It's the look in your eyes lately. It's the same look your father had before he died." Her words trail off.

There is nothing more to say now. Arluin and I could go on with more reassurances trying to make her feel better, but it would be pointless, so we leave it at that. None of us speaks much through breakfast, and nothing is said when we part ways for work.

*

Rana is waiting for me as I enter the infirmary, and she is not alone. Standing beside her is a young man and woman. They are wearing Healer uniforms though they both appear younger than the usual age required to be an understudy. I wonder what this is all about. They must be here for some type of instruction. Maybe they are meant to shadow us to make sure they have the stomach for the work.

"Hi Rana, what's up?" I ask while approaching the group.

"Kagen, this is Kesia," she says pointing to the young woman. "And this is Jace," she finishes motioning toward the young man.

Kesia gives a polite bow in my direction. Her eyes follow Rana and me intently, but her feet keep shuffling. There is nothing particularly distinctive in her appearance other than her age. Behind her attentive gaze is an imperfect complexion flanked by moderately dark and braided hair. After a moment, she notices her own fidgeting and tries to stand with a firm posture to conceal her nervousness.

Jace nods his head and stands silently. Even with a spindly and awkward build that has not yet been filled by age, he still looks much more confident than Kesia. Both of them lack the distinctive insignia of Leadership on their uniforms, but I still get the feeling that Kesia comes from it.

"I am pleased to meet you both," I say, nodding my head in their general direction. "To what do we owe the pleasure of their visit?" I ask Rana.

"We have both been assigned understudies," she says. Rana's voice and expression seems even, but if you have known her long enough, with the slight infliction in her words it is easy to tell she is uncomfortable with this.

"Jace will be working with me and Kesia will work under you. After a few months they'll switch positions," she says.

"I see. Well, we should get started orienting you then, Kesia. Go to the exam room and look around a bit, I'll be in shortly so we can get started," I say, still looking at Rana. Jace is smart enough to take the hint and goes to Rana's exam room, leaving us alone to talk.

"Not that we couldn't use the extra help, but doesn't this strike you as odd?" I ask her. "Neither of them looks old enough to be an understudy, and there was no advanced notice?"

"I do find it rather curious," she says. "I have already confirmed their positions with Leadership though, and you are correct about their age. They are both two years younger than usual, but then again, you are also younger than a typical mentor. I find it even more interesting that even though Leadership is so unhappy with you, they still trust you enough to start mentoring."

That point had not even crossed my mind. I cannot help but to wonder if part of their motivation is to limit my time alone as much as possible. What trouble can I get into with Leadership if most of my time is spent with an understudy?

"Are you ready to be a mentor, Kagen?" Rana asks.

"I learned from the best, Rana," I say, flashing a smile. "Besides, if I need any tips I know where to get help."

With that, I excuse myself and head toward my exam room. I still remember what it was like to go through all the rigorous courses that led to my first day as an understudy. Becoming a Healer was not initially my choice. Through aptitude testing by Leadership, I was found to score high in complex problem solving, multitasking, and performance under stress. These qualities, among other compassionate characteristics led them to assigning me to Healer training. I was unsure of whether it would really suit me until the specific educational courses began. Immediately, I became intrigued by the complexity and harmony of our internal biology.

Even though I excelled in those lessons, I still had no idea of what was coming. All the anatomy and physiology lessons do little to prepare you for the actual performance as a Healer. The first time I was allowed to interview a patient, my words to her came out as a stammering mess even though it was a very simple case of an outer ear infection. The complexities of caring for the ill and injured were still far beyond me. Managing the expectations, anger, fear and uncertainty experienced by the people that come to see us is not something one learns without the benefit of experience.

But as time passed, combined with Rana's instruction, each day the task ahead of me seemed less daunting. This gradual progress continued until I felt completely comfortable in my profession. What seemed like an impossibly complex and unmanageable task now feels more like a difficult challenge that can always be faced if approached in a thoughtful and systematic manner. It will be my responsibility to help Kesia make that transition as well.

I enter the room to find her working her way through the medical equipment. She appears to be familiar with most of it and looks more to be evaluating her tools than determining their purpose like Mr. Vaden was when he was here.

"So, Kesia, will this be your first time with direct

patient care?" I ask.

"Yes, I have completed all of my classroom anatomy, pathology, and physiology requirements. I was most of the way through the equipment training when we received the notice of advancement," she says proudly. Her nervousness is fading but still noticeable.

"Well, I expect it to be an interesting day for you then. We can go ever the usual preparation details in a minute. First is the ground rules," I tell her.

"Okay," she says and walks over to the gurney, waiting for me to continue.

"I'll start off with the first couple of patients and you will shadow. We'll talk about each case after we're done. After that, if it is a non-emergent case you can evaluate them first and tell me your findings and plan," I instruct.

"Sounds fair," she says.

"You are not to discuss your plan with the patient until we have talked about it and do not start any intervention without my approval unless it would be harmful to wait," I say. The amount of freedom is different with every understudy, but as inexperienced and nervous as Kesia is, I want to keep her autonomy to a minimum until she proves that she can handle it.

"Understood," she answers. Her shoulders relax with my words. I suspect knowing she will not be left alone on her first day is comforting.

"Now, you seem to be familiar with most of the standard equipment, but there are some unique pieces here as well. We'll go over their purpose and use as time allows," I continue.

Before I can finish the waiting room chime sounds. We both head to the waiting room to meet our first patient of the day. I was hoping to have some more time to get some background information on Kesia before we

started, but that will have to wait for now. In the front
room there is a worker with an arm injury waiting for us.
He has the sturdy look of a worker from the Deep Vents.
It is hard work keeping the massive generators supplying
energy to Securus, and they are frequent visitors to the
infirmary. While it is a difficult job, it is still not nearly as
dangerous as the Solar panel detail. Regardless, this
should be a good straightforward case for Kesia to get a
feel for the process.

"Hello, sir. I am Kagen, and this is my understudy,
Kesia. Follow us to the exam room and we'll get that arm
fixed up for you. What's your name?" I ask as we walk.

"Dalek, sir," he replies.

"Just call me Kagen," I say as we enter the room. "So,
how did you injure your arm?"

"We were moving some equipment around, and it got
smashed between the two pieces," he says, wincing from
a surge of pain.

There is some swelling, but the arm is not deformed.
More importantly, both his circulation and neurologic
function remain intact. I instruct Kesia to roll over the
portable X-ray machine. We have Dalek sit in the device,
and I show Kesia how to manipulate the arm to get the
correct angle for the X-ray. The image shows that his
forearm has hairline fractures through both bones but the
edges are not displaced, so a simple splint will do.

"Kesia, have you applied a splint before?" I ask while
retrieving the reusable splint. It has a thick but moveable
plastic lining that we fill with a hardened matrix of foam.
This foam, like many other things in Securus, is
completely recyclable. Using a specific solvent it turns
into a liquid and back into a firm matrix with the
application of another.

"No, I've only seen a demonstration," she reluctantly

replies.

"You can do this one then, it's pretty simple. The main part is positioning the arm correctly," I tell her.

I hold Dalek's arm still while Kesia slips on the splint and adds the solvent. The foam rapidly hardens and the splint is set. Though it is a relatively simple task, I see the pride and confidence she has from completing it. As we are walking Dalek back to the waiting room to release him, the chime sounds again. *It's going to be busy today*, I think to myself. What awaits us troubles me deeply. There are two patients, and both look critically ill. They are pale, confused, and soaked with their own perspiration. They were not able to come here under their own strength. Instead, they have been carried up by members of the Leadership Guard. The look of the ill men is unmistakable. It appears that Leland will not be the only one in Securus who contracted this form of aggressive meningitis.

"What happened to these men?" I ask the Guards while passing out respiratory masks and gloves to everyone in the room to lessen the chance of the infection being transmitted.

"They are researchers from The Caves," the Guard says. "We found them in the lounge near The Caves like this. They seemed tired when they first arrived this morning, but nothing like this."

The men are transported into my exam room while I call for Rana to come help. I can handle multiple cases at once, but when they are this ill, every minute matters, and it is better to have her reschedule appointments than to sacrifice precious time.

"Okay, Kesia, stay close to me. We have a lot to do," I tell her while preparing my equipment to begin the treatments and obtain blood samples for evaluation.

I look over the men to see who is in worse condition. While I do not know their names, I do know who they are. One has an unmistakable woolly beard, and the other has large glasses with a gangly appearance that could only belong to the research workers that inadvertently distracted the Guard when I entered The Caves. The bearded man has better vital signs so I start with the lanky man. Rana will be here soon to take care of his partner.

"Kesia, get the intravenous fluids and pour in three liters as quickly as you can," I tell her.

His blood pressure is low, and the extra fluids may help. My other immediate concern is his worsening confusion. He is no longer mumbling, and I fear that he is no longer in control of his breathing. He is at risk of aspirating into his lungs and that could compromise another vital organ system. I inject specialized medications through the intravenous access to facilitate the passage of an artificial breathing tube.

Using my old fashioned device, I peer into his oral cavity and find his vocal cords. There are more sophisticated devices with cameras embedded into the tip of the blade, but I still prefer this approach. Somehow it feels more natural to me. The streak of white cords that are nestled below the floppy epiglottis is my target. I pass the tube through the vocal cords and secure it in place. Now his airway is protected and the work of his breathing can be transferred to a ventilator machine. While I was placing the breathing tube, Rana and Jace arrived to start working on the bearded man.

"Looks like Leland's illness isn't an isolated case after all," Rana says to me as she works.

"Yeah, that's what I was thinking. These two also work in The Caves," I mention, knowing that may be important in identifying the exposure site of this disease.

This is something we will need to seriously consider later, after the men are stabilized.

Kesia already has the fluids running, so we move on to the sample collection. I know that we really need the cerebrospinal fluid, but he is in no condition to be manipulated for that procedure yet, so we run the standard battery of blood tests.

"Ok, while we're waiting to see if his blood pressure responds to the fluids, we should initiate a more direct treatment. What do you suggest, Kesia?" I ask while going to the cabinets to get the medicines we need.

"Well, we should start with broad spectrum antibiotics, I think. With his confusion, fever, and unstable cardiovascular system, I would suspect some infection. Maybe he has meningitis," she says, still considering her words.

"That's a good start," I tell her while bringing over the antiviral and antibiotic medications. "We very recently had a patient with severe viral meningitis, and I think these men have the same infection. However, with our limited information, we cannot yet assume that we know the diagnosis especially with both of them presenting at the same time. Have you considered a toxidrome such as neuroleptic malignant syndrome? That could also explain his fever, altered mental status, and unstable vital signs. He is a research worker and may be exposed to many chemicals. Plus, we have not yet accessed his records to see if he is on any medications that could trigger a toxidrome."

"I hadn't thought of that," she admits.

"It is always good practice to run down the list of possibilities and exclude as many things as possible before narrowing your focus to a single diagnosis," I say, almost bumping into Rana while moving over to start the infusions.

"Jace, what do you think about a toxidrome?" Rana asks as they continue their treatments.

"Well, they have some features of a toxidrome, but there are inconsistencies that make me doubt it. For instance, they don't have rigid muscles you would expect with NMS," he says.

"Since these men work in The Caves we also must consider the possibility of some kind of poisonous envenomation from any number of creatures. There are numerous odd insects and some small animals out there. Not all of them are benign," Rana tells the understudies.

All of these things are more for their education, preparing them to form their own differential diagnosis list. Both Rana and I know exactly what is going on and how fast the infection overwhelmed Leland. After the initial treatments are done, we both set up for the lumbar punctures. This time we talk our way through it so Jace and Kesia will understand exactly what we are doing. If this gets as bad as I fear, they will be doing this on their own sooner than anyone expected.

Now that the initial treatments, analysis, and stabilization have been started it is time to transport the men to the intensive care unit. Rana's patient is doing significantly better than mine, despite receiving identical treatment. He has not yet required the ventilator and is only requiring half the dose of medications to support his falling blood pressure.

"Can you take these men to the ICU?" I ask Jace and Kesia hoping Rana will not object to letting them do this on their own. I want to talk to her about this new outbreak privately.

"Sure, Rana showed us where it is when we toured the infirmary earlier," Jace answers.

"Tell Adara that they have the same infection as Leland and that I'll be back in a few minutes to speak with her," Rana adds as they prepare to leave. It looks like she has something on her mind as well.

## 12

"This is going to be bad, isn't it?" I ask Rana after the others have left.

"Three cases so close together and all very severe. We need to notify Leadership, it looks like the start of an epidemic," she warns. "We need to get Kesia and Jace up to speed as fast as possible. We may need their help more than we anticipated."

"Yeah, that's what I was thinking. But there is one other thing that's bothering me. So far, I've had some contact with all three men just before they became ill," I say.

"That's nothing to be concerned with," Rana reassures me. "If you had been exposed, you would've showed symptoms by now. And don't think for one second that you are a carrier of the virus. That pathogen is too aggressive to stay dormant in a carrier," she says anticipating my concern. Rana then pauses as if she is replaying something in her mind. "Wait, how did you come into contact with the two new cases?" she asks.

"During my excursion I saw them in the lounge area by the entrance to The Caves. They unwittingly distracted the Guard long enough for me to slip out the outer door," I tell her.

"That's not much contact. Sounds like you were far enough away to avoid any significant exposure," she says.

Rana's words comfort me, but they do not change the potential disaster facing Securus. We are going to have to enlist Leadership to help us ensure this outbreak does not spread. I can only hope that the Research Department is making some progress with their analysis of the samples we sent from Leland.

"I'll alert the other Healers of the new developments. In the meantime, we need to develop a treatment protocol that Jace and Kesia will be able to initiate in case we become inundated with a flood of patients. We should also have them split some time with Adara so they can flex positions to be more helpful," she says.

"Ok, I'll let them know the plan. You can tell Adara when you speak with her. Let's have them start with her now while I come up with the protocol. I'm sure you must have a backlog of appointments waiting by now," I say.

We make our way to the intensive care room to meet up with the others. Rana sends Kesia and Jace over to me while she speaks with Adara. I fill the understudies in on our new plan. Jace takes the news in stride and seems eager to continue. Kesia, on the other hand, is looking to the floor with her shuffling feet acting up again.

"If there are any questions or concerns, now is the time. Don't be afraid to speak up," I say looking directly at Kesia.

"It's nothing," Kesia says timidly. "Just, my instructors told us we were supposed to shadow one Healer at a time, and I was hoping to stay with you."

I feel my face turning warm and try to suppress the blushing caused by her words. I do not know if she is disappointed that she is not following her prior instructions or if she just wanted to learn from me. Either way, it is flattering that she wants to stick with me.

"Well, we all have to be flexible in this profession, especially when faced with a possible epidemic," I tell her.

"Besides, if things calm down, you will both do most of your instruction as we initially planned. We just need to make sure we're prepared first."

She looks as if she has more to say but does not voice the words. Before she can change her mind, I have them return to Rana and Adara. After checking to make sure no more patients are waiting to be seen, I return to my exam room to get to work on developing a standard treatment protocol for the understudies.

The rest of the morning passes quickly while I am engrossed in my work. There are a few more patients that come in but they are not infected with the new virus. By the time I have finished the protocol, it is already time for my lunch break. The morning was so busy that it slipped my mind that I was supposed to meet Hadwin and Sayda soon. There was no chance for me to figure out what to say. Before heading to the exit, I stop by Rana's exam room to let her know where I will be, in case she needs to call me back to help. Just before I reach the decontamination chamber, Kesia catches me in the hallway.

"Hey Kagen, you headed to lunch? I was gonna go now too. Is it okay if I go with you?" she asks.

Normally it would not be a problem for her to tag along except the coming conversation is not for her ears, so I think of an excuse. "I'll meet you there. First, can you to get the treatment protocol I left in the exam room and get a copy to Jace? You both need to get started studying it right away," I say to her obvious disappointment.

After enduring the decontamination chamber, I leave the infirmary to go to meet Sayda and Hadwin. We all arrive to the hall at nearly the same time. Without many words, we pick up our food, and then go to a more private area to talk. I urge them to hurry so we have as much time as possible, and more importantly, so we can disappear before Kesia finds us.

Sayda's quarters are the closest to the lunch hall, so after we pick up our food we make our way there. Sayda has been quiet so far, but at least she has not attacked me yet. I consider that progress. When we get into her quarters, Hadwin and I search the area to make sure there is nothing out of the ordinary that could indicate her room is under surveillance. The search does not take long since it is such a bare room. When I am satisfied we can talk, I turn to Sayda. To this point she has been quiet and calm, but there is nothing calm about the look in her eyes. This is not going to be easy.

"Hadwin told you what really happened the night Merrick died?" I ask.

"Yes," she says suspiciously. "But he also said you told him that there was more to the story." Hadwin and I sit on a bunk while Sayda continues to stand.

"Ok, so you already know there were some soldiers in the passage, equipped with guns and body armor. But, that was not all there was in that chamber. I saw a set of rail tracks behind the collapse. I don't know where they lead, but they were definitely there." I tell them.

"Are you sure you didn't just see some flashing lights or were so traumatized you could've imagined it?" she asks. Her words are not meant to be insulting, she is just naturally skeptical.

"I'm sure. I snuck back into The Caves to investigate, that's how I broke my ribs," I say clutching my chest and glancing at Hadwin.

"I was wondering how that happened. You fell, right?" Hadwin asks, assuming the injury was self-inflicted.

"No, I wish it was that simple. I ran into the soldiers again. When I went back into the passage, the collapse had been reinforced to form a complete wall and the tracks were hidden. So, I was photographing the area through the cracks when a door opened out of the rocks, and there they were," I say. Now they both are listening intently, no longer wanting to interrupt. Though she is listening, Sayda is still standing over me with her arms folded. I am not out of danger yet.

"The same two soldiers were patrolling the area, and I saw them open another door to what they called a supply room. There is no question in my mind that it was the same men because I will never forget their voices. The only thing I could do was crouch behind the rubble, but my movement accidentally dislodged a rock. They heard it and shot through a crack in the wall, trying to scare me out. I stayed still and they didn't see me. They assumed it was just a loose rock that had fallen, so they stopped looking. That was great, but during the commotion their gun blast dislodged another rock, and it fell right onto my chest. It took everything I had to stay silent and still," I whisper while showing them the healing injuries. With some time to heal, the bruise has darkened and dispersed, making it look even more impressive. Sayda subtly flinches at the site of it.

I retrieve my camera to show them the images. Hadwin looks on with anticipation while Sayda still has a look of disbelief. I point out the manipulated wall and the area where the man-made tunnel was. There is a slight protruding rock in the spot where I saw them men trigger a mechanism to open the door to the supply room. Unfortunately, the images of the soldiers are useless because the glare made them invisible.

"Looks an awful lot like a normal cavern to me," says Sayda.

"Yeah, but those rocks sure do look stacked. Why

would they put them back after getting Merrick's body out? It makes no sense unless they're hiding something," Hadwin tells Sayda.

It is a relief that Hadwin seems to believe me, but failing to convince Sayda is frustrating. I desperately need both of them to be with me on this. If I have to continue alone I will, but having both of their help would significantly increase my chances of succeeding. My only option is to change my approach.

"Look, Sayda, how long have we known each other? When have I ever been one to make up lies to cover my mistakes? I know that this whole thing is messed up, but try to put yourself in my position. What would you have done if you saw one of us get murdered and there was no way to stop it? Would you have let the rest of us get killed or would you have done whatever you could to save us?" I ask. Sayda remains silent, but her arms drop to the side and with them, I feel her defiance weakening ever so slightly.

"I would have done anything to save Merrick or to make his murderer pay, but not if that means sacrificing you, Hadwin, and Talia. I do feel guilty for not being able to save Merrick and for letting him get so far in that passage alone. I would have never allowed any of this if there was any way to stop it," I continue, now moving toward her. I place my hands on her shoulders and look directly into her eyes.

"Sayda, what happened couldn't have been stopped, but I am damn well going to find out what's going on out there and make those bastards pay. I need you with me on this. I can't do it alone, but I'll still try if need be," I plead.

A tear begins to form at the corner of her eye, and she reaches out to hug me. The honesty and resolve in my words finally broke through her remaining shreds of anger. The pressure of her squeeze aggravates my injury, but I do not flinch. Hadwin comes over to us and places a hand on each of our shoulders. He remains stoic, but I know he understands what I had to do, even if he does not say it.

"Okay, Kagen. I'm with you," Sayda says fighting off any further tears. After a few moments, we sit back down and begin nibbling at our food.

"Is there anything else that you left out?" she asks.

"Well, I'm fairly certain Leadership is involved in a cover up for a few reasons. First, I saw a symbol that looked similar to a Leadership insignia on the soldiers' armor. Then, the Healer that examined Merrick, Trent Riley, wrote a blatantly contrived report. Also, when Aamon came to tell me about my Solar Panel maintenance details, he acted as if he enjoyed it. I don't trust him at all," I say.

"Yeah, that guy always seemed like an arrogant bastard to me," Hadwin agrees. Sayda also nods in assent.

"On top of everything else, Mr. Vaden threatened me directly. Except I'm not sure if it was because of the cover up or if he was just being a protective father, since he made it clear he wants me to stay away from Talia," I continue. "Even after all of that, I still have no idea why they are out there or where those tracks lead."

"I think we should avoid Talia anyway, the daughter of Mr. Vaden has to know what's going on," Sayda suggests.

"I don't think she does. She covered for us in The Caves, and I think that's why Mr. Vaden didn't punish the two of you. On top of that, I bumped into her again when I snuck back into The Caves, and not only did she keep it a secret, she gave me cover getting back in past the Guards," I say.

"Did you tell her everything?" Sayda asks with a sharp stare. She obviously does not share my trust of Talia.

"No, I told her I just needed to see the area again to convince myself that there really was nothing that could've been done to help Merrick. I do trust her, but this is going to stay between us unless we have no other options. You two are the only ones that I have told the truth to, not that Arluin hasn't been poking and prodding me constantly," I say. Both Hadwin and Sayda laugh at that, knowing how perceptive and persistent my little brother can be.

"Kagen, you have to be careful. It's one thing for her to be helpful when she thinks you're trying to deal with Merrick's loss, but how can you really know how she'll react when she finds out you're directly undermining her father," Hadwin cautions.

"Yeah, I know," I admit, not having a good reason to contradict his logic.

"So what's our next move?" Hadwin asks.

"I want to get back in that passage with you guys. If we bring a little equipment I think we can get through that wall. I'm not sure if we can get to the tracks, but we can get in the supply room and that has to give us some clue to what they're doing out there," I say.

"We need to have some form of protection though, in case we see the soldiers," Sayda cautions.

"I'll see what I can do for that," Hadwin offers.

"Good," I say. "The other thing that has been bothering me is where they're getting the resources for the tracks and whatever else is out there. They may have found some new resources in some cavern, but I think the equipment would have to come from Securus. Can you two quietly look around for any signs of equipment being smuggled out into The Caves? If we find a source of supplies that would help us figure out how far the cover up goes."

We know what we want to do but have no clue to how we are going to do it. But, now that they are both involved, I am much more confident we will figure it out. It has been a while since we left the lunch hall, and I need to return soon so my absence does not become too apparent. So we finish our food and leave Sayda's quarters. When I reenter the lunch hall, Kesia is sitting alone at a table on the far end. I make my way over to her.

"There you are, I've been looking everywhere for you," I tell her. "I even went back to the infirmary."

"I was here, you must have missed me in the crowd," she says.

"Did you get the protocol to Jace?" I ask, keeping the focus on her and off of my absence.

"Yeah, he's going over it with Rana," she answers.

"So, what did you think of your first morning?" I ask, while sitting down.

"It was a lot more intense than I expected. I don't know how you and Rana do it," she admits.

"You'll get the hang of it; just give it some time," I tell her.

When Kesia is done with her lunch we return to the infirmary. Jace and Rana are deep in a discussion about something so we pass by and go to the intensive care unit. In the short time we were gone, the gangly man's condition has worsened severely. Adara is on top of the gurney, actively trying to restart his heart. I immediately run over to help. She had not had time to attach the automated chest compressor to him so she is doing manual compressions. I jump in to give her a rest and allow her the time to manage the medications more efficiently. With the first compression, I instantly regret my decision. A searing pain in my chest flares with each forced compression. If this keeps up, I will end up passing out from the pain. I look over to see Kesia still standing at the door, paralyzed by the sight in front of her.

"Kesia, come over and take over the compressions," I instruct. She breaks free of her fearful bonds long enough to take a position next to me. As I move away, she slides into position and timidly starts.

"Deeper, Kesia," I tell her. As she compresses his chest wall deeper, there is a horrified look that covers her face. The first time I had to perform chest compressions, I had that same look. When I pushed down, deep enough to effectively stimulate blood flow, there was a palpable crunch as ribs cracked beneath my hands. Even worse, it gave way to a sickening grinding of the bones with each compression as I tried to revive the person. Until you realize that this is expected, it is a terrifying sensation.

"I felt a pop. I think I broke a rib," she says contritely, but despite her hesitation, keeps the pace going.

"That's okay, it happens all the time. Better for him to wake up with a painful chest than to not get any circulation and never wake up at all," I reassure her. "Just keep going, you're doing great."

She continues on and soon, her fear fades. Adara adds in more medications to try and stimulate his failing circulatory system. The more we try, the more it is obvious that it is too late. His heart has completely shut down and is not responding to any of our efforts. I stop Kesia and check his heart with our ultrasound machine. There is no movement. It is not even responsive enough to try and shock it back to life. He has passed.

Despite being on the same treatment regimen, the

bearded man is relatively stable. His confusion has not progressed, and he has managed to fight off the need for the ventilator. Looking at his chart, his lab tests are much better than the others as well. He was a healthy man prior to this by the name of Delvin. I turn around to find Kesia slumped against the wall, still looking at the man we failed to revive.

There is nothing else we can do, so I try to refocus her attention and take her to our exam room to talk. These situations are difficult and everyone deals with them differently. We sit down to discuss the details of what happened and to help her understand how to approach it next time. I give her tips on how to remember what steps to take and ways to make the procedures physically easier for her to do. But there is a more important message that she needs to hear.

"This job can be a difficult one. There are so many things that are beyond our capability to heal. In the end, we must always be prepared to deal with death even while doing our best to fight it off. Sometimes, we need to step back to understand that some things are beyond our reach and not meant for us to change. There is only so much we can do, but we can take solace in the fact that we gave our best efforts," I tell her.

My own words cause me to stop and reflect. I have seen death in many forms, but as a Healer there is always a sense of separation. We subconsciously build a barrier to protect ourselves from the true destruction of the grief we are regularly confronted with. Those barriers are broken down from time to time and in situations like Merrick's, they are destroyed altogether. But my message also applies to his situation as well. I did do everything possible and still could not stop it. It was beyond my reach to change. I must accept that and let my guilt go.

That does not mean my pursuit of the truth should be abandoned. That *is* within my reach and I will not stop until it is discovered. I may not be able to bring Merrick back, but I can make sure that those responsible are held accountable for their deceit and crimes.

Kesia is looking down, lost in her own mind, just as I am. The patient chime goes off and shakes both of us from our introspection. It is another case of this new illness, and he looks every bit as sick and familiar to me as the others. Just like Leland, he is wearing the uniform of the Leadership Guard. *The outbreak is spreading*, I think to myself.

## 13

That night after dinner, I lay in my bunk, trying to escape the coincidences that have been following me. Arluin and my mother are still out in the dinner hall, giving me time alone to think. There had been three more cases of meningitis today, and I recently had close contact with all of them. The last man to come in ill was the Guard that had been distracted by the other two researchers. It seems that everyone I encounter in The Caves becomes ill. As that thought crosses my mind another one explodes to the forefront. Talia was also in The Caves. She had not come to the infirmary, but I cannot help but worry that she could be infected.

I am startled from my thoughts by the sound of the announcement tone. The light from the monitor fills the room and Mr. Vaden appears on the screen. I rise from my bunk to see what has provoked the unexpected evening announcement.

"Good evening, I am Mr. Vaden. I apologize for interrupting your free time this evening, but circumstances have arisen such that this announcement was necessary. Over the past few days there have been four cases of a severe illness. It is infectious in nature and has already claimed the lives of two of the four infected. The other two remain in critical condition. Our Healers are doing everything they can, but it appears to be an aggressive pathogen.

"While investigating the nature of this infection, it has

been discovered that the point of origin appears to be from The Caves. With the severity and virulence of this outbreak, aggressive measures must be taken to limit its spread. To that end, and until further notice, all access to The Caves will be restricted except for approved research personnel. The outer door will remain closed until we have determined there is no further risk to those of us here in Securus.

"Unfortunately this also means that we will be losing the resources that The Caves provide until we can safely return to harvest them. I urge every person to do what they can to ration our resources and be patient with these restrictions. Thank you for your attention, have a safe evening."

The news is bad. I had known there would be some kind of response to the outbreak, but the thought of Leadership closing off The Caves completely never crossed my mind. We rely heavily on the resources gathered from The Caves, and the health of our people could rapidly deteriorate without it. That was what we were faced with before the discovery of The Caves. Despite growth controls, our population had outgrown the nutrition generating capabilities of the facility. The food and water was spread thin enough to keep the people alive, but just barely. Those with less robust health were not able to cope with the lack of nutrients and many died. Mr. Vaden's discovery of The Caves changed that, and now he is taking it away from us.

I get up to go find Hadwin and Sayda because the lack of resources is not the only problem posed by this new restriction. If we can no longer get into The Caves, we need to find another path to uncovering the truth. Inside the social hall nearest to Hadwin's quarters, the area is so packed with people and loud with conversation that I can

135

barely stand it. I wade through the crowd, looking for my friends, but am immediately stopped and cornered by a concerned group of people. Some of them have recognized me as one of the Healers, and the frightened crowd is pleading for information about the illness.

"How did they catch it?" one woman asks.

Before I can answer, another woman shouts, "How do we know if we were exposed?"

This is followed by a man yelling, "What are the symptoms, what if we are already have it?"

I struggle to get some space. There are so many people yelling at once that it is getting overwhelming. With more people shoving their way forward to demand answers, the group is steadily herding me toward the wall. If I do not do something about it now, they are going to trample me. I look around for any escape, nearly falling from the growing pressure of the oncoming crowd. On my left, there is a large table. Seizing the opening, I leap on top of it, much to the surprise of those around me.

"Calm down," I roar to the crowd. The sight of me standing on the table and yelling at them temporarily halts the onslaught of questions.

"I will answer all the questions that I can, but you all need to calm down and listen," I say and wait for the attention of the group. I do not like the comparison, but standing here above the crowd, waiting to speak reminds me of Mr. Vaden patiently waiting for our attention when he starts the announcements. The prolonged pause is effective, and those around me now quietly await my words.

"Ok, so here is what we know so far. The illness is a type of meningitis. It is a virus that infects the natural fluid that surrounds our brain and spinal cord. It is a particularly aggressive type, and the symptoms progress rapidly. I do not think that it is easily transmitted from person to person, but more research is needed. I have no information on the source of the virus, but all of those infected so far work within The Caves.

"The warning signs to watch for are headache, fever, and neck stiffness. Unfortunately, this infection progresses rapidly to confusion and delirium, so if you or your family members start having any of those symptoms, either call for the rounding Healer or come to the infirmary immediately. However, I caution all of you to only use the Healers and infirmary if truly needed. There are only a handful of us, and we need to be as efficient as possible."

As soon as I finish, the crowd again barrages me with more questions. I try to calm them back down again, but this time it is not working. The noise from the group drowns out my voice. They are pushing each other closer to my table. The group moves forward, now completely surrounding my table. I look for an opening to get away, but there is none.

Suddenly, the group turns its attention, and the screaming voices fall silent. I look around, confused by the rapid change, and notice movement in the crowd. A figure is making its way toward me and inexplicably, the crowd of people is willingly accommodating the movement. I look on with bewilderment as the same people who were ready to trample me just a moment ago are letting someone push past them without protest. As the figure nears, it starts to make sense. It is not just another scared person, it is Talia. She seems to have a great sense of timing lately. She strolls through the remaining people with confidence and gracefully climbs on my table.

"Hi, Kagen. You were doing pretty well there for a

while, but it looks like I need to save you again," she says with a subtle smile.

"I'm just glad you think I'm worth saving," I counter, raising an eyebrow as if I was surprised by her decision.

"Sayda and Hadwin are in the back of the hall waiting for you. I'll finish here and meet up with you in a minute," she says calmly.

Talia begins to speak and as she does the entire hall falls silent, entranced by the eloquence of her voice. With Talia present, they have already forgotten me. I am able to walk through the crowd unnoticed to find Hadwin and Sayda. Talia's words are not very informative, which is expected since we still know very little about the origins and patterns of transmission of the virus. But, it is her presence and reassurance that does more for the people listening than any specific details could. She is a natural leader.

"Hey, Kagen, you looked like you were going to need a change of underwear before Talia saved you," Hadwin laughs.

"Don't pretend you were never saved by a girl, Hadwin. If Sayda wasn't here, that bully from when we were little, what was his name? Gerst? He'd probably still be following you and giving you daily wedgies," I counter. Even Sayda laughs at that. "Sometimes it takes a real man to know when you need to be saved by a strong woman," I say.

For a moment, it feels like we are just friends hanging out, but that cannot last long. Not with everything that has happened. There is no hiding from the reality we are faced with here in Securus. If we do not face it, then we cannot change it.

I look back to the crowd of people still gathered around Talia. They hang on her every word. In this moment, it is obvious that we need her. Discovering the truth is not our only mission. If there is something significant to find, we need a way to get the word to the people of Securus. Who would believe the ramblings of three insignificant people over the credibility of Leadership? If we had Talia deliver the message, it is hard to imagine it being dismissed. I know we need her help, but doubt that Hadwin and Sayda will be so eager to enlist it.

"Big setback today," I say to the others.

"Yeah, I hope the lockout doesn't last long. If it does, whatever is going on out there will be the least of our worries," Sayda responds.

"Since we can't return to that passage any time soon, I think we should concentrate on finding any supply lines. That could give us some answers. Plus you never know, if we find one, maybe it could lead to another route into The Caves," I say even though it is doubtful that another route could exist and go unnoticed.

"That's a start, but I was thinking, what's our end game? How do we do anything about whatever it is we find? There are only three of us against all of Leadership if it comes to that," Hadwin asks.

"Hadwin's right. We need a way to prove to everyone else what we find is true, and I don't think just a couple of pictures would do it. We need a way to get some real evidence and get everyone to see it," Sayda adds.

"I was just thinking the same thing," I tell them. "I have an idea, but you guys aren't going to like it."

They both look at me. Hadwin appears curious while Sayda narrows her eyes in suspicion. She must know where I am going with this.

"We need a voice. One that the people will listen to, and one that they will trust," I say.

"No, Kagen," Sayda says immediately. "We cannot trust anyone else until we find out more, especially anyone in Leadership."

"Am I missing something here?" Hadwin asks. Sayda remains silent, allowing me to explain myself.

"Look behind me, Hadwin. Look at the crowd huddled around Talia. She isn't telling them anything of substance, and they still hang on every word she says. What better way to get people to listen to us then to have her deliver the message?" I ask.

"I think you're both right. She would be the perfect person for the job, but how can we trust her? She is the daughter of Mr. Vaden after all. You don't get more entrenched in Leadership than that," Hadwin says.

"I trust her. She's already covered for me twice, and the second time she specifically knew I was disobeying her father's restriction. But mostly, I can feel it when I look in her eyes. She would do whatever was needed for the good of Securus, even if it was at the expense of Leadership," I try to explain.

"Yeah, I'm sure that's all you feel when you look in her eyes," Sayda mumbles, rolling her eyes.

"Look, I'm not saying we should tell her everything now," I continue, ignoring the look Sayda is giving me. "But unless you have a better idea, she's our best option."

"We need to wait until we really know what we're dealing with. There's no point in stirring things up unless we have to. When we do tell her what what's going on, we should leave her father out of it. That part may be too emotional for her to handle at first," Hadwin says.

"You're right, Hadwin," I say. "We have a lot of work to do first, and really, I'm not yet convinced that Mr. Vaden is involved, anyway. Aamon, on the other hand, I don't see any way that he's not directly involved."

"That sniveling little coward," Sayda hisses.

"Don't worry, Sayda, you'll get your chance," I reassure her. "What do you guys think, should we tell her anything?"

"I don't think we have a better option. I hope you're right, Kagen," Hadwin says. "But like I said, we should wait. We need some solid proof."

"Well, since I'm outnumbered, I have no choice. But when we do tell her, we only say what we have to in order to get her to help, agreed?" Sayda asks.

"Agreed," I answer. "We can start by telling her about Aamon being suspicious. That wouldn't reveal anything of significance, and maybe she could keep an eye on him."

They both agree, though Sayda is still not happy about it. We turn our attention back to the crowd of people around Talia. They are starting to disperse, and she is walking toward us with a satisfied grin.

"Thanks again for saving me," I tell her as she nears.

"You're very welcome, Kagen," she answers.

"I don't know how you do it. People always listen when you speak," I compliment her.

"I just reassured them. They were frightened by the unknown, and that's a natural response," she explains. "That's why Leadership sent people out to all the different sectors tonight, to help calm their fears. Lucky for you I was assigned to this hall."

"Talia, there's something we wanted to talk to you about, but we need some privacy first," I say.

"Okay, there's a research storage room nearby, we can go there," she says. Her forehead wrinkles as she looks at me with curiosity.

We walk away from the social gathering and down the hallway, to an inconspicuous doorway. Talia uses her identification badge to access the room. I have passed this room numerous times and yet, never really noticed it. I wonder how many more like it there are in Securus. It is not a large room, but inside there is a significant amount of equipment. Most of it is sophisticated electronic devices that I am completely unfamiliar with. Hadwin, on the other hand, appears to recognize some of it as he takes stock of the room. There is no way of knowing if this room is unmonitored, but I am not divulging everything now anyway.

"Talia, I'm concerned about something, but I don't have any direct evidence to support it," I start. Talia watches and waits for me to explain. "Aamon has been acting really suspicious lately, at least more than usual for him. Ever since the night Merrick died, he has been watching me. He's up to something, but I don't know what. I think somehow he got it in his head that I'm a threat to him."

"That's just Aamon. He gets very aggressive when he feels threatened or out of control. I can talk to him about it," she offers.

"No, it's more than that. I think he's hiding something significant. Please don't say anything to anyone, especially your father. He made it clear how displeased he would be if I distracted you," I tell her. A look of exasperation shows on Talia's face with my last words.

"I was just hoping you could keep an eye out. I don't want to stir things up unless there's actually something to it. I'm already in enough trouble as it is," I say.

"Okay, I'll keep it to myself. If anything pertinent comes up, I'll let you know," she says. "And Kagen, I'm sorry about how severe your punishment has been. I really tried to convince the others to suspend the Solar Panel detail, but by the time I found out, it had already been announced. Leadership felt they couldn't change it then, because it would send a conflicting message to the people."

"Thanks for trying, but I'll be fine. At least I get the Solar Panel detail done with and won't have to worry about it later," I say, trying to maintain a cheerful tone.

"What's all this stuff used for anyway?" Hadwin interrupts, pointing to the electronic devices. I had almost forgotten that he and Sayda were with us in here since they had both been so quiet.

"Most of it is either back up research equipment or partial inventions that some of the researchers have been tinkering with," Talia answers.

"Are there more rooms like this," he asks with a distant look on his face. Knowing him for as long as I have, it is clear something is bothering him.

"A couple, but not a lot," she says, now looking at him and trying to discover his intentions.

"I was just wondering because there are so many electronic pieces here. I didn't think we produced enough for this much extra equipment, but it makes sense if some of it is generated by the research team themselves," he explains.

"Well, I have a few more things to tend to before my day is over, so I gotta go," Talia says urging us out the door.

"Don't be a stranger, Talia," I say as we leave the room.

"Of course not, especially with your uncanny ability to get into trouble without me," Talia says as she walks down the hallway with a smile.

Her smile warms me, and the light sensation in my stomach returns. Sayda is looking at me with a smirk, but says nothing. Hadwin does not seem to notice any of this and is still looking back toward the supply room. Sayda notices his odd behavior as well.

"What is it Haddie?" she asks. I had not heard her use that nickname before.

"I recognized some of the pieces. They came from my department and are relatively new, but I don't recall any recent allotments for Leadership use. Most of our parts are supposed to be building up for the coming Solar Panel updates," he says. "It makes me wonder where else my parts are going."

"Well then, we need to figure that out," I say.

"I have an idea, but I need to try it out first. I'll let you know tomorrow if it'll work," Sayda says, already heading down the hall to get started.

"I may be limited on my time, depending on what comes into the infirmary over the next couple of days. I'm sure we'll have an overload of worried people because of the announcement. Watch Sayda so she doesn't get over excited and get into any trouble," I tell Hadwin.

"I'm all over her. I mean, I'm all over *it*," Hadwin says with a chuckle.

We both scatter to our own quarters for the night. It was good to see Talia doing well and without any signs of infection. I find my bunk and quickly fall asleep, knowing that I will need my rest for tomorrow at work. There is never a shortage of patients after an announcement like today's.

## 14

The next morning at breakfast, the tighter rationing of resources is already evident. I sit with Arluin and our mother trying to stomach the artificial gruel with the limited water we are given. Today there is no hint of natural food, only synthetic substitutes. Hopefully this does not last long.

"You looked in better spirits last night," Arluin says. "What were you up to?"

"Nothing, I was just talking with Hadwin and Sayda. They aren't avoiding me anymore," I answer.

"Abira was looking for you. Did you see her?" my mother asks hopefully. She has been getting more persistent lately.

"No, I didn't, but I'm sure she'll catch up to me later," I say and then finish my breakfast quickly, being anxious to get to the infirmary to see how the night went. When I arrive, Kesia is patiently waiting for me in my exam room.

"Do you ever get used to the decontamination chamber?" she asks. "I felt nauseated just walking past it this morning."

"Not really. I hate that thing too, but it's a necessary evil," I say. "Let's find Rana and see what we missed last night."

We hear Rana and Jace talking about a patient they had seen earlier when we near her exam room. Not wanting to interrupt, we wait quietly at the door for a break in their discussion.

"Don't be afraid to come in," Rana says.

"How was the night?" I ask as we enter the room.

"One more case, the other two are stable," Rana says. "I do expect a busy day today though."

"Yeah, that's what I was thinking. We're going to check with Adara and then get ready. We'll let you know if we need help," I tell her.

Kesia and I leave the appointment area and go in to find Adara. She is busy with the three ill patients in the intensive care unit. The two men from before, Delvin and Grant, look about the same as they did yesterday. This is encouraging since they are not declining as quickly as the others did. The new patient is a woman that is completely unfamiliar to me. I almost feel glad that it is someone I do not know, but the thought immediately causes me to feel guilty. I do not wish this illness on anyone, it is just that the constant connection the other patients had to me was getting disturbing.

"Hi, Adara, any progress in our patients' condition?" I ask, hoping for some good news.

"Unfortunately, not. Delvin is holding steady, but the labs for Grant are concerning, though you couldn't tell by looking at him now. Our new patient, Sonela, is already showing troubling signs that her infection is worsening," she answers.

"Well, just let us know if you need any help. We'll be close by," I tell her as we exit the room.

While preparing for the day, I show Kesia the important equipment and supply checks she will be responsible for while working with me. While we are doing this, I remember something that has been bothering me.

"Kesia, can I ask you a personal question? I wouldn't be offended if you declined," I ask.

"Sure, ask away," she says without hesitation.

"Does your family come from Leadership? I had the feeling when we first met that you did, but you don't have the Leadership marker on your uniform," I ask her.

"Well, yes and no," she answers sheepishly. "I didn't think anyone remembered since it's been so long."

"I don't remember anything. It was just a feeling," I say. "What do you mean by yes and no?"

"We used to be, but long ago, before I can even remember, my father was invited to the Detention Center by Leadership. He never talks to us about what he did or about his time in there. Ever since then, we've been stripped of all the privileges of Leadership. So, yes we were in Leadership, but not really anymore. I guess that's always been one of the things that motivated me. I feel like if I work hard enough, maybe I can restore my family's good name and standing in Leadership." Kesia looks down at her feet and lets out a faint sigh when she finishes explaining.

I feel bad for bringing it up, but there was no way of knowing her circumstances. The reminder of her situation strips the enthusiasm from her. She must have felt obligated to tell me, though I am sure she would rather avoid the subject entirely.

"I understand. I don't like to talk about it either, but my father also spent time in the Detention Center. After that, he was never the same. The stigma and emotional toll it takes on everyone is difficult to bear, but not impossible," I tell her with one hand on her shoulder.

She looks at me with surprise. Most people do not know about my father except those old enough to have first-hand knowledge. With our limited physical space, Securus does not afford a lot of privacy, so most information and rumors are spread quickly. But some subjects, such as the Detention Center, are avoided in conversation. There are certain things that are too taboo for idle gossip.

Before we can say another word, the patient chime goes off twice in succession. The flow of patients is starting. It is not long until the waiting area is full. For the most part, there are waves of frightened people with no significant symptoms, yet are still convinced they have contracted the new disease. The subtle intricacies of the Healers craft is often considered somewhat of an art form, and convincing worried people that they do not have a life threatening disease is definitely one of the more complex aspects of it. It is a hectic day, but it is filled with good lessons for Kesia.

Luckily, the flow of patients begins to slow as we near lunch time. That is another sign that most are not as ill as they fear. I dismiss Kesia and go to check on Adara before heading to lunch, hoping the detour will give me enough time to avoid Kesia following me. It turns out that Adara was right about Grant's condition, as he had passed halfway through the morning. It is becoming increasingly clear that anyone who becomes infected has a grim prognosis. Enough time has passed, so I go through the decontamination process and emerge from the infirmary only to find Kesia waiting for me. Apparently, time alone is not a privilege I will be afforded today.

We arrive at the lunch hall and gather our food. It looks like the same artificial sludge we had for breakfast accompanied by another miniscule portion of water. Hadwin and Sayda are already seated, so we join them.

"Hadwin, Sayda, this is Kesia, my new understudy," I introduce them as we sit.

"What did she do to deserve that kind of punishment?" Hadwin exclaims with an exaggerated empathy for her.

"It's a good thing they assigned two new understudies early because we need the help with everything going on now," I say, ignoring Hadwin's joke.

While we are eating, I notice Jace on the far side of the hall, sitting alone. Rana must have dismissed him early.

"Hey, Kesia, Jace is over there by himself," I say pointing to his table. "Why don't you go join him so he doesn't look so lonely?"

Kesia hesitates, but agrees and goes to accompany him. Finally, I have a moment to check in with Hadwin and Sayda.

"You guys find out anything new?" I ask while continuing to force my food down. Even though we are not in a private area, most people are actively avoiding each other out of fear of contamination. This is probably the most privacy we have ever had at lunch.

"I didn't, but someone else did," Sayda admits while looking at Hadwin. I have noticed that they seem closer lately.

"Well, since I do possess the sharpest mind in Securus, would you expect anything less?" Hadwin asks.

"Yeah, sharp as a well-worn plastic spoon," I counter.

"Okay kids, can we get to the point," Sayda interrupts.

"You can't rush this kind of investigative prowess," Hadwin protests, but Sayda's icy stare stops his joking.

"So, I was thinking about all the electronic pieces we saw. I figured that if they came from my department, there should be some electronic record of them somewhere. People here love their paperwork way too much to not leave some trail.

There are only two distributing managers, and one of them is me. Since I know I didn't authorize the shipments, it had to have been Bara. I *let myself in* to her office and found her logs just waiting for me in a hidden file on her computer. We were both right," he says, the smugness he was displaying has eroded. Now he leans closer to us and lowers his voice. "And it's a lot more pervasive than we thought. It seems the majority of our electronic pieces are not going toward their intended purpose. Or at lease what we expected their intended purpose to be."

I try to process this new development. The news is good for us but disturbing at the same time. If there are stored records, that will make it easier for us to get evidence when needed. But how could the majority of the pieces be siphoned off for an alternate use, and how was this misappropriation never noticed before? What about all the equipment that we need to maintain and upgrade the facility?

"Did it say where the pieces were being diverted to?" I ask.

"Just some vague reference to something called Caelum," he answers.

"We need copies of that file," I say.

Hadwin's self-satisfaction returns. "Already done," he says. "I made a copy. It's hidden for whenever we need it."

I lean back in my chair and feel the gravity of the cover-up increase. There has to be an extensive involvement in Leadership for this to go unnoticed. Though I am still certain that Talia can be trusted, maybe it is good that we did not divulge too much.

"Well, getting you involved wasn't as big of a waste of time as Sayda said it would be," I tell Hadwin. He looks at Sayda to protest before he realizes that she never said anything.

"What about the idea you mentioned, Sayda?" I ask.

"I'm trying to set up a tracking device to put in the outgoing electronics. I got one to work, but it was too bulky. I have to work on making it smaller. It's going to take some time," she says.

"That's a good idea. Let us know when it's ready. I have to get back to the infirmary, it's one of those days," I say. When I get up, my eyes are drawn to a man at the other end of the hall in a Leadership uniform that looks to be watching us. "Hey, do you guys know that guy?"

"I don't know him, but I've seen him before," Hadwin says. "He popped up after I was in Bara's office. He said he was looking for her."

"Did he see you in there?" Sayda asks.

"I don't think so," Hadwin says, sounding unsure.

"Well, keep an eye on him and Sayda, keep Hadwin out of trouble," I say while starting to leave.

The man leaves the hall as I walk in his direction. I feel like I am getting paranoid and try to tell myself that is just a coincidence. On my way out, I collect Kesia and Jace. I feel bad for having to get rid of her all the time, but she will get used to her independence, and as she gains confidence will be less attached to me.

"Rana keeping you busy, Jace?" I ask him as we walk.

"Oh yeah, she's sneaky sometimes. Just when I think she's not paying attention to me or is getting off subject, she makes a point or observation that is surprisingly insightful," he says.

"Yeah, eerie isn't it?" I say.

When we near the infirmary we find a lone figure waiting outside. Normally, I would expect it to be a patient waiting to be seen, but his uniform tells otherwise. He turns as he hears us coming, and my suspicions are confirmed. I find it curious that Aamon waited outside the infirmary this time. I guess that is the one benefit of the new virus, it is keeping him outside.

"Go find Rana. She'll get you started while I have a word with our friend here," I tell Kesia and Jace. Calling Aamon a friend, even if it was sarcastically, makes me feel ill.

"What can I do for you, Aamon?" I ask when the understudies are gone.

"I just came to see how our Healers are dealing with the outbreak," he says causally.

"We're doing everything we can. Let's just hope that the cases don't spread like the flu did before," I answer.

"Are the new understudies performing adequately?" he asks.

"They're doing fine," I say, becoming annoyed that he is not getting to the point.

"You know, I find it interesting that this outbreak started after *you* led us to a new cave system, and the first victim was the man that *you* confronted to help arrange the rescue team," he says. I think I liked it better when he was skirting his intended topic. "Are you sure you didn't have any interaction with the other victims?" he asks looking at me expectantly.

"I'm sure," I answer while forcing myself to unclench my jaw and maintain a calm façade. "I would definitely remember that beard of Delvin's. What about you? As I recall, *you* were there that whole night and *you* spent more time than I did with Leland. Are you sure that *you* haven't been interacting with any of them?" I ask, using the same annoying emphasis on my words that he had.

As I accuse him, the thought causes a chill. Even Aamon is not sadistic enough to unleash something as dangerous as this, but hearing him imply that I had something to do with it is infuriating. Turning the words on him helps keep me from losing my control.

"Oh, I am very sure as well," he says.

There is an uncomfortable silence held between us. I have nothing further to say and simply wait for him to finish. He watches me closely. I think he is trying to unsettle me, but he greatly overestimates his ability to intimidate. Aamon just does not have the presence of someone like Mr. Vaden.

"Oh, by the way," he finally says. "The death detail, excuse me, the *Solar Panel maintenance* detail is fast approaching, and there are some mandatory training sessions before it starts. Since the infirmary is too busy now to have you go during regular hours, special sessions will be set up during your free time. I will have the schedule sent to you later this afternoon."

I had been trying to avoiding the subject of the Solar Panels as much as possible. For me, the best way to handle these types of situations is to try not to worry about things you have no control over. There is always plenty of time for that when the day comes, but it appears now I no longer have a choice. Aamon knows the seventeen percent mortality rate the detail carries and is more than happy to remind me of it.

"Okay, I look forward to fulfilling my duties," I say while walking past him to enter the infirmary. "You coming in, or were you done?" I taunt him.

Aamon leaves, but his words linger with me. He was just trying to throw me off, but it makes me wonder if he knows more than he is letting on. The question of me interacting with the other ill patients was more pointed than simple instigation. *I'm just being paranoid*, I repeat to myself in my mind. If he really knew about my trip to The Caves, he would have just thrown me in the Detention Center instead of toying around like this.

I sneak past Rana's exam room. Inside, she is lecturing

Kesia and Jace, so they should be busy for a while. Back in my exam room, I pull up the records from the last detail. Since it is already on my mind, I may as well search the records for the injuries and deaths that have occurred on past Solar Panel details. There was one death over the week of work and multiple other injuries. Unfortunately, that is the average toll for the detail. The man who had died was a high ranking member in Leadership. I open his record and read the last entry.

*I was called to examine the patient in the decontamination hold. It appears that while working, he sustained a cut in his bio-suit that exposed him to the atmosphere. He displayed all the typical symptoms of an infection consistent with The Agent. He had intense visual hallucinations and began screaming incoherently. His symptoms progressed, and his bodily secretions dried up. In his delirious state, the dryness of his mouth and eyes agitated him to the point that he attempted to rip his own eyes out and then tried to fill his mouth with his own blood. He was placed in a five point restraint harness to prevent further self-mutilation.*

*When his agitation slowed, he began to develop involuntary muscle spasms and twitches that eventually gave way to the flaccid paralysis of all of his musculature. With this, his heart and lungs ceased to function and he passed. As per protocol, the body was returned to the surface for disposal in order to maintain the safety of Securus. The family has been notified.*

The Author of the record was Trent Riley. He has been given special consideration for volunteering to care for those that are ill or injured while on Solar Panel detail. In exchange for the inherently dangerous duty, he is exempted from ever having to serve on the detail himself. I am not sure that I would have taken the same deal, though right about now it is starting to sound a lot better than the alternative.

The new virus we are facing in Securus is nothing compared to The Agent. It was a weapon made to specifically target human physiology and is one-hundred percent lethal once it fully infects someone. The people that originally made the virus had placed a death protocol within it that was supposed to inactivate it after one month. Unfortunately for all of humanity, that never happened. The Agent spread across the entire planet, driving the sole group of survivors into Securus. Now, here I am one-hundred years later, being forced to expose myself to this invisible killer.

Before I have a chance to search the rest of the records from that trip, the sound of footsteps approaching interrupts. I close the files and open my charting that still needs to be completed from the morning rush.

"Hi, was there any important news from that Leadership official?" Kesia asks from the doorway.

"Official? That was just Aamon. He wanted to let me know some details for the upcoming Solar Panel detail," I tell her.

"Is that coming soon?" she asks. "I don't think the infirmary can spare you. Maybe Leadership would grant an exemption if you told them how busy we are," she says.

She is still naïve to many of the workings in Securus. The detail is dangerous but also vital to keeping Securus running. The deep Thermal Vents alone cannot supply our energy needs, so it is imperative that we maintain the Solar Panels. There was no way that Leadership would grant an exception, even if they were not trying to make an example of me. There is nothing I can do but accept it and move forward. So, I turn my attention back to my work, trying to push the account of The Agent's gruesome effects out of my mind.

# 15

The afternoon patient flow was similar to that of the morning. Our time was spent reassuring worried patients as well as caring for some scattered people with the usual maladies. Kesia stayed glued to my side for the rest of the day up until it was time to exit through the decontamination chamber. When I left, she lingered, waiting for something. I assumed she was waiting for Jace. Whatever the reason, I left and now am enjoying the first few moments alone that I have had for a while. It can be easy to forget how useful and recharging time alone can be when the rest of your waking hours are filled with the presence of others.

I walk into the dinner hall with a sense of hope that proves to be foolish. The food is still the same bland sludge as before. Some of the natural food is grown within Securus itself, so why has it completely been cut off? I understand not having the resources of The Caves, but not why the shortage has reached even further than that. My only guess is that Leadership is stockpiling for a prolonged drought of resources. Whatever the reason, there is no point in dwelling on the misfortune. I have too many other things to occupy my mind and this is the least urgent of my problems. The rest of my family is not here yet, so I find an empty table. A few more moments alone would be nice, but my solitude is not long lasting.

"Hello there, Kagen," Abira says cheerfully as she sits next to me. She sets her food tray down and settles in for dinner.

"Hey, Abira, what's up?" I ask. "I heard you were looking for me?" I give her a playful look of concern.

"It was nothing important. How's the infirmary been?" she asks, avoiding my question.

"It has been really busy, but all things considered, it's going as well as can be expected," I say. By the way she is pushing her food around on her plate, it is obvious she has something on her mind. I am not in the mood for prodding, so I pretend not to notice and continue eating.

After a few moments, she looks at me and draws a deep breath, as if she is about to speak, but then stops. Instead, she greets Arluin as he joins us at the table. I had not even seen him coming. Through the rest of dinner, Abira makes small talk with us, but never gets back to what was really on her mind. Whatever it was, it will have to wait. I had received my training schedule from Aamon's messenger during the afternoon and tonight is the first session. I excuse myself to go to the training area. The session is being held in a room near the surface, since that is where the equipment we will be using is stored. I walk up a seemingly endless spiral of stairs and have to pause a few times to prevent my legs from cramping. I have not been up here before, but Securus is well mapped, making it easy to find the way.

Aamon is waiting for me when I arrive, and he is not alone. There is another Leadership member neatly arranging the pieces of a bio-suit on a table at the front of the room. Once inside, I realize that this special training schedule is not just for me. Balum, one of the Leadership boys that Arluin had overhead talking about volunteering, is sitting near the front table. Behind him is a woman that I do not recognize.

"Glad you could make it, Kagen," Aamon says, as if I

had a choice. "Have a seat and we'll get started."

"You going out there with us, Aamon, or are you just here for the show?" I ask trying to irritate him.

"Leadership wants to make sure everything goes smoothly, so I agreed to oversee this detail," he says.

"Kagen, Balum, Nyree, this is Rupert. He will be explaining the bio-suit's features and functions," Aamon says, pointing to the man in the front of the room.

Our attention is drawn to the elderly man in front of us. Based on his appearance, he must be one of the oldest inhabitants of Securus. His thinned hair and furrowed brow, mounted on a tremulous frame, has the look of one that has withstood many long years in this facility.

"I would advise you all to pay close attention, these details will not be repeated, and your lives do depend on them," Rupert says in a strong baritone that clashes with his frail appearance.

"First is getting into the suit, which is a tedious process in itself. Balum, we will demonstrate with you." He waves for him to come up front. Balum strolls at a leisurely pace, eventually winding up next to Rupert. He has a young face and is around the same age as Arluin. Despite his age, he has a muscular build that is almost too big for the bio-suit. He rolls his eyes at Rupert's instructions, exuding arrogance in a manner that reminds me of Aamon.

With Rupert's sluggish help, the process takes double the time that it should have. Surprisingly, Balum maintains some level of patience through it. After the suit is on, they carefully seal the few exposed joints and affix the helmet. Once this is locked in place, Rupert turns on the suit's life support systems. The external system is impressively small and is carried like a backpack. The control panel for the systems sits on the left forearm of the suit. Rupert opens it and shows us how to perform a diagnostic of the various systems. Among these is an air filtration system that is combined with a temperature control and humidifying mechanism, which maintains comfort within the suit for its wearer.

Another system continuously monitors the integrity of the suit and warns immediately of any breech in the seals or the suit's lining. In case of a breach in any of the extremities, Rupert shows us the compartmentalizing safety system that must be manually activated. When activated, it compresses the extremity at the most proximal joint, encasing the rest of the body safely away from the breech. The compression is tight enough that blood flow to the extremity is also limited. This is painful but intentional. If The Agent infects the exposed extremity it cannot make it past this barrier. The infected extremity would still need to be amputated, but losing an extremity is preferable to the alternative. It is an interesting feature, but I do not find it particularly comforting. Like in the case file I read, it cannot help if the operator panics and is unable to activate it.

The next feature Rupert displays looks rather uncomfortable. Once above ground, no one is allowed to return to Securus until the end of the work day. This limits potential exposures to The Agent, but has also made it necessary to have an additional system installed that allows for human waste collection and disposal. I cringe from the instructions Rupert gives us to the systems attachment. I am definitely not looking forward to putting that piece on. On top of the physical discomfort, it will be more than a little weird to have to relieve myself in a suit I have to wear the entire day.

Rupert moves on to the last piece of the suit, the helmet. I look around the room, watching the others as he explains how the dispenser for water, and a semi-liquid nutrient mix, works. Aamon and Balum are nearly asleep, while Nyree keeps shifting back and forth in her chair. I understand her irritation. None of us want to be here, except Balum, for some reason.

By the time we finish going over the controls and accessory functions, it is getting late into the night, so we are all excused. Not wanting to spend any more time here than is required, I exit the room before Aamon wakes up and corrals me into another one of his annoying talks. Nyree jumps up as fast as I do, and we almost collide trying to get out the door. She is a tall woman who stands shoulder to shoulder with me as we walk.

"Sorry about that, I'm just anxious to get out of here," I say, matching her rapid strides. She looks about ten years older than me, but by her fitness you would never be able to tell.

"Tell me about it. Just the thought of going up there makes me nervous," she says. "I don't even like being this close to the surface."

"Yeah, I know what you mean. So, what area are you from?" I ask. Since we are going to be working together above ground, it will be useful to know more about her skill sets.

"The lower levels. Most of my family, myself included, works in the Deep Vents. I do a lot of the general maintenance," she answers. "You don't have to tell me what you do, everyone knows about your recent experience and why you're on this detail."

Straight to the point then, I think I like Nyree. No nonsense or veiled insinuations. "I figured as much. It's hard to avoid the scrutiny of a special announcement in your honor," I say. "If you don't mind answering, what's the general feel about what happened that night and the fallout after?" It is an unexpected chance to see what the perception of me is in a circle outside of my own.

"It's kind of a mix. Some people say it was just a tragic accident that could have happened to anyone. Others think you were being too reckless," she says evenly.

"And what do you think?" I ask, almost afraid of the answer because I get the feeling she is not going to hold her tongue, even if she is of the latter group.

"I think there's more to the story than we're being told. Singling one person out after a tragic event is peculiar. If I know anything about Leadership, it's that there is always a specific purpose to their actions and messages," she says, looking toward me. "Don't worry; I won't bother asking if I'm right because I know you wouldn't say anyway."

The pace of her steps increases, and I almost break out in a trot trying to keep up with her. By the time I find a rhythm to keep up, we reach a divergence in our paths. We go our separate ways, and no departing words are spoken. I make a note to myself that if there is any trouble or problems on the surface, she would be a good person to have nearby.

\*

Back in my quarters, I prepare for bed in the silence of an empty room. The day was so busy that there was no time to rest or even acknowledge the emotional fatigue that has been mounting over the recent days. It hits me now. I want nothing more than to just fall asleep and become lost in my dreams. But even in sleep, there is no respite for me tonight. No dreams come, and I wake every hour only to find that the night has not yet passed. By the time the power is activated, I am frustrated enough with my insomnia that it is a relief the night has ended. I go through my morning routine in a trance, slowly shaking off my fatigue.

Later that morning, just after breakfast, I get Arluin alone. "So, apparently volunteering for the Solar Panel detail was more than just brave words for Balum," I say. "He's on the detail with me. Is there anything you think I should know about him?"

"I don't know him well, but even so, I don't like him at all. He acts like he's above everyone else. I'll keep an eye out and let you know if anything catches my attention," Arluin says. "Is there anything you want to tell me?" he counters.

"You never give up do you?" I say with resignation. "We're getting closer to the truth. As it turns out, going on the Solar Panel detail may actually be a source of useful information. Stay strong, you'll know more than you want to soon enough," I reassure him.

"We? Let me guess, you told Hadwin and Sayda everything," he says, annoyed that others know the very secret that he has been seeking.

"Yes, I did. I needed the help, and they were already involved. Don't worry, your time will come," I say while turning to leave to the infirmary.

*

When I get there, Rana is in the hallway. "Good morning, Rana. Were there any new cases or significant changes for the others?" I ask.

"There was one more case last night," she says. "Sonela's deteriorating rapidly and the new patient isn't far off. So far, only Delvin looks to have any chance to survive this infection."

She leaves it at that, but we both know the news is dire for more than the obvious reason. It means that there are still new cases despite The Caves being closed. So, either the incubation period for the disease to show itself is longer than we thought, or even worse, that the virus is being transmitted within Securus. This makes it less likely that Leadership's aggressive actions have contained the outbreak. Not to mention that the longer it takes to completely contain this disease means even an even longer time until we can access The Caves resources again.

Unfortunately, this is not the only problem on my mind today. Since our understudies are not here yet, I go to my exam room to further look into the medical records from the last Solar Panel detail. The rest of the injuries were more mundane that the first. There was a man with a sprained ankle, another person that had an anxiety attack from the stress of the detail, and a third person whose suit malfunctioned causing her to become dehydrated from the day of work without adequate water. All of them were relatively benign occurrences. I turn off the records interface and rise from my chair. When I turn around, Kesia is watching me from the door.

"Good morning, Kesia. Are you ready for another busy day?" I ask, hoping she did not see what was on my computer screen. Not that it would really matter if she did, but I want to keep some privacy.

"Absolutely," she says while entering the room. "What are you up to so early?"

"I came in early to go over things with Rana and finish some charting from yesterday," I say.

The patient chime sounds, and our day begins. It is much like the morning before, very busy but uneventful. When it is time to go to lunch, I dismiss Kesia, fully expecting her to find me again at the decontamination chamber. After finishing my medical records from the morning rush, I make a delayed exit. To my surprise, Kesia is nowhere to be seen. I guess she is finally giving me a break today.

As usual, I meet Hadwin and Sayda for lunch. There is no new information for any of us to share, and her tracking device is still not ready, so we just have lunch. Today, almost feels like everything was normal. We joke with each other and reminisce of the amusing antics of our past. But this pleasant illusion cannot last long. Lunch is soon, over and I have no choice but to return to the reality of my present situation.

When I reenter the infirmary, an annoying change awaits me. The computer system has gone down. There is a worker in the other room troubleshooting the system. She assures me it is just a temporary problem that will be fixed soon. It is an extra irritation to have to revert to actual paper charting. The others will be upset that we cannot pull up old information on patients, but I am annoyed because it precludes me from continuing my search of the old Solar Panel detail records. Not to mention, it means I actually have to write out everything by hand. Despite having a steady hand for medical procedures, when it comes to writing my coordination fails me. Plus, we have a very limited supply of paper for this, which forces me to write smaller than what is natural to me. The resulting words are harsh and nearly impossible to decipher. That means anyone who ever reviews the chart will always need to come find me to interpret my hieroglyphic entries.

We deal with the inconvenience and work through the rest of the day. There is one more case of the new meningitis, and like the last case, I have no connection to the patient. Kesia is showing improved confidence if not improved skill, and most of the remaining patients are routine. Delvin continues to hold steady, but is still not able to speak. If he would only wake up, we may actual get some clue to how he became infected. My emotions are mixed when I leave the infirmary. The computer system is still down, so I am glad that the day is over, except it means I have to go from one annoyance to another. Tonight, Aamon and Rupert await me for another session.

# 16

That night I return to the upper levels for another training session. Aamon and Rupert are already inside, organizing a spread of tools on the tables up front. When he notices my arrival, Aamon slithers over to me with a confident smile.

"Kagen, I trust all is well," he says.

"Get to the point, Aamon," I say, tired of his meandering conversations.

"It seems the stress of your upcoming privilege is affecting your manners," he says dismissively.

I do not reply. Instead I lean back in my chair and place my feet on the table in front of me. My shoes are nearly poking him in his midsection. I look him directly in the eye and lazily place my hands behind my head in a relaxed position. Though he tries to hide it, the slight flush in his cheeks and bulging veins in his neck make it clear that my disrespectful behavior is frustrating him. *Good, he's taking the bait*, I think to myself. I did not intend it, but a satisfied sneer completes my relaxed posture. I wait until he is just about to speak and then interrupt him.

"Actually, I'm just a little tired," I say with a yawn. "Meeting with you is not the most stimulating experience."

"You must be tired from a long day. Having some computer problems in the infirmary?" he asks.

*Interesting*, I think to myself while raising an eyebrow at the comment. That is such a trivial thing for him to bring up. I was hoping for him to say something more revealing in his anger, but this is intriguing. If he is bringing it up, he must have had something to do with it and wants me to know it. I must have been getting close to finding something he does not want me to see. On the other hand, that also means he is watching me closer than I realized. Either way, I know more now than before. More importantly, it also shows me that though he may do well with the politics in Leadership, he can still be provoked to lose his composure.

"No big deal, it'll be back up in no time," I say. My lack of concern angers him even more, to the point where he is getting a slight twitch in his eye.

"Well, you may be too busy to enjoy it when it's fixed. I'm considering pulling you from the infirmary so you may better prepare for the detail," he says, leaning forward to assume a position looking down at me.

He probably thinks his posture is intimidating, but I find it a little awkward on him and more entertaining than anything else. His words, on the other hand, are not entertaining at all. It is not my welfare that I am concerned with, rather my worry is what could happen in my absence in the infirmary. There is only so much time that the others can cover for me before fatigue sets in, and we are going to be pushing it with my absence for the Solar Panel detail in itself. I did not intend to provoke him this far, but maybe I can use this as well.

"If you do that, you better hope the outbreak doesn't spread. Otherwise, your decision will be questioned thoroughly by all levels of Leadership. It would be a shame for you to look bad so soon after your promotion," I say.

Now he is backed into a corner. Either he follows through with his threat and risks looking bad to

Leadership, or he backs down from it and looks foolish for even mentioning it. I can see him playing those scenarios in his mind, looking for another way out.

"It is not my standing you should be concerned with. After all, I will be sitting in here quite safe while you are out on the death detail. You should be concentrating on trying to make sure you aren't the one in six who doesn't make it back," he says, referring to the average death rate for the detail. "I will inform you of any changes in your schedule as it suits me," he finishes before returning to the front table with Rupert.

Nyree arrives and takes a chair without acknowledging anyone. Soon after, Balum joins the group, and we begin. Rupert shows one tool after another, discussing their function and how to use them properly. Throughout the lecture Aamon continues to watch me closely, while impatiently tapping his fingers against his desk. I ignore him and focus on Rupert's words, though his methodic explanation of the equipment nearly puts me to sleep.

The only thing that saves me from giving in to the urge to close my eyes is the entertainment I get from watching the blatantly obvious irritation that Nyree shows every time Balum asks a question. The content of the lecture is simple, and I suspect it is even more so for someone as technically inclined as Nyree. Despite the simplicity, Balum struggles to grasp the concepts, and the time it takes Rupert to repeat the explanations for him infuriates her. At the end of the lecture she nearly sprints out of the room. I rush to catch her in the hall, still intent on trying to gain her favor.

"Balum isn't the brightest one, is he?" I say as we speed walk.

"I have no idea why they're letting him on the detail. His incompetence could be dangerous," she says.

"Yeah, tell me about it…" I start to say before my words trail off, seeing a man heading toward us. We both instinctively stop and move to the side so he may pass. I am hoping he will keep walking past us, though there is no chance of that happening.

"Kagen, is the lecture over already?" Mr. Vaden asks as he stops in front of me.

"Yes, Rupert went over everything twice," I say.

"You must be Nyree," he says, shifting his attention. "I thank you for your service in this imperative task."

She remains silent and nods respectfully. Mr. Vaden turns back to me but continues to speak to Nyree. "If you would be so kind as to excuse us, I was hoping to have a word with Kagen here," he says.

Nyree starts to leave, but does so slowly. I am not sure if she is curious to hear our conversation or just stunned by Mr. Vaden himself, but there is an awkward silence until she is gone.

"What can I do for you, Mr. Vaden?" I ask.

"Walk with me, Kagen. There is something I want you to see," he replies.

We go back down the hallway and continue through a secure doorway. After entering in his security code we emerge into another hallway. The structure of this area is the same as the rest of Securus, but the decoration of it is an abrupt contrast. The cold, bland walls have been painted with warm, colorful tones and there are scattered pieces of artwork lining the path. Even the floors have been covered with a soft, cushioned surface that subdues the force of our steps. I have never felt anything like it. This must be Mr. Vaden's private offices and quarters. He notices my curiosity as I absorb the new surroundings and waits for me to return my focus before he starts to speak.

"I trust things are going smoothly in the infirmary. How are the new understudies performing?" he asks as we continue down the hall.

"As well as can be expected, considering how inexperienced they are and the extra pressure with the new outbreak," I say.

He leads me into a side room. This one is full of viewing screens and other audiovisual equipment. I recognize the area behind the desk on the right as the one we see during our announcements. There is a large Leadership insignia embroidered on a light silver base, draped on the wall behind him. He sits behind the desk and assumes the same authoritative posture I have seen countless times.

With the push of a button, he activates a control panel and all of the screens turn on. On them I can see various halls and other important locations with a few scattered people still lingering on the free time. I also see The Caves and there are, what looks to be, research workers scurrying about throughout the initial cavern. From this chair, all he has to do is flip a switch and he can see most of Securus. When my eyes make it down to the last two screens in the bottom corner of the display, if feels as if I were punched in the stomach. One shows the entrance to The Caves, and the other shows my work station in the infirmary. If Mr. Vaden was watching, he knows that I am up to something.

"I wanted to bring you here to remind you of something. Take a good look at the screens," he says gesturing toward them. "So many people struggling to endure and all of them have a valuable role in each other's survival. Securus is a powerful testament to that survival but despite the strength that has built it, just like life itself, it can be quite frail.

"All it takes is a few pieces of this intricate puzzle to become lost and the entire foundation crumbles beneath us. Even a single person selfishly pursuing his own agenda could lead enough people astray to start a chain reaction that could compromise our very existence. We desperately need to reopen The Caves and regain the use of its resources, but it is a difficult task when reckless behavior leads to the exposure of dangerous pathogens.

"The delicate balance is being shifted dangerously close to the edge. In times like these, we must all ask ourselves what we can do to better serve the colony, preserve our way of life, and to protect the lives of all the people you see on these screens. It is a hard decision to make for some, and even more so when there are extenuating circumstances or strong emotions that cloud one's ability to think rationally. When these things happen, there comes a point when I must do whatever is necessary to ensure the security of our people," Mr. Vaden says, finishing his speech and watching for my response.

What could he possibly expect me to say? He is obviously referring to me in his speech, and I find it meaningful that he would ascribe such power to my actions. He wants me to know he is watching everything on these monitors and he wants me to abandon my search. I do not believe that finding the truth would lead to the destruction of Securus, as he is insinuating. Hiding the truth is the real danger. You cannot conceal something important from people and expect them not to search for the answer. Perhaps that is the real purpose of his message. He knows that if I bring to light whatever he is trying to shield in the darkness of The Caves, the people will not be able to forget or ignore it. What he is doing, I do not know, and to some level I do not care. I just need to know what it is, and so does everyone else. The one thing that is confusing me is his mention of the outbreak. He has to know it has nothing to do with me.

"What does the new outbreak have to do with this?" I ask.

"Do you really think it is a mere coincidence?" he asks. "You find this new chamber, and as soon as you return, people fall ill. The only ones infected are those with direct contact with you, or one of the others that has already been infected. "

The blood drains from my head and I feel faint for a moment. He could be right. If I did bring this virus back, the newer patients could have been exposed second hand from the original patients. After all, they did work in the same area. On the other hand, if that were the case, then why has no one from my group of friends shown any symptoms? They would have had the most exposure, and all are symptom free. I think he is just trying to use this to gain my cooperation.

"I understand," I say, hoping he will believe that he has convinced me.

"Good. I would hate to have to revisit the subject as I have always found the confines of the Detention Center rather distasteful," he says, causing a chill to run through me.

The gentle demeanor he has had through his speech is gone and now there is only malice in his eyes. The coldness of his gaze makes me question my resolve. I am shocked by the power of a single look.

"You may leave now. I trust you remember the way," he says.

Just like that, I am dismissed. He does not even bother walking me out. There is no point, he can see me every step of the way on his monitors. I am being watched, and it is clear that it is my life that is delicately on the verge of being extinguished. There is a difficult decision for me to make, either I continue my search and risk my very existence, or leave it alone and live on in shame for having abandoned my convictions. It was a lot easier to stay focused when all I had to deal with was the clumsy threats from Aamon. The danger then felt more like an idle threat. Now, the peril feels overwhelmingly real.

Alone, I slowly walk back to my quarters. The chill of Mr. Vaden's stare evaporates as I realize something that had not occurred to me before. There is something holding him back. He could have easily discarded me in the very beginning if he thought I was so dangerous, but he did not. He knows I am up to something, and yet, he has not thrown me in the Detention Center. Maybe Talia has somehow convinced him that I am not a threat or at least persuaded him to be lenient. Maybe there is something deeper involved that I have yet to discover. Whatever it is, I have some small advantage that is allowing me to continue. I am not powerless against him, and if I find something of substance my power will only grow. By the time I reach my quarters, my resolve has returned as strong as ever.

*

The next few days feel like a blur. Aamon made good on his promise to pull me from the infirmary, but only for the afternoon half of my days. I am kept constantly busy and away from my friends and family except when it is time for sleep. Even then, I am so exhausted that I cannot manage many words to them before lying down for the night. The only positive is that so far, no more cases of meningitis have been brought to the infirmary. The outbreak has been successfully contained and casualties were very low for such a potentially disastrous pathogen. But even so, all those infected have succumbed to the disease except for Delvin, who remains in the intensive care unit. The work in the infirmary is easily manageable with the extra help of the understudies, even with my partial absence.

The Caves remain closed, and our resources are running dangerously low. When I do walk through the halls of Securus, it is easy to see the change this has affected. There is far less enthusiasm and energy in the inhabitants of Securus. Part of that is from the psychological factors associated with the fears of the outbreak, despite its reprieve, combined with the increasing restrictions Leadership has placed on our free time. But the more significant factor is the physical hardship of the rationing of our resources. We are simply not getting enough food to keep our energy and spirits up.

My schedule eases when there are only two days left before the beginning of the detail. I have completed all of the required training and am returned to my normal work. There is something comforting in a familiar routine. When I arrive to the infirmary, Kesia is already waiting for me outside, as she has taken to doing over the last few days.

"Good morning, Kagen. I've already restocked our exam room and checked with Trent before he left. There are still no new cases, and, Delvin is talking today," she says cheerfully.

"Excellent," I respond. "I don't have any extra lectures today, so I'll be in the infirmary all day. You'll stay with me this afternoon."

In my absence, Kesia had been splitting her afternoons working with Rana and Adara. Judging by her wide, crooked smile, I think the change pleases her. I am excited to see what Delvin can remember. Being the sole survivor of the disease, his input may be of particular help. Especially since the research team has made no progress with finding a better way to fight this disease or in discovering its true origins.

"We have some free time until we get a patient. You can use the internet interface if you like. There's a lot of good information in there. You just have to figure out what's legitimate and what isn't. I have some links set up to the more reliable sources," I say.

"Okay, what're you gonna do? In case I need you," she asks.

"I want to go and talk with Delvin. That is unless Rana already beat me to him," I say, knowing she probably has.

Once inside the intensive care unit, my suspicion proves correct. Rana is seated next to him already engaged in a conversation. Without privacy, I cannot ask all the questions that are on my mind, but at least I can say hello.

"Look at this guy!" I say to Rana while reaching out to shake Delvin's hand. "Hi, I'm Kagen, another one of the Healers," I tell him. We have never actually met before, at least not while he was cognizant of his surroundings. Despite this, his eyes narrow slightly when he sees me, as if he recognizes me. He does not give away his thoughts though, and simply shakes my hand while flashing a brief smile through his thick beard.

"What did I miss?" I ask Rana.

"Unfortunately, Delvin's memory is still very hazy. He cannot recall anything out of the ordinary that led to his exposure," she says. Delvin grumbles as she reminds him of his difficulty. He wants to help but cannot. I know that feeling all too well.

"But at least he's doing well," she says, looking at him.

"That's what matters most," I add, trying to reassure him.

I leave them to finish talking. I can come back another time and try to jog his memory with some of the details from my forbidden excursion.

The rest of my work day felt amazingly normal. There were very few patients, so I lectured Kesia on various diseases. I was unable to distract her long enough for any privacy throughout the day, including during lunch. Hadwin and Sayda have become used to her presence and took it in stride. That evening, my spirits are high enough that I do not even mind the persistence of the same bland food, if it can even be called that. Even my nagging rib injury is starting to feel a lot better. When I get to bed, I fall asleep instantly. Might as well enjoy it, with the detail so close, I will not be sleeping so lightly soon enough.

## 17

It is the day before my Solar Panel detail begins, and as our tradition dictates, my entire day has been designated as free time. Despite this, I still wake up to the sound of the morning alert. The persistence of that revolting device never relents. I get dressed as usual and slowly make my way to breakfast with my mother and Arluin. We all pretend that it is just another day, but the growing tension is obvious with the terse conversations we force. During breakfast, Arluin waits until he has a chance to pull me aside and speak alone.

"Kagen, I've been watching Balum, and I'm completely confused by his behavior," he whispers.

*This is interesting,* I think to myself. Arluin usually has such a good feel for people. Balum must be acting really odd to throw him off.

"What's he doing that has you so confused?" I ask.

"Well, Balum is being... nice," he says. "He's never like that. And it's not just to his friends; he's being nice to everyone."

"Sometimes when we're forced to consider our own mortality, we reevaluate how we treat others. Maybe this experience is helping him to mature," I suggest, though as the words come out, they do not feel right. "But, I doubt that's what you're thinking."

"You're right. I don't think that's it. I would've bought that if he didn't seem so genuinely happy. It's like he can't wait to start the Solar Panel detail. I would understand trying to have a pleasant goodbye if he actually seemed worried about the possibility of dying, but that's just it, he doesn't," Arluin says.

"I don't know what that means either. I do know he isn't as much of a sophisticated thinker as you are, so his psychological defense mechanisms may seem foreign to you. But, whatever's going on, I'll keep a close eye on him while we're up there," I say.

After breakfast has finished, I find myself in a disturbingly unfamiliar position. There is nothing to do and nowhere that I am supposed to be. I could return to my quarters, but sitting in there alone for the entire day would bore me to the verge of insanity. Instead, I decide to go to the infirmary despite not being scheduled to work.

I leisurely stroll through the endless halls of Securus. There is no point in hurrying through these barren paths when there is no schedule for me to keep. Taking a long route to get to my destination, I watch the different people scurry about performing their daily duties. One thing strikes me as I really look at those around me for the first time in a while. They all look weary. It is not the fog of the early morning but rather the fatigue that is setting in from the continued lack of adequate nutrition. It is overtly clear that unless something changes very soon, we will slowly atrophy into oblivion. We really need to find some way to safely reopen The Caves.

I am able to make it into the infirmary unnoticed by anyone. Back to the intensive care unit, Adara is sitting at her small desk, completing what looks to be patient charts. I look through the room, and begin to fear that it is too late. I came to find Delvin, but he is not in here. Did his condition really spiral down that quickly? He looked so good yesterday.

"What happened to Delvin?" I ask Adara.

"He was transferred back to his own quarters," she says happily. "He needs more recovery time, but all our testing shows that his immune system has cleared all remnants of the virus. So, it was deemed safe to allow him to leave the infirmary."

"That's great news," I say. Not only is he making strides toward his recovery, but now I can speak with him in private. "Where are his quarters located? I wanted to talk with him a bit."

"Level 18, hallway 12, number 8," she says. "And, Kagen, good luck tomorrow. Hurry up and get back in here, we need you," she says optimistically.

"Thanks, Adara," I say while turning to leave.

Walking down the hall, I hear Rana speaking with a patient in my exam room. Not wanting to interrupt, I continue out of the infirmary and head toward Delvin's quarters. There will be more than enough time to see her later today. The halls are devoid of life on my way down. I walk through multiple identical hallways, all with the same bare steel walls. The only way to differentiate them is by looking for the identifying number system painted in plain white symbols near each formal entrance. Now standing outside his door, it is eerily quiet. I knock and call his name.

"Come in, it's open," he yells back.

I enter his quarters and greet him, "Hi Delvin, it's me, Kagen, from the infirmary. I just wanted to come by to talk a bit and see how you're doing."

"I was hoping you would," he says, appearing genuine. "Adara filled me in on everything that's been going on since I've been in there."

"What made you want to speak with me about it?" I ask suspiciously.

"I didn't tell them the entire truth. I've been starting to remember some things, but it wasn't until after they told me about you and your punishment that it triggered my memory. You were the one in the lounge that day at lunch. I didn't think anything of it at the time, and I wasn't even sure it was you until you came to the ICU yesterday. You were there when you weren't supposed to be, why?" he asks gruffly.

So, he was paying more attention than I had thought and for some reason he has kept this information to himself. There is no good explanation for my presence in that lounge, and I do not have time to come up with a reasonable excuse.

"There were things I needed answers for and those answers could only be found in The Caves," I answer honestly since it would not make a difference to conceal the truth now. If Delvin decided to tell Leadership, and Mr. Vaden found out someone else in the colony knew of my trip, whatever is holding him back would not be enough to save me.

"Even when Leadership expressly forbade you. Interesting," he says, pensively scratching his thick beard. He sounds as if he is thinking out loud rather than making a statement to me.

"There are some things that are more important than the whims of Leadership," I say brashly, and immediately regret saying it aloud.

He looks at me quizzically for a moment and then shows a knowing smile. "That's exactly what I was hoping to hear," he says.

"Why is that?" I ask, baffled by his response.

"Because I may know where the virus came from, and I can't tell just anybody. Not if I want to stay alive, at least," he says. "I suspected there was more to the story when I heard about your punishment, and even more so when I realized you were disobeying Leaderships orders. Whatever is going on, it has you at odds with Leadership, and that makes you my ally."

"You're not saying what I think you are, are you?" I ask, afraid of the answer. That cannot be it. He has to be delirious from his infection still. Even if the virus is gone, he could still have some residual inflammation and edema around his brain, causing him to become intermittently confused. Only, he is not confused. He looks to be in complete control of his faculties.

"I don't know for sure; it's only a suspicion. I thought it odd at the time when Trent came down to administer updated vaccinations instead of just setting up the usual appointment for us to come to the infirmary," he says. "That was the only abnormal exposure I can recall prior to becoming ill. Though, for the life of me I cannot think of any reason why Leadership would want to introduce a virus like this into Securus."

"I can," I say and stop then myself, before revealing too much.

Trent, I should have known. First, he covered up for Leadership in The Caves and now this. I always knew he was more than a little insensitive, but this is just outright heartless. Now that I think about it, while the act itself is atrocious, releasing this virus was also a deceptively clever action by Leadership. What better way to close off access to The Caves without being questioned so they are free to hide all traces of whatever it is they are doing out there? It makes sense, but I do not want to believe it. How could anyone be so callous as to inflict this kind of suffering not only on those infected, but also on those forced to cope with the withdrawal of the resources from The Caves? The more frightening question is, what could be so significant that they would go to these lengths to hide it? Delvin has been watching me progress through a mixture of emotions and waits for me to regain focus before speaking again.

"I know how you feel because I didn't want to believe it either. I was hoping it was just my imagination, but seeing your reaction tells me otherwise," he says. "Can you share with me what you think is going on?"

"I'm sorry, but I can't," I say. "When the time is right, everyone will know the truth. That's all I can offer you for now." I cannot risk telling him because there is no way of telling if this is a ruse to get me to reveal what I know, though that is unlikely.

We spend some more time talking in general and going over the specific details of his vaccination by Trent. Both Delvin and his partner, Gareth, were injected not long before the symptoms started. He clearly remembers what happened before the vaccination, but afterward it all became a nightmarish haze. Trent had used a standard vaccination injector that he carried in a sophisticated, metallic case. It was internally cooled and used a key code for access. If nothing else, I now know what to look for. A case like that is not a common item, even in the Research Department.

When we are done, I return to my quarters to rest until the standard lunch time. While walking, the walls around me feel like they are moving. With everything that is happening, it is as if the entire world is disintegrating around me. Not only that, but it is not even certain that I will be around to see this through. What if I do not make it through the Solar Panel detail alive? I lie on my bunk and force a slow deep breath.

"I will be okay and with the help of my friends, we will find the truth," I tell myself out loud. I repeat this enough times in my head that it almost starts to feel true. I again remind myself that there is nothing that can be done about the past, and there is still a chance for me to set things right. It is already noon, so I walk up to my normal lunch hall to find Hadwin and Sayda. They need to know what Delvin told me.

There is a noticeable change in the lunch hall as I enter it. The loud conversations cease, and the collective gaze of the hall focuses on me. I can feel the morbid curiosity of the others watching the man who may soon die. I continue to walk and try to fight the sensation of being a condemned man trudging toward the gallows in the stories of humanities distant past. Luckily, their attention does not last long, and as I am gathering my food the volume of conversation returns to normal. Hadwin and Sayda are just reaching a table on the side of the hall, so I move quickly to join them.

"Hey guys, I feel like a dead man walking in here," I tell them.

"Don't pay attention, it's just human nature to be curious," Hadwin says. "Besides, we have something to get your mind off that."

"We? I don't recall you spending all those hours working on the design or meticulous fabrication," Sayda says, teasing Hadwin.

"The design and fabrication of what?" I ask.

"It's ready," Sayda says, obviously pleased with her achievement. "My tracker is functional. I made two of them, just in case. I already gave the first one to Haddie this morning so he could put it in the next outgoing electronics shipment."

"It's about time," I say in an exasperated groan, trying to suppress my smile. "I almost thought we were going to have to have Hadwin take that task over."

"Hey, I can't do everything for you guys," Hadwin protests.

"I should probably take the other tracker with me tomorrow, just in case I notice anything suspicious. It could come in handy," I tell Sayda.

"Okay, I'll get it for you later," she offers.

"Sounds good. I also have something important to share, when we have a moment," I say in a serious tone to let them know the urgency of my message. They both understand the insinuation. After we all finish our lunch, we head back to Sayda's quarters to talk, hidden from the ears of curious onlookers.

"Well, what is it?" Sayda asks immediately as the door closes. She never did have much patience.

"Delvin started talking again yesterday. At first, he said he didn't remember much about what happened. But when I visited him in his quarters this morning, his story was very different," I tell them.

Sayda sits down to stop herself from pacing, and braces for bad news. Hadwin stands with his arms crossed, waiting for me to continue.

"I was hoping he would be able to shed some light on where he may have contracted the disease, and I think he has. That morning just before he became ill, Trent came down to give him and Gareth a vaccination. The problem is he never does that. If we need to update someone, we either schedule them an appointment or have the rounding Healer take care of it. Trent is far too lazy to take over someone else's duties for no reason." I finish and wait for them to absorb the implications.

Hadwin looks as though he may become ill and sits down on the bunk while taking in a deep breath. Sayda is turning red and looks like she may become more lethal than the virus itself. I understand their reactions because I felt a little of both when Delvin told me this as well.

"I can't vouch for Delvin or the authenticity of what he told me, but I thought the both of you should know," I say.

"Leadership using The Caves as their own little playground is one thing, but this goes far beyond that. If this is true, we need to do something now!" Sayda fumes.

"I can't believe that anyone could do something like that. What is there to gain from it?" Hadwin asks, trying to make sense of it.

"I don't know," I admit. "But we're going to find out. I'll see what I can do to find the vaccination guns Trent used. If we can get that, combined with the evidence from the equipment siphoning and the storage room in The Caves, we'll have everything we need to make something happen. If this is all true, we're gonna need Talia more than we thought."

"If this is all true, we may need more than just her help. If Leadership already went to these depths to hide the truth, I don't want to know what else they would do to keep it secret," Hadwin warns.

Their time for lunch is running out, and they have to return to work. I, on the other hand, have nothing to do except fixate on the new revelation. Instead of returning to the solitude of my quarters, I decide to head back to the infirmary. There is someone else there that may be of help. While walking up the stairs, I am intercepted by a familiar face.

"Hi, Kagen," Abira says. The lack of enthusiasm in her voice makes it clear she is not in nearly as good of a mood as normal. I am sure she is just worried about my upcoming detail.

"Hi, Abira. Don't look so down, everything will be fine," I reassure her.

"Kagen, can we talk for a minute?" she asks and looks away, as though she immediately regrets speaking.

"I have nothing but time today, but don't you have to get back to your classroom?" I ask, offering her a way out.

"I do, but this is important," she says, gaining conviction.

I follow her out of the stairs and around the hallway, toward the main Learning Center. When we enter the area, the change in decoration is obvious. Instead of bare steel walls, they are lined with images of our history. There is a schematic of the original structure of Securus, images of the founding members of Leadership, and a magnified model of The Agent itself. Just looking at the actual physical structure of The Agent, with its numerous sharp tentacles flanked by a diffuse matrix of hooks used to entrap its prey, unnerves me.

Abira leads me to a small supply room and looks around to make sure we are not noticed by anyone. She keeps nervously tugging at a lock of hair, and her anxiety is making me uneasy. We move past the various supplies used in the classes, as well as the mix of other cleaning supplies, and maintenance equipment. She turns and faces me in the dim light, but the look on her face tells me this is not the type of conversation I thought it was going to be. My day is about to get even more interesting.

## 18

What I see while looking into Abira's eyes in the pale light is completely unexpected. She is nearly in tears. I hesitate to even ask what has led her to feel like this, but it is why she brought me here.

"Abira, what's wrong?" I ask, placing a comforting hand on her shoulder.

"I'm so sorry, Kagen," she says with a slight quiver in her voice.

I wait for her to continue, but she just looks at me in silence. "Sorry for what? What's going on?" I ask, urging her to continue.

"Aamon came to me the day after Merrick died," she starts.

With the mention of his name, I removed my hand from her shoulder. What has Aamon done now, and why is Abira the one that is sorry?

"He said that you were being elusive with Leadership and may be dangerous to Securus. I didn't believe him for a second and that's why I agreed to help, because I knew you would never do anything to endanger us. I wanted to prove your innocence," she says, grabbing both my arms and pleading for forgiveness with her eyes.

"Help him do what, Abira?" I ask, trying to suppress my rising anger.

"At first it was just supposed to be one conversation. I was to ask you about Merrick and record your response for him. So, I did. And I was right, you didn't do anything wrong. I thought it would be over after that, but he wouldn't let it go," Abira says, no longer able to look me in the eye.

I remember that day. She looked hesitant to ask about it. I thought it was because of concern for my emotions, but apparently there was more to it than that.

"Then he wanted me to keep an eye on you and report back to him. I tried to say no, but he threatened my little sister. I figured there wouldn't be anything to tell him, so I went along with it," she says.

"If you've been spying on me for Aamon, tell me why I should believe anything you say now?" I ask coldly.

"Kagen, I never thought it would hurt you. I would never do anything to hurt you," Abira says through her sobs. She looks up through tear-soaked eyes and again reaches for me. "After the first day, I didn't tell him anything. I just let him think I was doing what he asked."

"So what did you tell him the first day?" I ask with my anger already fading, knowing she is sincere and is truly remorseful. She just did not know the magnitude of that night, and how could she? No one could.

"I just gave him the recording and told him about your temporary uniform," she says and manages a slight grin at the memory. "There's one other thing," she continues with her fleeting smile already gone. "I got the feeling I wasn't the only one he had watching you."

So that is how he knew about my clothing change that day. The information she could have given Aamon is inconsequential, but I think she was meant to serve more of a purpose by just keeping tabs on my general habits. Aamon has been even more thorough than I thought, having multiple people watching me. Even if Abira does not know who the other spy is, I have a strong suspicion of who it could be.

"Okay, Abira, I understand why you did it, but why are you telling me this now?" I ask, confused by her timing.

"Because of something else he said," she says in a barely audible whimper. "I told him I didn't want to do this anymore, and he said not to worry because it won't be an issue for much longer. Oh, Kagen, I'm so sorry."

She reaches out and clings to me, burying her tears in my arms. We both know the significance of Aamon's words. It is not a coincidence that he would say such a thing right before I am scheduled to start the Solar Panel detail that he is overseeing.

"It's not your fault, Abira," I tell her firmly. "If it wasn't you, he would have found another way. At least I know he's planning something, and can look out for it. That's a lot better than being ignorant of his plotting. If nothing else, you've given me a fighting chance."

It is a few minutes more before her tears relent. My outward strength is somewhat fabricated as this news has shaken me deeply. But, the more I tell myself that I must be strong for her and everyone else, the more real it feels. As I accept the reality of my situation, it almost starts to feel easier. No matter what I do, it cannot make things worse. Either it helps or the outcome remains the same inevitable conclusion. More importantly, it does not change what must be done.

"I have to go, Abira," I say gently, breaking the silence. "Thank you for telling me the truth. I may need your help before all of this is over. Can I count on you if the time comes?"

"Anything, all you have to do is ask," she says sincerely. She looks up and softly kisses me on my cheek. "You take care of yourself, Kagen."

I compose myself and leave the Learning Center. It is

hard to blame Abira for what she did, but even so, it will be difficult to ever fully trust her again. It is surprising how calm I feel walking back to the infirmary, particularly given the events of this day. Determined to continue with my ultimate goal, I go to find Rana. She does not need to know everything that is going on, but if she found out later that I withheld what Trent did, she would never forgive me.

On my way, I walk alone through the empty halls and staircases. Despite this, it feels like someone is watching me. I look around for any of the scattered security cameras, and find one at the end of the hall, pointed directly at me. Even if Mr. Vaden knows where I am, there is no way that he knows what I am up to.

When I reenter the infirmary, once again, all of the infection control warnings have been deactivated. That will make it easier for me to go in and out as needed today. I already know from the schedule that Rana is working in my exam room, and since the intensive care unit is finally empty, Adara is filling in for the appointments. I activate the patient arrival chime to summon Rana. When she and Jace come to meet me, a smile crosses her face. Nice to see I can still surprise her sometimes.

"This one looks really bad, don't you think, Rana?" Jace jokes.

"I agree, terminal case of smugness," Rana plays along. "We probably should just euthanize him now and rid ourselves of the hassle."

"Thanks, I feel so much better knowing I'll be treated so well," I say, forcing a smile and trying to stop myself from cringing. It is clear they are not really in a playful mood and are just trying to keep my spirits up, but the joke hits too close to reality for me. Euthanizing me is exactly what Aamon would prefer. "I really do have an issue though, but it's kind of sensitive," I say, glancing toward Jace.

He gets the message and excuses himself while I follow Rana back to my exam room. It feels weird being on the opposite end of this encounter, even if it is a charade to speak with Rana in privacy. Even when we are alone, it is still not safe to speak freely since I know Mr. Vaden has a camera hidden in here. I need a way to avoid it and any other spying devices.

"What can we do for you today?" Rana asks expectantly.

"I think I need an X-ray, I tripped and really hurt my upper arm," I say despite obviously not being injured. She understands what I am trying to do and plays along.

"Well, let's take a look first," she says. "Hmmm, probably not broken, but there's only one way to find out for sure."

She is doing better than I expected with this. Crafty Rana, she is always full of surprises. I get positioned into the X-ray machine. Nestled in the chair, I motion for her to come in closer. She activates one half of the automated barrier that is meant to keep radiation in. We pull the other end as far closed as we can without decapitating Rana, who has her head inside the machine with me. The slightly open end is facing a wall, so in a whisper, we should be free to talk.

"What's going on, Kagen?" she asks.

"I went to talk with Delvin this morning, and he remembers more than he was admitting earlier," I say.

"Why would he lie about that?" she asks.

"He was protecting himself. He needed to know that he could trust me before he could say anything. I can't vouch for what he said, but if it's true, things are a lot worse than I feared," I say. Rana does not interrupt, but she does look around the room again to make sure we are still alone.

"Trent went down to his research lab and gave him and Gareth some kind of vaccination. He told them it was just a regular update. Shortly afterward is when he started to feel sick," I tell Rana while watching her response to the news.

"I know there weren't any scheduled updates, and even so, Trent wouldn't have been the one doing them," she says, putting the pieces together. The anger in her eyes startles me. I have never seen that look from Rana before. I can see her thoughts continue to race, searching in vain for another explanation of why Trent would have been there giving shots to the men.

"We need to confront him. This is too sinister to let it go unpunished," Rana says.

"No, you have to keep this between us for now, Rana," I plead. "I know Leadership has some role in this, and we need to know the full extent of it before we do anything. I need you to trust me. This is not the only revelation I've had to deal with lately. It's part of a larger conspiracy, and I need to put it all together. Otherwise, we may end up doing nothing but condemning ourselves by acting too soon. Then what good would we be able to do for the rest of Securus?"

She takes a breath, as if she was about to start a rebuttal, but stops before it comes out. She knows I would not have come to this decision lightly, and reluctantly agrees to the plan. "Then why are you telling me this now?" she demands.

"Because you would kill me if I didn't. Plus, even though I promised not to involve you, I need your help," I say. The other reason is too difficult for me to say aloud. Someone needs to know this, in case I do not live past the next few days.

"Just tell me what you have in mind," she says eagerly.

"We need to find the case and vaccination guns that Trent used. That way we will know for sure that Delvin is telling the truth, and we'll have hard evidence to back it up. Delvin told me exactly what it looked like so we know what to look for. For my plan to work, we need to get Talia to help us, but she'll need to be convinced. I think giving her the case to test for the virus will be all the evidence she needs," I say, not even realizing that was my plan until the words came out.

I give Rana all of the details that Delvin had told me about the case. I leave out most of the other occurrences because she is already worried enough. She does not need the added shock of knowing what awaits me on the death detail.

"And, Rana, don't trust anyone. I think we're being watched," I warn her.

We finish my X-ray and luckily, my arm was not broken after all. Soon after we finished, Jace and Kesia come to the exam room to see if I am alright. I assure them it was nothing to worry about and get up to leave.

"Well, I should let you all get back to work. You are coming to my dinner tonight, aren't you?" I ask Rana. Part of the tradition of being selected for the Solar Panel detail is that a dinner is held in your honor the night before it starts. It serves as a chance to say goodbye to friends and family in case you do not make it back. Leadership treats this as a special night since it only happens once a year, unless an emergency forces an additional detail. So for this night only, people are allowed to move their dinner designation to other halls in order to be with the ones they care for.

"I wouldn't miss it," she assures me.

"We'll be there, too," Kesia cheerfully offers.

"Okay, I'll see you all then," I say while turning to leave.

There is still a lot of time left in the afternoon work session, so I need to find a way to occupy myself until Hadwin and Sayda are finished for the day. After everything that has happened today, I cannot sit alone in my room with nothing but my thoughts. That would be like torture, so I just keep walking. My legs carry me down through an endless maze of identical hallways and numerous flights of stairs.

I find myself walking into a familiar space that is nearly identical to my dinner hall. There is the same arrangement of tables, a food distribution area, and high vacant walls. As I look around, there is a subtle difference. On the back wall there are images of some of the Deep Vent's machinery and a list of names. I recognize the memorial and realize where I am. The list is a tribute to those who have lost their lives working in the depths of Securus. I have been here once before and had not returned until now. My father's name is on that list.

"I didn't expect to have company so soon," a voice calls out, startling me from my thoughts.

Nyree is off to my right, sitting alone at one of the tables. I was so preoccupied by the memorial that I did not notice her until now. She looks different than before. The tension and annoyance that were always present during our required training courses has been replaced with a calm acceptance. It is the first time I have seen her relaxed. I walk over to sit with her.

"Me neither," I respond. "I didn't see you over there."

"Yeah, I noticed that," she laughs. "What brings you down here?"

"Honestly, nothing. I was just wandering around, killing time," I say.

"Weird, isn't it? I always complain that we don't have enough time to ourselves with our hectic schedules, and now that I do, I'm bored out of my mind. I guess we get so used to our routine we don't know what to do without it," she says.

As we talk about nothing, I notice something had not been obvious before. Despite her brutally honest affect, there is kindness beneath her hardened exterior. It just took a more comfortable environment for her to let her guard down.

"Okay, I have to ask, what was that about with Mr. Vaden the other night?" Nyree asks and intently awaits my response.

"Let's just say I'm not on Mr. Vaden's list of favorite people," I say with a wry smile. "Especially since his daughter was with me the night of the incident in The Caves."

She raises her brows with hearing that. "Funny, he didn't mention that Talia was in The Caves during the announcement. How convenient for her," she says sarcastically.

"It's not Talia's fault. She actually tried to take the blame for me, but Mr. Vaden didn't like me endangering or distracting his daughter," I explain. There is a camera in the corner of the ceiling, fixated on us as we speak, so I leave my story at that.

"Ah, I get it now," she says with a beaming smile.

"No, it's not what you think," I say, guessing what is behind her smile.

"Sure, keep telling yourself that, but you can't hide from the truth. I can see it in your eyes and your red cheeks," she says with her smile getting even bigger.

"Anyway," I say, trying to change the subject. "Do you know Kesia Pack? I think her family is from this area."

"Yeah, I've seen them around, but I've never spoken with any of them. I tend to avoid Leadership members. Why do you ask?" she answers.

"Kesia was recently assigned as my understudy, so I was just curious," I say. "Do you know where her father works? It would be interesting to meet him."

"Good luck with that. It's not easy to get a meeting with such a high ranking Leadership official. Then again, you've had private meetings with the Vaden's, so it shouldn't be a problem for you," she jokes.

"Thanks," I say. "I think I'm going to walk around for a bit, you wanna come," I offer, hoping she does not accept.

"No thanks, I just want to sit here and relax for a little while," she says. "I'll see you bright and early tomorrow."

I exit the hall and again am alone with my thoughts. Will this day and its constant revelations never end? So, Kesia's dad is a high ranking member of Leadership. That is not quite in line with her sob story of trying to restore her family's standing and them being stripped of all Leadership privileges. It was a clever ploy, most people would not ask much about her father since the story she told me involved the Detention Center. I would have never questioned it myself if it were not for Abira's admission and warning. Now, I know who is watching me. The only question for me is do I confront her or use this knowledge to my advantage? I can already feed Aamon false information through Abira if need be, so I must evaluate what further use Kesia could be.

It is hard for me to get past the anger I feel from her deceit. Especially with the fabricated story that was obviously meant to generate sympathy from me. Even worse, it had worked. I really did feel for her and her family's situation. Now, the truth has revealed her as a fraud. The more of the truth I discover, the less I like it. But that is exactly why I must continue. I no longer have the time or luxury of worrying about how these things affect me.

## 19

I want to find Hadwin and Sayda, but right now they will be busy at work. With nowhere else to go, I head to the dinner hall early. The room is empty except for the few workers that are preparing the food. Though tonight's dinner is meant to be a celebration, no decorations are hung on the lifeless walls. I prefer it this way because celebrating the likelihood of my impending death is not something that interests me. The large, plain, steel box room seems an appropriate place for what could be my last evening. Anything I do could be the last time I ever do it. That thought is depressing. I need a distraction.

Arluin and my mother are the first to arrive. Both of them try to keep a strong front, and they both fail. We exchange hallow reassurances that everything will turn out okay. Oddly, it feels like it is more for their sake than mine.

"I'm sure you'll be fine. After all, even when you injure yourself, you always seem to be able to avoid anything major," Arluin offers.

"Thanks, I think," I say, giving Arluin an awkward stare. "More than anything, I just want to try and have a semi-normal dinner tonight. I don't want to worry about tomorrow until I have to, okay?"

"Of course, plus we don't have anything to worry about. Arluin is right," my mother says, getting in one last comment before granting my request.

Soon, the table is full with my family and friends. There is my mother, Arluin, Sayda, Hadwin, Abira, Rana, and Kesia. Of course I did not want to invite Kesia, but there was no inconspicuous way to keep her from coming. I decide to not say anything about her father for now. That can wait. Besides, what good would it do unless I make it through the detail alive?

Our food is served to us for this night. It feels weird to have others do for me what I am more than capable of doing myself. I do not fight it though, since it is tradition. Being the honoree for the night I am allowed a double ration of food. Normally that would be a treat but with the gruel we are forced to endure now, it almost feels like an added punishment. I have to repeatedly remind myself that it is much better than having no food at all. Unlike the food, the extra water is something I eagerly enjoy. The constant mild dehydration is draining on my body and emotions.

Despite having such a large group, my table is relatively quiet. Even Hadwin is not his usual boisterous self. It is hard to be cheerful in times like these. At the end of the meal, I reluctantly prepare for my next task, the goodbyes. Even though the average is one death per detail, making it five times more likely you will return than not, the goodbyes are treated as our last. I am set up with a private table in the corner of the hall, and those who wish to speak with me come one at a time. Since they will see me in our quarters tonight, my mother and Arluin do not get in line. Rana is the first to come to speak with me and as she does, the hall turns silent. Everyone holds their conversations out of respect for ours.

"Rough day, huh?" she says.

"Even more than you know," I respond.

"Just remember to always keep your calm and focus. You'll need them for whatever challenges you may face. I'll be anxiously waiting for your return. You can't leave me with them alone," she says, motioning to Jace and Kesia.

I smile and thank her for her words. Then look for the next person in line. Somehow Abira has managed to get in front of Hadwin and Sayda. As Rana gets up, Abira starts walking toward my table but before she can make it, a late arrival cuts her off.

"You are going to have to wait a couple more minutes," Talia tells her sharply, before turning to me and sitting at my table. Surprised by Talia's arrival, Abira reluctantly returns to her place in line. I had hoped Talia would be able to come but had already given up hope since it was getting so late.

"I didn't think you were gonna be able to make it tonight," I say, my smile too large to hide. The timing of her appearance seemed deliberate, especially with her words being so harsh to Abira.

"I wouldn't have missed it," she says. "I'm going to try and get in the Control Room as much as possible during the detail, just in case you need me."

"Thanks, that actually does make me feel a little bit better," I say, knowing it will be harder for Aamon to conspire if he is being watched.

"You were right about that guy you mentioned, I've been watching and he's definitely up to something. He hasn't given his secret away yet, but I'll figure it out. I know you wanted it kept quiet, but my father needed to know. Don't worry, your name was left out of it," she says.

"You were always so stubborn," I say, already forgiving her for telling Mr. Vaden. She had no way of knowing what is really going on, especially since I have been keeping her in the dark. Talia is just doing what she thinks is right to help. "If things work out, I may soon have everything you need delivered to you. Just keep an open mind," I tell her.

She scoots closer to me and lowers her voice so that no one else can hear. "Be careful, Kagen. I need you to come back," she pleads.

"You can't get rid of me so easily," I reassure her.

Sitting here, looking into her angelic almond eyes, I become lost in them. Without thought or reason, I reach out for her. Before realizing what is happening, I pull her closer to me. I feel the delicate silkiness of her lips against mine while stealing a kiss. When the reality of my action confronts me, it is already too late to stop. To my surprise, Talia does not resist. *If am going to die, I might as well do this just once*, I think to myself. It is not as if I can upset Mr. Vaden and Aamon any more than I already have. Even if I do, any punishment they could administer would be worth it.

I lean back and see the surprise on her face, but that is nothing compared to the shock of those who were watching nearby. Rana is the only one who does not look surprised at all. The room was quiet before, but now there is a deafening silence. I had not only stolen a kiss from one of the highest ranking and most important women in Securus, but also broke a deeply imbedded taboo in doing so. It took the harsh reality of facing my death to give me the courage to acknowledge my true feelings for Talia, and now everyone knows. I wonder if Mr. Vaden is sitting in his office watching the whole thing on one of his many monitors. If he is, I bet he fell out of his chair when it happened. I lean back and again look her in her eyes.

"I'm sorry. I didn't plan to do that. I, I just…" my words trail off. The kiss has left me slightly lightheaded from the swirling emotions, and unable to compose a rational though. Talia waits for me to continue. "I just can't lie to myself about my feelings for you anymore," I finally get out. "Even though I tried to fight it, you have always been the one in my heart."

Talia looks at me with a stoic expression. I cannot tell if she is angry, happy, or anywhere in between. She was always hard to read and right now she is impossible. I brace myself for whatever is in store for me. Then, without a word she reaches back for me and pulls me in for another kiss. This time I think I am as surprised as everyone else. For a second, all of my worries dissipate. Nothing matters except the warmth of her embrace. When she lets go, she finally breaks her silence.

"I think we're both in trouble now," she says with a mischievous smile. "You just make sure to take care of yourself and come back to me so we can figure this out together."

Talia rises from our table and walks away. No one moves or speaks until she has left the hall. When she is gone, Hadwin is the first one to break the silence.

"High five!" he yells out to me with his hand raised above his head. Sayda stands next to him, shaking her head at his joke.

After this, the rest of my visitors are less eventful. Abira and the others come and give tearful wishes for my safe return. By the time it is over, I am exhausted from the flood of emotional conversations, and there is still more to come. I still need to tell Hadwin and Sayda about the day's events. It is more private now that the majority of the crowd of people has dispersed. We excuse ourselves and head to Hadwin's quarters.

\*

"I know you wanted to get Talia to help us, but I didn't think that was how you planned to do it," Hadwin laughs.

"If you didn't have enough attention from Leadership before, I'm sure you fixed that now," Sayda scolds me, being less amused than Hadwin. Her words are not out of anger. Knowing her for as long as I have, it only shows her protective worry.

"I didn't plan that, it just kind of happened," I explain. "Not that I regret it, especially after the day I had."

"Yeah, I've been thinking about you going up there all day too," Hadwin says, pointing upward and with his expression becoming serious. Sayda does not say it, but the pained look on her face tells me she is has been thinking about it as well.

"Unfortunately, that's not the worst part of the day," I say.

"What happened?" Sayda asks, nervously shifting her position.

"It started with the news about Trent. Rana is looking for the only possible link we have to prove it, but that isn't the only thing I discovered today," I say.

"What else could there be?" Hadwin asks.

"Sayda, promise you will listen to my whole explanation before you do anything?" I ask before continuing, anticipating her reaction.

"Just spit it out, Kagen," she snaps.

"Aamon has two spies keeping tabs on me. I only found out because one of them was coerced into it and couldn't take the deception anymore. She didn't reveal anything of importance to him, and now we can use her to our advantage by feeding Aamon false information if we need to," I say.

"Who is it," Sayda demands as she begins to tremble from her spiking anger.

"She also warned me that Aamon may be planning something for me real soon. Most likely when I'm on the Solar Panel detail," I continue.

"Who is it, Kagen?" she repeats.

There is no way she will ever relent, I have to tell her. "Abira," I finally say.

Hadwin nearly has to tackle Sayda to prevent her from sprinting out of the room to find Abira. We cannot have Sayda pummeling Abira because then Aamon will know for sure that we are on to him. I think Hadwin knows the advantage of keeping Abira on our side. Sayda will too, as soon as she calms down.

"I have an idea of who the other spy is, but haven't had a chance to confirm it yet. Since I know you won't let it go, Sayda, I think it's Kesia," I finish.

"That is one messed up day," Hadwin says. "No wonder you lost your mind." He slumps against the wall, as if it was the only thing keeping him standing.

"How about the tracker you made for the equipment?" I ask Sayda, hoping the change of subject will calm her.

"It's in place," she says looking at Hadwin. "But the pickup isn't scheduled until tomorrow."

"If I don't make it, I need you guys to tell Arluin everything. He'll drive himself crazy if he doesn't know," I say.

"Don't talk like that," Sayda says, interrupting me. "You have to make it back."

"We're gonna finish this together," Hadwin adds, struggling to sound confident, though he fails miserably.

With nothing left to say, they both hug me tightly. We all fight back tears, knowing this could be the last time we ever see each other. Before I go, they both remind me to be careful, and give me tips they gathered from survivors of prior details that they had sought out.

The walk back to my quarters seems like a never ending trek. When I do arrive, Arluin and my mother are patiently waiting for me. There have been so many tearful goodbyes already that I cannot take another. Thankfully they know me well enough to see this, and like when Merrick died, we embrace silently.

\*

The night passes rapidly in my sleep. A special alert disturbs my rest before the others are scheduled to rise. It is surprising that I slept so well considering what this day has in store for me. I dress as quietly as possible, trying not to disturb my mother and Arluin from their sleep, but am not successful. They both wake up in time to see me off. To my surprise, when leaving my quarters, I do not feel sad or frightened. Inside me is a sense of determination. I am not helpless and have the ability to control my fate, but only if I remain focused. In a weird way I feel truly free for the first time in my life. I am no longer bound to the regimented life of Securus or the will of Leadership.

My orders are to report to the same room that we had our training sessions in. From there, we will get further instructions. I climb the stairs at a slow and steady pace, trying to preserve my energy for whatever surprises the day will hold. Still, it does not take long to reach the upper levels. Passing through the hallway, my speed increases when I realize how close Mr. Vaden's quarters are. I hope to be able to avoid another encounter with him, especially after what happened last night. There is no way he does not know about the kiss by now.

When I approach my destination, there are already

multiple voices coming from inside. The typical detail is made up of six individuals as well as a host of support personnel. I have already met two of my teammates but have not received any information on the other three. Remembering Abira's warning, I enter the room cautiously. It is doubtful Aamon would try something so soon, but it is prudent to keep my guard up. Rupert is the first person I see, standing in front of the others. Today, his involuntary tremor is so pronounced that I worry he might lose balance and fall. As usual, his true strength is only revealed by his voice.

"Kagen, welcome to the first day of the detail," he says.

The others look back at me as I come to join them. Balum is already here and appears anxious to get the day started. Next to him is another light-haired woman bearing the insignia of Leadership. She looks to be slightly older than I, but the dullness in her eyes makes me think she is about as bright as Balum. There is another familiar looking man standing next to them. He is not from Leadership, so I already want to like him. He has much darker skin than the others and also lacks their simple minded stare. I am sure that we have met before, but am unable to place him.

"Kagen, this is Eldin and Jadyn. You already know Balum," Rupert says introducing me to the others.

Soon after I arrive, Nyree comes in and also meets the rest of the group. We both sit away from the others as we wait for the final member of our detail.

"You ready?" I ask her.

"As ready as I ever will be, at least," she says

"It looks like we have our work cut out for us. I get the feeling Jadyn's going to make Balum look like a genius," I say.

Nyree laughs, as she was apparently thinking the same thing. Finally, the last man on our team slowly walks into the room. Though he is a young man in his early twenties, he is built nearly as frail as Rupert, and his overt fear is making him tremble almost as much. His pale skin contrasts against his dark hair and eyes to amplify his trepidation.

"This is a sad looking team," Nyree whispers as the newcomer reaches the front group.

"Everyone, this is Ardal. He is an electronics expert and will be taking care of the more technical issues we need to fix," Rupert announces.

I examine the group and try to figure out if any of them could be a threat. I already trust Nyree, so she is off the list. Ardal is only a threat to soil himself, so he is out. Jadyn does not seem clever enough to be involved with any covert plans. That only leaves Balum and Eldin. I really need to remember why Eldin looks so familiar. That would make it easier to figure out how closely he needs to be watched. From what I know of Balum, he is definitely one that would collude with Aamon. So for now he is my top priority to monitor.

Sitting here waiting for Aamon is making me anxious, I would much rather just get started. Eventually, I hear his voice in the hall as he approaches. A tremor runs through my spine when seeing that he is not alone. This is exactly what I hoped to avoid.

# 20

Mr. Vaden walks into the room with Aamon attentively following behind him. His eyes scan the area before locking onto their intended target. I look down, trying to avoid his piercing stare. This time, Nyree does not hesitate to briskly walk away as he comes toward us.

"Kagen, when this detail is over we need to have a discussion. It seems I was not clear with my instructions regarding my daughter. I will not make that mistake again," he says. The calmness in his voice masks his true emotions from those in the room who could hear his words. But from my vantage point, there is no mistaking the fury in his eyes.

"Of course, Mr. Vaden, although I expect Talia will want to be present for that conversation," I say, emboldened by the fact that I may not even be alive when this detail is done. For the first time, Mr. Vaden does not have the words to respond. Or maybe he knows he cannot say what he wants to in front of the others. He takes a moment before continuing.

"I'll worry about my daughter, you have other things you should be concerned with," he says, before turning to leave the room.

Any other time his words would have stricken me with fear, but now they are robbed of their power. *You can only kill me once, but if I am successful you will be the one who has other things to be concerned with,* I think to myself.

"Kagen, come and join us," Rupert calls out. All of the

others have already gathered around him and Aamon. It is about time we got started. As soon as I am with the group, Aamon begins giving our instruction.

"We're going to have different assignments for each day of the detail. Today we're going to focus on clearing the fields of plant overgrowth. We cannot have an obstruction in our paths or allow the forming roots to compromise the equipment. Take the stairs one flight up and they'll lead you to the exit chamber. In there you'll find your bio-suits. I'll be waiting in the substation. Once you're ready, I'll split you into teams and give you your specific objectives for the day. Now go," Aamon commands.

The substation occupies a large part of the upper level. Most of us have never been to that level because it houses most of the technology used to convert and store the power that is generated by the Solar Panels. Only the people directly maintaining the equipment and those that work in the adjacent operational center, called the Control Room, are allowed up there.

We ascend the stairs to the upper level. In the hallway just outside the staircase, we find a sign labeling the room in front of us, *Exit Chamber*. We open the door and find the room set up in two distinct areas. The initial half is a changing area for us to get into our bio-suits. On the other side of the room is a large open area that is separated from this half by a familiar nuisance, a decontamination chamber. It makes sense that we would have to return through the chamber each day to protect Securus.

I turn my attention to the changing stall in front of me. There is a bio-suit with my name on a label placed above it. The changing stalls have short walls made just long enough to afford privacy when the outer curtain is closed. The wall in front of me is lined with seven identical stalls, with the one to my right being empty. I glance at the stall next to me and see Balum's name on a label identical to mine.

When the others are enclosed in their individual stalls, I reach for the extra bio-suit in the empty stall. It is reserved for use as a backup in case anyone else needs to go to the surface while we are out on the detail. I decide to switch it with mine just in case Aamon has tampered with it in any way. Meticulously, I go through the process of securing my bio-suit, making sure any accident will not be my fault. There is no room for careless mistakes now. To my surprise, when I emerge from my stall, nearly half of the others are still not ready. They are being every bit as careful as I.

When we are all dressed, Aamon joins us in our changing room. He intentionally avoids direct contact with me and addresses the group as a whole. It must be harder for him to look me in the eye knowing he has something planned.

"Okay, time to split up into teams. Balum and Jadyn, you'll work on clearing the central field. Ardal and Eldin will clear the north field. Kagen and Nyree, you're responsible for the south end. All the equipment needed will be in the storage bunker located just outside the exit. You all have been given the code to get in. Any questions?" Aamon asks.

No one speaks. The only sound comes from the incessant nervous shuffling of Ardal.

"Okay, be safe and productive," Aamon says as he dismisses us.

I almost laugh when hearing him steal Mr. Vaden's closing line from the announcements. He is trying hard to appear important, and I suppose his way of doing that is by emulating the most powerful man in Securus. He sees my amusement as he looks at me in the eye for the first time today. Only this time he does not look upset by my reaction, and that concerns me. I decide against another confrontation and instead turn my attention to Nyree.

"No point in procrastinating; let's get this over with," I tell her.

She nods in agreement, and we both walk through the inactivated decontamination chamber, toward the ladder that leads out to the surface. While the chamber is not currently set for decontamination, it still has a pressurized system that prevents airflow from passing into the changing area of the room. This prevents The Agent from entering the main room when the outer hatch is opened. The others follow our lead and form a line behind us.

My legs feel heavier and heavier as I climb the ladder. I am both nervous and excited at the same time. Now that the time is here, there is no avoiding the painfully real threat that awaits me on the surface, but that is not the only thing that is driving my emotions. I have always dreamed of being free to explore the surface of this beautiful planet. The scenery from past images on my computer has always visited me in my fantasies and now, I finally have a chance to see some of it with my own eyes.

The first thing that strikes me when I emerge from the tunneled exit is the intensity of the Sun's light. Though we have many levels of artificial light, with some of them modified to mimic some of the Sun's properties, I had never known how different the real thing would be. The blinding warmth holds me in a trance, so much so that my movements halt and I am inadvertently blocking Nyree from finishing her ascent. Her not so gentle push returns my focus, and I move to the side to allow her and the others to join me on the surface. The light strains my eyes, so I activate the tinting function of my visor to limit the glare.

Now that the Sun no longer holds my attention, I look to the sky. The immensity of it is overwhelming. I have never been in any place that did not have a ceiling of some kind. Even in the largest chambers in the depths of The Caves, there is always a stone covering above. Now, there is nothing but openness. Nyree is much less impressed by the beauty and vastness of our surroundings.

"Hey, Kagen, if you're done absently drooling at the sky, maybe we can get our work done. I don't want to spend any more time up here than we have to. I swear I can already feel The Agent trying to pry its way into my suit," she says.

"Sorry, but you have to admit, this place is amazing," I respond while turning toward the supply bunker.

"I hear that sometimes the most beautiful things can be the most dangerous," Nyree mutters as she follows me.

The storage bunker is much larger than I could have imagined. There is a massive steel double door entrance that protrudes from a hill covered with soil and wild grass. Even from here, the raised biohazard symbols on each of the steel doors are clearly visible. The entrance is large enough to obscure our view of the entire Solar Panel field. I remember being told early in school that this was the original entrance to Securus and after the facility was filled to capacity, the stairway was sealed off to add a double layer of protection.

Standing here makes me think of the horror that faced the desperate hoards of people trying to escape The

Agent. Their only hope for salvation was denied by these immense doors and the solid steel floor inside. A barrier so efficient we left it in place and created another exit when it was safe. The ghostly remains of the countless people stuck outside were removed years ago. Now, the only reminder of their futile attempts to find a way inside Securus is the numerous dents and gouges in the steel barrier. It is a depressing thought, and it makes me glad I was not the one who had to make that decision.

Nyree enters the security code into the keypad on the side of the entrance, and the doors shriek as the automated system pulls them open. Before going inside, I turn around and look out from the entrance, surveying the rest of the area. The view is limited but stunning none the less. There is a high metal chain fence that encloses us from the magnificent forest beyond. The fence is emitting a gentle hum that I can only assume means it is electrified to keep the animals out. There is a rapid transition from our relatively barren land within the fence to the thick cluster of thriving life just beyond it. *Nature is doing quite well without us*, I think to myself.

To avoid irritating Nyree any further, I return to the task at hand. Inside the storage bunker are numerous piles of different equipment, tools, and supplies. Seeing the amount of equipment in here makes me glad we do not have to haul it up from Securus and sterilize it every day. That would probably double the time needed to complete the detail. Close to the entrance are the machines we need for today's work. We each have a motorized vehicle assigned to us, a Land Clearer, as Leadership calls them. They are big enough for two passengers though we each will operate our own.

I walk to my Land Clearer and see why the workers have nicknamed this fierce piece of machinery, The

Grinder. Attached to the front of it sits intimidating, hardened claws that rotate to clear the unwanted plant life that encroaches on the Solar Panel fields. Behind the claws is an encapsulated compartment for the operator, perched atop spiked wheels that can maintain grip on any terrain. I disconnect the battery charger and get inside. Before getting started, the system diagnostics need to be checked. The batteries are fully charged and the attached Solar Panels are functional. I am ready to go. Sitting in this machine makes me feel safe, but unfortunately, I cannot stay in it for the entire detail.

With my progress initially slowed by my awe of nature's surroundings, the others have passed me and are already clumsily maneuvering their Grinder's out of the bunker. Nyree and I follow. Despite the relatively simple controls it takes a lot of effort to get a feel for the movement of the machine. We did not have enough room for a full demonstration inside Securus, so this is the first time any of us have actually operated these machines. My Grinder lurches around the side of the bunker as the Solar Panel field fills my view. The panels are so large that they obscure the forest behind them. The field is an impressive maze of endless machinery that forms its own metallic forest, constantly rotating on their bases to efficiently absorb precious energy from the moving sun.

As I continue toward our designated area, the true size of the monstrous panels becomes apparent. They are mounted on a base as large as the tree trunks that dwarf me in my small Grinder. Driving through the field in the shade of these mechanical trees feels unnatural. With the light being mostly blocked by the panels, the plant life below is significantly stunted. Still, the fields are vast and will take most of the day to clear, especially with our uncoordinated operation of the Grinders.

*

Our helmets are equipped with communicators and there are multiple frequencies so each team can communicate with each other without annoying the entire group unless they need to. Even with this function, Nyree has been quiet for a while. She must be used to working in silence, but I am not.

"So, Nyree, are you getting the hang of your Grinder yet?" I ask trying to break the monotony of the work.

"Actually, I was thinking that they should get one of the electronics people to make these things remote controlled. Seems like they could cut back on some of the detail's work and lower our risk that way," she says.

"That would be nice. These things are tricky to operate, just imagine what Ardal looks like driving his," I say, laughing at the thought.

Nyree laughs with me before her thoughts are interrupted. "We have a problem, Kagen," she says.

"What is it?" I ask, already fearing the worst.

"The fence over here has a big hole in it. It's ripped open so wide I can almost drive through it," she answers.

"What could've done that?" I ask knowing she is just as puzzled as I am.

"I don't want to find out, but we're gonna need to fix that soon," she says.

I drive over to where she is working and see the gaping defect. She was not exaggerating and it does not look like something that would happen from simple aging of the fence. We need to let the Controllers in the substation know so they can advise us what steps to take. I change the communication channel to the main frequency.

"Substation, this is Kagen, we have an issue with the

fence," I say through my communicator. "There is a very large defect in it, I don't have any idea how it happened."

"Don't concern yourself with that for now. You'll have a chance to fix it tomorrow," Aamon answers.

"Do you know how it happened?" I ask, starting to become suspicious.

"Your orders are to continue clearing the field. When you need further information I will let you know," Aamon replies sharply.

There is no point in trying to argue now, so I return to my work. We both focus on clearing the area by the fence so we can move away from it as soon as possible. Neither of us wants to find out what it was that is capable of creating that damage.

It is more comfortable in the bio-suit than I had anticipated, that is, once you adjust to the discomfort of the waste collectors. The temperature control system shields us from the heat of the Sun as well as the heat generated by our own bodies. I am trying to keep my guard up, but it is easy to relax while feeling secure with the added protection of my Grinder. It is also hard not to be distracted by the wonders of nature that beckon just beyond the fences. While we are working, my eyes are constantly drawn out to the towering trees as I yearn to be able to walk amongst them. I am so close, but it may as well be just another image on my computer screen. It is far too dangerous to wander out into the wild forest with The Agent lurking about, waiting for its chance to infect me.

The morning passes quickly with my Grinder doing most of the work. When lunch comes, we return to the bunker for a break. Nyree and I are the first to arrive. We arrange some of the loose equipment to form makeshift chairs. Sitting down, I activate the nutrition supplier in my bio-suit. It is a thin tube normally hidden within the helmet that delivers a slow steady stream of semi-liquid nutrient slurry that is similar to what we have been getting in Securus lately. Only now it feels as if it is being forced into me by the unrelenting flow. I could turn it off, but I need the energy and prefer to get it over with. The water attachment is much more pleasant. It functions more like a straw and allows me to sip the water at my own pace. While resting, we turn off our electronic communicators since we are close enough to hear each other without it and more importantly, because I do not like the Controllers in the substation being able to listen to our every word.

"Well, I hope the rest of the detail goes this smooth," Nyree says while sipping some water.

"I wouldn't count on it," I reply. I had been internally debating how much to share with her since we are working so closely today and likely for the rest of the detail. I do not want her to needlessly expose herself to any potential danger that is intended for me. "Nyree, there's something you should know," I say, motioning her to come closer so no one can overhear us.

"What is it?" she asks tentatively.

"There's a strong possibility that Aamon may be planning an accident for me," I answer as truthfully as safely possible. "I can't tell you what or why, I just wanted you to know so you don't get mixed up in it."

"You have to tell me more than that. Why can't you just go over his head in Leadership?" she asks.

"It's complicated, but he's not the only one in Leadership that's involved," I say.

"It has to do with that night in The Caves, doesn't it?" she asks.

"Yes, but the less you know the better. Plausible

deniability will save your life if it comes down to it," I warn.

"Okay, I understand. I don't like it, but I understand. Thanks for the heads up," she says. That was much easier than convincing Arluin. I suppose it is because she understands the workings of Securus more than most people. There is no more time to talk anyway because the others are starting to arrive.

## 21

There is a noticeable difference in the degree of mastery of the Grinder's controls between the different operators. Ardal is surprisingly efficient while Eldin is struggling significantly. His Grinder stutters as he awkwardly guides it into the bunker. I take another sip of water and check my control panel to see how much is left to ration through the afternoon.

Suddenly, a high pitched whine draws my attention back to bunker's entrance. Eldin's Grinder is accelerating rapidly in my direction with its churning metal talons reach out for me. I pounce to my feet and try to dive to the side to avoid the grips of the ravenous machine. As I do, my foot sinks into a crack in my makeshift chair, collapsing me onto the floor. I yank my foot loose and now, lying face down on the floor, hear the Grinder rapidly converging on me. My arms reach out to pull me away from danger, but my hands only slide across the loose soil covering the steel floor below. *This is it, my life is about to end here*, I think to myself. I never imagined it would happen like this.

Just when my fate seems inevitable, a pair of strong hands locks onto mine. I instinctively pull on them as they in turn pull me away from the runaway machine. Still, it is not enough to escape it completely. My leg is twisted as the talons lock onto it. Nyree pulls harder, freeing me from the machine and pulling me out of the way of the oncoming wheels. The Grinder finally comes to a stop on top of the equipment we were just resting on.

I look down at my leg and see the sole of my shoe has been clipped by the destructive teeth of the Grinder, twisting my ankle and ripping a piece of the bottom lining off. Ignoring the pain in my ankle, I frantically grab my foot to search for a penetrating defect in my suit. If the suit is compromised, I need to activate the compartmentalizing function before The Agent gets too far in. The piece that was ripped from my shoe was just a cushioning pad and luckily, my suit remains intact. In my rush to examine the damage I had not realized that my system controls have remained silent, indicating the suit had not been compromised. I take a deep breath and calm my racing thoughts, knowing I need to stay focused. *I'm okay*, I reassure myself. Eldin climbs out of his Grinder and rushes over to me.

"Are you okay, Kagen?" he shouts. "I don't know what happened. It was like the Grinder just took off on its own. The throttle and steering locked up on me."

"I'm okay, thanks to Nyree," I say giving her a grateful look. "Just a trim of my shoes and a sprained ankle, nothing permanent."

I try to remain stoic, though the throbbing in my ankle is increasing as the adrenaline begins to wear off. I do not want to show any vulnerability in front of my assailant. After pressing on the bones of my ankle to check for pain and stability, I get up to further test it. Despite the pain, it feels sturdy enough to walk on. Satisfied that it is not broken, I sit back down to recover. Balum and Jadyn are just arriving and come over to see what happened. Eldin tells them how the Grinder ended up in its current position.

I was more concerned with Balum than Eldin, but

with what just happened that needs to be reconsidered. It could easily have been an accident, especially given his lack of skill with the Grinder's controls. Then again, it seems all too convenient to be a simple coincidence or mechanical failure. He had to have done it intentionally. Either that or Aamon has found a way to remotely operate the Grinder from the Control Room, but that seems too blatant even for him. Balum notifies the Controllers of the incident and soon after a voice calls me on my communicator.

"Kagen, are you injured?" Aamon asks, sounding more hopeful than concerned.

"I'm fine," I respond.

"Do you need Trent to take a look at you?" he asks.

That is the last thing I need. There is no way I would trust him to evaluate me in these circumstances, especially given his involvement with the outbreak. Even if it was Rana doing the exam, I would still refuse because my injury is minor.

"No, I can continue working," I answer. "Hey, has Talia arrived yet?" I ask, remembering that she was going to try and get in the Control Room.

"There are more pressing issues that require your attention than the whereabouts of my daughter," Mr. Vaden snaps through the communicator.

I had not known that he was watching the detail personally. There is no way Talia will be able to get into the substation with her father around. Undoubtedly, that was his intention. Now that I think about it, he has been trying to keep us from each other for longer than we ever realized. I do not think the timing of her switch to Leadership training was a coincidence all those years ago.

Without Talia in the Control Room there will be no one to interfere with Aamon's plans, except Nyree, I thankfully remember. I was right about her. Here we are on the first day of the detail, and she has already saved my life.

"You need a little more practice on that thing, Eldin," I say while limping back to my own Grinder. I feel safer in there right now with my sore ankle than being out in the open next to Eldin and Balum.

Nyree follows my lead and we both drive out of the bunker, toward our assigned section of the Solar Panel fields. I find a spot nestled at the base of one of the Solar Panels that is out of view of the scattered surveillance cameras. There are many blind spots from the cameras because their focus is toward the outer fences. I exit my Grinder and motion for Nyree to join me.

"Thank you, Nyree," I tell her while gingerly moving toward the Solar Panel base. The support of the pole takes the weight off of my throbbing ankle.

"It's no big deal," she says, trying to downplay her actions. "I was hoping you were just being paranoid, but apparently not."

"Yeah, so was I," I say with a nervous laugh. "Maybe that really was just an accident, but I can't afford to believe that right now."

"It's time you tell me exactly what's going on. I was willing to let it go before, but we're way past that now," she demands.

"I wish I knew," I say honestly.

I struggle with whether to tell her everything or not. She did save my life and also gave me valuable information about Kesia, but what if she is another one of Aamon's spies? It could be a ploy to gain my trust and find out what I really know. Then again, what would be the point of that now? I think Aamon already has a plan for me no matter what. Nyree is watching me while I internally debate how much to reveal and expectantly waiting for me to continue.

"I'm still trying to put it all together, but it started in The Caves. Someone that shouldn't have been there murdered my friend Merrick, and Leadership has been covering it up. They're up to something out there but I just don't know what yet. It gets worse too. I think the recent outbreak was introduced by Leadership as a ploy to allow them to close The Caves for as long as they need to cover all their tracks. They didn't think I knew anything at first, but the more suspicious they get, the more dangerous it becomes for me. I'm guessing they've grown tired of speculating and just want to rid themselves of their problem now," I tell her, being careful to leave out the involvement of the others, just in case.

"That's a bit out there. It seems so ridiculous but plausible at the same time. No wonder you were keeping that to yourself," Nyree says. "So what are you going to do? It's not like there's anyone else you can appeal to. Leadership is it."

"I'm getting all the evidence I can. After that, I need to find a way to tell as much of Securus as possible. Leadership can't continue whatever they're doing if they don't have the support of the workers. Other than trying to live through this detail, my next problem is that I need to get back into The Caves one more time," I say, becoming frustrated. There is just one barrier after the other. It would be so much easier to just give up and spare anyone else from sharing my fate.

"Well, there may be a way to get around the last part," Nyree offers.

"Really?" I ask.

"I never really thought anything of it before, but there's a passage in the Deep Vents that leads out to The

Caves. I always figured it was just a random tunnel since no one uses it," she says.

"Do you know where it leads?" I ask, tempering my growing excitement. There are so many different tunnel systems and most are isolated or abruptly end without communicating to another system. Being that the start of it is that deep down, it likely never communicates with the system I need to access.

"I went through it when I was younger and more curious," she says. "It's a difficult path, but it eventually leads up to a chamber just outside of the fishing pools."

My heart races, this is exactly what I need, an unwatched entrance to The Caves. I could get back to the supply room with Hadwin and Sayda without Leadership ever knowing we are gone. If we can do that, and if Rana finds the vaccinations guns Trent used, we would have everything that we need to force Leadership to reveal the truth.

"Where is it?" I ask, encouraged by the prospects.

"It's really hard to find. You would easily walk right past it if you didn't know it was there. I can show you when this detail is over," she says.

"Well, we might as well get back to work. There's still a lot of land to clear," I say.

"The sooner we finish, the sooner we get back into Securus," she agrees.

As I walk toward my Grinder there is a flash of black that whizzes by. It narrowly misses me and crashes into the ground at my feet with a ghastly thud. I look at the now dead bird nervously. It nearly exploded from the impact, and there are scattered feathers still floating down from the rebounding force of its fall. These falling birds are dangerous, but at least I know they are not part of Leadership's plan.

"What's up with these birds?" Nyree asks after stopping to look.

"Weird, huh? I've seen them spread around the field. I have no idea why they just crash down like that. Some of the panels are damaged from their impacts too," I say, just as confused as her.

"I'm going to ask the Controllers, maybe they can be useful for once," she says while activating her communicator.

I leave mine off, being in no mood to listen to Aamon right now. After a couple minutes and a frustrated look on her face, she has their answer.

"They were hypothesizing that the glare from the reflected light might be blinding them or that the magnetic field created by all the electricity is disorienting them. In other words, they don't know but don't want to admit it," she relays to me, irritated with the lack of honesty from the Controllers.

Back in the relative safety of my machine, I return to the task assigned to us for the day. While clearing the fields, I try to avoid the morbid thought of the birds being further dismembered by the claws of my Grinder. One benefit of working up here on the surface is that it is easy to distract your mind. There is color and life everywhere you look, unlike the dark, drab steel and stone walls that we are accustomed to.

The electrified fence is a menacing barrier, but just beyond it lays a fluid mixture of beauty. The thick weaving trunks and branches of the trees form intricate layers that give way to the numerous deep green leaves sprouting from them. In the open areas beyond the fence and before the forest takes root, the ground is vibrant with colors. There are dense carpets of short plants that blossom with wild flowers of unimaginable variety and color. The sound of the birds and other small forest creatures breaks the trance-inducing dull hum emanating from the fence and the electricity transmission lines. This is life the way we were meant to live it. Surrounded by other natural life and not hidden in the depths of the Earth, cowering away from our own devious creation. I have to remind myself that not everything we create is ugly. Looking at the Solar Panels above, I must admit there is a strange beauty in them as well.

As we move further toward the center of the field while clearing the ground, my attention is drawn to the varying forms our Solar Panels have taken. I remember from my lessons as a child that the original Solar Panel system had to be expanded upon as the structure of Securus was enlarged. Additional fields were added to the one I am working in before The Agent reached our area. The first Solar Panels simply absorb the Sun's energy and convert it to useable power in one of the substations. The additional fields function differently, and now that I see them, they are as astonishing as anything I have ever seen in my life or in the images on my computer.

There are circles of formed mirrors just as large as the Solar Panels in my field that are reflecting a brilliant light onto a central spire. The golden light surrounds the spire with a majestic incandescence. This is not only breathtaking, but efficient at the same time. The heat generated from the concentrated light coalescing on the tower and its inner components is harnessed and converted into useable energy. The height of the spire itself is amazing and frightening at the same time. I am glad that it was serviced on the last detail and climbing it is not necessary for us.

The rest of the afternoon passes without another incident, and we are treated to our first sunset. Pictures and words alone cannot describe the wonders of nature, and this sunset is clearly one of them. I force myself to break from my idle thoughts because it is time to return to Securus. Things are more dangerous for me when I am in the group than when alone with Nyree. Though I am not anxious to return to the others, I am more than ready to get this bio-suit off of me, especially the waste disposal system.

"It looks like we're done for the day. Finally we can go back inside," Nyree says happily.

"How can you not appreciate the scenery up here?" I ask as we drive back toward the bunker.

"I do appreciate it. But I appreciate being alive much more, and the chances of that steadily decrease the longer we're out here," she says analytically.

*Me too, I just don't know where I'm more in danger at this point*, I think to myself. We are the first ones back, which is not surprising. It is going to take Eldin a lot longer to clear his assigned territory and Balum's field was a lot farther away from the bunker. Not wanting to wait for the others after what happened this afternoon, I park my Grinder and head straight for the exit hatch, with Nyree following close behind me. For once, I am moving faster than her. When we are both inside, the hatch locks and the decontamination begins. We have to go through two cycles. The first cycle sterilizes our outer bio-suits. After that, we take off our helmets and open the seals in the joints of our bio-suits so we can undergo the standard decontamination. I have endured this many times in the infirmary, but this is going to be the first time for Nyree.

"Just a fair warning, this process is uncomfortable to say it politely," I tell her.

"It's all that's keeping me from getting inside Securus, so right now I welcome it," she says.

The first cycle is painless. We prepare for the second cycle and activate the system. The mist creeps into the chamber and envelops us. Nyree staggers toward the side of the chamber from its disorienting effects. I reach out for her, but with her sight impaired, she crashes into the side wall of the chamber a second time before steadying herself. Now as the heavy mist fills our lungs and sets our bodies ablaze, she gasps for a breath of air. There is no relief and the gasp only deepens the burn, as it allows more chemicals to enter her lungs. It will be over soon, so I stop trying to help her up and focus on my own breathing. Mercifully, the mist recedes and our sight is returned as the burning subsides. We are now able to reenter Securus. She carefully steps out of the chamber and comes to a rest at her changing station.

"You weren't lying about that decontamination. That was horrible. How can you do that all the time?" she asks, still clutching her chest.

"I only use it when absolutely necessary. It doesn't get any better, but at least you know what to expect for next time," I offer, knowing that is of little consolation.

I return to my own stall and begin to take the bio-suit off piece by piece. This one needs to be quietly switched back with my original bio-suit, except for the shoe that was damaged, so no one notices. Then I can continue to use this bio-suit without worry of tampering. By the time the suit is off, the others have all arrived. When they are all changing, I start making the switch. Nyree notices, but does not say anything as she leaves the room. After the switch is complete, I follow her. We are free of the surface for the day, but that does not mean I am out of danger. Soon the others will join us, and I need to stay vigilant.

# 22

Before the others arrive, Nyree and I head down the hall to another room that is designated as our sleeping quarters during the detail. The room is much larger than our standard quarters, with enough space for six beds to be lined along the walls without stacking. The flooring is soft, just like in Mr. Vaden's quarters. In the center of the room there is a couch and multiple chairs arranged as an additional resting area. I may not be looking forward to the company, but at least the room looks comfortable.

By the time I finish surveying the area, Nyree is already resting on the bunk she has chosen. I pick the one that is closest to hers and pull back the blanket to mark it as mine before going to the couch. We typically do not get such a large and cushioned seat, so I take full advantage of the small benefit. It does not take long for me to start shifting back and forth, already bored. From my chair, there is nothing to occupy my mind, and all I can see are the bare walls. They are colored with a warm, earthy-brown tone, which is a pleasing change compared to the typical metal grey in most areas. It is an expansive and luxurious room, but after spending the day on the surface it feels cramped and suffocating. The others trickle in until the room is full, making it feel even more confined.

"Good thing you had your partner nearby. How's the ankle?" Balum asks while sitting down across from me.

"It's fine," I answer tersely, not wanting to engage him

in a conversation.

Eldin sits alone on his bed. The only words he speaks is another apology to me for the nearly disastrous accident. Ardal quickly falls asleep on the opposite side of the room, while Jadyn comes to join Balum on the chairs. The latter two are the only ones that seem comfortable here. Now that they are here, I suddenly yearn for my boredom to return.

I check the time, mentally willing it to move faster. Finally, Rupert appears at the door. Since there were no incidents or potential contaminations, he releases us for a limited amount of free time. Nyree and I immediately leave the room. Neither of us wants to spend any more time with our detail group than is necessary. There is no point in asking Nyree where she is going, knowing she will be well on her way down to the lower levels before I would be able to finish the question. Besides, I am in a hurry myself, even if my movements are not as fast. I head toward the infirmary first to get a brace to help stabilize my ankle. It will not heal my injury but it should help prevent me from aggravating it.

Standing just outside the infirmary, I pause to calm my mind, preparing myself for a potential interaction with Trent. Slowly, I make my way down the hall. When approaching my exam room, his muffled voice can be heard inside. He must be speaking with a patient. Maybe I can get a brace from Rana's room without having to see him. I slip into the room across the hall and carefully close the door behind me.

Now safely inside, I walk over to far wall where Rana keeps the supplies. I reach out to open the cabinet, but freeze in place when a faint rustling comes from behind the gurney. Someone must have followed me! My muscles tense, preparing for the confrontation. Quietly, I move to the side for a better angle. Peaking around the gurney, I get my first glimpse of the spy, and it is definitely not the person I expected to find. Seeing the cowering figure concealed by a flowing veil of grey hair, I nearly burst out with laughter.

"Rana, what are you doing down there?" I ask, suppressing a chuckle at her awkward position.

"Oh, it's you, Kagen. I thought it was Trent," she says, holding her chest and taking a deep breath.

"Yeah, I came to get an ankle brace. I sprained it today," I tell her. "What're you up to?"

"Exactly what you asked me to do. I looked during the day but the case was nowhere to be found. When he came in tonight he had it in his hand. He was just walking around with it this whole time," she says incredulously. "I was waiting for a chance to switch the vaccination guns."

"Rana, you have many talents, but hiding is clearly not one of them. How were you going to open it up anyway? It needs a code," I laugh for a moment before catching myself. I do not want to make too much noise or Trent will find us both.

"Well, sneaking about is not something I'm well practiced at," she admits. "But I do know Trent. He always uses the same password because he's too lazy to memorize another."

"Of course, I should've known that," I say. "I might have a way to make this easier on you."

"What do you have in mind?" she asks.

"You get to hide while I distract Trent. I'll get him in here and keep him busy long enough for you to make the switch. Just ring the patient chime on your way out so I know when to stop stalling," I say.

"Where should I hide?" she asks.

"Your best bet would be the waiting room, or at least

around the corner near it. As soon as you hear Trent come in here, you go in. Oh, and I have another idea. Take this and hide it in the case," I say pulling out Sayda's tracking device. "Sayda can use it to track his movements. We might be able to find where the virus originated from if he goes back to the source."

"You obviously have had way too much practice with this recently. That's a decent plan," Rana says as she takes the tracker.

Now I need to figure out how to distract Trent. I peek out the door just as he is walking his patient out of the infirmary. When he returns to the exam room, I signal Rana to go back down the hall. As soon as she is fully out of sight, I open the door and turn around to knock over a metal container, spilling its contents on the floor. The vibrating clang it makes is as loud as I had hoped it would be. While I am cleaning up the resulting mess, Trent appears at the door.

"Having some trouble there?" he asks sarcastically.

"I was looking for the ankle braces and this thing got in my way," I say, throwing the syringes back into the container with a feigned annoyance. "I didn't want to interrupt you while you were with a patient, so I came in here to get one. I sprained it on the detail today and wanted some support before going back tomorrow."

"You know you could have asked for me to bring you one up there," he says.

"I didn't want to bother you for something so minor. Besides, I can handle it just fine on my own," I reply. "Since you're here, would you mind helping me out with this mess? I'm exhausted from the day, and it would be nice to get out of here to get some rest before the morning arrives."

He reluctantly agrees and starts helping me clean up

the mess. I look over at him kneeling over, picking up the syringes and needles from the floor in such a vulnerable position. He is lucky I have some self-control because nothing would please me more at the moment than to turn and maul him. Instead, fighting that urge, I clumsily continue to clean the mess. Even with me slowing the process, by the time we finish cleaning the mess the patient chime still has not gone off, and Trent is about to leave.

"Do you know where Rana keeps the braces?" I ask doing my best to stall for her.

He walks over the shelf next to me and pulls a brace out. I pretend to be perplexed to how my search missed it. He turns to leave and I am running out of ideas to stall him. As he reaches the door, the patient chime rings. I exhale, knowing Rana has made the switch and is safely out of the infirmary. Trent leaves to greet his new patient, still shaking his head at my uncoordinated efforts. I stay behind and put on the brace before making my own exit. That went as smoothly as I had hoped. *It's about time something went right*, I think to myself.

My feet stop moving when I see Trent coming back around the corner accompanying an ill looking woman. That means it was not Rana that triggered the chime and that she is still in the exam room. Trent is going to find her! I try to think of a good way to distract him, but everything that comes to mind is too obvious. My only choice is to trust that Rana will find a way out of this, but still, I cannot leave her alone to deal with Trent.

"Ah, I forgot to get some of the cooling packs for my ankle," I mumble loud enough for Trent to hear as he passes. I slowly return to Rana's room while listening for any reaction from Trent, but can only hear him speaking to the ill woman. Back in the exam room, I pause to try and form a new plan. I have to find a way to get her out of there because like she proved earlier, Rana can only hide for so long. While thinking, I start to pace the room, becoming more and more upset with myself for placing her in this position. Then, my concentration is broken by an unexpected sound. It is a faint laugh. I turn to look for its source and there she is.

"How did you get in here?" I ask with my mouth still agape from the surprise. "I was getting worried and trying to figure out how to rescue you from Trent."

"I have a few tricks up my sleeve," Rana boasts while holding up two vaccination guns.

"Sneaky," I tell her. "Now I hope those guns are what we think they are. If I see Talia before you do, I'll tell her to come find you, but I can't mention why. There's no way we'll have enough privacy for that conversation."

"I'll keep them safe for her," she says.

Looking at the clock, it is later than I thought. I had not realized how long this side trip had taken, and now there is not enough time to go down to see my mother and Arluin. They will have to wait until tomorrow. I leave the infirmary and climb the stairs, with my mind occupied by concern for my friends. Seeing Rana sneak around has made me realize how much my actions are endangering them. I remember the men watching Hadwin and Sayda when we talked during lunch. It had not seemed like a danger at the time, but now I know better. I should have kept this to myself. Now if things go bad, I will have jeopardized everyone who matters to me. I almost wish I could go back and just leave it alone, even though it would have still eaten away at me for the rest of my life. But at least then all of the others would be safe and blissfully unaware that anything was wrong. I try to remind myself not to dwell on things that cannot be changed, but now it is not so simple. Regardless of how I feel, now that they do know, there is no going back.

*

When entering the upper level hallway, I am greeted by a group of familiar, yet unexpected faces. My mother, Arluin, Hadwin, and Sayda have all come to see me.

"Hey, what're you guys doing up here?" I ask while limping toward them.

"I was worried when you didn't come down, and I don't care if we aren't allowed on this level," my mother answers, turning her head when she notices my affected gait.

"What happened to your leg?" Sayda asks before I have a chance to explain.

"It's just a sprain. I went to the infirmary to get a brace and some cooling packs," I say, showing them my supplies. "It wasn't as bad as I thought it was going to be on the surface, and, the view is amazing."

Only a few more words are spoken before Aamon appears down the hall and interrupts. "This is a restricted level. All visitors must exit," he calls out, but does not come near to enforce it.

"Don't worry about me," I say looking at my mother, since she is the one who will worry the most. "I'll make sure to come down sooner tomorrow."

We say goodbye, and they all turn toward the staircase to leave. I catch Hadwin by the arm and stop him.

"Wait," I whisper to him. "We have a way to get into The Caves. Nyree knows of a tunnel in the Deep Vents. As soon as the detail is over I'm going back in. The other good news is Rana has the vaccination guns Trent used. She put the other tracker in his case, so have Sayda monitor it. We almost have everything we need."

"*We* are going. I'm not letting you go alone again," he

says quietly, but with absolute determination in his eyes. "One way or the other, we're going to end this."

He turns and follows the others into the staircase. I can feel Aamon still watching me from down the hallway. While turning toward him, I am careful to display a carefree smile for his benefit. I do not want him to even think that he knows what we were talking about. As far as he knows, we were just making more jokes. He crosses his arms and starts impatiently tapping his foot, waiting for me to get back to the sleeping room. So, I slow my pace to a relaxed saunter.

"Is your injury too much for you?" he asks as I move past him.

"I'm just fine, thank you for your concern. I guess Mr. Vaden doesn't trust you as much as you think since he had to personally oversee the detail," I say in a mocking tone.

"I'm in charge of this detail, make no mistake about that," he snaps back. "He only checked in briefly, since I have everything under control."

"Yeah, you're in control. Just like Eldin has complete control of his Grinder," I mutter.

"It's time you return to your quarters," he orders.

Aamon looks as though he is desperately trying to hold his tongue. There is something he wants to say, and I think I know what it is. He wants me to know it was not an accident today and that he controls my fate, at least he thinks he does. I am getting tired, so I stop instigating him and walk back into my temporary quarters. Nyree has also just returned and is settling in for the night while the others are nearly asleep already. She turns to me as I sit on my bunk.

"I asked around some, the rumor is that there are large predators on the surface that have mutated since we've been down here. I don't know if it's true or just frightened imaginations conjuring up monsters, but we need to be careful repairing that fence tomorrow," she warns.

"That's been worrying me too, especially since Aamon refuses to tell us anything about it. Hopefully, we don't meet whatever caused that damage," I respond. The fatigue of the day is starting to sink in, so I get comfortable in my bunk for the night. I quickly drift off to sleep, and tonight my dreams return to me.

*I am walking on the surface without my bio-suit. The warmth of the sun energizes my steps and the trees bristle with life. I am happy and free of the weight of my bonds from Securus. While exploring the forest, the distinct sound of heavy footsteps starts following me. Suddenly, all of the sounds from the creatures in the forest cease. There is only the increasing cadence of the footsteps drawing near. They turn into a rapid gallop, and I instinctively run.*

*I circle around through fallen branches and emerge onto the Solar Panels fields. The fence has completely disappeared. The sounds of my pursuer vanish, and I am again alone. I search the field, and at the base of the central tower there is a security coded box. It stands twice my height and is colored black. There is the distinctive Leadership insignia brightly painted near the top. Somehow, I know all the answers I seek lay within this box. I sprint to it, and go straight to the key pad, which is actually a keyboard for a computer. Without thinking, my fingers type in the code: T-R-U-T-H.*

*There is a hiss from the released pressurized gas within when the box opens. I strain to see what is inside, but it appears to be empty. My throat starts to itch. I try to clear it but the dryness becomes overwhelming. My muscles twitch and begin to weaken. Falling to the floor I realize what I have done. The box contained The Agent, and I released it. My eyes look up and see that everyone I care for is now standing in a circle around me, gasping for air. They have been infected because of my heedless impetuosity.*

*The world begins to darken as the Sun is swallowed by foreboding clouds. An electrical storm is nearing, and the thunder becomes deafening.*

At first there is a single burst, but soon after another follows. It gives way to rhythmic bursts of thunder that in turn morphs into the shrieking of our special morning alert. I wake up and try to shake off the terror and anguish from my nightmare but cannot. I must face my guilt for leading those that care for me into the path of harm. My appointment in life is to help those in need and to do no harm, but in that I fear I may fail.

The others are now awake and getting ready to start the detail for the day. As we dress, Aamon and Rupert enter the room. Aamon briefly whispers to Rupert before leaving.

"As soon as you're ready, grab some breakfast across the hall then make your way to the exit chamber. You have twenty minutes to eat. We need to be efficient if we're to stay on schedule today," Rupert tells us.

There is very little conversation amongst us as we finish dressing and go to get our food. When we enter the small room across the hall, a pleasant surprise awaits us. The room is the size of the average domestic quarters, but has been outfitted with a table just large enough for the six of us. On the table is our food, and it is not the synthetic gruel that we were expecting. There is a filet of fresh fish served with a mix of vegetables and a large glass of a strawberry flavored drink. At least that is what they tell us the flavor is, since none of us have ever actually had a real strawberry.

The surprising treat elevates the mood of our entire group. It has been a while since we had any natural food and to get this type of meal is exceptionally rare. Our plates are emptied rapidly. There is something about the natural food that just feels more energizing. Our food is so unexpected that it worries me. It feels kind of like a last meal. If I am not careful, it may well be.

## 23

After breakfast, we make our way back into the changing room. It easier than expected to switch the bio-suits again since everyone else is so preoccupied with their own preparations. When we are nearly ready to start, Aamon reappears.

"It's time for today's assignments. Your main task is going to be maintenance and repair of the underground electric transmission lines. We'll keep the same teams and field sections as yesterday. When you're out there, the Controllers will help guide you to the locations of the specific lines that require servicing. Kagen and Nyree, you will also have to fix the security fence. I suggest you work efficiently because you all have a lot of work to do today. Are there any questions? No? Then get to work," Aamon instructs.

"What? You're not gonna tell us to be safe and productive today?" I ask, mocking his speech from yesterday.

He does not respond to my comment but does give me what he seems to think is a menacing stare. I think it is better to try to keep him off balance. He does not think as clearly when he is agitated, plus it amuses me to see him flustered. He stomps out of the room while we turn toward the exit to start the day.

Before making it to the decontamination chamber, my movement is halted by an unexpected tug on my arm. I instinctively jerk back and swing around to get in a position to defend myself from the attacker. Talia nearly falls down from the force of my harsh turn.

"Oh, I'm so sorry, Talia. I didn't know it was you. I've been a little jumpy up here," I explain, checking to make sure she is okay.

"It's no big deal, at least I know you're being watchful," she reassures me.

"What're you doing in here?" I ask.

"It's my only chance to see you. My father took what happened even worse than I thought he would. He's getting ready for the morning announcements right now, that's the only way I was able to sneak past him. I just wanted to let you know why I can't be in the substation," she says, resting a gentle hand on the side of my helmet where my cheek would be.

"Yeah, I figured that part out when I asked the Controllers about you yesterday and your father replied," I tell her while checking to make sure my communicator is turned off. "There is something else you can do to help though. Find Rana and keep an open mind to what she has to say; it'll be shocking. You'll understand everything then. The only others you can trust with what you find are Hadwin and Sayda. Remember, this isn't just for me. It's for all of Securus. I'm sorry I can't say more, but it's not safe."

She looks confused but understands that we cannot discuss it further without privacy. Hadwin and Sayda may not be convinced, but I am confident Talia will do the right thing. I take her hand and hold it with both of mine. I yearn to feel the softness of her hand against mine and the comfort of her embrace, but in this bio-suit that is not possible. Without that, being able to look into her eyes still gives me all the strength I need.

"Thank you for coming to see me; it means more than

you know. I have to get to work now so I can hurry up and come back to you," I say, recalling her words after the kiss.

Talia manages a warm smile and replies, "I'm gonna hold you to that." She glides gracefully out of the room. Even with everything that is going on you would never be able to tell she was troubled if you did not see the concern in her eyes. I turn back to the exit. Nyree has waited for me, watching from the other side of the decontamination chamber. She is kind enough to spare me meaningless encouragement or questions about Talia. Instead, we focus on the task ahead and climb through the exit hatch.

We have started the detail earlier today, and the Sun is just beginning to peer over the tree tops. The indirect light casts a subtle glow on everything around us. The others have already opened the bunker, so we enter and organize our equipment. We will again use the Grinders today, but this time the teams will each share one of them to carry the various tools needed for the day. Though I am as comfortable as Nyree with operating the Grinder, she prefers to drive the machine herself. I suspect that being in command of something gives her some comfort up here where so much is out of our control. She maneuvers the Grinder back toward the defect in the outer fence and backs the machine up to the fence line for easier unloading of our tools as well as a faster escape if needed.

I get out and study the fence. Its structure is more complex than it appeared at first. There are three separate layers. The inner layer is a grid of thick interlocking metal links that forms a barrier to anything larger than the width of a few fingers. Behind that is the middle layer, which is composed of multiple electrical wires running horizontally in parallel to a height that is above the reach of my outstretched arms. The outer layer consists of a coiled wire spread across the base and top of the electric components. It has razor sharp edges and small hooks, making it particularly perilous to try to go over or under the fence.

I get next to the edge of the defect in the fence and listen to the wire to make sure there is no electrified hum emanating from it. The only sounds I can hear are the songs of the birds and insects in the forest beyond. To start the repair, our instructions are to first secure another support post in the middle of the open area. Then we can weld the edges of the fence to it and reconnect the electric wires.

"Let's get the hole dug out. Then we can work on the other components," I suggest to Nyree.

She nods and gets out our tools. We each grab one of the two handles of our electric hole-digger, and turn on the drill. Nyree and I constantly watch for any signs of danger, as we make the hole and place the post. We secure it with a quick hardening synthetic substance that is similar to the hardener in our medical splints. The missing chunks of the outer layer are much larger than the other sections so we cannot connect the edges. This is good news since neither of us was looking forward to handling the sharp edges and risk puncturing our bio-suits. Now we can move on to reconnecting the electric components.

"Substation, this is Nyree, can you confirm the power for the fence is off so we can continue repair?" she asks through her communicator.

"The power is off, you may continue," Aamon replies.

Somehow, it is less than comforting that he was the one to answer. I get the wire connecting tool from the

Grinder. The upper wires are too high to reach on foot, so we stand on the back of the Grinder to get to them. Nyree is skilled at welding, so I use the clamp-like edges of my tool to pull the wires together while she connects them. Even with my eyes focused on our task, I continue to listen diligently for any new sounds from the forest.

We are halfway through connecting the electric wires when there is a rustle in the woods. We both stop and look outward. There is no visible movement. We freeze in place, positioned to make a quick turn to get to the Grinder. The sound stops for a few moments then again, I hear the shuffling of leaves on the ground. This time I recognize it as the rhythmic pattern of slow footsteps, and they are headed directly toward us. We start to carefully inch backward, trying not to make any noise.

"What are you two doing?" Aamon demands through the communicators. We do not answer. "What are you two doing?" his voice loudly calls out to us from the Grinder's built in communication system.

The sound makes me cringe because whatever is out there must have heard it. I turn back to the forest. The footsteps have stopped. Suddenly, there is more movement, and I see what looks to be a large animal, racing through the trees. It flashes in front of us and then vanishes back into the forest just as fast as it appeared. Nyree is already in the Grinder, but I remained in place, having recognized the animal from some of my internet searches. It moved gracefully on four hooved legs and had light brown fur topped with a crown of jagged spikes. It is called a deer. From what I read, they are skittish creatures and typically not a threat to people.

"We were being still because we heard something in the forest. Thanks for drawing attention to us," I scold Aamon. "Luckily, it was just a deer."

Aamon does not reply. I can picture him in the substation fuming from my insubordinate tone. Smiling from that thought, I reassure Nyree that it is safe to come out and continue working. I almost feel a little embarrassed being so excitable and looking for a creature that probably does not even exist. Even so, I want to hurry up and finish. Just knowing that we have no form of self-protection from any predators in the forest is unsettling to the point that it is becoming emotionally draining.

We quickly finish connecting the electric wires. Now we just need to attach the inner fence to the new post and hook it to the electric wires. Then we can move on to a safer location, deeper in the Solar Panel fields. I pull the edges of the fence to the post but they are over one foot away from closing. The wire connector tool has another attachment that can hook the edges of the mangled fence for us to repair it, but the defect is too large, and we need to inset a patch into the fence to connect the free edges.

With Nyree and I working together, the fence quickly begins to take form. Before we can fully connect the inner layer, we need to reconnect the outer electric wires to it. I slide through the remaining opening being careful to avoid the exposed rough edges that Nyree is holding away from me. To tie the two fences together, I use a flexible conducting wire that will allow the flow of electricity to secure both layers. As I am starting the last connection, the footsteps in the forest return. They sound similar to the ones we had heard before. *It must be another deer*, I think to myself while continuing to work. The connection is nearly complete when I see movement out of the corner of my eye.

I turn, expecting to see another deer. But instead, there is a massive beast stalking me through the trees. It is down on four legs but still stands taller than I, with its black, beady eyes fixed on me. It is hard to see where the animal ends and the forest begins because the thick fur coat that covers it is a dirty, deep brown, which blends in with the soil and bark of the trees. One thing that is not obscured is its bulky claws, which look about as wide as the size of the defect in the fence. I am paralyzed with fear, unsure of what to do. This creature vaguely resembles some of the bears that I have read about but is significantly larger than any of them. I remember reading that running could trigger a predator's natural instinct to chase and attack, but there is no way I want to stand up to this colossal wild animal.

"Nyree, slowly back into the Grinder. Do not make a sudden move and do not turn away," I say, trying to keep my voice calm and steady.

Nyree was watching me and had not yet noticed the beast. She gasps when she looks into the forest and sees it. I try to back out of the fence, but with Nyree no longer holding it open, the sharp edges grab at my bio-suit. I am stuck in place and am absolutely helpless. Either I stay to face the animal or pull away from the sharp edges of the fence and risk being exposed to The Agent. I continue meeting the stare of the monstrous bear until a sharp crack and feral growl from deeper in the forest, rings out through the trees, grabbing the beast's attention. It turns from me, and I let out an exhausted sigh as it stomps off deeper into the forest to investigate the more interesting noise.

"Nyree, it's gone. I only have one more connection to finish. Then we can close this fence," I tell her.

She comes back out of the Grinder and waits for me to finish. My hands shake from the lingering fear while I try to connect the wire. It takes longer than before, but eventually I complete the connection. Now that it is done, Nyree uses a tool with large hooks to pull the fence open again, so I can come back inside the protective barrier. While sliding through the fence, an eerie tingling starts in my extremities and then radiates inward. The small hairs on my arms and neck stand up against my bio-suit. *Is that still the effects of the adrenaline from the bear encounter or is something wrong?* I ask myself.

My heart jumps when I hear the unmistakable hum of the electricity being activated for the fence. I spring backward, but Nyree let go of the hooks and the fence collapses onto the arm of my bio-suit. I struggle to pull my arm free as the energy permeates the fence. Sparks shoot out from my bio-suit's control panel as the electricity jumps into me. All of my muscles spasm and lock into a rigid contraction while the electricity assaults my body and nervous system. The force of my spasm rips me free of the fence, collapsing me to the ground. My muscles burn and continue fasciculating from the electrocution, but surprisingly, my mind is still clear.

"Kagen, are you okay," Nyree shouts as she comes to my aid.

"Not really," I answer back, trying to get up but my muscles and coordination resist. "A second more and the shock would have stunned my diaphragm as well as interfered with the conduction within my heart. Thankfully, I wasn't holding on to anything so when my muscles forcefully contracted, it pulled me free of the fence and limited the damage."

"I think it fried your brain because I have no idea what you just said," she says with a smile and relief that I am still alive.

"Sorry, I guess being analytical is one of my defense mechanisms," I tell her before changing the channel on my communicator. "Substation, would you care to explain what the hell just happened," I demand.

"It was an accident," Aamon explains. "Something must have tripped the systems automatic defense mechanism. When it senses a potential threat, the system activates itself."

"Don't you think it would've been a good idea to deactivate that function while we were working on it, or is that too complicated a procedure for you to handle, Aamon?" I respond, becoming more agitated by his lame excuse.

"You still have a job to do, can you continue or shall I call the Healer for an evaluation?" Aamon says, ignoring my comment.

I check my bio-suit's control panel. The readout on the screen is unintelligible, so I try resetting it. While it is rebooting, Nyree assists me to my feet. I feel sore everywhere, but still have enough strength to support myself. Fortunately the reset works, and the control panel for my bio-suit turns back on. It appears that most of the electricity jumped straight to me and did not damage the circuits significantly. Somehow, with my aching muscles, that does not necessarily feel like a lucky break. But at least I do not have to be at the mercy of Trent. That though makes me wonder if that is what Aamon is trying to arrange, since he has been so quick to repeatedly offer Trent's services.

"I just need a short break. Then I can continue," I reassure him and then switch off my communicator.

"Why don't you just let the Healer check you?" Nyree asks.

"Because I trust Trent about as much as Aamon," I reply. Nyree nods in understanding and turns to the fence. The hum has ceased as the electricity has again been deactivated. She seals the remaining defect while I continue to recover. When the repair is complete, we do not waste any time moving further into the field where we will have to work on some of the transmission lines.

I activate my hydration attachment and try to continually sip water. With the damaging jolt, it is important for me to stay hydrated so my kidneys do not become overwhelmed and shut down from a clogging buildup of enzymes released by the injured muscles. As we drive into the field, Nyree tells me that it is time for a lunch break, so we rest under one of the Solar Panels. We agree to stay away from the bunker today because I feel too vulnerable there with the others. Even though she still says very little, I think that Nyree is getting a little more comfortable with being on the surface, especially since she agreed to stay here with me for lunch. After a short rest, I feel less shaky and ready to resume work.

Nyree has left her communicator on so the Controllers can guide us to where we can find the transmission lines that need maintenance. Most of the lines in our sector are in good shape, but some need to have the insulation reinforced to protect the energy flow. They give us the general location, and we use another portable locator that uses ultrasound waves to more accurately define the location of the lines.

With all of our sophisticated tools and equipment, we still only have manual shovels for digging around the transmission lines. This is in part because they do not want workers unfamiliar with dangerous tools compromising the lines because of poor technique. That makes for the most physically difficult task so far on the detail. Combined with my fatigue from the shock I received earlier, it makes for a painful afternoon. My only consolation is that for now, aching muscles and a sore ankle are my only injuries. It could have been much worse.

By the time we finish recoating the affected lines with new insulation, the Sun is nearly setting again. Today I have no interest in staying for the view. I just want to get back inside Securus and try to get some rest, though that is not likely to happen.

## 24

Today, Nyree and I are the last ones to make it back into Securus from the detail. By the time we pass through the decontamination chamber the others have already finished shedding their bio-suits. I slowly take mine off, having to constantly stop because of the soreness in my muscles. Afterward, I search through our standard first aid kit and take a mild pain relieving medication. It is not much, but it should help some. Even though my fatigued body needs the rest, I cannot lay down just yet. There is a promise I have to keep, especially after not being able to go down to visit everyone yesterday.

Instead of waiting in our temporary quarters for Rupert to tell us when we are cleared for free time, I head down toward my usual dinner hall. At this point, it is not like I could get into more trouble with him or Aamon. I do my best to walk normally when entering the hall, so the others do not get concerned. My ankle is not as sore as yesterday, but my muscles resist every move that I make. They are all sitting at a large table waiting for me, already having finished their food long ago. On one side is my mother, Arluin and his friend Varian. On the other side sits Sayda, Hadwin and Abira. I cannot help but notice the irritated look on Sayda's face and the strategic position Hadwin has taken to keep Abira safe. Abira is the first to see me coming, and greets me with a relieved smile.

"Hi, Kagen, how was the day?" she asks cheerfully.

"It was a long one. But hey, that's two down and only three more to go," I say.

"You look tired. Have you been getting enough food and rest?" my mother asks.

"Yes, I have. We just had a lot of manual labor today, so I'm a bit worn down," I reassure her.

Arluin does not speak. By the way he is looking at me, I know why. He knows I am withholding the truth, but he does not want to call me out on that in front of our mother. Neither of us wants to make her worry. We spend some time just trying to be normal, and though nothing feels normal now, it is still comforting. My time is limited however, since they will be closing down the upper levels soon. I hug my mother and Arluin before walking toward the exit. Hadwin, Sayda, and Abira all follow under the pretense of walking me up to my quarters. I know it does not really fool my mother because she is too smart for that, but she plays along anyway. Now in the hallway, away from potential spies, I turn back to the others.

"Did anything happen up there today?" Sayda asks before I can speak.

"I think Aamon tried to electrocute me. Hopefully he doesn't have too many more surprises planned," I answer. Hadwin takes a deep breath and Sayda clenches her fists when they hear that part. "How about you guys, any new developments?" I ask, trying to deflect the focus, so they do not concentrate on their worry for me.

Sayda glances at Abira and hesitates. She obviously has something to tell me but does not want her to hear it.

"Abira, if you see Aamon, make sure to mention that I looked in good spirits. I don't want him to think he's getting to me," I say.

"I will. I hope you don't mind me waiting for you. I

just needed to see that you were still okay. If there's anything else I can do to help, just tell me. Some people may never be able to forgive me for giving in to Aamon, but I want to try to make up for it," she says and is brave enough to look over at Sayda when she says the last part.

"Thanks, I appreciate that," I tell her. She hugs me and wishes me luck before leaving the rest of us alone.

"What's on your mind, Sayda?" I ask as soon as Abira is out of sight.

"I've been monitoring the tracker in the equipment, and it has left Securus. It's still on the move, but as of now it's already far into The Caves. If it goes too much farther, I'll lose the signal," she replies.

"Looks like we were right about that, but where are they taking it?" I ask, knowing that none of us has an answer. "How about the tracker in Trent's case?"

"Just ordinary movement so far. I'll keep watching," she says.

"There is one other thing," Hadwin says. "Talia got a message to me today. She wanted you to meet her outside of the Control Room in the substation when you go back up there tonight."

"And why didn't you tell me about this?" Sayda demands, poking him with her finger as she speaks.

"Because if I told you earlier, you would've mentioned something about it to Abira, just to irritate her. We both have seen how she cringes when Talia is mentioned. I don't think you could've passed up the opportunity to throw that at her, and I figured it would be better to keep it quiet," Hadwin explains.

"You're gonna get it for that," she says with a playful push. "No more secrets. I can be discrete when it's needed."

"Is there something else I should know?" I ask them

both, noticing how they have been closer lately.

"No, that's it," Hadwin says. He clearly did not understand what I meant. Sayda, on the other hand, is giving me a wide-eyed stare intended to make me drop it. That look combined with her silence answers my question.

"Alright, I'll see you guys tomorrow. I have to get back up there before they close the level down and put me in the Detention Center. Have fun with your secret admirer," I say motioning to the man that has been loitering in the hall, unsuccessfully trying to look like he is not watching us. He must be another of Aamon's spies.

\*

The upper level is quiet when I arrive. Inside our temporary quarters, everyone is already asleep except for Nyree. She has still not returned from the lower levels and is going to be cutting it close. I bunch up the blankets and pillow on my bunk to make it appear occupied, just in case anyone checks on us. When it looks convincing, I sneak back out and head to the Control Room.

Surprisingly, there is very little security or cameras on this level. I suppose that since it is usually just Leadership personnel up here, they are less concerned with oversight. Nearing the entrance to the Control Room, I peer around the corner to see what awaits me. Talia is standing alone, fidgeting with her fingers while waiting for me. The area looks clear, so I walk to her.

When Talia sees me coming, she reaches out to me. I embrace her with more force than intended and accidently lift her from the ground. I ease my grip and look at her. As I do she leans in for another kiss. That was unexpected, but unlike all of the other surprises that have been following me lately, this one is welcome.

"Are you okay? I heard about what happened with the

fence," she says.

"I'm okay, just really sore," I tell her. "I wanted to ask you about that. Is there really an automated system that would turn the fence on like that?"

"Yes there is, but it has to be separately activated. Normally, when you shut the power down, everything is off. It was created to conserve energy, only activating the fences when needed. The system ended up being too erratic, so we don't typically use it unless absolutely necessary," Talia explains.

"Yeah, that's what I thought," I say. "Is there any way for me to see the security system in the Control Room? I want to know what else Aamon has access to."

"That's one of the reasons I wanted to meet you here. There's only one operator at night and tonight it's my friend, Cyrina. She's waiting for my signal so we can go in there alone," Talia says.

She knocks on the door with three faint, spaced taps. The door opens, and a tall woman with a natural dark complexion appears. She nods at Talia as she passes us and continues down the hall. Her slender frame moves quickly, and she soon disappears around the corner.

We enter the room and close the door behind us. I walk by the main control panel and try to make sense of the sophisticated setup. There are four work stations facing the various gauges, readouts, controlling levers, and buttons. Most of them look like they are controls for the Solar Panels themselves. Behind the workstations is a larger, elevated chair positioned to give its inhabitant an overview of the entire operation. This must be where Mr. Vaden or Aamon sits during the detail. I move to the chair and sit in it. It feels even softer than the luxurious couch in our temporary quarters.

From here, I can also see a panel of screens similar to

those in Mr. Vaden's office that shows the visible areas in the fields. Now the images all have a green hue that Talia explains is a special setting for when there is no visible light. The overall coverage of the fields and fence by the cameras is far less thorough than I had thought it would be. It turns out that the areas I had been assigned to work just happen to have the best coverage by the cameras. Other than the controls for the Solar Panels and outer fence, most of the equipment seems to be either surveillance oriented or directly related to the power generation.

I look over the rest of the room. Off to the side are monitors for the energy levels. Most of the information is beyond my understanding, but one of them catches my attention. It has a small label underneath it that reads, *Caelum*. I remember that name from when Hadwin was looking into the electronics diversion.

"What's that?" I ask, pointing to the display.

"I'm not sure, I'll ask Cyrina later," she offers.

After finishing my examination of the controls and screens, I turn back to Talia. "Did you see Rana today?" I ask.

She shifts her stance and tilts her head before answering. "Yes, she gave me the vaccination guns. I agree that something is going on with Aamon, but I doubt it goes that far. I'm analyzing their contents and should get the result by tomorrow. I'm sure it'll turn out to be nothing," she says.

"I hope you're right, but you don't know everything that has happened so far. Whatever the result, I need to know for sure. Then I can tell you everything. I've been trying to keep things quiet as much as possible so no one else is put in danger," I explain. "Unfortunately, the situation has been forcing my hand, and one way or another something is going to happen soon. The farther this goes, the more I wish none of it ever happened. Well, except for getting the courage to tell you how I felt."

She stops me from my rambling speech and hugs me again. Her touch erases the pain of my aching muscles and temporarily replaces it with a delirious contentment.

"We have to go, but I'll try to see you again tomorrow unless my father finds out. I'll get word to you," she says.

"Just say where, and I'll be there," I tell her as she lets go.

My fatigue is becoming overwhelming and now, even Talia cannot keep me distracted from it. We part ways, and I sneak back into my bunk. The soft bed and smooth blanket is a merciful end to this grueling day.

Even with the comfortable bed, for a while sleep eludes me. My body tosses and turns as my mind wonders what could happen next. Eventually I do get to sleep, but as has been the trend lately, it is not long enough. It feels as if I had just closed my eyes when my alert wakes me again for another day on the detail. The exhaustion from the physical and mental rigors of the detail is becoming evident within our group. Everyone looks tired and has already settled into a routine. Nyree and I have been keeping to ourselves as much as possible. Eldin barely speaks a word to anyone while Balum speaks too much, and most of what he says is annoying, condescending, or both. I have given up trying to remember why Eldin is so familiar to me, and after almost running me over, I do not want to ask. Jadyn fumbles her way through the work and everyone is losing patience with her incompetence while Ardal has been surprisingly efficient. Despite this, he has kept persistently withdrawn from the rest of the group.

While we are dressing, another special breakfast is announced. The meal is different than the day before, but is equally delicious. This time we have a mix of small crab meat with a vegetable soup and another fruit flavored drink to go with it. I almost feel guilty enjoying such good food while the rest of Securus continues to slowly wither away. After breakfast, we return to the exit chamber to get ready for another trip to the surface. My routine of switching the suits is becoming efficient. I even have some time to sit and rest before Aamon shows up to tell us our assignments.

"Good morning and welcome to the third day of the detail. Today we'll be switching up the teams. Jadyn, you'll be paired with Eldin. Nyree will work with Ardal, and Balum will team with Kagen. Today we begin the replacement and repair of the Solar Panels themselves. Since this is going to take the next three days, you'll no longer be assigned specific areas in the field. Instead, we'll direct you where to go as you work. If there are no questions, you may start your day. Be safe and productive," he says, looking directly at me with the last sentence.

This is not a welcomed change in plans. While working with Nyree, I could focus more on the work itself and avoiding accidents, but now a lot of my attention will have to be given to watching Balum. With her narrowed eyes and obvious frown, I think it is safe to say Nyree is also less than happy with the change. Ardal has been working better than expected, but she knows his nervous affect can easily lead to an accident. Resigned to the new hardship, I walk over to Balum.

"Let's get to work," I tell him as we head toward the stairs.

Back up in the light of the surface, I take a moment to look at the clouds and their varying shapes drifting across the sky. With the angle of the rising sun casting shadows and sprinkling colors on them, the sky looks more like an artist's creation than a physical reality. I turn from my distraction, remembering that today it would be unwise to divert my attention, and walk into the bunker. We pack as much of the equipment into the Grinders as possible before driving into the fields. I do not trust Balum to drive the Grinder, even though it is doubtful he would do anything to endanger himself. Still, there is no reason to take any unnecessary risks.

The controllers direct us to a nearby Solar Panel that needs repair. I park the Grinder near the base and check my equipment before getting started. I look up to the small platform we need to climb onto so we can replace a small section of the panel. It will be challenging getting everything up there.

"I'll carry the tools up. We can hoist the panel up when we get to the base plate. You go first so if anything falls, it won't hit you," I tell Balum while gathering the tools.

He agrees to the plan, likely because it keeps him safe while I do the harder work. Placing the tools in a cloth bag, I sling it over my shoulder and carry it up the ladder with me. My ankle feels stable, and even my aching muscles have improved greatly since the electric shock yesterday. But as soon as I step onto the ladder, a deep burn reminds me that they are nowhere near being fully recovered. After a few steps, the tension in my legs lightens slightly, making the ascent bearable.

In my life, I have climbed more stairs than I could ever count, but none of them were like these. The restriction in movement caused by the bio-suit, combined with the dizzying height of the Solar Panel makes for a frightening climb. For some reason, it feels a lot more intimidating than climbing rock walls in The Caves. It is not only because of my situation and injuries, but also because out here I can see the height so much clearer than in the darkness of The Caves. I continue going up, focusing on one step at a time until the top is near. There is a safety strap and clip attached at our waist that is meant to secure us to the base plate to prevent a fall. Seeing Balum standing on top makes me realize that I should have gone first. He is crowding the entrance and could easily knock me off the platform before I secure myself.

"You're moving too slow. Do you need a hand?" he asks as I approach.

"I got it; just give me some space to get up there," I tell him while motioning for him to back up.

He takes a single step back. Before releasing my grip from the ladder, I lock my legs around the rungs to solidify my position. Now that my legs are firmly holding me in place, I reach out to clip my safety strap to the support above. With the strap is securely fastened, it is safe for me to let go of the ladder and step onto the platform. I force myself to look away from the stunning view of the tree canopy, stretching across the rolling landscape.

"Let's get the replacement panel up, that is, if you're done daydreaming," Balum says.

Ignoring his comment, I place the tools onto the floor and attach the rope that I carried up here to a pulley. The other end is already connected to the panel, so we can hoist it up to us. Balum is as strong as he looks, and it takes little time to get it onto our platform. Balum signals the Controllers to position the panel for repair. With a vibrating, mechanical groan, the enormous panel above moves its angle so that the damaged section is directly over us. I instinctively crouch down though its movement is restricted, so it cannot crush us. Even knowing this, it still feels like it is trying to do just that.

Now that it is close enough to touch, it is easy to distinguish all of the smaller sections of the Solar Panel that make up what looked to be a single piece from the ground. I use one of the electric tools with an impact function to effortlessly shake the bolts free of the locking adhesive so we can remove the individual panel. When the segment is loose, Balum uses another multi-armed tool to deal with the electrical components. He extends the gripping arm, which grabs and cuts the wires. Then another arm adds a connector to the exposed end. Removing the damaged piece is surprisingly fast and sets us up to secure the new piece just as easily.

We gently lower it to the platform and find the source of its defect. There is a small crater formed in the middle of the panel with a feather still embedded in it. This segment was a victim of the falling birds. After securing the replacement in place, we attach the broken segment to the rope to lower it back down to the Grinder. Like most things in Securus, it will be repaired and reused on another detail. With this panel done, we can climb down and move on to the next repair. *If only the rest of the day would go so smoothly,* I think to myself. Just as the thought comes to mind, I look over to see the sinister smile on Balum's face as he starts down the ladder, erasing any hope of a quiet day.

# 25

Balum is the first one to climb down the ladder of the Solar Panel. When he is at the bottom, I begin my own descent. I am still carrying the extra tools, but am prepared to drop them if needed. Balum watches me from the ground. When I get close to the bottom, he starts to speak.

"You know, Kagen, I've heard a lot about you lately from my friends in Leadership. Now that I've met you, I don't understand why there was ever so much concern. But that won't really matter anymore, anyway," he says ominously.

I stop my descent and turn to look back at him. He is pressing some buttons on his bio-suit's control unit. Whatever he is trying to activate, it will not be good for me. I move faster down the steps to get onto solid ground and into a better position to defend myself.

"How's the air up there?" he asks with an arrogant laugh.

"It was just fine until you started blowing so much hot air around," I answer while reaching the bottom of the ladder.

He almost jumps when hearing me answer, then frantically starts fumbling with his control panel again. Again he looks back at me, but nothing happens. I think he expected something to already have happened.

"What's the matter, Balum, having trouble with your controls? I understand. Such complex machinery can be vexing for a mind as simple as yours," I say while cautiously moving past him on my way to the Grinder.

Whatever he was up to, it apparently did not work. From the Grinder, I can see him yelling in his helmet. He must have turned it to a private channel since I can no longer hear him. It is a good thing that I have been switching the bio-suits because it looked like he was trying to activate something in my suit. After he finishes packing the damaged segment into the Grinder, he joins me in the cabin.

"All I meant was that it no longer mattered since we're so far into the detail, so your punishment is almost over. Then everyone can forget the matter. I didn't mean it to sound insulting," he explains meekly.

"It's not really close to complete. I still have another detail to do after this one. But I appreciate the explanation," I tell him.

I do not believe a word he is saying, but it is easier to play along for now. One of the Controllers informs us that the next Solar Panel we need to work on is nearby, so I drive the Grinder in the given direction and unload the tools again to repeat the same process. This time I decide to keep Balum just behind me going up the ladder and close below me going down. This way he cannot cause me to fall without being in danger of being taken down with me.

We climb the ladder, and for once, Balum is silent. The quiet is a nice change, but it makes me worry at the same time. He avoids eye contact with me as we start removing another segment. This time when he finishes setting up the wires to accept the replacement segment, he forgets to retract the tool's working arms before he lowers it. I move to the side to give him room to set the tool down, while continuing to hold the loose segment in place. As I do, my left sleeve is pulled. My eyes dart toward the tugging sensation in time to see that the cutting arm of the tool is extended and has clamped onto the sleeve of my bio-suit with its cutting function starting to engage.

In a panic, I drop the segment. It crashes to the platform, striking Balum and I while ripping my arm free of the tool. We are both knocked off of our feet and if it were not for the safety strap, Balum would have gone over the edge.

Before I can assess my bio-suit for damage, red lights flash inside my helmet and a warning alarm sounds. The words appear in front of me on a display projected onto my visor: *Warning, bio-suit breech. Left arm compartment compromised.*

My entire body tingles with disbelief. How did I not see this coming? I reach for my control panel and activate the tourniquet function to seal my arm off from the inner suit. The pain from the tourniquet collapsing around my upper arm nearly causes me to crumble onto the floor again.

There is still a small chance to save my arm from amputation if I can get into the decontamination chamber in time. That is, unless the tool has cut through the skin or if I hesitated to long to activate it. The lack of blood flow is already numbing my entire arm, so it is impossible for me to feel if it is cut. I try to look for a laceration but although the bio-suit is compromised, it is still intact enough to hide my underlying skin. Everything feels surreal with the blinking lights and numbness in my arm making it feel like it is no longer a part of me.

I force myself to stop trying to analyze my situation, because none of it will matter unless I get back into the decontamination chamber immediately. Even if the compartmentalizing function was successful, if it takes me too long to get back, Securus protocol dictates that the infectious risk is too high, and my reentry will be denied. I get up and move to the stairs. Turning around to get onto the ladder leaves me face to face with Balum, who is now staring at me with a wild look in his eyes. Without a word, he lunges at me. I unhook my safety strap and glide down the stairs as fast as possible, barely in time to avoid his grasp.

I am moving as fast as my limbs will allow, but it is too slow. Needed to increase my speed, I lean toward the left and grip the rail tightly with my good hand while placing both feet on the outside edges of the ladder. Now I am falling with a controlled slide down the ladder. The soles of my shoes are digging into the metal as they burn down the ladder. I can only hope this does not tear all the way through them and compromise another compartment.

I tense my grips to slow my motion down to a safe speed just before reaching the bottom. Still, the force of my landing is too strong and causes me to collapse to the ground. Through the blaring warning signs on my inner visor, still only indicating a single breech, I can see Balum coming down the ladder after me. I get up and sprint to the Grinder without looking back. Once inside, I speed off toward the exit hatch. In my panic, I could only hear the alert from the bio-suit and have been oblivious to the Controllers screaming through my communicator.

"Kagen, what happened? We need you in the decontamination chamber now!" the frantic voice repeats over and over.

"I'm on my way," I finally answer, when the voice penetrates my concentration. The glare of the alarms obscures my vision and makes driving the Grinder much harder than normal.

"You have sixty seconds before the lockout protocol is engaged," Aamon says calmly into the communicator.

The hill covering the bunker is directly in front of me, but there is not enough time. I slam the accelerator to the floor. The Grinders engines release a high pitched squeal as it taps into its maximum power output and starts climbing the back side of the hill. If I am to make it in time, my only option is to go over the bunker instead of around it. I veer off to the left side of the hill, hoping the drop will be lower there than directly over the top of it.

The squeal of the engines reaches an even higher pitch as the wheels pass the edge of the cliff, and I become airborne. My stomach becomes weightless. It feels like I am hanging in the air for an eternity until gravity takes hold and pulls my Grinder crashing into the ground, nose first. The machine lurches forward and threatens to flip before falling backwards and finally coming to a rest. The sudden stop slams my head into the control panel, and my vision explodes with a brief flash of an intense white light. It does not matter because my Grinder has landed right side up and exactly where I had hoped.

I ignore the lightheadedness and black shroud now trying to shield my vision while disconnecting my safety restraints. I fall out of the Grinder as Aamon counts down the remaining time in my ear.

"Ten, nine, eight...," he says with a detached, rhythmic cadence.

I crawl to the exit hatch, open it, and fall in just as he finishes his countdown. Somehow, I manage to twist in mid-air, landing squarely on my back. Surprisingly, at this moment I feel no pain. There is only a euphoric tingling that swims through my body. I made it back and somehow am still alive. Like everything else, this does not last long and the pain soon creeps through me. I crawl into the decontamination chamber and activate it, still unable to lift myself from the floor. This is the first time I have ever been relieved to see the fog of the chamber engulf me.

My mind feels like it is slipping away, but I am still able to set my communicator to broadcast on all channels to make sure everyone knows what really happened. "Balum tried to kill me!" I shout.

When the fog recedes, I try to get up but am forced back down by a team of Leadership personnel. Among them I see Trent, and he has a vaccination gun in his hand. *Great, I escape The Agent only to be delivered to another monster*, I think to myself. Knowing what is in the gun, I lash out at the men, trying to free myself from their grips. It is of no use, I cannot escape them or the injection.

"This is an antiviral medication. It's of limited use against The Agent, but it's better than nothing," Trent yells as he injects the poison into my arm.

It is too late to fight now, and there is no evading my fate, so I stop resisting. My head falls to the side and by the wall I see the same metallic case that he used to carry the new virus to his other victims. Maybe I will be as lucky as Delvin. As they detach my bio-suit and move me to the isolation room, I think of everyone I will be leaving behind. Maybe they can do what I could not. Maybe they will be able to set things right. My biggest fear is that they might follow me to the same fate. I cling to my last shred of hope as the darkness completely envelopes my sight, and I lose consciousness.

*

A faint sound pierces through the rigid silence. It is slow and steady. The mechanical chirp starts to ring louder and louder, echoing within my growing consciousness. It is familiar, but I cannot place it. The rhythmic chirp continues. Slowly, I realize its source. It is a monitor announcing my heartbeat. I normally do not leave the function on because the incessant chirping can be irritating, but now it is one of the most beautiful sounds that I have ever heard. It means that I am still alive. When everything turned dark, I did not expect to ever wake up again. Now that my mind is starting to clear, I wonder how long I was unconscious, and where am I now?

I open my eyes, but can only see the blur of a single bright light overhead. The glare of the light hurts my eyes and adds to the throbbing that is swimming through my head and body. I try to get up, but my movements are restricted by the straps holding me against the gurney. Slowly, my vision begins to form, and I recognize my surroundings as one of the isolation rooms. I could not have been out for a long time otherwise they would have transferred me to the infirmary by now. I struggle against my aching body and bonds that hold me in place. The chirping monitor increases as my pulse hastens from my agitation. It is of no use, the straps are designed for this very purpose, and I am at the mercy of my captor.

In the end, it does not even matter since Trent already injected me with his new virus. It is only a matter of time before I succumb to the disease. Or did my body fight it off, and I am awakening from the delirium as Delvin did? Does my body still ache from the crash in the Grinder and my fall into Securus, or is it the result of a prolonged fight with the virus?

I look around the room, searching for some clue or answer. The only thing visible, other than the blinding light above me, is the blank steel walls. When straining to look behind me, I catch a glimpse of a window in the fringes of my peripheral vision. I try to angle my head for a better look, but it is useless. My movements are too restricted to see anything.

"It's about time you woke up." A soothing voice calls from a speaker perched near the light. It takes me a few seconds to recognize its source. It is Rana!

"Rana, what's going on and why am I tied down?" I call out to the speaker.

"That's more for our protection than yours. When you first got back in, you were attacking everyone around you. Trent's nose will never look the same," she says, not able to mask her amusement even through the speaker.

"How long have I been in here?" I ask.

"It's only been a few hours. Long enough to get the blood tests back, you managed to escape The Agent," she says cheerfully. "Give me a second, I'll have someone come in and release your restraints."

"Tell them to hurry, these things are driving me crazy," I shout back. "By the way, why are you here and not Trent? Not that I mind."

"When I heard what was going on, I insisted on being involved with your care. Plus, Trent did not take the pain of his deformed nose well, so after I set it, he took a handful of painkillers and some sedatives before going to his quarters," Rana explains. "We can talk more when we get you out of there."

The door opens and I hear footsteps approach. Rana's helper silently begins loosening the restraints. Then without explanation, the helper stops. I get an uneasy feeling that this could be one of Aamon's men getting ready to attack. I brace for whatever pain is coming. Instead, I feel a soft hand against my cheek as the helper leans over and looks into my eyes.

"I'm not sure if I should keep you here as punishment for not telling me everything that was going on right away," Talia says with her mischievous smile.

I smile back while looking into her caring eyes. With the bright light above, she looks as though she is glowing. She is my angel coming to set me free. Before I am completely lost in the grace of her beauty, a realization grabs my attention. Mr. Vaden would also have to be aware of everything that happened by now.

"How did you convince your father to let you in here?" I ask.

"I didn't ask him, I *told* him I was coming," Talia answers as she restarts releasing the restraints.

When my arm is free I pull it up to inspect it for damage. It is still partially numb, but there are no lacerations from the incident and above all, it is still attached to me. As I sit up the room starts to spin, making me sick to my stomach.

"You have a concussion, but there is no skull fracture or intracranial bleeding," Rana reassures me as she joins us in the room. "All of your blood tests came out negative as well. So, other than a slew of sprains and muscular injures, you're doing quite well."

"How am I okay? I saw Trent inject me with the vaccination gun. I should be infected by now," I ask Rana.

"He injected you with the gun that I placed into his case. It had a small amount of saline, so all he did was improve your hydration some," she answers.

Neither Talia nor Rana are smiling, and both look concerned. They are troubled and are keeping something from me. It is fitting for me to be in this situation when I have been on the other side of this encounter so often recently. It is rather frustrating and makes me realize I have been torturing Arluin like this for too long. It is time to tell him the truth. I remind myself to do so next time I see him.

"What are you two not telling me?" I ask suspiciously.

"That will have to wait," Talia answers firmly.

"Since your tests were negative, you are no longer confined to the isolation room. I've informed Leadership that we'll be transferring you down to the infirmary for a few more tests," Rana says.

That is good news. In the infirmary my surroundings will be familiar and the people I can trust will be nearby. I try to get up to walk with them, but Rana stops me. She insists that I be wheeled down to the infirmary for my safety. Either she has a concern she has not yet mentioned, or it is part of her ruse to get me out of the isolation room. Regardless of the reason, I know better than to fight her.

When we arrive to the infirmary, I am wheeled into Rana's exam room instead of mine or the intensive care unit. That confuses me because this room is less equipped for additional testing than the others are. They leave me alone and walk back to the intensive care unit to get the equipment Rana needs. After a brief span alone, the door jolts open, but it is not Rana or Talia that walks in.

"Kesia, what're you doing here?" I ask. She is not the person I wanted to see.

"I heard you were injured, and wanted to see how you were doing. You look a lot better than I expected," she says enthusiastically.

I have no patience for her deceit now. Not with everything that has happened in these past few days. I do not even try to think of an excuse to get her to leave because she is too persistent to be dismissed so easily. So, I decide on a far less subtle tactic.

"Hey, something interesting happened," I say as she looks on, anxiously awaiting my next words. "I ran into you father the other day. Not quite what I was expecting, you know, given that he's a little different than you described him."

She looks at me with surprise and horror in her eyes. "I can explain," she pleads, hoping to salvage her lie.

"Don't bother. I'm growing weary of Aamon's little games. Tell him I know you're working for him and that he should be man enough to do his own dirty work," I say, not hiding my contempt for the both of them.

Kesia relaxes and an arrogant smile creeps into the corner of her expression. She no longer looks like the eager but insecure helper I have become used to. Now she looks a lot like Aamon; calculating, pompous, and self-serving.

"Well, I was tired of pretending to be your admiring understudy anyway," she says. "Now I can move on to better things."

"As long as your moving takes you out of this room, that's just fine with me," I say dismissively.

She rolls her eyes and walks away. Even if Aamon knows I have uncovered this part of his ruse, it does not tell him the extent of my discoveries. But at least it rids me of one annoyance so now I can wait in peace for Rana and Talia to return and tell me what is bothering them.

## 26

It is not long before the door to the exam room opens again. This time it is Talia and Rana that enter.

"Why are we in this room instead of one of the others?" I ask when the door is closed.

"Because we need to talk," Talia answers.

"And we know it's safe, otherwise Trent would've known about vaccination gun switch and we wouldn't be here in the first place," Rana adds.

"You finished analyzing the contents in the other guns. I was right, wasn't I? He thought he was infecting me with that virus," I say to Talia.

"Yes and no. He was trying to kill you, but not with the new virus. One of the vaccination guns did have that virus in it, but the other didn't. He thought he was injecting you with The Agent," Talia answers with her voice falling to a whisper.

Her unexpected words stun me. I had known that Trent was being reckless with that virus, but never imagined he would consider introducing The Agent into Securus.

"I haven't told anyone about this yet. I had just received the results and was going to tell my father when Rana got word to me of your incident. So I came here first," Talia reassures me.

"Talia, I know he's your father, but you know there's no way he doesn't know what's going on," I tell her. There is protest in her eyes, but I continue before she can speak. "It's about time you knew the entire truth of what really happened that night in The Caves," I say with my head bowed and eyes fixed on the floor.

I can barely look them in the eyes while telling the story of how Merrick was murdered. There has not been enough time passed to dull the anger and frustration of that night. I tell them about the mysterious rail tracks, the hidden supply room, disappearing equipment, the enigmatic name on the electric grid, and of course about Aamon's spies. After hearing the last part, Rana checks the hallway to make sure Kesia did not come back. She will never be allowed in the infirmary again, but past that, there is nothing else we can do with her unless we finish what I have started. There is an overwhelming silence that overtakes the room. I understand how they feel. What is someone supposed to say to something like that?

"I'm sorry it took so long for me to tell you all of this. I just needed to get enough evidence and make sure no one else was put in danger until I knew what to do. It has been my plan to tell you everything once I figured it out, because the people of Securus deserve to know the truth, and there isn't anyone they would trust more than you, Talia," I say softly, hoping she will accept my apology. "There is one more thing."

"What else could there be?" she asks, clearly frustrated.

"Your father brought me into his office to have a discussion. He implied that he knows what's going on and that my trying to uncover it is endangering Securus," I tell her.

"My father can be rigid and even coldly analytical when needed, but I don't believe he would be actively involved in all of this. Aamon must be misleading him," she rationalizes.

"There's only one way to find out for sure," I say. "When the detail is over, I'm going back into The Caves to get into that supply room. I've been told of a hidden tunnel that can get me in without having to go through the main entrance. After that, we can take everything we have, plus whatever I find there, and present it to him."

"We should tell him now so he can stop whatever they're doing immediately," she demands.

"Talia, I know all of this is completely unexpected and difficult to accept, but we need to be careful. Even if he doesn't know, we need to have irrefutable evidence so Aamon or whoever is behind this cannot twist our words and evidence to make it seem benign. All I ask is for two more days. Please, just wait that long. Then we'll both go directly to him," I plead with her.

There is another prolonged silence. Rana watches us both but does not interfere. Talia has the same look on her face that she gets when she is trying to solve a problem. She is analyzing everything that has been said and deciding what to do. I simply sit and wait, hoping she will agree.

"Okay, two days and two days only. After that I tell him no matter what. There is one condition though," she says, finally breaking the silence.

"Just name it," I agree before even hearing her demand.

"I'm going with you into The Caves," she says.

"No, it's too dangerous, and I'm not going to risk losing you, Talia," I snap back.

"You don't have a choice, I *am* going," she says.

By the look in her eyes, I can tell there is no way for me to stop her. Besides, I had not known how adorable she looked when she gets angry and that cripples my resolve to deny her wishes. Plus, we will not be alone.

Hadwin and Sayda will be with us. She can go, but I will make her wait outside of the tunnel so she will never be anywhere close to those soldiers.

"So stubborn," I say with a smile, trying to ease the tension. "Okay, but if you go, you have to do what I say in there, got it? You can't use that cute, stubborn look to get your way again, it's not fair!"

With that, Rana starts laughing. Even Talia calms down, though she looks slightly frustrated that her angry look made me smile.

"Fine, you're in charge," Talia says. "There is one other minor detail. We need to keep you alive for the next two days. There's no way anyone is going to keep me out of the Control Room now, so at least I can keep an eye on Aamon."

"That'll make me feel a lot safer," I say. "Now, Rana, what tests were we supposed to be doing?"

"I told them we needed to do an abdominal ultrasound and some neurologic monitoring. Looks like we're done with both," she says with a wry smile. "I did arrange for dinner here for you since you can't go to the main hall. After that, you're free until the upper level gets locked down."

"I'm going to stay here as long as possible to get some rest. I definitely need it. Can one of you tell the others where I am?" I ask.

"I'll do it. It'll be less obvious if I'm the one walking around rather than Talia," Rana offers.

Rana helps Talia get me into the gurney before she leaves. I get more of plain gruel for dinner along with plenty of water. It is not an extravagant meal, but more than I need right now. When my meal is finished, I rest my eyes and soon fall into a deep sleep.

My rest does not last long, but I get the most pleasant

wake-up of my life. Talia gently kisses me and whispers in my ear telling me that the others are here. I rise in time to see them walk into the room. My mother nearly cries when she sees me on the gurney. I sit up to try and reassure her that I am alright.

"What happened?" she asks while looking me over.

"I *might* have crashed one of the Grinders. Then I *may have* fallen off a ladder into the exit chamber," I say coyly, trying to keep her from getting too worked up.

Arluin is looking at me expectantly, knowing there is more to the story. I try to ignore it, but this time he does not relent. He stands firm in front of me, waiting for me to continue.

"Okay, Arluin, I was getting ready to tell you anyway," I say giving in.

"Tell him what?" my mother asks.

"That none of this has been an accident, and it's time you both knew why," I confess, and then stop, choking on the words.

It is hard enough to be forced to repeatedly relive everything that happened, but now it is even worse, knowing how my mother will feel about it. Sensing my reluctance to continue, Hadwin starts the story for me.

"It started the night we went to The Caves. After the earthquake, Merrick was trapped and stumbled upon some men with guns. Before we knew what was happening, they shot him. Kagen got our group out of there before they could find the rest of us," he says, making me seem more heroic than what I know is true. "It turns out Leadership is up to something, and they've been covering it up. There's a hidden storage room with stolen electronics from my work as well as a railway that leads deeper into The Caves," he continues.

"Unfortunately, it gets a lot worse than that," Talia

picks up when Hadwin pauses. "Trent Riley instigated the recent outbreak and tried to kill Kagen to cover their tracks."

"I just found out today where he got the virus from. I followed the tracker Rana put in his case to a hidden room in the research labs. After he left, I went in and found an entire storage room full of hazardous viral storage containers. He has an endless supply," Sayda adds.

"I don't know what they're doing, but Merrick didn't deserve to die to keep their secret. I have proof to back up most of those things, but we need to get back to The Caves one more time to find out what they're up to. Then we will make sure everyone knows the truth," I say.

"When are you planning on going," Arluin asks with the obvious intent of joining us.

"Right after I finish the last day of the detail," I answer. Seeing the horrified look on my mother's face, I stop him before he can demand to go with us. "But you can't go, Arluin. There's already too many of us in danger, and we can't afford to let the truth die with us if something happens."

"You can't expect me to do nothing while they try to kill you, Kagen," he argues.

"I don't, otherwise I wouldn't have told you yet. We need you to keep copies of everything in case we are caught. Plus, I need to make sure that we can get to the hidden entrance and into The Caves. Nyree told me she has seen your friend Varian down in the Deep Vents before. Since he apparently knows his way around, I need you both to be lookouts for us when we go down there and to make sure it's safe to reenter when we get back," I say, offering him a limited role that should keep him out of trouble. After noticing the piercing stare from our mother, he agrees to the task.

"I'm sorry Mom, I wanted to tell you, but didn't know how. I didn't want to worry you," I manage to say before my voice gives way.

"You're just like your father, Kagen. I'm proud of you for standing up for what is right and what you believe in," she says. Her response leaves me utterly speechless. That is not at all how I expected her to react. "I won't get in the way, but please, try not to take any unnecessary risks. I can't lose either of you," she says, pulling Arluin and I together to hug us both.

"I have a guardian angel for the rest of my detail, so you don't need to worry," I tell her while looking at Talia.

"I always wondered why you never went for Abira or any of the other girls from our sector," Arluin says with an understanding smile. Talia gets a small wrinkle in her nose when Arluin mentions Abira's name. It seems as if the very sound of that name irritates her. She and Sayda have that in common.

After they have had enough time to come to terms with the disturbing revelations, we discuss the plan for how we are going to approach the reentry and the needed steps after. The hardest part will be how Talia is going to get the message out if her father does not want to cooperate. She does not see this as a potential problem, but I know better. Sayda mentions that the electronics she was tracking stopped in the vicinity of the supply room in The Caves. That is why Hadwin said there were electronics in there. Then it continued deeper into the tunnels until she lost the signal. Wherever it eventually went, it is farther in than I had thought the tracks would lead.

I want to stay in the infirmary for the rest of the night, but it is getting close to lockdown on the upper level, so it is time to leave. It was a lot easier to tell everyone what was happening than I had anticipated. After getting the weighty load off of my shoulders, I feel a little better about what needs to be done. But in the end, it does not change the fact that everyone is in danger. For that, my guilt will never relent unless we can finish what I have started.

After another goodbye, I return to my temporary quarters. When I arrive, Nyree is the only one there. It is good for me that the others are still out on their free time since I do not have the energy to confront Balum right now.

"I was waiting for you to get back," Nyree says as I limp toward my bunk.

"I was trying to get as much rest as possible before coming back," I reply, sitting on the edge of my bunk and facing her.

"A lot happened after your accident," she starts.

"Accident? There was nothing accidental about it," I interrupt. "That was quite deliberate."

"Well, that's what Leadership is calling it, anyway. Balum kind of lost it after that. He was babbling through the communicator, making no sense at all. They said he had an acute stress reaction from the rigors of the detail. I thought he looked psychotic. I'm not sure if they're going to let him continue," she says.

"I'm not that lucky. Everything else is ready, by the way," I say trying not to give away my true meaning in case anyone is listening. "Just that one last piece left."

"I'll get you there soon," she says. "Now, get some more rest; you look like you need it. I'll keep an eye out for a while, until the others are back and asleep."

"Thanks," I say awhile crawling under the inviting blanket to go back to sleep again.

*

The morning comes, and I feel more rested than I have in a while. That is probably because I have been asleep for the better part of the last eighteen hours. I still ache with every movement, but am starting to get accustomed to the constant stiffness. The pain is tolerable enough for me to fight through it for the short time that is left on the detail. Looking around the room, I notice that there are only five of us in here. Balum is conspicuously absent. The others are groggily getting out of their beds and preparing for breakfast. It is a little entertaining to see them fumble around, still half asleep. *This is what Arluin must feel like watching me all the time*, I think to myself.

No one is in a talkative mood this morning, but the others are constantly watching me from the corners of their eyes. It is obvious that all of the accidents that keep following me are more than a coincidence, but no one says it out loud.

At breakfast, we are served a less exceptional but still sizable meal. It consists of some of the pasty gruel that has become the main food source lately with a piece of fresh bread and an orange flavored drink. Needing the energy, I rapidly clean my plate. Afterwards, we all head back to the exit chamber to start the detail. When we arrive, I am met with an unpleasant surprise. Aamon and Balum are both waiting for me next to my changing station. Balum is slouching over, staring at his own feet, while Aamon is his usual annoying self.

"Kagen, we wanted to talk with you before the detail started," he says, nudging Balum to continue.

"I wanted you to know how sorry I am for what happened. I kinda lost it and blacked out. When they told me what happened, I felt terrible about it," Balum says trying to sound apologetic. Do they really think I am that easily fooled?

"Being the youngest member of the detail has taken a toll on Balum. Trent has diagnosed him with an acute stress disorder. As you know, he was not really himself yesterday. But things are better now. He started a medication to help him relax and deal with the stress," Aamon reassures me.

"I'll keep that in mind," I say, knowing every word was a lie. Even if he was medicated, that could make him more dangerous. Being under the influence of mind altering medications is not a good idea when working with the equipment and conditions we are in.

"If it was so bad, why don't you just give him the day off? We can manage without him," I offer.

"He'll be fine, I assure you," Aamon says while motioning for Balum to go and put on his bio-suit. When Balum leaves, he continues in a near whisper, "Just so you know, Kesia was just making sure that you were maintaining an acceptable performance as a Healer. It is a vital function and you have been through a lot lately. It was necessary to have another evaluation because Rana is too attached to objectively assess you."

"Seriously Aamon, you need a better imagination. Your excuses are pathetically transparent. Now, if you don't mind, I have another vital function to prepare for," I say, unable to contain my contempt for him any longer.

He gives a dismissive smile and simply walks away. *Here we go again. He has something else planned*, I think to myself.

## 27

As soon as Aamon leaves, I again switch my bio-suit, knowing that either of them could be tampered with. The one I had on yesterday had to be replaced because of the damage. So my options are to either use the new one or the one that was originally intended for me. If they try anything it should be with the new suit, at least that is what I am hoping. When we are all dressed, Aamon reappears but this time he is not alone. Talia enters the room with him, much to the surprise of everyone except me. Just seeing her calm determination gives me strength.

"Okay, everyone, there will be new teams for today. Jadyn and Nyree will work together. Eldin, you're with Ardal and Kagen is again with Balum," Aamon says. "Let's try to make it through the day without another incident. Be safe and productive."

Talia gives an incredulous look to Aamon when she hears the last sentence. Apparently I am not the only one who notices his penchant for trying to imitate her father.

"Balum, I'll be keeping an eye on you. If you step out of line even once, I'll make sure you regret it," Talia says in an icy tone that I had not even known she was capable of. She must have learned that from her father.

Balum nods in understanding and along with the others, waits for me to walk to the exit hatch first. I try to appear confident on my way to the ladder and while climbing to the surface. With everything that has happened, I no longer have any desire to enjoy the scenery of the surface. Instead, my thoughts are focused on what could be planned for the day. I must stay vigilant, because there is no question that it is only a matter of time before they try something else.

Like before, we start by retrieving our charged Grinders from the bunker. It is easy to find mine, since it is the only one with a caved-in and mangled front end. Luckily, the damage is only cosmetic and the machine itself is still functional. We pack our equipment and drive out of the bunker to start the day. The Solar Panel that we are directed to is near the center of the field and close to the panels that the others will be working on. I get out of the Grinder to start unpacking the tools and equipment.

"Why do you continue working on this detail? Why not just admit it's too much and plead for Leadership to relieve you?" Balum asks while still sitting in the cab of our Grinder.

"Because we have a duty to the people of Securus, and I do not hide from my responsibilities," I answer. "It's called pride and discipline. Maybe you'll learn about those things someday."

"I'm growing tired of your insubordination toward Leadership," he says, getting out of the Grinder.

I do not like where this is going. He must have turned his communicator to a private channel otherwise Talia would have said something by now. I look around and notice that for the first time, there are no cameras around. We are in a blind spot. When he comes into view in the periphery of my vision, there is something in his hand. From this angle, it looks like a spear. I am careful not to look directly at him, so he is unaware that his weapon has been revealed.

Subtly, I try to activate my communicator to call for

help, but it has been disabled. Apparently I chose the wrong bio-suit. I take a deep breath and try to look for a way to defend myself. There is nothing out here except the tools we brought. Moving to the pile of equipment, I make sure to keep him just at the edge of my vision. Most of the tools are useless as a weapon or for defense. The only viable option is the replacement Solar Panel segment. I pull it out and pretend to start tying it to the rope. Balum has slipped behind me, but I am intentionally facing away from the Sun. His long shadow tells me exactly what he is doing. My adrenaline surges as he draws near. His shadow raises the spear in a position to strike.

Balum lets out a yell as he plunges the spear down, aimed at my back. I dodge to the side and try to catch the spear in my shield, but he pulls back at the last moment. We face each other and he circles around, looking for another opening to attack. While mirroring his movements and keeping my shield between us, I see someone else coming in the distance. I really hope it is Nyree, because if it is Eldin, any chance there is for me to make it through this will be erased.

Balum again lunges at me with his spear. I step slightly to the side and angle my shield to deflect the blow. Even with the shield, I cannot keep doing this for long. Eventually he is going to connect with one of his thrusts. I try to control my breathing and conserve my limited energy. There is nowhere to escape to, so I watch his eyes and try to anticipate his next move. He looks disoriented and even downright psychotic through his tinted visor. Nyree might have been right about him. That makes him even more dangerous and tells me I need to do something, fast.

Without any other options, I do the first thing that

comes to mind. Releasing a guttural scream, I attack. He is surprised by the aggressive move and is slow to react. By the time he raises his spear to defend himself I am already bringing down my shield onto his arms and knock the weapon from his grip. The thud of contused flesh and crack of breaking bone rings through the air with the blow. Before he has a chance to regain his balance, I leap onto him. We both fall to the ground and struggle to gain a superior position. The ground and sky spin in my vision as we wrestle for an advantage. Somehow, I manage to get on top of him and lock my legs around his to secure myself. He continues flailing at me, ignoring his broken arm.

Needing to break his will to fight, I sit up in a better position to attack. Avoiding the harder helmet, I focus on his exposed ribs and reign down blow after blow. The rage that has been building since the night Merrick was murdered is taking over. All I see while pummeling Balum are the soldiers that killed Merrick and Aamon's conniving face. The only thing that stops me from completely losing control are the same crunching and nauseating grinding that I have felt while trying to save lives with chest compressions. Except this time, I feel it as Balum's ribs crumble against the savage onslaught of my blows. Even though Balum deserves to be punished, I need to control myself and calm my emotions. I stop my attack and hold him down, while trying to catch my breath.

The other person coming is now close enough to see. To my relief it is Ardal and not Eldin. Balum is no longer resisting, so I get off of him and grab the rope to tie him up. I can already hear Aamon's explanation of how Balum had a psychotic reaction to the medications.

"What happened?" Ardal asks as he approaches.

"Balum lost it, he tried to spear me. Help me tie him up. Then we can return him to Securus. He needs to get to the infirmary," I say. It is a good thing that Ardal is here because now that I am starting to calm down, my body feels broken.

"Okay, hold him still and I'll tie up his legs," Ardal offers. "I can't believe he flipped out."

Carefully, I circle Balum and fall back on him before he can try to kick me. Surprisingly he still does not resist. The broken arm and ribs have finally taken the fight out of him. As Ardal binds Balum's feet, I sit on the ground, needing the rest. There is a shuffling sound behind me. I look back to check Ardal's progress in time to see the segment that was my shield come crashing down onto my helmet with a resonating blow that blurs my vision. Falling to the ground, I can only hear a ringing in my ears and cannot see past my visor. The disorientation is brief, but lasts long enough for Ardal and Balum to get into position over me.

"Did you really think I was all alone out here, Kagen? You're not as smart as you think," Balum laughs. His smile is ghastly, showing the moist glistening of fresh blood stains covering his teeth. I see more movement as another person approaches from behind them. Eldin is coming to join them. I might have had a chance against the two of them, but with Eldin helping, my chances are rapidly diminishing. I try to slowly back up and keep them busy while searching for a way to escape.

"I knew you would have help, Balum, there's no way they would trust someone so incompetent to do anything by himself," I say, getting to my feet. Ardal anticipates my plan and moves to cut me off from the Grinder.

"You're so sure of yourself, Kagen. Don't you realize that it's over? Even if by some miracle you get away from us, Aamon will never let you back into Securus. You're locked out," Ardal says.

"We'll see about that," I say. "He isn't alone in that Control Room today." Balum moves in closer to Ardal and they tense up as they prepare to attack.

"Are you going to call Eldin to come save you now?" I taunt them, trying to stall for a moment longer.

Ardal laughs, "That brute. He's too thick to realize what's going on. He never even figured out that I rigged his Grinder with a remote control to make him run you over. My aim was a little off, but I can fix that mistake now."

His words confuse me. Eldin did not try to kill me? Then why is he standing with them right now? I look again and realize that he is not standing with them, but *behind* them. They are not even aware of his presence.

"Is that so?" Eldin asks.

His voice startles the other two long enough for me to react. I do not know whose side Eldin is on, but right now it does not matter. I jump to my feet and kick Ardal square in the chest. He was already unbalanced because of the distraction, so the blow knocks him into Eldin and they both fall.

I turn to run for the Grinder, only to find it is farther than expected. I sprint as fast as my legs can carry me toward its shelter, and for some reason, the others are not following. When reaching the Grinder, I jump inside and attempt to power on the engine, but it does not respond. I try again to engage the machine, but it remains lifeless. No wonder they were in no hurry to run after me, Ardal must have tampered with this Grinder as well. I cannot sit in here and wait for them to surround me. My only choices are to face them here or try to make it back to the exit chamber.

I get out and look for an opening. It looks like the others are helping each other get to their feet. Why are they still not coming after me? I soon realize why. Ardal and Balum are attacking Eldin instead of trying to help him to his feet.

I race back to them. Ardal turns in time to see me coming, but he is not fast enough to avoid the blow right in the soft spot between his stomach and chest. He collapses to the ground in a panic, unable to breath. Alone, he is easily controlled. Without Ardal helping, Eldin quickly subdues Balum as well. I get the rope and tie both of them together.

"I thought you were with them," I tell Eldin while securing the two attackers.

"You really don't remember me, do you?" he asks.

"I knew you were familiar, but couldn't place where or when we've met before," I say.

"Two years ago, we met in the infirmary," he explains. "My mother had a bad accident, and you saved her life. I volunteered for this detail after your punishment was announced figuring if the chance arose, I could pay you back for what you did for us."

The memory floods back as he speaks. His mother was caught under some large equipment that had fallen over during an earthquake. By the time she got to me, she was near death from a ruptured spleen. She barely made it through the surgery but did end up recovering over the next few weeks.

"I remember her alright," I say. "She was such a strong fighter. Apparently you got that from her. Thank you for helping me. Does your communicator work? Mine has been disabled."

"Yeah, it works fine. Should I tell the Controllers what happened?" he asks.

"No, they'll find out soon enough. Can you get Nyree over here? Use a private channel though," I tell him.

*

Either Eldin told Nyree what happened, or Jadyn really annoyed her because when they arrive, Jadyn is tied up to the back hatch of the Grinder.

"Real subtle, Nyree," I say, trying not to laugh at the sight of Jadyn as a decoration on Nyree's Grinder.

"I didn't want any problems," she says. "What's the next move?"

"I can't risk this detail anymore. I need to go to The Caves now, before Aamon realizes his plan has failed again. Can you show me that entrance or at least give me some good directions?" I ask.

"Umm, what exactly is going on?" Eldin asks.

I give him a shortened explanation of the situation while we tie Jadyn up to the other two. I do not know or care if she is involved, but we cannot afford to trust her right now. We pack into Nyree's Grinder and drive back to the exit hatch, leaving the trio for Leadership to save later. As we drive, Aamon's voice fills the Grinder through its inbuilt speakers instead of our communicators.

"What's going on, and why aren't you working, Nyree?" he demands.

"Jadyn had a bit of an issue, and I need to get her back into Securus," she tells him.

"Negative, no reentry until you tell me exactly what happened," he insists.

We are getting close to the chamber. As soon as I get out of the Grinder he will see me and know what is happening. I whisper for Nyree to make sure Talia is listening.

"This sort of issue would be better understood by

another woman," Nyree explains. "Is Talia Vaden there?"

"I'm here, Nyree. What's wrong?" Talia's voice responds through the speakers, strengthening my hope.

"Talia, make sure that hatch is unsealed. I'm coming in now," I yell to her as we all jump out of the Grinder and run to the hatch.

I grab the handle and turn it to open the portal, but it does not budge. If Talia cannot get this unlocked, all three of us will die. We look around to see if there is a way to pry the hatch open, but there is nothing strong enough to penetrate it. Eldin and I try again. This time the handle turns and is followed by a hiss of air as the pressure releases from the opening. We are in, now we need to make it pass the Guards that will be coming any moment.

There is no time to change out of our bio-suits, but we still must pass through the decontamination chamber. It will cost us precious time, but I will not risk exposing the entire colony to The Agent for our own self-preservation. Just as we exit the decontamination chamber the door to the hallway opens. We get in position to fight, but instead of the Guards that I expected, Talia bursts into the room.

"We have no time; the Guards are on their way," she says in broken words, trying to catch her breath.

"I have an idea. Eldin, turn your communicator on and run down the hallway. Pretend like you're talking to us and don't realize you left the communicator on. It may give us enough time to escape," I tell him, hoping he will not object.

"Okay, good luck," he says to us and runs out into the hall. I can hear him ranting as he disappears around the corner, "What the hell is going on and why are we running? Kagen, you're not making any sense; we should wait for Leadership to…"

Talia, Nyree and I go in the opposite direction and start to make our way down toward the Deep Vents.

"We need Hadwin, or this is going to be useless. The rocks in the tunnel are too large for us to move alone," I say as we rush down the stairs.

"That's taken care of. When I left the Control Room, I instructed Cyrina to have him meet us down there," Talia says.

"I'm glad you were more prepared for this than me. How did you even get out of there with Aamon around?" I ask.

"When I unlocked the exit hatch he tried to have me detained, but the only Guard that was in there is my friend and he refused. After that, Aamon tried to grab me himself, so I kicked him in the groin and ran out," she answers in a calm tone, as if it were no big deal.

"I can't even count how many times I owe you now," I say, wishing I was there to see that happen.

"I'm just trying to keep you alive so I can collect," she answers.

The trip down is surprisingly quiet. There are no Guards following us yet. I hope Eldin did not get injured distracting them for us. Every surveillance camera we pass makes me cringe. It is only a matter of time before they realize where we are, but they have no way of knowing where we are going. It is a small advantage, but we will take anything we can get.

## 28

As we move down the stairway near the entrance to the Deep Vents, muted voices become audible from below us. We slow down and strain to hear the words. When we get a little closer, I recognize the voices.

"Hadwin, Sayda? It's us. Did anyone see you guys come down here?" I ask.

"No, I don't think so. When this is over, we need to talk about your planning and getting your watch fixed. This is not exactly on schedule," Hadwin says with a reassuring smile.

"Nyree, are you coming with us or are you staying in Securus?" I ask.

"I'm coming with you. If they catch me here, there's nowhere else to go except the Detention Center," she says.

"Okay, we need to move fast; don't stop for anything. Just get in the tunnel and go. Is everyone ready?" I ask.

I look everyone in the eyes one last time. They are all prepared to continue. Nyree is the first to exit the stairs and the rest of us follow her. Talia is careful to stay between Hadwin and Sayda to decrease the chances of her being noticed. I follow behind the group, keeping watch.

We pass through a short and narrow hallway that looks like any other in Securus before we can enter the main chamber. Nyree uses her identification code to open the door. Inside, it looks more like The Caves than a part of Securus. We enter a chamber with a highly vaulted ceiling and jagged rock walls all around, except for the steel wall of the entrance. The biggest difference from The Caves is that all of the natural formations have been cleared. We head directly toward the massive, metal spires that have been built around the thermal vents. The sheer size of these energy harnessing machines rivals that of the Solar Panels above. While we march, my eyes follow the spires high above, where the towers taper and merge with the rock ceiling into elaborate channels that ultimately vent on the surface. Even with the surface vents, we are not in danger of being exposed to The Agent down here because the pressure and constant flow of the rising hot air prevents any backflow. I am thankful for that, because the recent events brought me far closer to The Agent than I ever wish to be again.

The other thing that strikes me is the relative lack of workers. I had expected it to be teeming with activity, but there are only a few scattered workers in the distance. I suppose it is a fortuitous break, since we can make it through unnoticed even in our bio-suits. We stop at a work station set up near one of the closer towers to grab some extra illuminators and tools.

"Look over there," Nyree says, pointing to the far end of the chamber. "If you follow that tower halfway up and look where the stairs go next to the rock wall, you can see a dark spot under a ledge. That's where we're going."

My eyes follow her extended finger to the tower and the spiraling stairs wrapped around it. The stairs are normally used by the workers for maintenance of the inner turbines that harness power from the movement of the heated air, but for us they are an escape route. She was right about it being completely hidden. From here, the spot she is pointing at looks like just another shadow on the wall. That gives me hope we can make it out and back without Leadership finding our portal.

We continue toward the hidden tunnel. To get there, we need to walk in the open, and when we do, the workers on the other side of the chamber notice our unusual group for the first time. Like Nyree, most of the workers in the Deep Vents keep to themselves, so I doubt they would be in a rush to report us to Leadership. Still, I urge the others to move quicker. The area still looks clear when we near the base of the stairs. As we are about to reach the stairs, a voice calls out to me.

"Going somewhere, Kagen Meldon?" the man says is a mocking tone.

I turn around and almost stumble from the shock of seeing a group of Leadership Guards waiting in ambush for us. How did they know we were here, and how did they get into position so fast?

"Just going for a stroll," I say casually, trying to stall as we back toward the stairs. They were waiting for us, but they do not know our escape plan. Otherwise, the tower would have been blocked. Standing firm, I nudge Talia and Sayda up onto the stairs. I can feel Hadwin and Nyree standing next to me facing the Guards. They form an arc around us, blocking what they think is our only escape.

"You have nowhere to go, release your hostage and then we can calmly talk this over," the lead Guard offers.

So, Mr. Vaden has declared his daughter my hostage now. That is clever. For all of his faults, it is obvious that he does love his daughter and keeps trying to protect her.

"We're gonna talk it over a bit, I'll be with you in a minute on that," I say, now backing onto the steps.

It is too narrow to stand together now, so I push Hadwin behind me and motion for him to get the others into the passage. If I cannot make it, at least I can hold the Guards long enough so the others can. I take a deep breath and prepare to attack. Before I can make a move, Nyree does. She charges them without saying a word. Her unexpected move startles them long enough for her to crash into the lead Guard.

"Go, Kagen, go!" she shouts as the other Guards pile on top of her. I try to move but cannot. I am torn between helping Nyree and returning to The Caves. The sight of her being attacked by the Guards sickens me, and I want to fight back. But logically, I know the only way to help her now is to finish what we have started.

Reluctantly, I turn to race up the stairs. I circle around, out of view of the Guards. Even this close the passage would be hidden from me except I can see Hadwin inside, waiting for us to follow. I climb onto the outer edge of the stairs and leap into the passage. While I am in the air, a gunshot rings out. *Not again*, the words roar in my mind. As soon as my feet touch ground, I turn to jump back to the stairs. Before I can, two hands pull me back into the tunnel and force me to the ground with surprising strength. Hadwin is stopping me from going back. He could not have seen what happened, but the sound of the gunshot told him everything he needed to know.

"We need to keep moving. We can't help Nyree unless we keep moving," he says while pulling me further in the tunnel.

After stumbling backwards through the tunnel, I finally turn to face him, knowing he is right. There is nothing I can do back there now. She could have been shot, or they might have been shooting at me. Either way, the only real option we have is to continue. I follow him through the darkness of the tunnel, trying to catch up to the others.

"Did you see what happened?" he asks as we crawl.

"She bought us some time. We both had the same plan, but she acted first," I say remorsefully. "I didn't see the shot though."

Hadwin does not question any more now. This far in, it should be safe to turn on our lights without giving away our position. He turns on his illuminator, and I activate the external lights of my bio-suit. The tunnel gets bigger, allowing us to stand just as we are faced with a choice of four paths. There is nothing distinctive about any of the tunnels.

"Should we split up?" Hadwin asks.

"No, look there," I tell him pointing to the ground. There is only one path has tracks, telling us that someone has been through here before. "They went this way."

We continue to climb and crawl our way upward. I do not say it out loud, but I hope the tracks were there before Sayda and Talia went through there or we could be lost. I take the lead since the bio-suit gives me more protection and its lights are even brighter than Hadwin's illuminator. Soon, we reach another divergence and stop to look for more tracks.

"Where is Nyree?" Talia asks, emerging from the shadows.

My heart jumped into my throat when I heard her voice. Hadwin was just as scared and almost fell over. We had not seen either of them hiding in here.

"She attacked the Guards before I could stop her," I say, unable to look Talia in the eye.

"Well, then we must make sure her sacrifice is not wasted," Talia says resolutely. She understands even more than the rest of us what Nyree's actions mean. Attacking the Leadership Guard is an action that will be punished severely, if she is even alive to be punished.

"Okay, let's keep moving," Sayda says.

She leads us to the next path, following more tracks in the dirt. With our quick pace, it is not long before we hear running water. We dim our lights as we emerge into a large cavern that contains one of the fishing pools.

"I know this area; we're close to the main chamber just outside of Securus. It's still closed down because of the quarantine," Talia whispers.

"Good, I need to stop for a minute and get this bio-suit off. It's too bulky for the narrow tunnels we have left, and I probably couldn't climb that last rock wall in it, either," I say.

No one objects. They all look as though they need a brief rest as much as I do. We drink some fresh water from the pools, and I share the stored nutrient mix from my bio-suit before we leave it behind and continue on. This path is becoming familiar to me and is getting easier to manage with low lights. Even though The Caves are closed, some of the Leadership Guards could be in here, so I remain on guard.

We are still alone by the time we reach the entrance to Merrick's cavern. After fastening the tools we acquired from the Deep Vents in preparation, we go to the rock wall. With the experience of my other two climbs I have found a good path that should be safe for us to follow.

"Ready to try again?" I ask Sayda, and instantly regret my poor choice of words.

"I'll be fine," she says, shooting me an annoyed look at the mention of her previous incident.

"Talia, you wait here and keep watch. We'll go up and get what we can," I tell her. I can see her formulating an argument for why she needs to go, but before she starts, we are both interrupted.

"Kagen, stop being overprotective," Sayda scolds me. "She has every right to see for herself what's going on."

Hadwin stands with Sayda and though he does not speak, it is obvious that he agrees with her. I try to find a reason why it would be better for Talia to wait, but there is no excuse that they would accept. I reluctantly agree, and we prepare for the climb.

I go first to lead them to the safest path. Talia goes next, followed by Sayda and Hadwin. I move deliberately, making sure that each hand and foothold is secure enough for the others. Talia eyes are wide, and she is silent as she climbs. Soon, I am up on the ledge and turn to help the others climb up. Talia looks to be in a trance-like state as she moves. Apparently, she really is afraid of heights. When Sayda and Hadwin get safely up, we stop to catch our breath.

"We have to be careful in there. Keep the lights low. If you hear any sounds, turn the lights off and hide," I instruct before we continue.

I make Talia and Sayda stay behind Hadwin and me, despite their vigorous protests. At least Hadwin supports me with this demand. We slowly make our way through the winding passage until we come to the wall of fallen rocks. I show them the smaller rocks that Leadership stacked, solidifying the edge of the wall as well as the locations of the hidden doors.

"That's where we can get through. But once we open a path, there's nothing to keep those soldiers away from us," I warn them.

Hadwin takes the pry bar he has been carrying and positions it to wedge the rocks loose. I give Sayda and Talia some hammer-like tools to hold. The tools will not help move the rocks, but can be used as weapons if needed. With Hadwin and me pulling on the lever, the boulder starts to move. We rock it back and forth until there is enough momentum to finally jar it loose. The rock was supporting a larger piece of the wall than we realized and with it removed, an entire section collapses with it. The rocks fall to the ground with an exploding cannonade that reverberates through the tunnels.

"If the soldiers are anywhere close, they had to have heard that," Hadwin laments.

We retreat outward through the tunnel and wait to see if they appear. After an eternity in the cold, dark silence, we decide it is safe to go back in. The dust has settled, making it easier to climb through the hole in the barrier and into the opposite chamber. I look for the hidden lever the soldiers used to open the door to the tracks, but cannot find it. Everything on the wall just looks like normal rocks and mineral deposits. Not wanting to waste time, so I move to the storage room. The lever is easy to find since I saw them activate it before. I reach up and push on the protruding rock. There is a muted, mechanical hum as the door opens.

The others are stunned at the sight of the cave wall opening into a doorway. When it fully opens, the internal lights activate. Now that I can finally see the inside, it looks nearly identical to the storage room in Securus that Talia had brought us to, with piles of various pieces of Hadwin's electronics. The one big difference is the armored gear for the soldiers. Looking at the inside walls, I notice an activation switch just inside the door that must be another mechanism to control the door. I am drawn to the table with the soldier's gear and shuffle through the drawers. Inside is an assault rifle that is a duplicate of the ones that the soldiers carry.

"This is what they used," I say, showing the gun to the others.

Hadwin grabs the gun and hold it up to get a better look. "It looks like it needs to be manually activated. There's a slot here for some kind of key," he says to my disappointment.

He takes it out to the rubble and tries to shoot it. As he suspected, it does not work. Even if we cannot use the weapon, it may work as a deterrent and will be useful to show the people what is hidden out here. The contents of the supply room will be helpful, but do not give me the answer I was looking for. I still have no idea what they are doing out here. While we are walking back toward the supply room, there is a faint vibration in the ground. I start to brace myself, expecting another earthquake until I notice that a part of the wall is moving.

"Get inside, they're coming," I warn the others and dart onto the supply room.

I activate the internal lever and the doors close, encasing us inside. We all find separate hiding areas to wait out the soldiers. After a period of silence, there is a muffled blast of a rifle coming through the walls. They had to have found the opening in the rubble. Hopefully they will decide it was just a natural occurrence. After a few more minutes, as expected, the door to the supply room begins to open. We just need to hide long enough to convince them that no one has been here. I hold my breath as one of the soldiers walks past me. He looks around and walks over toward the stored gear.

"Did you leave the rifle out," the soldier growls to the other. My muscles tense at the sound of his voice. It is the same man as before, the one that killed Merrick. This time there is no wall to separate us. If we are found, they will do the same to us. A mixture of fear and rage surges within me. Despite the danger, I have to fight the overwhelming urge to attack them.

"No, I put it in its case," the mechanical man responds.

He comes in to investigate and from my hiding spot, I can see both of the men examining the gear. They raise their rifles and start to search the area. *Stay calm and quiet*, I tell myself and try to project the thought to the others.

"I can see you behind that table, come out or I will shoot," the mechanical man demands.

To my horror, Talia stands up and faces the man with her arms raised in surrender, just as Merrick had that night. His murder replays in my mind as I see the men train their guns on Talia. I start to get the same helpless feeling as before, except this time there is no rock wall blocking me. Without a plan, I spring out of my hidden position behind the men and charge them. It seems futile, but I have to try to save her. I could not bear to watch her die as I did Merrick.

The soldiers are focused on Talia and do not see me coming soon enough to get out of the way. The force of my collision knocks the soldier on the left into the wall head first. He bounces back and crumbles to the floor with his rifle lodged under him. I turn to the other startled soldier to attack, but he has already steadied himself and is aiming his weapon at me. Talia shouts out for the soldier to stop, but he ignores her plea and pulls the trigger.

I see a shadow behind the rifle followed by an intense blast of light. The next thing I know, I am on the ground, stunned from the impact and cringing from the wave a pain that swells through me. There are loud yells and grunts all around me in the room. I shake the haze of confusion and force myself to get up. There is no time to look at my wound, even if I am to die, there is still a chance to save the others first. Hadwin is already on top

303

of the soldier who shot me, rabidly flailing at him. Sayda flies past me to help Hadwin and starts to wrestle the rifle from the soldier's hands. I look back at the other soldier and see Talia trying to pry the rifle lose from under him, but he is starting to regain consciousness.

I jump on top of him before he can get up and start smashing the back of his helmet with the first solid object that my hands find. Stunned by the blows, his handle on the gun weakens and Talia is able to pry it from his grips. She hands it to me, and I turn to the others. Hadwin is trying to keep the soldier on the ground, but he is nearly upright. The soldier lands an elbow to Hadwin's midsection that frees him from his grasp and gives him enough leverage to pull his rifle back from Sayda. He turns toward Hadwin and starts to raise his weapon.

"Stop," I yell as he stands over Hadwin, poised to shoot.

The soldier ignores me and his finger reaches for the trigger. There is another flash of light as the soldier falls to the floor, limp and lifeless. It was my gun that fired first. I could not let him take another life. I turn to the remaining soldier and motion for Talia to stand clear.

"Get up," I shout at the man as he struggles to gain his balance.

"Okay, I surrender," the mechanical man says when he sees the rifle pointed at his head.

While I focus on this soldier, Hadwin checks the fallen one. He confirms that the shot was indeed lethal. I step back to a safe distance while keeping aim on the man with the mechanical voice.

"Are any of you injured?" I ask.

"We're all okay, some bumps and bruises, but nothing permanent," Hadwin assures me, still catching his breath.

"Grab the gun, I need to see where I was shot," I tell

him.

"Umm, Kagen, you weren't shot," Hadwin laughs.

"I saw the blast and was knocked to the floor. How else did that happen?" I argue while searching for my wound.

"That was the work of our little spider monkey," he says, still chuckling. "When you attacked, Sayda and I came out of hiding to help. I tried to get his gun, but wasn't fast enough. Sayda tackled you just in time."

It feels embarrassing to realize that I had mistaken the jolt from Sayda as a gunshot. The pain must have been from my already sore body absorbing the impact of the fall. But it is better to be embarrassed than shot. Still shaking and nervous from the adrenaline, I go over to look at the dead soldier. He is much less intimidating now than what I remember. With the other soldier captured, it is about time we found out what they are doing out here.

## 29

"What's your name?" I ask the soldier. For the first time, the image on the chest plate of his armor is clearly visible, and I was right. It is an eight pointed sun but is different than our Leadership insignia. There is no biohazard symbol, and the color of the glowing sun seems more intense. I am not sure what to make of it.

"Kerad," he answers.

"What are you doing out here?" Talia demands.

"We were guarding the tracks," he says.

"You're going to have to tell us more than that," I say.

"You don't know what you're dealing with," he replies.

"Try us," Sayda hisses.

"Do you really think you're alone here?" he says, mocking us. "We protect the tracks to Munitus. We can't have your groups interacting, so we monitor the tracks."

"What is Munitus?" Talia asks.

"Another facility, just like Securus," he answers.

His words twirl through my mind, making me feel dizzy. We are not alone. There is another facility, and that is why his insignia is different than ours. When I had thought of the potential reasons for the tracks, this never felt like a real possibility. I thought that Leadership was trying to build its own secret lair or was stockpiling precious resources for their own use.

"If there are others, then why is it being kept a secret, and why are we being kept separate?" I ask.

"I have told you all I can. You can threaten my life all

you want, but they will kill my entire family. You have no power over me. So do what you must, but I'm done talking," he says with a conviction that I do not doubt.

"That's still not good enough," Talia tells him.

"You can ask your father the rest, Talia Vaden," Kerad snorts.

His recognition of her leaves Talia speechless. There is no denying Mr. Vaden's involvement any more. Of all of the surprises I have had, this is the most difficult to comprehend. There is another facility, and Mr. Vaden knows about it. By the way Kerad was speaking, there could even be more. He did say *'we can't have the groups interacting.'*

Kerad stops speaking, so we decide to return to Securus, We bind Kerad and leave him in the supply room until we can come back for him. Before we leave, we strip away both of the soldiers' weapons and armor for Hadwin and me to use. They can help us on our return and I do not want to chance him getting free to use them against us. I look at him for the first time without his intimidating helmet and mask. I do not know what I expected, but it feels surprising that he looks like an ordinary man. He stands taller than the rest of us, but is not built much differently. In a way, he looks a lot like many of our workers, with a tired brow and face than has seen more years in the past than he has left in the future.

I turn away from the soldiers, and we leave the supply room. Closing the door behind us effectively entombs Kerad in the room with his fallen partner. One of us will return for him later and if we cannot, the punishment for his treachery will be to forever remain in this room. There is no point in trying to follow the tracks now since we know where they lead. We can explore them another time if we are successful in our return. Now, we need to get back to Securus to finish what we started.

No one knows what to say as we travel back toward the fishing pools. This discovery is more significant than any of us could have anticipated, and I still do not completely understand it. I am excited to learn that we are not alone but frightened by the possibilities of how this forced isolation came to be. Whatever the ultimate reason for the deception, Mr. Vaden is the only one who can reveal the truth to us now.

I look over to Talia. She is silently trudging forward with an absent stare, not speaking a word to anyone. She was rocked by Kerad's words, and is lost in her own mind. Though I knew she would have to eventually face the truth that her father was not oblivious to these events, there was no way to know how she would ultimately react to it. I know she is strong enough to overcome this, but seeing her plunged this deep into distress magnifies my own emotions.

I try to break from the confusion and focus on our next step. I am sure that the Leadership Guards figured out where our tunnel is, leaving us with no safe point of reentry. I have no ideas on how we can all make it back in without being captured immediately. If we cannot make it safely back in, then all of this will have been for nothing, and no one will ever know the truth.

"So, how are we supposed to get back in Securus? The Guards have to be watching our tunnel in the Deep Vents," Hadwin asks.

We all know Securus was designed as an impenetrable fortress. There are no other entrances, and I am left with no other option. "There's only one way. We don't all need to go back in. I can go and give up my hostage," I say, motioning to Talia. "They'll finally have their target, and Talia will be free to set things right while they're distracted with me."

"I don't like that idea at all. They've already tried to kill you so many times, what would keep them from finishing the job before Talia could stop them?" Sayda says.

"Well, anyone else have a better idea?" I ask. Both Hadwin and Sayda are silent, knowing there is no other way but not wanting to accept it.

"I do," Talia says to our surprise, momentarily breaking through her mental anguish. "I figured we might have this problem. So I came prepared."

I wrap my arm around Talia and pull her close to me. She is still distracted by her thoughts and barely seems to see us as she speaks. I want to help her, but what can I do? Her own father is in control of this whole sordid mess. There is nothing I can do to change that. I place a gentle hand on her cheek and turn her to look in my eyes.

"Talia, I'm sorry how this is turning out. I just want you to know that no matter what, I'm here for you," I say gently.

She rests her head on my shoulder and embraces me. Tears pour out as she finally embraces the truth. We all sit, silently sharing in the devastation of these events. After a few minutes, she lifts her head and looks back into my eyes. There is a small glimmer of her strength returning of her eyes. She kisses my cheek and then steps back, pulling something from her pocket.

"Your little brother is relentless. He came to see me, and I agreed to give him a communicator in case we needed help when we went into The Caves. I guess it's a good thing he didn't wait until the detail was over. Let's find out who's waiting for us," she says, giving me the communicator.

I activate it and call out to my brother, "Arluin, are you there?"

"Yeah, I'm here. You guys are in serious trouble. Mr. Vaden did a special announcement saying you abducted Talia. Everyone is looking for you," he says.

"That doesn't matter. I need you to find out how many Guards there are in the Deep Vents. Have Varian check, if they see you there, they'll get suspicious. We're ready to come back in, but they saw us leave. We're trying to figure out a new plan," I tell him.

"Okay, I'll let you know as soon as I can," he says.

With nothing else we can do, we sit and wait for Arluin to tell us what we are facing. Talia and I sit together with her leaning against me. I rest my cheek against her head while the others and try to think of an alternative plan. Hadwin is staring at the ground, moving small pebbles mindlessly while he is consumed by his internal thoughts. Sayda keeps looking back toward him as if she wants to say something but hesitates. If we make it through this, I need to talk to Hadwin. He is often surprisingly insightful, except right now he seems to be missing something really important. I am the last one that should be giving advice about these things, but one thing I have learned through this mess is that you need to take advantage of whatever time you have with loved ones before it is too late.

"Kagen, are you still there?" Arluin's voice finally calls back through the communicator.

"Yeah, how does it look in there?" I ask.

"Not good, the place is crawling with Guards. There's no way you can make it through there," he says.

"Have you heard anything about Nyree or Eldin?" I ask.

"Nothing for sure, but Mr. Vaden did say something about a conspirator being detained," he says.

"There has to be another way," Sayda says, throwing a

small rock against the wall in frustration.

"Maybe there is," I say, remembering something from the last time I had to sneak back in.

"Give us a minute, Arluin," I say into the communicator.

"What do you have in mind?" Talia asks.

"Do you think Cyrina could get to the Guards in the main entrance?" I ask.

"Sure, but what then?" she replies.

"She tells them you managed to escape from me and need them to open the main entry for you. But she needs to convince them to keep it quiet. Maybe she could say I have a mole in the Leadership Guard somewhere. I don't think any of those guys would pass on the chance to be the one who saves you," I say, remembering how they all looked at her.

"That might work, but as soon as they see you guys it would be over. Unless..." she says, pausing in mid-sentence with her eyes opening wide.

"I like that look," Hadwin says.

"If there are that many Guards waiting for us in the Deep Vents, they would've had to pull them from the entrance post. They probably left only a single man there since it's closed anyway. Even so, I still need a way to neutralize him when I get in," she says.

"We have access to a couple of strong and eager young men," I say with a coy smile.

"That sounds a lot better than your suicide mission," Sayda says.

"Arluin, looks like it's time you got your wish. I need your help, and it's not going to be easy," I say, imagining his excitement at finally being able to do something.

I spell out the plan, and as expected, he is more than willing to help. I do not like having my little brother engage a man with a gun, but with Talia's distraction and the help of his friends, the risk will be substantially decreased. With renewed hope for our chances, we wait for the pieces to fall into place. Arluin checks in when they are ready before turning the communicator over to Cyrina. Not long after that, she calls to Talia.

"Talia, I'm here with Branek, are you still alone?" she asks.

"Yeah, they haven't found me yet. Is he going to save me?" Talia asks, trying to sound like a helpless victim.

"As soon as you get close, he'll open the door. Be careful, we don't want anyone to catch you," Cyrina instructs.

Talia bravely walks into the open alone, and heads toward Securus, while the rest of us hide behind one of the massive stalagmites near the edge of the cavern. It is as close as we can safely get without being seen. I am not overly worried for her safety since the Guards would never harm her, but Arluin has no such luxury. Sayda gives me a reassuring look before turning her attention to listen for the door to Securus to open.

The creaking of the mechanical control breaks the silence in the Cavern as the door opens. The first part is going well, strengthening the hope that our plan will work. We quietly wait in place for Talia's signal. Our vigil is interrupted by the sound of approaching footsteps. Just in case it is not who we expect, Hadwin and I position ourselves to fight. Arluin rounds the corner and out of joy I pounce on him. By reflex Hadwin follows and we form a pile, nearly crushing him.

"This is the thanks I get for saving you guys," Arluin complains as we get up and help him to his feet.

"Hey, you never can be too careful," Hadwin says with a wicked smile.

"Is it safe?" I ask.

"Was there ever any doubt?" Arluin boasts. "Maybe next time you'll remember how useful I can be."

"I would prefer there not to be a next time like this," I say as we walk toward Securus.

Just inside the main door, we find the tied up Guard with Varian and his brother, Reed, hovering over him, preventing an escape. Cyrina is sitting in the lounge with Talia, calmly waiting for us.

"Thanks guys," I tell them as we enter the lounge. To be honest, with everything that has happened, I was never really sure we would even make it to this point.

"So, how are we going to end this?" Hadwin asks.

"I think it's best if we go straight to Mr. Vaden. He has a lot of answering to do," I say while putting on the armored helmet.

"You look scary in that, Kagen. That alone might get you past the Guards," Arluin says.

"That's the whole point, hopefully it works," I say through the mask and see the disconcerted look on Arluin's face when he hears the mechanical manipulation of my voice.

Before we can move on, Branek interrupts us, "You're not going anywhere. You will all surrender now or face the consequences."

He has managed to get free and is holding Reed as a hostage. Varian had wandered over to the rest of the group to look at the armor. That left Branek alone with Reed, and he was able to get loose. Next to me, Varian has a horrified look on his face, seeing his younger brother with a gun pointed at his head. Making things even worse, there is a flashing light from the alarm that he activated. More Guards will be here soon.

There is no way out of this without Reed getting hurt.

The only option we have is to give up and hope that Talia can fix this. Just as I am lowering my weapon, Varian lunges at Branek. Hadwin tries to stop him, but it is too late. Branek aims his pistol and fires. Reed sinks his teeth into the Guard's arm, causing his hold to release. Now that Branek is exposed, Hadwin fires his weapon. The Guard crumbles to the ground next to Varian.

I rush to help Varian, but when I turn him over, there is no life left in him. It was a lethal shot, and Varian has already passed. Reed sobs while clutching his dead brother.

We are all stunned by what happened. By the time I regain focus, two more Guards burst into the room. They look confused and frightened by our group, especially with us wearing the soldiers' armor. We need to move fast, so I fire a warning shot just above their heads. Seeing that they are outgunned, they immediately retreat back into the stairway, shooting wildly as they run.

"Is everyone else okay?" I ask, checking the group.

"Not really," Sayda says, trying to hold in the pulsating flow of blood pouring out of her arm.

I run over to help her. The sickening guilt of what happened to Varian and now Sayda nearly overwhelms me. I force my mind to concentrate on her wound. She was grazed by a bullet but it nicked an artery and blood is pooling all around her. The wound needs to be fixed fast or it will turn fatal. The only place that has the tools needed is the infirmary, so I need to slow the bleeding to buy some time. I rip her sleeve and use it as a tourniquet. Tying it in place only slows the pulsating flow of blood, but does not stop it.

"Sayda, Listen to me. Take your right thumb, put it right here, and hold it down hard," I tell her trying to get the best point pressure we can on the wound to prevent exsanguination. "We can fix this, but only if we get her to the infirmary before she loses too much blood."

Hadwin helps Sayda to her feet, while I keep her arm still and help put pressure on it. When we get her upright, her eyes roll back, and she nearly passes out from the blood loss. After a moment, her eyes come forward and she looks right at me. Her already fair skin has tuned pale and clammy. She is starting to look a lot like the patients who were poisoned by Trent with his new virus just before they died. While we are moving Sayda, I hear Talia instruct Cyrina and Arluin to help Reed with his fallen brother.

"Can Rana fix this?" Hadwin asks as we enter the stairway and start climbing.

"Yes, but I've already seen the wound. I'll get it done faster," I tell him. Rana is more than capable of helping Sayda but I do not want to leave her side. We cannot have any delays, or she will die. I cannot lose anyone else because of my actions.

"No, if we all go, we'll get caught and you know that. I'll take care of Sayda. You and Talia need to finish this. We can't stop now, not after everything that's happened," he demands.

Hadwin is right. Rana can handle it, and we cannot let the deaths of our friends be meaningless. We need to get to Mr. Vaden before it is too late. There is no time for goodbyes, so we part ways unceremoniously and continue on.

Not long after we split up, a loud alarm fills the halls. The pulsatile grunt of the alarm indicates that Leadership is ordering a lockdown of the facility. I have seen practice drills before, but there has never been an official lockdown in my lifetime. They are trying to keep the people inside their quarters and away from the truth.

Talia and I continue to climb the stairs. We encounter many hurried workers trying to get back to their quarters. When they see me and my weapon, the reaction is as expected. Confusion and fear strikes while they run back the way they came. The stairs begin to vibrate. I look up and see a large contingent marching down toward us. It must be the Leadership Guard. I expected this, but hopefully we can still avoid them. We exit the stairs and move through the halls, trying to make it to a different stairway.

We navigate through the turns in the hallway until the next stairway is directly in front of us. Before we can reach it, the door opens and five Guards emerge with their guns already in hand. They form a line to stop us from continuing. We are completely exposed in this hallway. There is nothing to hide behind and the footsteps of the other Guards are getting louder behind us.

"Stop right where you are," the center Guard demands, with a pronounced fear in his voice.

"Sorry, I can't do that. Get out of the way or I will shoot," I say with a deeper than normal voice, taking advantage of the eerie manipulation and its frightening effect.

Despite their obviously fear, they hold their ground. We must get past them. I know what needs to be done, though I wish there was another option. *I really hope this armor is not just for show*, I think to myself.

"Stay behind me, Talia," I tell her while raising my weapon.

The Guards do not know how to react. One drops his gun and seeks shelter in the stairway. A second Guard panics and starts stepping back and forth not knowing where to go or what to do. The other three keep their guns aimed at me until one of them fires. The shot misses and careens harmlessly down the hallway, but the sound of the gun firing triggers the others to shoot as well. I feel a bullet crash into my chest with tremendous force. Another strikes my abdomen. I nearly crash to the floor from the pain, but remembering Talia behind me, force myself to stay upright.

I cannot take the pain much longer, so I fire back. The flash of light explodes down the hall and hits the door behind the men, leaving a gaping hole in it. The sight of me still standing and the display of my weapons power is more than enough to make them all flee for their lives. I hold on until they disappear into the stairwell, then fall to the floor.

"Kagen, are you okay?" Talia shouts as she comes to my aid.

"I don't know. It hurts so bad I can't tell if the bullets went through or not," I tell her, temporarily immobilized by the pain.

"I don't see any holes, just some dents in the armor," she says while frantically searching for wounds.

"Then help me up, we have to move," I tell her.

She drags me up to my feet and I stumble into the staircase. I have to continue on. We cannot stop now that we are so close to the end. I look upward, searching for more Guards, but there are none. My foolish gamble has worked. We are getting close to the upper level. There is only a short way to go.

## 30

Surprisingly, we make it the rest of the way to the upper level without encountering another Guard. I stop to listen at the door before opening it. There are no sounds on the other side. I have Talia wait for me to clear the area, so she will not be exposed to any more danger. I step into the hallway, expecting an ambush. The area is not empty, but there is no ambush. Mr. Vaden is waiting for us by himself. He is calm and confident, like nothing unexpected has occurred at all.

I take off my helmet and look him in the eye. He does not flinch or show any hint of surprise at the sight of my armor and weapon. He pulls his hand from behind his back, and suddenly, there is a pistol pointed at my forehead. I had not realized he had a weapon, and it catches me completely off guard.

"Where is my daughter?" he demands. There is a fleeting look of concern with his words. He is not sure if Talia is unharmed.

"Talia," I call out, signaling for her to come out of the stairwell.

"What are you doing?" she yells as soon as she sees the gun pointed at me.

"What is necessary to protect you and our people," Mr. Vaden says, after looking to make sure she is not injured.

Talia jumps in front of me. "If you really want Kagen dead, you're going to have to shoot me first," she shouts.

For the first time, Mr. Vaden's rigid exterior is broken. There is uncertainty in his eyes. He looks away from me and turns to Talia. When Mr. Vaden sees the way his daughter is looking at him, it is as if he were stabbed in the heart. I was right about him; he does truly love his daughter.

"Let's go to my office where we can talk," he tells me while lowering his gun.

"Okay, but like I said before, Talia needs to be here for this conversation," I answer. It is obvious with him around, she is not in danger. But without her around, I definitely am.

"Of course, Talia is central to this matter after all," he says.

We walk back into the same hallway he brought me through that night during the training sessions. The serene atmosphere is comically opposed to the surging chaos enveloping Securus. We settle into his office and he takes a seat at his desk. He does not have the same calculating stare that he normally does. Instead, he looks tired.

"I must apologize for Aamon and the overzealous Guards, Talia. I called them off after they displayed that astounding lack of control in the hallway," he tells her.

"Stop stalling and tell us what's going on," Talia demands.

"Aamon has become completely out of control with his desire for power. That situation will be rectified shortly. He was supposed to contain the incident in The Caves. His escalating failures forced our hand until it has become this confusing mess we are now faced with," he says, still not directly answering her question.

"I'm tired of playing games," I interrupt him. "I've learned a lot since that night in The Caves. How about I tell you what we know, then you fill in the blanks, so we can skip past the lies and cover-ups?"

"Sounds fair," Mr. Vaden concedes. He leans back in his chair with his stoic façade returning. Even with his deception unraveling in front of him, he no longer looks concerned. It is confusing to me. A second ago he looked broken, but now he is impossible to read.

"Kerad and his partner murdered Merrick to hide the tracks and supply room located in The Caves. They lead to another facility called Munitus. Trent instigated the recent viral outbreak using stored pathogens from the Research Labs in order to close The Caves. Electricity and electronic supplies are being siphoned off for some use outside of Securus. I don't know to what end, but it has to do with something called Caelum. Aamon has been blundering his way through attempts to kill me for the last four days. What I don't understand, is why you didn't just kill me in the first place. Why such an elaborate scheme when a simple one would have done?" I ask.

"Well, you have been much busier than we realized. First, I must applaud your stubborn determination. Most others would have relented long ago. To answer your question, at first we thought you had no knowledge of the Soldier Guards or the tracks, so it was not necessary. Plus, I have always known Talia had an attachment to you, and I did not want to see her in pain. Still, the further we looked into it, the more obvious it became that you knew more than we initially believed.

"I was hopeful we could find a less messy solution, and turned it over for Aamon to handle. That was my mistake. I had hoped you could be persuaded to abandon your pursuit, obviously that did not happen. An outright reprimand would have been too obvious and would have given credibility to anything you may have mentioned to any others. It needed to be more subtle, without turning you into a martyr. Aamon was far more forceful in his approach than I had hoped for. Especially when he infected those he felt failed Leadership with that virus. His intent was to secure The Caves and distract the people with a short lived hardship. It seems your penchant for instigating him has continued to push him further and further from reason. Plus, he did not take both of your behavior the night before the detail well, either," Mr. Vaden confesses.

"Why are we even keeping this secret from the people? What is so dangerous that they couldn't handle?" Talia asks. By the look in her eyes, it is obvious she is hoping for a redeeming answer.

"I knew you couldn't be kept from this forever," Mr. Vaden says, resigning himself to finally revealing the truth. He takes a deep breath and looks Talia in the eyes as he starts. "It started long before I was even born. Securus has been under the control of Caelum since The Agent became inactive on the surface."

*Inactive?* I think to myself. How could that be, I have seen the effects of The Agent for myself. But as soon as I think it, the answer becomes obvious. The never ending supply of the virus they keep stored in the Research Labs. They have been infecting people with The Agent for many years in order to control us. The question is why would they do that? By the confused look on Talia's face, she must be going through the same internal struggle. Mr. Vaden waits for our attention to return before continuing.

"The people of Caelum were the first to emerge from the devastation of The Agent and saw an opportunity to build a utopian society. They wanted to make a life for themselves without hardship or suffering at the hands of poverty or war. The problem was that this is an impossible goal. Because of our very nature, there will always be inequalities and divides in our societies. They realized they needed someone to do the distasteful work for them to allow their people to live the lifestyle they so desperately desired. Only then could they get as close to their goal as possible, all the while condemning the rest of us.

"So, before the other colonies could emerge from their underground confines, they enlisted the members of Leadership to control their new workforce. The offer was simple. Supply them with the energy and manufactured goods they desired or they would release The Agent into the air filtration systems killing everyone. How they were able to access our systems without our knowledge is unclear, but they have demonstrated their power in the past and would not hesitate to do so again. The fact that the surface was habitable was too dangerous in their view, so we were forced to perpetuate the deception of The Agent's continued viability. Unfortunately, even without The Agent, escaping to the surface is not an option. Caelum is completely prepared for that as well, and no one would survive.

"Munitus is just like Securus, happily unaware of the truth. If Caelum were to ever realize the people of Securus have discovered the truth, they would eliminate us all. All they would need to do is push a single button, and we will be no more. That is why it was so important that this was contained. I have nothing against you personally, Kagen. My actions were only meant to protect the people of Securus from extinction. Now I see the only way to stop this is to tell you both the truth."

"Why have you never told me this before," Talia says with rage in her eyes.

"You have so much of your mother in you," he says

with a mournful longing. "I wanted to tell you, Talia, but what would you have done? There would have been nothing that could have kept you from trying to free us, but ultimately, that would have led to our destruction."

My mind is whirling with thoughts and memories that no longer seem real. Everything has been tarnished. Anything would be better than to know that we are being used as slaves for the pleasure of the despicable people of Caelum. Locked up underground and robbed of any free will is far worse than anything else we could have imagined. I almost wish I had been killed while on the detail instead of having to know this. I try to find a hole in his explanation that will reveal this as another intricate layer of deception.

"Why would they demand this to be kept a secret? If they have the power to kill us, why not just tell us and coerce our cooperation?" I ask

"Power and control are very delicate things. If you lord your power over people, they will invariably resist it. But, if you give them the illusion of free will and solidarity with Leadership, they are much easier to pacify. The focus is turned to survival and fellowship rather than bundling their energy into anger and opposition aimed at their oppressors. I know you have read the old world's history on the internet, is that not how governments and corporations have operated for centuries? They pretend to be concerned with their workers or subjects and even enlist their opinions. All the while they are secretly steering them toward their own ideals and pursuing their own agenda," Mr. Vaden answers.

I think of my many internet searches through human history during my spare moments in the infirmary. There are countless stories of corruption overwhelming the moral judgment of those in power. Every bit of my heart wants to reject this as absurd, but my logic knows better. It would take a hideous alteration of one's moral judgment to consider something so atrocious, but it would not be the first time that power and fear has led to such a dark path in human history. Another thought springs to mind that gives me hope that this is not the truth.

"If The Agent is inactive, then why do so many people die on the Solar Panel maintenance details?" I ask, mentally willing him to not have a logical answer.

"As a reward for our service, certain members of Leadership are granted access to live in Caelum. Fabricated deaths are a simple way to extract them while simultaneously reinforcing the dangers of trying to leave the safety of Securus. For my service, I was offered a spot for Talia and myself. I never accepted that offer, knowing what it would do to you to discover the truth," he says to Talia. "You would never have accepted living there while leaving the rest of our people behind. So, I stayed here with you."

"This can't be true," Talia says. Her anger has weakened. She wipes the tears from her eyes.

"I am afraid it is, Talia. Think about it, isn't it odd how we are always able to find just the right resources in new areas of The Caves? That is not an accident. We are given what we need to survive and continue supplying Caelum. Kagen, how else could any portion of the internet be available? Now, you both have an important decision to make," Mr. Vaden says.

"And what is that?" I ask, though I do not want to hear the answer.

It is hard to even look at him now, knowing the depth of his deceptions. I cannot even imagine how Talia feels, hearing this from her own father. I look behind Mr.

Vaden at the Leadership insignia draped on the wall. It has new meaning now. No longer does it symbolize the light rising through the destruction of The Agent. It only shows how The Agent was used to enslave the light. How the illusion of democracy has kept us from discovering or questioning our true captors.

"You two still have the power to save our people from their impending doom. Even though Caelum constantly monitors our population and productivity, the daily details are entrusted to the select members of Leadership who are allowed to know of their existence. Since neither our population numbers nor production has been altered, we have not attracted additional scrutiny. They are unaware that their secret has been discovered.

"It is quite simple really. All you have to do is hold this dark secret as I have for these many years. Talia, if you choose to leave to Caelum, that can be arranged, but I doubt that would be the case. Assuming you choose to stay, we will set up a timeline for you to succeed me as head of Leadership. Then you can be assured that you will have the authority to do everything possible to improve our lives here. Also, I will not interfere if you choose to be with Kagen. This is not an easy path, but you must choose whether you will accept this or if you will continue on your current course and lead Securus to its end.

"You are my daughter and I will not stop you, no matter what you decide. Everything I have ever done has been to try to keep you safe. You are all I have left in my life. I have always been able to take solace in knowing that whatever evil I have been forced to do has always been outweighed by the goodness and light of the one thing in my life I was not forced to corrupt or compromise. That is you."

Talia can no longer fight her tears. The confusing mix of anger, love, and regret drowns her resolve and throws her into distress. All I can do is hold her close while she processes the emotions and then we both must face the overwhelming weight of the truth.

"How often does Caelum check our population numbers?" I ask, still hoping for an alternative.

"They have sensors that can pick up our biological signatures within Securus, and they check them daily. They do allow for slight deviations to account for workers in The Caves or those maintaining the Solar Panels," he answers.

"Then why can't we just sneak out after they do their check, and keep moving away from here until we're safe?" I ask.

"Because that gun and The Agent are not the only weapons they have available to them. Caelum knows that is the first thing the workers would try if they found out the truth, and have planned for it. They cannot risk a revolution. I would welcome that option if it had a reasonable chance of success, but the outcome would be inevitable," he answers.

My head tilts down as I run out of ways to deny the revolting truth. There is a prolonged silence while Talia and I consider his words.

When Talia is able to speak again, she answers the only way she ever could. "I cannot accept that, father. I will not lead our people deeper into slavery. There has to be a way to liberate them, and I will find it," she says with surprising strength.

Mr. Vaden does not argue. He only looks at her with proud acceptance. It looks as though he plans on being true to his word. "Then we can only hope you are able to do what I never could. Like I said, I will not resist," he says, abdicating himself to her.

"If you won't, I will," Aamon shouts from the door.

I had not noticed his presence before he spoke, and judging by Mr. Vaden's reaction, neither did he. Aamon stands in the doorway with a fierce intensity, flanked by Ardal and Balum. The group would not be intimidating, especially with Balum hobbled, if it was not for Aamon's weapon.

"We are not going to let you stop us from getting to Caelum," Ardal barks.

Instinctively, I stand and move to cover Talia. To my surprise, Mr. Vaden comes from behind his desk and stands beside me.

"Aamon, this has gone far enough. You will stop now or not only will you be denied access to Caelum, but you will never see anything outside the walls of the Detention Center again," Mr. Vaden warns.

"I looked up to you. I thought you were strong and courageous enough to do what needed to be done. It looks like I was wrong. I was wrong about you both," Aamon says motioning to him and Talia with his gun.

During the tense confrontation I can feel Talia moving slowly behind me. At first I do not realize what she was doing, but then feel her gently nudge my arm with the assault rifle. She is giving us a chance to fight back.

"Your only way out of this is to give up now, Aamon," I warn, worried by the disappearance of the sliver of internal conflict that was initially in his eyes. "Your actions have been misguided, but we can work something out."

"My actions were misguided? I'm not the one trying to kill us all, Kagen. That is what you are doing. How can you not realize that? I'll save Securus and reap the rewards that I deserve in Caelum," he says, raising his gun.

Before I can grip the weapon that Talia is trying to pass to me, Aamon fires. I hear the sound of two shots and feel one of the bullets sneak through a gap in my armor. The searing pain of the torn flesh in my left shoulder instantly erases any doubt that this time that I have been shot. *It is only my arm*, I think to myself while grabbing the weapon with my right arm. Without hesitation I fire back, but Aamon has seen me aiming and jumped behind Balum. The flash of my rifle reaches out and finds Balum as its target. He collapses to the ground, clutching at his gaping abdominal wound. Seeing the damage, I know it will not kill him instantly, but that amount of damage cannot be salvaged. With Balum nearing death, Ardal immediately lays on the ground in surrender.

With his advantage erased, Aamon runs down the hallway, trying to escape. I sprint after him. Blood pours down my arm and the last shreds of my energy are consumed. We must stop him before he finds a way to communicate to the Soldier Guards or to Caelum itself. My legs do not have the strength to keep up with him, not with the beating I have taken. He is too fast. Aamon disappears through the outer door. All is lost. Aamon will kill us all in a last attempt to save himself.

I try to mentally will myself to move faster, but the effort only creates an awkward step that sends me tumbling to the floor. Lying on the floor, looking at the empty doorway, I lose all hope. To my astonishment, a moment later, Aamon flies backward into the hallway and crashes against the wall. His gun falls from his hand. He reaches for it, but Arluin kicks it away before he can reach it. Hadwin, still dressed in the Soldier Guard's armor, kicks him again in the chest, forcing him back against the wall. He then lifts his rifle, placing it directly on Aamon's forehead. Aamon immediately stops fighting.

"I'm so glad to see you two," I say, now sitting on the floor and trying to get my armor off. I need to stop the bleeding from my wound.

I go back into the office to get Talia's help with the armor. My heart sinks when I see her clutching her father on the ground. Aamon had not shot at me twice as I had thought. Mr. Vaden's uniform is stained with his own blood. He has been shot in his upper abdomen and is already getting very pale. If the bullet hit a major blood vessel he does not have much time to live. He is in worse shape than I, and we need to act fast.

"Arluin, cover Ardal and Aamon. Hadwin, help me get Mr. Vaden to the infirmary now," I shout, trying to lift him to his feet so we can move him.

I secure his upper body and Hadwin grabs his legs. Talia opens the doors for us and then returns to her father's side immediately. As we move, I hear him trying to talk to her.

"Talia, I'm sorry for what I've done. In my desk, there's a black book with our insignia on it. It has all the information you need to keep Securus safe," he says meekly, through stuttering breaths.

"You can show it to me later," she cries.

"Just remember, I always loved you. You were always my reason for life, and I was always proud of you, my little angel," his voice trails off.

"I love you too," she sobs as the life slowly drains from him.

We burst into the infirmary, and Rana follows us into the surgical room. We frantically start trying to resuscitate him, but it is too late. He has lost too much blood, and our efforts are in vain. Mr. Vaden, Talia's father, has died.

## 31

Talia retreats into herself, mourning for her lost father. She sits next to him and asks to be alone. We leave the room, letting her deal with the loss in her own way.

So much has happened, and so much has changed. I am finally able to tell the others the truth of what happened and what we still face. Only, the truth has not set me free like I believed it would. It has devastated everything I have ever known. Everyone has suffered from this in one way or another, and the price is difficult to bear. I turn to Rana.

"How's Sayda?" I ask.

"She did well. The artery was intact enough to repair. She's angry, but she'll recover just fine," Rana answers.

"Do you know what happened to Nyree or Eldin?" I ask.

"Nyree was beaten severely. She's in the ICU now. It'll take some time, but I think she'll recover. Eldin was taken to the Detention Center immediately after I splinted his broken leg," she answers.

"We need to get back to Mr. Vaden's office," I tell Hadwin.

Talia appears at the door, her eyes swollen from the tears. "I'll go with you, there is still much to do," she says.

Rana stays to tend the infirmary and make the final arrangements for Mr. Vaden and Varian. The rest of us return to the upper level. When we arrive, Arluin is still guarding Aamon and Ardal, who he has sitting side by side in a corner. Talia summons the Leadership Guard and has them immediately taken to the Detention Center. The Guards are also given instructions to release Eldin. I watch as Talia sits at her father's desk, closes her eyes, and takes a deep breath. When she is ready, she opens her eyes and activates the announcement system.

"Hello, I am Talia Vaden. I bring to you, the people of Securus, sad news. My Father, Mr. Vaden, has died. He was murdered by a viscous sect of Leadership that has been deceiving us all. Today, Kagen Meldon has led us to discover that we are not alone. Securus is not the only colony left on this planet. There are at least two more that we now know of, and one of them is not an ally. They have been secretly imprisoning us while using our people as slave labor to supply their energy needs.

"The continued danger of The Agent is a lie. They have been poisoning us to make us believe that The Agent was still active. It is not. I know this is a startling discovery and one that is difficult to believe. But it is the truth.

"Even without The Agent, there is a very real threat to our existence that still remains. The controlling colony, Caelum, has weapons beyond anything we possess. If they find out we have discovered their treachery, they would destroy every member of Securus rather than risk us liberating ourselves or another colony.

"This is a dire situation, but not one that we cannot overcome. Before he died, my father entrusted me with his role as head of Leadership and has given me all the information we need to continue to survive. If you, the people of Securus wish it, I will embrace this challenge. While we shall not concede our lives to our oppressors, we do need to be careful in our coming actions.

"As a people, we have survived the original onslaught

of The Agent. We have lived in this unnatural setting and thrived for many years. We have shown our strength and ingenuity countless times. I ask you to do this once more. With your trust and cooperation, we will rise above our subterranean prison and finally emerge onto the surface to live a life we could only dream of before. This change will not be immediate, but when we reach the brilliant light at the end of our journey, it will be transformative. I ask for everyone to convene in their dinner halls if you have not already done so. Please have one representative from each hall bring me your answer.

"No matter what you decide, I want you to know who has sacrificed so much to uncover this deception. Kagen Meldon has risked his own life numerous times in search of this truth. He would have never been able to make it without the help of Hadwin Chon, Sayda White, Rana McPheeters, Nyree Imelda, Eldin Rankyn, Arluin Meldon, Varian Barand, Reed Barand, and Cyrina Brown," she says bringing Hadwin, Sayda and I in front of the camera.

"I think you left one very important name off that list, Talia," I interrupt, to her surprise. "Without your strength, courage, and leadership, I would not be here right now. Your father sacrificed himself because he knew you are the one person who can free us from our bonds."

"Thank you, Kagen," she says. "I await your response, Securus."

Talia ends the announcement. The hopeless despair that has been building since I have learned the truth starts to fade. Listening to the elegance and poise in her words reminded me of what we are capable of. With Talia leading us, we can overcome this. It is encouraging to learn that I am not the only one that feels this way. One by one, the representatives come and pledge their support for Talia. When the stream of representatives has finished, the two figures that have been waiting in the hallway burst into the room. My mother and Arluin nearly knock me over when they come to hug me. My mother demands I return to the infirmary immediately to have Rana tend to my wound. I have no strength left to resist.

*

Over the next couple of days, Securus settles back into its previous routine. The Caves have been reopened and its resources restored to the people. We are slowly rebuilding our health from the drought of resources that had loomed over us since The Caves were closed.

Kerad tried to escape when we returned to the supply room, and was killed in the struggle. The bodies of the two soldiers were redressed in their armor and meticulously staged to appear as if they were killed in an accidental collapse.

Talia has started reorganizing Leadership, with some of the prior members now occupying the Detention Center, and new members called up from the ranks of the workers. While we plan how to free our people from Caelum, our workers continue to supply their energy and manufactured electronic pieces as if nothing ever happened. We will be patient and deliberate, knowing our time will come soon.

*

I lay in bed with my eyes wide open, too anxious to sleep. The extensive safety testing of the surface air and soil is finally complete. Tomorrow, we get to walk on the surface without the bio-suits for the first time. I look next to me, at Talia, who is sound asleep. I gently stroke her hair until my mind is calm enough to allow me to fall asleep as well.

My eyes open before my morning alert sounds. I am too excited to oversleep today. Talia is already dressed,

333

having been awake long before me. I cannot hear her, but still know where she is. I sit up and look to the attached office in our private quarters. There is a light on and a moving shadow, confirming she is in there. Talia is always the first to rise, and often does work in the early hours while everyone else is still sleeping. She hears me shifting in bed and comes to the doorway.

"Are you ready for your big day?" Talia asks. She walks over and gives me a loving kiss.

"Almost," I say pulling her back for another kiss, using her own mischievous smile against her. "Okay, now I am."

After I get ready, we go to the exit chamber where we are met by Hadwin, Sayda, Arluin, my mother, and Rana. Nyree and Eldin are still not fully healed from their injuries, and even if they were healthy, I am not sure Nyree would have accepted the invitation anyway.

"Are you sure it's safe?" Hadwin asks.

"Don't worry, Haddie, I helped with the testing myself. It's safe," Sayda reassures him.

"Maybe Hadwin should wear the bottom half of the bio-suit in case he has an accident," Arluin teases.

"Ha, Ha," Hadwin responds sarcastically.

"Let's go," I say, pulling Talia with me to the Ladder.

I emerge into the cool air of the early morning above. The wind softly passes, giving me bumps on my arms from the chill. Talia steps off of the ladder and looks out, toward the rising Sun. The rays of the Sun gently caress her soft skin while the breeze lightly stirs her hair. Seeing her in this moment, it is obvious that her father was right. She is an angel.

I turn to the others and smile at their stunned expressions, just like Merrick had when he brought us to his chamber. After a brief moment, Hadwin starts to rub his nose. Soon after, his eyes dart all around as he becomes increasingly agitated.

"Something's wrong!" he shouts. "My nose is getting clogged, my eyes are burning, and my head is starting to throb. I think I'm dying!"

The others look at him then one another, trying to figure out if we were wrong and have all exposed ourselves to The Agent. As they help Hadwin back toward the ladder, I start to laugh uncontrollably. Confused by the mixture of my laughter and Hadwin's concern, they all stop and stare at me.

"Why are you laughing?" Arluin demands.

"Because, nothing's wrong," I say, catching my breath. "You wouldn't get any of those symptoms from The Agent. I've read all about this, it's called allergies. You'll be fine Hadwin."

"Thanks for warning me, jerk!" he says, now starting to laugh at his own reaction.

For the first time I can remember, my heart is filed with excitement and hope. We have a chance to renew our lives, and I have someone to share that new life with. From the truth of Merrick's death, a rebirth of Securus can begin.

The End

# ABOUT THE AUTHOR

Anthony Maldonado was born in southern California on August 18, 1979. He earned a degree in biomedical sciences from University of California, Riverside in 2001 as well as a MD from UCLA's school of medicine in 2004. He then went on to complete his internship and residency in Emergency Medicine, in which he currently practices. He currently lives in Southern California with his wife, Bernice.

Aside from writing, Anthony enjoys running, hiking, and dabbles in a bit of woodworking in his garage. He is fully in touch with his inner (really outer) nerd and enjoys video/computer games as well a range of entertaining movies and cartoons.

If you enjoyed this book, please watch out for the second installment of The Securus Trilogy, *The Controller.*

For more details, visit www.TheSecurusTrilogy.com

Made in the USA
Charleston, SC
15 December 2013